What She Wished For...

...*a Cautionary Tale*

ELLEN L. EKSTROM

Whyte Rose & Violet, Scribes

I've had knights ride in and out of my life, but this is for one knight in particular.

What She Wished For...

...a Cautionary Tale

1

Once Upon a Time... the Computer Crashed

RICHARD OF GLOUCESTER stood behind a wall of household knights and waited. Somewhere on the field his brother the King and the York vanguard was drawing up new battle lines and regrouping. Off in the distance, in the fog, he could see shapes moving and the unmistakable silhouette of Edward astride a great warhorse and screaming orders, his banner of the Sunne in Splendour a beacon for the Yorkists who fought their way to rally with him.

To Richard's left the duke of Clarence's men shifted and changed position. They were positioned in the center with the King where Edward could keep his eyes on them, but now Clarence was ordering his men towards Hastings' flank. Why would it not surprise Richard if his brother of Clarence changed heart yet again? Of the Plantagenet brothers, one never knew where George stood. Today, Richard hoped it would be with Edward. George only claimed kinship when it suited his political ambitions, or as it recently happened, to save his own neck.

Every man waiting with Richard held their breath as they watched for a sign that the day would be theirs.

Richard was ready to send a herald to the King and ask for further orders when cries went up in his army. Men were pointing towards the field where the Black Bull banner of Clarence appeared through the fog and took the Lancastrian center by surprise.

That was it! That was the signal!

"Now!" Richard shouted at his men. "For God, Edward and York! For York!"

Slamming down his helmet visor Richard led his vanguard in a charge and would have clashed with the earl of Oxford's men had the computer not suddenly frozen up and the Blue Screen of Death appeared with a message.

'DISK ERROR 23 READING DRIVE A. ABORT? CANCEL? RETRY?'

"Sonofabitch!"

Violet could see her reflection in the monitor screen gone dark and glanced up at the Kit-Kat clock wagging tail and googly eyes from its position above the kitchen door. Twelve thirty-three. She drew in a ragged breath and puffed out a sigh, then tried a few DOS commands, offering a prayer to the God of Microprocessors. The hard drive vented an excruciating whine comparable to her '67 Mustang on cold mornings. She tried another command, then a few more.

Nothing. Nothing at all.

"Noooo! No, no, no, *no!"*

Violet banged her head gently against the monitor screen. Four hours of work had crashed on the information highway, made an irreparable detour into Cyberspace.

Nothing like modern technology to shock one out of the sanctuary of imagination and back to the autumn of 1995—well, that and remembering the garbage cans needed to be dragged out to the curb.

The September night was cold and clear, the air sweetly pungent. A platinum moon slid from behind layers of mist and fog and came to fullness, as bright as a street lamp. Somewhere in the neighborhood a musician banged on a piano and a dog barked frantically.

Everything in Violet's world was the same; her

comfortable, safe, predictable, world.

Except there was a man standing at the corner of Oxford and Cedar.

He didn't belong in the neighborhood; that much Violet knew. The blanching light of the street lamp made his features distinct: he was blond, attractive, wore expensive European clothing, carried a suitcase and looked hopelessly lost.

Quite by accident they made eye contact and he smiled, taking hesitant steps in her direction. She shoved the cans up against the driveway gate and then made a dash for the door, pausing only a moment to glance back.

He was walking up toward Rose Street, just passing the front gate. They made eye contact again, and again he stopped. Violet ducked behind the lace curtains, then peeked out one last time before she turned her attention to the laundry on the sofa. Laundry seemed to grow there, like mushrooms on a forest floor. If you plucked up one dishtowel, another would replace it by next afternoon; another sock would sprout from the overstuffed cushions.

Violet dug under the towels and sheets in search of the remote control and found a cookie instead. She had second thoughts about eating the cookie, even if it was double fudge; she didn't know which of the children had left it there. A second hunt recovered the remote control and eighty-seven cents.

Towels were folded into neat stacks beside pillow cases and fitted sheets—though how one ever folded a fitted sheet into a neat square, Violet had still to figure— while Jay Leno interviewed an aging sixties rock star about her comeback and past lovers. This made Violet laugh. Pity the poor fool who had to try so hard to be in the spotlight once it had been switched off and on again. While the aging hippy chick told stories of nights that turned into mornings in Soho, Paris and at Studio 54, socks were rolled into egg-shapes and clothes were sorted and laid out on the back of the sofa to be claimed by their owners in the morning. Violet glanced up sharply when she heard a name. The rock star was waxing poetically about Fortinbras, a British invasion band that followed the Rolling Stones and Moody Blues to America, especially her escapades with their front man, Christian Walsh, during the Summer of Love in San Francisco.

"Hardly!" Violet laughed at the television screen. "You're old enough to be his mother."

She settled onto the sofa with that night's writing and a bottle of beer. *The Tonight Show* became white noise, the drone of voices and music, flickering images held no interest as she worked. With precision, speed, and a red Flair pen, she marked up twenty pages and stopped only when the grandfather clock in the hall chimed three in the morning. No, she couldn't stop just yet. The paper was due in a week and there was more research needed. Violet took off her reading glasses and laid her head against the arm rest of the sofa.

I'll just close my eyes for a moment...

She woke just before dawn to a glaring, hissing, static, television.

The living room took on different perspectives in the blue-gray darkness. It became a chamber crammed with gargoyles and dragons that sprang to life from tables, cupboards, bookshelves, and chairs. Family ghosts sat in the chairs and watched, asked her how she was getting on, waited for answers, wondered why.

Why? Why, Violet?

"I don't know; I wish I knew."

This was her favorite time of day, the hour before dawn. The blue-grey light was strangely soothing; it was comforting to lie in a semi-conscious state while listening to the sounds of morning. Everything was clean and everything was new. It was God's way of giving her another chance to get it right...

"There's nothing for breakfast."

Violet opened her eyes and found seven year-old Alex

glaring at her. He pulled the stuffed rabbit she was using for a pillow out from under her so that Violet's head thumped softly onto the sofa arm. She was awake now and sat up.

"What do you mean? I bought a box of cereal yesterday," she yawned.

"No there isn't!" Alex pointed behind him to Max, who was clutching the box of oat cereal and shoving handfuls into his mouth. The two-year old was assessing the situation with large dark blue eyes and eating as fast as he could.

In one movement, Violet scooped up Max and handed off the cereal box to Alex. "*Now* there is."

The day began in earnest with Max's howls of protest. "Faffles! Faffles, peeze, Mamma!" he sobbed as Violet carried Max into the kitchen and set him in the high chair with a cup of juice and a chubby-board book. Alex followed, demanding to know why his little brother could have two breakfasts and he only one.

"Because he knew where to find the cereal. And I better find another place for the cereal. Let's see, is there time for waffles?" Violet mused as she paused to kiss the top of her daughter Elisabet's head. Elisabet was hunched over a bowl of Shredded Wheat with the New York Times.

"I can do it," Elisabet offered. "My first class isn't until ten and your bus is coming in fifteen minutes."

"Sonofa –!" Violet gasped, glancing at the clock. She spun about madly and almost careened into Alex, who thought it was a game and blocked his mother's exit. When she finally got past him, however, she headed for the coffee maker, which was cold and held a pot of yesterday's brew. Violet dashed out, calling over her shoulder, "I don't have time! Maybe Sam can give me a ride to the city? Where's your dad?"

"Airporter came at dawn. He said to tell you he'll be back tonight. Gone to save the Soda Company. He left a bunch of notes on the fridge. Said you need to read them."

"Babysitter!" Violet exclaimed. She was back in the kitchen, grabbing for the phone. "We don't have—"

"Go. I got this. I already called Grammy Am; she'll be here in a few minutes. See you tonight, Mom," Elisabet chuckled and reached for the waffle iron on top of the refrigerator.

THE LINE AT the French Hotel take out window was already down to the sidewalk and Violet quickened her pace. She was late and a bad day was in the offing, if one judged life by minor domestic crises and the number of notes left on the refrigerator. Late or not, Violet needed coffee. She shifted the Macy's shopping bag full of manuscript pages and notebooks and hoped it wouldn't break. That was another thing. He always took her briefcase.

"What'll it be? Want coffee or pastry?"

Violet smiled up at the barista waiting and tapping a finger on the Formica counter as Violet struggled with the bag as she fished on the bottom of her purse for change.

"Want a loan?"

"No, I've got it. Yeah, hi… Uh… cappuccino, no cinnamon, whatever you make cappuccinos with, uh, large."

"Grandissimo?"

"Sorry. Just not into the coffee culture…a bag of beans from the Co-Op and a coffee grinder works for me," Violet groused, and then smiled at the barista as she handed over a fist full of coins, some of which spun and then reeled off the counter and on to the pavement.

"Wait a minute!" Violet called as she knelt down to catch the quarters traveling into the street. "I got it, I got it!"

"No. *I* do."

A man's voice, soft, sensual, British in lilt, made Violet look up and she found herself staring directly at a man with striking, classically handsome features.

He was over six feet tall and looked about forty-seven, forty-eight, though he might have been younger. His eyes were violet-blue.

The blond man under the street lamp.

He offered a knee-disintegrating smile. Violet managed a 'thanks' while she tried to balance her purse and the overstuffed Macy's bag. Shifting the bag caused disaster. It split open, spilling the contents onto the sidewalk. As she reached down, the blond man did the same and their hands met briefly. Violet recoiled and her movements propelled a wire-bound sketchbook, box of number two pencils from his hands. She stammered an apology and reached for them.

He was fabulously backlit with sunlight burning through the fog; his hair—tawny, gold-streaked and starting to thin—was tousled and damp, yet casting gloriously light of its own, like a halo. No one had a right to look so damned gorgeous so early in the day.

Violet piled everything into a stack and would have tucked it in the crook her left arm if the barista hadn't offered a shopping bag with the cup of coffee shoved in her direction.

"So how've you been, Violet?" he asked exchanging notebooks.

"I'm sorry; do I know you?" Violet asked, smiling up at him.

"I guess after so many years you wouldn't remember me, though you haven't changed," he was saying now. "Lovely smile; just as I remembered it."

Violet laughed nervously. "If I were more awake I'd be in a better position to remember who you are; your voice and face are so familiar—I know! The Historical Society dinner at Chez Panisse last week?"

"Chez what? Oh no, long before."

Violet fished around in her purse for her sunglasses and slipped them on, growing uncomfortable under his scrutiny. She tucked stray locks of hair falling out of her chignon behind her right ear and continued smiling.

"You used to do that whenever a boy would look at you. Glad to see nothing's different."

She wanted to say that the charm went with the looks, but when she made eye contact again, Violet felt as tongue-tied and nervous as a sixteen-year old. "You really do look familiar—" she began, and then spotted the Transbay bus rolling up to the stop halfway down the block. "Oh geez, look at the time," she stammered, glancing at her watch.

"We could always catch each other up another time…"

She offered a look of panic and a weak smile. "Damn! My bus—I'm so sorry, but I'm going to be late—bye!"

The rest of his invitation was lost in the sudden blast of a police siren as she made for the bus. When she sank into one of the back seats, Violet glanced out the window and saw him wave. If she had looked back, she would have seen that he was still at the corner near the French Hotel, looking.

FROM THE INCLINE to Treasure Island, traffic on the Bay Bridge was at a standstill. This was nothing new, especially for a Thursday morning. Violet sensed the change in rhythm and glanced up from proofreading to see how far the bus had traveled in the last forty minutes. Nothing was visible in front of them. The fog had made a spectacular entry from the Golden Gate and now blanketed everything from Treasure Island eastward. As soon as the bus maneuvered around a stalled delivery truck in the tunnel and emerged on the western side, the fog thinned and San Francisco materialized under a pale autumn sky. With threads of sunlight and wisps of fog interlacing skyscrapers, the monoliths and spires of the Financial District reminded Violet of a castle. The Black Knight, her guardian of childhood, would live in such a place…

The squeal of brakes and wailing of car horns, the lunging of the bus as it skidded to a halt, made Violet curse and grab the papers and books sliding off her lap. She was still picking up pages and notebooks when the bus creaked and groaned its way around the elevated lane into the Transbay Terminal. Violet disembarked; the last passenger off. One of the passengers, an attorney called Will, offered to help organize her things, but Violet smiled her thanks and said she could manage for herself.

". . .'Scuse me, Ma'am, didja drop sumptin'?"

Violet started at the janitor's voice, and turning, smiled. The old janitor leaning on his broom gestured with the handle to the chess piece at her feet. Violet recognized it as an Isle of Lewis chess piece, the knight, an early medieval design from the tenth maybe eleventh century, primitive and beautiful.

A Suit-in-a-Hurry excused himself and navigated around Violet as she knelt to retrieve this unexpected treasure. Made of granite or composite stone, the knight was smooth and polished under its light film of grime.

The morning itself seemed brighter now that the little knight was tucked in Violet's sweater pocket and would be so the rest of the day. "Looks like you've finally got your knight on horseback, Violet Ellison!" she sighed.

"MORNING, VI; SAFE to come up?"

Ned Percy was at the foot of the stairs, waiting. It was his office, his law practice, but Violet was his secretary. He knew who was boss.

"Don't call me Vi."

Well, it was more satisfactory than the greeting he'd expected. Ned dragged himself up to the loft above the reception area and library, his head still pounding, the smoky taste of last night's bourbon coating his tongue and palate.

"Sorry 'bout the rush."

"I live for the stress, Edmund…"

"*Don't* call me Edmund."

Violet peered over her reading glasses and from the stern set of her large eyes and round mouth, Ned knew she was making an entry into his catalogue of sins, something to be recalled later, and something to be used against him. The way she stared made Ned glance nervously down to his fly. Satisfied he was spared humiliation for the moment, Ned turned to inspect last night's damage in the picture mirror hanging over the sofa beside his office door.

An incongruous smear of burgundy lipstick rode the collar of his only passable white dress shirt; the cloying bouquet of a designer perfume saturated his rumpled suit. Not too bad; there'd been worse mornings...

A cough made Ned turn and the morning's livery was thrust at him: a mug of strong coffee, a boiled egg, a bottle of Excedrin and a small container of Minute Maid orange juice. Grunting something akin to thanks, Ned disappeared into his office at the eastern end of the loft and thanked his lucky stars for a woman as easy-going as Violet Ellison.

Throughout the morning he could hear the reassuring tap-a-tap of her fingers on the keyboard, her low, soft, voice as she fielded telephone calls and put out fires, saved his bacon yet another time, the uneven clip of her heels on the oak flooring. Once in a while, though, Ned wished he could have back the old Violet, could see a smile now and then, and hear her laugh...

"Yeah, Violet! C'mon in."

Ned didn't bother looking up when the door opened. He knew it was Violet by the trademark scent of freesia announcing her. The tentative raps on the door were another giveaway. Violet was the only one who bothered knocking.

A thirty-five-page mediation brief was presented to him in a manila folder decorated by pen and ink doodles, most notably a castle and dragon, a damsel in distress. Ned had always wondered which one was Violet: the rock-solid castle on a hill, the dragon with brass scales, or the damsel.

Looking up now, he decided on rock-solid castle.

For the first time in weeks she smiled back. When some women smiled at Ned, it was device to initiate flirting, with Violet it was absolution for past sins, sanctification and assurance that all was well. Besides, no one had a smile like Violet's.

"Sorry about the rush," he apologized for the tenth time that day; "I totally forgot."

"You've said that already. How'd yesterday's ex parte go? Is the trial getting moved?"

"Nope. Looks like I'm spending the holidays in L.A. Better get started on the reservations, and get a suite at the Wilshire Beverly Hills."

"If you get a suite at the Marriott, we can pay the rent on this place, pay the employee taxes, and Emma and I can get paid at the end of the month."

"That bad?"

"Let's just say we might have to sell your old Bentley to make ends meet if you insist on the Wilshire."

"Marriott. Thanks, Vi."

"*Don't* call me Vi. I'm going to lunch now. Want anything on the way back?" she offered, starting to tidy up the desk. Ned always wondered why she did that, especially when in an hour everything would be in a state of upheaval again. He did like watching her hands, though: perfect ovals with long, elegant fingers. The polish on the nails was always chipped and the fingers stained with ink, but the hands were graceful as they moved deliberately across the scratched walnut veneer of the desktop.

"Twelve already?" he murmured; now glancing at the brief. "Sonofabitch! You found that precedent! Good work!"

"Lunch special at the green awning place?"

"Chicken chow mein, no broccoli."

"Uh, Ned? I'm kind of short today…"

He winked and grinning, said, "I thought you were short every day!"

"You know what I mean."

"Violet, if you need a loan…"

"It's just lunch—"

"Chicken chow mein, no broccoli. For two."

Ned watched the color rise in her cheeks, how a slender finger ran over the broken stitching on the strap to the worn leather bag slung across her torso, watched as she avoided his eyes when a rumpled twenty passed from his pocket to her trembling hand.

"Thanks, Ned. My treat next time."

He wanted to offer a clever retort, something that would launch Violet's humor to infinite boundaries, to bring a smile and more color to that now-pale face, but he knew how quickly Sweet Violet could go from hot to cold in the snap of a finger when she was troubled. Something in those beautiful green eyes told him to let it go.

"All you have to do is ask," he murmured softly as she went out the door.

THAT THURSDAY LUNCH hour Violet trekked up California Street to Grace Cathedral. Making it up the steep incline of Nob Hill made the prayers she routinely offered worthwhile, especially those concerned with publication. Tucked under her arm was a seven-hundred-page history of the Wars of the Roses she'd been invited to submit to the Boston publishing house of Gladstone & James. In the same package was an eight-hundred-page historical novel she decided to throw in as a bonus, throwing caution and publishing protocol to the wind. If the editors didn't like politics in fifteenth century England, maybe they'd settle for sex and violence in fourteenth century Tuscany.

She bypassed tourists wandering about in the gray, cavernous nave and skirted clusters of sketching art students, took a circuitous route around the Labyrinth where barefoot, twentieth-century pilgrims followed their own path to spirituality, and traced the northern wall to the

Chapel of the Nativity. The echo of her footsteps kept cadence with the prayers now being offered in the Chapel of Grace, rose like candle smoke to God.

No one was in the Chapel of the Nativity. Here, as on other days, Violet knelt before the altar and stared at nothing in particular. The antiseptic smells of the cathedral —candle wax, cleaning fluid and stone—sharpened her senses. Voices rose and fell, footsteps reverberated as tourists wandered quietly in and out of chapels and vestibules. The worldly and mundane grabbed her attention when she ought to have been praying.

That was happening too frequently of late.

She was still trying to hear answers to her prayers when the bells of the cathedral shook the nave, ringing one o'clock.

"Damn!" she swore, and skidded out of the cathedral, leaving her package behind.

Ned heard Violet's spectacular entry and came cautiously out of his office, peering around the door to be certain that all was clear before venturing out. She was slumped down like a blob of Silly Putty, head in hands, her chair back against the filing cabinets on the other side of the loft, the asparagus fern dislodged from its pot and lying in a heap of soil and clay shards.

"Everything okay?" Ned asked, leaning against the countertop on the walnut partition and offering what Violet often called 'the oily smile' – a smile that was insincere, but a smile nevertheless.

"Peachy...just peachy," Violet muttered, sliding the chair back to her neatly organized desk. She made a production of digging about in her purse, pulling up a small envelope of postcards. One of the postcards, a modern illustration of the poet/theologian John Donne, was added to a row of family photographs and children's artwork decorating the bulletin board of the partition. A moment was spent meditating on the postcard.

"It's one-thirty-five, and you're never late. For a

moment I thought…is everything —?" Ned began, cut off by the sharp glance directed at him.

"I know, I know; look, I'm sorry. I lost a package of manuscripts up at the cathedral. I had to go back to find it."

"Did you?"

"Yes, thankfully. The Verger found them."

"You left them at the cathedral? Shouldn't you have put them in the mail box?" Ned's attempt at humor was lost.

"I always—you'll just think it's silly. I like to offer a prayer before sending them. For luck."

"I would guess prayer works better than a rabbit's foot." Ned was pointing at the purple rabbit's foot hanging on the bulletin board.

"Great, now you're mocking me."

"No. Just wish I had a tenth of the faith and determination you had."

"Look, I'm sorry, Ned. I won't be late again."

"No, it's okay. You're never late for anything. You had me worried when you didn't come up at one." Ned was ready to go back into his office when he paused and came around the partition and started cleaning up the asparagus fern mess. "I *am* worried about you, though. I know it hasn't been that long…have you seen anybody? Are you talking to a counselor, or —?"

"I'll be okay." Violet clicked on the Dictaphone and smiled. "I'll survive this. Hey, I've got three kids; I work for you. I'm not afraid of anything. I'll be okay."

"Well, if you need anything, you know I'm always here."

"Thanks," Violet sighed, and then looking she smiled and said, "Thanks, really. Now, go away, Ned. I'm fine. Really."

"I suppose our lunch is up at the cathedral?"

"Oh geez, I forgot! Damn it all, d'you want me to go and get it? Nothing's going on right now."

"Sure." Ned was trying his best to re-pot the fern. "Isn't this the plant —?"

"Yeah, I'm surprised it's lasted this long. Here, use this," Violet took a plastic spoon off her desk and tossed it., missing Ned's open palms. She scrambled on the floor after it. "Got it!" she laughed.

"No, I do!" Ned replied, lunging for it. He grabbed the spoon off the carpet and chuckled, "Christ, Violet! It's just a spoon! You look like you've seen a ghost!"

"Nope; you reminded me of someone just now."

"An old boyfriend, maybe?"

"Go away, Ned…" Violet sighed in mock frustration. She winked and reached for the phone and pressed a speed-dial button. "I'll have the green awning place deliver."

"Sure."

He pushed himself up, bringing the potted fern with him. It was a sorry attempt to salvage the poor thing and Violet tried not to laugh. "So all is right in Violet's enchanted world and life?" Ned asked, still hovering.

"I'm fine. Go proofread those jury instructions already."

Ned believed her after watching the lines in her brow relax as soon as she started transcribing his dictation, the rhythmic tap of her fingers on the computer keyboard, the rock n'roll music playing softly out of her clock radio. He retreated into his office and was still wondering about her when Violet came in with his lunch an hour later. Things were back to normal when she placed the take-out box before him with napkins and plastic cutlery, sliding his case files and papers out of the way, removed the half-empty coffee cups and plates of old pizza off the coffee table, calling him a slob on her way out. At five-thirty he found Violet clearing up for the day. The case files she was working on were arranged in alphabetical order by client in a sorting rack; the asparagus fern had been expertly repotted and was back on its space on the filing cabinet;

the volumes of California Appellate Reports were replaced on the bookshelves above the sofa.

"Beer at MacArthur Park?" Ned queried.

"Not tonight. I have a paper due, and Sam went out out of town again, so I have to rescue my mother-in-law from the boys. Thanks all the same," Violet answered, not looking up from her filing of documents in case files. "Don't forget your settlement conference over the Tenby contract. Nine-thirty, Department Eight, Santa Clara."

"You owe me a beer."

She looked up and smiled. "Since when?"

"Since you told me that Dana Carter would never sign with Apple Tree Records."

"I'll buy you a beer when she cuts a single that makes it in the top ten or can carry a tune." Violet said as she grabbed her papers and notebooks and tried to stuff them into her purse. "I'm calling it a day."

"Day," Ned quipped as he came around the counter and opened up a bottom file cabinet, pulling out an oversized department store shopping bag—this one from Sears—and helped her dump her things in. "Y'know, Violet, anytime you need to talk about what's happened…"

"Thanks. See you in the morning." Violet breezed past him, winking, as she skipped downstairs. "Later, Ned. Behave."

"If I don't?" he called down after her.

"At least have fun!" she called back. The tinkle of the antique bell above the door sash told Ned she was gone.

2

Play it again, Sam...On Second Thought, Don't...

HE WAS HOME.

Violet's borrowed briefcase—sporting a new stain—his battered Pullman and garment bag were dumped in the hallway, making an obstacle course out of the four foot walk from the front doorway to the kitchen. The aroma of spaghetti and meatballs simmering in a pot on the stove, the laughter of the children were like an embrace to Violet as she entered and was greeted by smiles and squeals. Elisabet waved hello with a wooden spoon as she cradled the telephone between ear and shoulder, nodding up and down and reciting "Uh huh, uh huh," like a mantra.

"Boom!" Max crowed as he pressed his thumb and forefinger around a cherry tomato, and then exploded with laughter as the fruit burst and its juice was shot into Alex's face.

"Max! What did I tell you!" Elisabet shouted, and then into the receiver, "Sorry, Ben! Little brother shit."

"Beth, really!" Violet said, trying not to laugh.

"Mom!" Alex wailed. "Tell him to stop it!"

Elisabet hung up the phone and skidded across the tiled floor. "Max! How many times do I have to tell you? Stop being such a brat!" she growled and snatched the cherry tomatoes out of Max's fingers, the fruit exploding on Violet's silk blouse. "Shit! Damn, Mamma! I'm so sorry!"

"It's just a shirt. And if everything was normal whenever I walked in the door I'd wonder if it was really our home, Beth," Violet said as she went up on tiptoe to kiss Elisabet's forehead and then bent down to kiss both boys. "Do I need two guesses who taught Max that new game?"

"Grandpa Stanley. Who else? He also showed them

how to shoot peas on the ceiling," Elisabet commented, pointing upwards as she handed Violet plates to set.

Violet glanced up at the constellation of peas near the light fixture. "Who gets to clean that up, I wonder? Is he here?"

Elisabet shook her head. "He brought Dad home from the airport, got into it with Dad, and then left after teaching the boys more new tricks with vegetables they don't want to eat."

"So where's your father?"

"He muttered something about an abyss, an abysmal failure, and damning all soft drink companies to hell, and went upstairs with a bottle of scotch."

"I don't suppose he wants dinner."

Elisabet banged the spoon on the rim of the sauce pan and shook her head. "I think the scotch and a bagel was it."

Sighing, Violet pulled up a chair between Alex and Max and then took the ceramic bowl of steaming spaghetti and meatballs from Elisabet, dishing out equal portions on four plates, leaving the fifth plate empty.

Another quiet family dinner, she mused.

"Y'KNOW WHAT I love most about you, Beth?"

Violet took a plate from Elisabet and dried it with the cotton dish towel, letting it squeak as she passed the towel around it several times.

"That I have Dad's eyes and Grammy Am's big mouth?"

"You're the grown up in this family."

Violet winked as she put the last of the dinner plates in the cupboard. "It's Psych 101. Why art majors are forced to take Psych..."

"I'd be sorry if you were a legal secretary or went into the family business."

"To me law is as exciting as watching paint dry, and lawyers, all except Uncle Ned, lack sincerity and hearts.

And I have no desire to a bi-coastal spaz in a futile pursuit to save a soda company account. It would make me bi-polar." Elisabet squeezed out the sponge then and said, "God forgive me, I've used the *blue* sponge for the floor and the *yellow* sponge for the dishes! And now, I have to go draw my foot."

She tossed the sponge at Violet, who caught it expertly with her left hand and said, "Oh dear, Beth, you missed a spot!" And wiped the floor with the blue sponge.

"You're not a very good role model, you know," Elisabet quipped as she left.

"Think how boring your life would be if I was," Violet called after her and added, "You wouldn't love me if I was normal!"

"True. Nighty night, Mommy…"

Violet sat at the drafting table and switched on the computer, holding her breath. No blue screen of death greeted her and it was just as well, as she had a paper to finish. It was after two when she finally called it a night and quietly slipped into her enormous bed, trying not to wake Sam. This gargantuan bed set into a recessed corner of the room and hidden by curtains was her sanctuary, a wedding gift from him. Right after they were married, Violet mentioned that she'd always liked the bed in Zeffirelli's *Romeo and Juliet*. It took three months of Sam's hard labor in his parents' garage, but here it was. This single feat of carpentry filled their tiny bedroom.

Sam hadn't bothered taking measurements.

Or finish the six-foot headboard decorated with medieval roses set in lozenges. What mattered then was pleasing his bride. The novelty soon wore off, and now, seventeen years later, Sam wanted to get rid of the monstrosity. Violet insisted that it stay and stay it did. The bare wood was now stained with the patina of age and the oil of hands, color crayon scribbles and coffee spills. Tiny indentations marked where their daughter Elisabet had used the mattress rail as a teething toy, where their sons

Alex and Max still ran Hot Wheels cars.

She found Sam buried under the handmade comforter and quits, under a mountain of pillows that had long lost their plumpness, yet another reminder of their modest beginnings in this more than modest Victorian, a fixer-upper that had yet to be fixed up.

He'd been there a while, given the depth and gravity of his snoring. Violet gently shoved him onto his side and for a moment the grumbling and growling stopped.

Sam sensed Violet's presence and turned to face her, shoving the pillow off his face and opening his eyes. In the dark she knew their color: a yellow-gold hazel, like a great cat's.

"I didn't hear you come in," he yawned.

"How was the trip?"

Sam grunted and put the pillow back on his face. Shifting, Violet moved away, claiming some of the blankets and turned to face the window, staring at the shadows of tree branches on the curtain. Just as she was drifting off, she felt Sam's arm around her and a kiss on her neck.

"You're wearing my pajamas," he murmured.

"Want 'em?" Violet whispered. He smelled good, that sexy, musky, scent particular only to Sam Peters. Violet turned in his arms slid a hand down the taut, smooth, skin of his washboard chest and abdomen.

It was almost two when Sam fell away from her, exhausted, saying: "I always know when you're having trouble with the writing. There's only one cure."

Yet Violet lay awake, staring at the shadows of trees and rooftops on the wall, the silvery arrows of moonlight piercing the heavy lace bed curtains. Her eyes smarted with tears, just as her throat constricted with a lump. If she gave way, a sob would break the silence.

Violet turned over in bed to trace the exquisite outline of her husband's face.

If you looked hard and in just right light, small lines

were evident around his eyes, small white slivers midst the tan, where his eyes rose and sparkled when he smiled or laughed. His lips were in a perpetual pout, soft and sensual. The moonlight fell in his hair and highlighted a thatch of curls always struggling to stay in place. She leaned over and kissed him, a tear spilling onto his cheek.

"Vi?" Gratification and fatigue slurred Sam's voice.

"I love you!" she whispered huskily.

"You're precious, Vi; you're a saint, D'you know that? 'Night, swee'heart…"

Violet watched him fall to sleep again and sought comfort from childhood thoughts, images of daylight hours, until unnamed fears, fears that had plagued her for months, surfaced.

And then Granny Mowbray's words came to her.

If you didn't get what you prayed for, you didn't pray hard enough.

A prayer from childhood came to Violet now. She stumbled over the words, trying to remember, finding that nothing made sense. The more she tried, the wearier she became, both in body and spirit.

As she was drifting off, Sam started snoring again, those ugly, reverberating, spasms that made sleep impossible. She was still awake when Sam hit the snooze button at six o'clock.

"Hey," he whispered, kissing her good morning; "have you been awake all night again?"

"Problems with the writing. The computer's ready to give up the ghost. There's no money for a new one; there are just too many problems right now, things I wish could be fixed, just, problems."

"And other things," Sam murmured and nuzzled her bare shoulder. "It's been a couple of weeks, and I know."

"No, that's not it. I don't know what it is. It's like walking in a fog. I don't know what's up or down."

"You're exhausted, Vi, and that's when you get morose and see things in the shadows that aren't there.

Tell you what; maybe we should get away for a few days. Don't you have vacation coming?"

"Isn't going to happen," Violet sighed, easing out of bed. "Ned couldn't get the trial continued so we're going out in December. It'll run into January for sure."

She disappeared through the curtains to open drawers and cupboards in search of clothing. "Well," Sam yawned after a time; "I've got another idea. Remember that new client I told you about, the one my old firm passed on, Castle Records of London? One of the perks is a backstage pass to their artists' concerts."

"You need revenues, Sam, not backstage passes."

"Y'know who started Castle, don't you? Fortinbras. And I've got two VIP passes to their December concert in Oakland."

"That's the second time in two days someone's brought up Fortinbras. They're going to be in Oakland? It's amazing they're still together and still alive."

"And still pack 'em in. Tickets still sell out an hour after they announce a concert. And I know somebody who really, *really* likes their lead singer."

"Don't start!" Violet laughed from the bathroom.

"'*Come into the dark forest, my love...*' Sam sang, and then, "God that's a hokey, whiney, song! Wanna go? You'll get to meet him in the flesh. Don't tell me it hasn't crossed your mind since I brought it up."

"He's probably fat, balding, wrinkled. Face it, Sam, not every guy can age as nicely as you."

"I made a pact with the devil! Vi, you haven't answered my question. Are we going?"

"When were you going to tell me this?" Violet laughed as she reappeared, leaning over him to grab her faux lapis earrings on the headboard shelf, and then melted into Sam's open arms.

"Right before I told you I have to go to Chicago and New York again —"

"Sam!"

"Only a few days this time, I swear!"

"The bakery, the software company, or let me guess, soda company again?"

"Yeah, something 'bout the print ads."

"Are you getting reimbursed for your expenses? We can't afford to pay for another transcontinental flight. The cards are almost maxed out. And the creditors started calling again."

"This account is important, Vi, you know that..."

"Having food on the table's a little more important. It's been three years and still there's no real income. You should have never left Braithwaite, Peters and Tooker. They'll be the only agency still standing in San Francisco when the bottom finally falls out."

"We've been through all this; you knew it was a risk. I don't see why you always bring it up just when things really start cooking."

"I'm just wondering how much longer."

"I was just wondering the same thing," Sam whispered kissing her neck. 'C'mon, Vi, let's make it happen this time!"

He ignored her weak protests, the admonishments to be careful with her business suit, the only decent work clothes she owned, and crumpled the smooth gabardine of her tailored skirt as he slid a hand along the silky hosiery covering her thigh to up and under the teddy. He met with feeble resistance.

Violet had managed to discard her jacket and her heels thudded onto the braided rug. Sam parted her lips with his tongue and explored her mouth while searching under her blouse with his free hand. He had managed to pull away the teddy and now let his mouth fall upon a breast gently.

Violet drew in her breath at his touch, the familiar and welcome heat of his body as he rolled her onto her back and pressed her into the mattress, tugging at his boxer shorts and the rest of her clothes until they were both unrestricted yet tangled in the bed linens.

She could hear Max squealing his way downstairs to steal another box of cereal; Alex making car noises and threatening his younger brother with death if he touched the last of the frozen waffles; Elisabet grumbling about the unfairness of a life that included brothers...Someone pounded on the door, something about the Soda Company on the phone.

Max was howling and Alex proclaiming that he didn't do it, no matter what it was.

Violet reached for the covers that had been tossed to the floor while Sam slid lower down the bed, huskily whispering, "I know what'll do the trick!"

Again the pounding at the door. Did she remember to lock it? The soda company.

Sam had disappeared under the covers.

Max had taken the last of the cereal again, was there anything else to eat?

"Take a message! Make waffles or something!" she gasped, trying to keep her voice even, though soon, any moment now, her body would betray her...

And there it was.

"MORNING, VI."

"Morning, Ned. *Don't* call me Vi."

Violet handed over the bottle of Excedrin, boiled egg and bottle of Minute Maid as Ned paused by the counter to check the briefs Violet had placed there.

"Ned, d'you want to go to lunch later?"

"Oh God, you're quitting!"

"No! I just need to talk to someone."

"Sure."

Ned went into his office and shut the door, opening it a moment later to see Violet glaring at him and he smiled back. "Glad I can finally be of some help, Violet," he murmured.

As soon as the grandfather clock struck twelve, they

walked around the corner to Clown Alley and ordered two bacon cheese burgers with double fries. Ned watched Violet eat, waiting. When she didn't speak, he said, "Are you leaving Sam?" Violet looked up, a stunned look on her face, her eyes large and frightened. All the color was gone from her face. "Oh shit, I stepped in it, didn't I? The look on your face…"

"No! It's nothing like you're thinking. But there's this guy. He looks so damned familiar. You know when I saw him, I thought of the time after my mom died in sixty-nine, and all these memories came back. I know I've seen him before, Ned. I'm trying to put a finger on it. Ever since I saw him… can't get him out of my mind, y'know? It scares me. I wanted to talk to Sam, but—"

"When have you ever been able to talk to Sam about anything?"

"Just this morning we talked about the importance of the Soda Company account."

"And you'll do that while washing up after dinner, or waving goodbye as he jumps into another cab to the airport. I was at your wedding, Vi. Don't lie to your Ned."

"D'you think I want to have an affair?" Violet laughed.

"I don't know. Do you?"

"I'm married!"

"This must be some guy to shake your foundation. Solid, dependable, true and loyal Violet Ellison all shook up over . . . what's this guy look like?"

"Tall, blond, gorgeous. British."

"Hmmmm. I see a pattern here. First Christian Walsh, then Sam."

"At least I don't have Farrah Fawcett's poster in my walk-in closet."

"Hey, I told you, it was there when I bought the place."

Violet nodded, studying the labyrinth of catsup she'd made with a French fry. "Sometimes, the impossible crushes are the easiest to live with. You know they'll come to nothing and you don't get hurt."

Ned shrugged and took the last of the fries.

THE CORRUGATED METAL walls and the bright blue door of the warehouse on Delaware and Fourth Streets were deceptive; it might have been a machine shop, but once you passed through the blue door and went up the freight elevator, the top floor gave way to gigantic posters of bright, garish, advertising art, the only indication that this was the headquarters for Peters ADF, a struggling advertising agency.

Sam's assistants, Carrie and Thornton, were bent over drafting tables at one end of the cluttered loft, receiving heat from portable electric heaters and light from cheap fluorescent fixtures that dangled from rafters. The 'Executive Office' was at the end of the loft behind an eight-by-twelve-foot screen decorated with everything from campaign ideas to the children's school art projects.

Carrie and Thornton paused for a nanosecond to acknowledge Violet with deferential smiles, returning their attention to the troublesome soda company campaign. Sam heard the familiar uneven cadence of her footsteps and slid his chair out from behind the screen to acknowledge her with a wink.

"Hey! What you brings you down here?" Sam asked, genuinely pleased to see her. "You okay? You look perturbed."

"Me? No, I'm fine. I was thinking we should pick up a pizza and a movie for tonight. It's Friday."

"Sounds like a plan."

"Hey, maybe you can help me with this. Do you remember the spring of sixty-nine, when my mother died? You came home from college right after my birthday."

"Yeah. Hey, stuff comes up in times like this, Vi."

"No, listen. Isobel came back from Oxford with Colin. They just started dating, remember?"

"So did we."

"Not really. Not yet, at least. Didn't they bring a friend?"

Sam nodded and started pushing the mouse around on the pad, closing down files. "They brought lots of friends if I remember right. Geeky, tweedy, musicians, historians and scientists. The only thing cool about them was that they got together on Saturday nights and smoked pot and had kick-ass political debates."

"No, there was one in particular – you got into a fight with him about something."

"He was jealous."

"Of what?"

"This," Sam replied and pulled Violet and the chair out of view of the others. He drew her down onto his lap and gave Violet a kiss that left her limp. "I gave you your first kiss. Now, how about getting that pizza?"

"How 'bout getting a hotel room?" Violet murmured.

"Mmmmm… sounds like a plan."

Violet's hopes soared. "Really?"

"Why not? I know three excellent reasons why we should and we should tell the oldest she needs to stay in tonight because we'll be really, really, late. Use the phone on Carrie's desk and get a room at the Hotel Durant, okay? I'll only be a sec," Sam instructed and set Violet on her feet. He suddenly spun the ergonomically correct, hi-tech studio chair and dished a small book out of a cubicle on his drafting table, handing it off to Violet.

"'Come live with me, and be my love, and we will some new pleasures prove, of golden sands, and crystal brooks, with silken lines and silver hooks.'" Sam recited in his deep, melodic, voice. "John Donne, I believe?"

"*The Bait.*"

"I thought it would be."

"I love the little things," she purred between featherweight kisses.

"I knew it would cheer you up. Thornton! The

software artwork is done. You can pull it up on the Pendragon directory!" Sam shouted as he shut down the computer and reached for a worn corduroy jacket draped over a filing cabinet.

As Violet was gathering up a portfolio, briefcase and lunch tote, the telephone rang and she stopped short, throwing her hands up in the universal sign of frustration.

"It's probably nothing," Sam answered her unasked question, and then turned to ask Thornton who it was.

"Sorry, but New York's on two... the soda company shoot in Paris," Thornton replied, handing over the phone.

"I'm sorry, Vi," Sam apologized as he picked up the receiver. "I'll make this quick and meet you downstairs."

"'All here in one bed lay'... see you in a bit?"

Sam blew a kiss before moving away to press the flashing button on his phone and greet the caller in his most charming, oily, voice. Violet smiled at Carrie when she leaned over the drafting table to get the phone. She picked up the receiver and after hesitating, replaced it carefully. Ten minutes later Sam was still on the phone. Violet departed quietly.

3

If You Wanna Hear the Song, You Gotta Pay the Piper…

VIOLET HAD EXPERIENCED this nightmare before.

Gathering papers and books, frantically searching for car keys, frantically searching for a parking space, only the last time, she had been naked. Tonight, it was horribly real.

The panic, which made her chest tighten with every labored breath, grew worse as she ran, her footsteps clattering and bouncing off the shiny linoleum floor; the same profound anxiety as she slid into her appointed, alphabetically placed chair in the lecture hall. The same tang of night air and freesia followed her and the same relief overwhelmed her as she got out her notebook knowing the professor hadn't —

"Why don't we start with Missus Peters? Missus Peters, we were just fielding questions about good lordship. Would you like to explain it?"

Damn!

Her eyes darted up and met the Professor's. He was not your stereotypical, tweedy, academic: he looked more like a linebacker for the San Francisco Forty-Niners – a powerfully built man with a jar-shaped head and neck like a redwood tree. His eyes were constantly moving and his smile had every woman in the class wondering how he looked stepping out of a shower – every woman but Violet Ellison, who now matched smile for smile as she settled in.

"Good lordship?" Violet asked, retrieving the pen that had fallen under her chair. She pushed back her mop of hair and noticed that a few of the men in the class were smiling appreciatively, including the professor.

"The essay topic for last week."

"Good lordship," Violet sighed, scratching her head. "In what context, Professor? Good lordship as in, 'I'll let you farm my lands and live on the swampy fens if you ride under my banner and fight for me? That's feudalism in its simplest form. Or, good lordship as in patronage in exchange for service and grants?"

"Offering me a challenge, Missus Peters?" the professor laughed, his dimples deepening. Violet thought she heard every woman in the room sigh – every woman but her. "Patronage, Missus Peters."

"Well, a good example would be, that, if Richard of Gloucester, I guess, when he became King Richard the Third, had practiced the good lordship of building an affinity such as he did while lord of the north, northern England, that is, if he had repeated the eleven years of building trust and affection, of granting offices and lands, of placing trust and responsibility where it was needed the most, to his affinity in the south, and particularly in London, he might have won the battle of Redmore Plain – excuse me, Bosworth, I guess, and we would not be here talking about it, because Henry Tudor wouldn't have become Henry the Seventh and his son, Henry the Eighth wouldn't have become king and split from the Roman Catholic Church in order to get his way in just about everything from religion to marriage. I guess. But I think the split would have happened, with the Lollards, if Henry the Fourth hadn't died... but that's another story."

"That's a fair explanation. But I know you can do better. Care to do more research and put it on paper for a presentation to the class?"

"Uhhhh..." Violet glanced around at the graduate students in her corner of the hall and watched their faces, waiting for an indication of a set-up. The professor had a nasty habit of choosing a 'victim' every semester and using that poor fool to start discussions and frame opinions. He was one of the most popular faculty members of the History Department at Cal despite this proclivity and women tended to vie for his attention. Violet ran a hand through her hair, watching the women, who were egging her on.

"Sure!"

The lecture on medieval history continued without further incident. When two hours were spent, Violet gathered up her things and tried to disappear into the crowd of undergraduates heading for the parking lots.

But then the Professor called Violet's name.

Violet winced and found that her feet would not move; she was rooted to the floor by a wad of old chewing gum and a Post-It. She wheeled about and smiled, inclined her face to that of the demi-God before her, the fluorescent lights bleaching out his summer tan.

"Do you have a moment, Missus Peters?" "Ellison; my name is Ellison."

"I don't want to drop you from the section," he said as he leaned against the wall, shoving his hands into the pockets of his tight jeans.

"I've turned in my work on time, I show up for class."

"Late. You know my rules – you have the syllabus and requirements. One more late…"

"I have to come over from San Francisco every Monday night and when I get home there's always something

– like tonight it was – never mind, you don't care about that, do you? I'm sure the other working parents in the class."

"You're it."

"Oh. Well then, lucky me… look, nothing I could say would work in my defense —" "Then don't offer an excuse. Why exactly are you taking this class, Missus Peters?" "Ellison. I'd like to finish my history degree," Violet sighed.

"Excellent, because that interest clearly shows up in your fiction."

A copy of one of Violet's short stories came out from the briefcase resting on the floor, thrust at Violet with the force of a cannon blast.

"So that's where it went to," she muttered, taking it.

"I've read better."

"I bet you have... I can write better—well, I've sent a manuscript to Gladstone and James."

"Gladstone and James? *My* publisher?"

"Is it? I didn't know. They were recommended to me. Anyway, it's a history of the Wars of Roses. It's done in the style of James Burke. You remember *Connections*? Well, I thought if I made it clever in some way, connected events and identified the players—"

"A popular history?"

"Yes; but you make it sound like it's pulp fiction or worse. I think that, if you want to get people interested in history, if you want children interested in history, you have to make it palatable. You can't force dates and names down someone's throat and expect them to like it. It's bad enough you need a score card to keep track of who's doing what to whom and when between York and Lancaster."

"What are your sources?"

"The extant ones: Commynes, Mancini, Vergil. The Arrival."

"Not Thomas More?"

"Can't prove Thomas More wrote his history of Richard. Besides, More was living in Bishop Morton's household, and I think Morton of Ely—"

"Do you think you've got a chance?"

"As much as an ice cube in Hell. If I promise not to be late, would you ease up on me a bit? I get the idea sometimes that you like to yank my chain because I'm the oldest student in the class."

"Sorry if it seemed that way. You turn in the best work in the class. In fact, you've got a natural talent for history. You have a gift for detail and research."

Violet's eyes darted up and widened to the size of the full moon shining through the window.

"What's your point?" she finally asked and Violet was sorry to have opened her mouth, noticing the Professor wince at her bite. It should have been something akin to gratitude.

"Try something meatier than popular histories, Missus Peters. You love Richard so much—"

"Like. Intrigued. Don't get me confused with the loyal fans who practically light candles before his portrait and write time-travel stories about going back to the fifteenth century and sleeping with him."

"People write that stuff? I had no idea. Anyway, why not delve into his career before the crisis of 1471, or his career as lord of the North? No one's undertaken his brief career in Wales. Perhaps it was in Wales that his character took shape. The Oxford and University of California Presses are looking for new authors for their monograph series. Take yourself more seriously, Missus Peters—"

"Ellison. My last name is Ellison."

"Missus Ellison. Bring your assignments tomorrow evening and we'll discuss the Fellowship."

Violet swallowed hard, hearing this. "Fellowship? What fellowship? You didn't say—"

The Professor offered his dimpled smile. "Gotcha. There's a twelve-week fellowship at Oxford, winter term, coming up, January through March. Studying, doing some serious, scholarly research, papers published in the historical journals, all that. It's all paid for—room, board. You have to pay for your airfare and meals. It counts for credit towards a degree. I've nominated you. Meet me here tomorrow night? In the faculty lounge?"

"Sure."

"We'll go over the application and requirements then."

The Professor turned heel and disappeared into the lecture hall. Violet was unaware of the students jostling her as she struggled with her things and headed for the parking lot. The Professor's words were like a tambour in her ear: *Fellowship! Fellowship!'*

"Fellowship," she repeated to Sam that night in bed.

"Whaddya mean? Fellowship?" Sam asked and reached for the carton of Haagen-Daz on his end table, retrieving a delectable chunk of pecans with pralines. He moaned with delight as he devoured it, and then offered Violet a lick.

"Just what I said. It's a twelve–week program at Oxford, room, board, tuition paid for. It will look very nice on a resume and it gives me a leg up for teaching jobs when I finish my degree next spring," Violet answered as she took another bite of ice cream.

"You don't have to give them an answer right away, do you?" Sam asked, spoon-feeding teases of ice cream.

"Maybe you could ask your clients to pay their bills, or I could work something out with Ned," Violet replied, playfully licking the ice cream off his mouth.

"Ned can't afford to pay you for a twelve-week sabbatical."

"How do you know what Ned can and can't afford? How about getting your friend Marjorie Rotherwell to pay her bills on time? Or the Soda Company?"

Groaning, Sam stabbed his spoon into the ice cream. He shoved himself up against the headboard with all of the good pillows at his back and after a moment of considering her, brought Violet with him.

"Ned'll have a cardiac if you go."

"How do you know? I've known Ned—"

"I know Ned like you know Ned," Sam murmured into her hair. "I know he couldn't afford to give you a decent raise or a Christmas bonus last year, and how you've put in more overtime than there are hours in a day and I know he's got one hell of a crush on you."

"He doesn't! We've been friends for too long. Please... things'll get better at the office. Ned promised."

"I hope to God not!" Sam laughed.

"That's not what I meant and you know it!"

"Okay. *I'll* have a cardiac if you go. The kids..."

"Think of it this way. Add up all the rescue missions

for the Soda Company, the trips to Pennsylvania for the furniture company, the bi-coastal meetings for the record company account, not to mention the weeks spent in New York for Marjorie Rotherwell's account, and that comes to more than twelve weeks."

"Yes, but I'm getting paid," Sam sighed.

"Are you?"

"I had Carrie send out the invoices. The Soda Company alone owes me forty thousand and that's not including costs."

The hand Violet now placed on his naked chest was ice cold and Sam yelped at her delicate touch, and then dove under the covers.

"Let's hope that's in dollars not pennies. C'mon, Sam; *pleeze*? I know I'll never be able to give up my day job for a writing career but I can lecture in history at a university while I write, and getting that fellowship and my degree should do it. I'm tired of being a legal secretary. It was only supposed to be a temporary thing. I want to do something else," Violet murmured as she peppered Sam with kisses on his ear and neck.

"Twelve weeks, Vi! We can't afford it!" Sam argued, trying to keep the moment serious and not give in to what his body was demanding.

"Twelve weeks. That's a small sacrifice in exchange for all that I've done to help Peters ADF. C'mon!"

"What about the kids?"

"I'll talk to Elisabet. She's been wanting to take a semester off to get a portfolio together and she can work here at the house. And if we can sweet talk your Mom and Dad, maybe they can help with the airfare for you all to join me in England for Spring Break unless you're riding off to save the Soda Company account, then it'll be just the kids."

"Where would we all stay? We can't afford it, Vi."

"I can ask Colin's parents to rent their house in Oxford. C'mon. You know I'm right."

"That's what you keep telling me. Good night, Vi. Hey, could you put the ice cream away?"

"Sure – no, I think I'll finish it off."

Violet picked up the carton and let gobs of soupy, porridge-like ice cream slide off the spoon and puddle at the bottom of the carton.

"Just like my dreams," she murmured.

THE PROFESSOR WAS waiting in the faculty lounge when Violet arrived as promised – and on time – the next evening. He even thanked her when she offered a Peet's coffee. In exchange, the Professor opened a folder and removed a packet of papers that smelled delightfully of book glue and printer's ink.

Before long, Violet was thumbing through the application. "So... wow, I never seen an application with so many pages, and directions. Do I need a number two pencil, or what?"

"Funny. Read it first, then fill in the required information. If you can manage a short essay, do that. They just want two paragraphs. Shouldn't take you too long," the Professor murmured as he began making entries in a grade book. He glanced over the reading glasses balanced on his nose and winked, dimpling in a smile. "You're welcome, Miz Ellison."

"Thank you!" Violet whispered happily.

Violet's pen scudding softly over the application and the Professor's clearing of his throat and labored sighs were the only sounds until the lounge door creaked open. The Professor looked up and muttered something, then ignored the man who had entered and was rummaging through the refrigerator.

"Desolate... nothing worth eating here," the intruder groused.

The voice was English – Midlands, maybe. Violet prided herself on knowing most of the English dialects. Her mother's voice had been rich, melodious Midlands.

When she finally inclined her head to catch a glance, all Violet saw was a blond head, a suede varsity-style jacket and jeans. Men in jeans did look good from behind.

It was The Blond Man.

She returned to business at hand, though every now and then, Violet would glance up and look away just as quickly. An hour later, the application was completed and handed over to the Professor with trembling hands. Flipping through it, the Professor nodded. "Excellent – I expected no less," he murmured as he read. "I'll add my own recommendation and we can cross our fingers. The first and most painful phase is done."

"What's the second?"

"Oral examination and interview. I don't think you'll have trouble with that. 'Night, Miz Ellison." The application was placed into the folder and spirited away as the Professor left.

Controlling the urge to laugh or dance across the lounge was hard. Violet settled for smiling like a fool as she gathered up her things, softly humming a Fortinbras tune. When she knelt to retrieve her purse from the floor, it was equally difficult to avoid the smile The Blond Man threw her way.

She smiled back and was delighted when The Blond Man winked.

"HEY!" SAM GREETED with a kiss when Violet arrived home, and then resumed his review of slides on a light box. "You missed Beth's first attempt at pot roast – I saved you a slice. Ned called, said something about changes to the jury instructions for the trial in L.A. Are you guys always in trial?"

"No, we're always getting ready for trial – we're lucky if it gets that far," Violet said.

"So where'd you go to? Beth said something about school. I didn't think you had classes on Tuesdays."

"The professor asked to talk to me; he wanted to go

over some assignments."

"Trouble in paradise? You've only got a couple of months to go."

"Nothing like that at all. He wanted to review my papers and attach them to the Fellowship application —"

Sam fell back in his chair and shoved aside the light box, scattering slides over the kitchen table and on to the floor. "Damn it, Vi! I thought we —"

"I want to go. I'm going. I don't know how, but I'm going," Violet said quietly.

"If I said no? What then?"

"You know better than to say no. You owe me this."

"Vi, you're not thinking straight."

"You owe me this!"

The tone of Violet's voice made the pit of Sam's stomach churn. Sweat was starting to bead on his face – precursors to one of their infrequent quarrels. Violet Ellison was a rare woman, a woman who refused to fight, and one that withdrew quietly and licked her wounds. Violet always walked away from a quarrel and found solace in her writing or watercolor illustrations. From the stance she took and from the hard set of her eyes now, however, Sam knew this was a rare battle and one that would be hard fought.

"Think what it'll do to our finances," he begged, reaching for her. He wasn't surprised when she backed away and started to organize the stacks of notebooks and papers on the drafting table she used as a computer desk.

"I want this," she said in the same calm voice. "If we can creatively finance your agency, we can find twelve weeks of grocery money."

"We've got creditors banging on the doors, and I got served with papers yesterday for one of the Agency's debts."

"You'll have to make payment arrangements, won't you? Ask one of your clients to pay their damn bills!"

"A lot can happen in twelve weeks."

"What's that supposed to mean?" she asked, thumping a stack of drawings on another stack of folders stuffed with research notes. Violet turned at looked at him head on.

Violet's incredible green eyes threw Sam back in time to the evening of her mother's funeral. So long ago, it was, the spring of 1969. That was the last time he saw fright and unhappiness in those beautiful eyes; it was right before he kissed her for the first time. That's what he saw now. He wanted to kiss her, but was afraid.

"Christ!" he muttered as he shoved himself out of the chair and the kitchen. Violet continued to neatly stack and organize the books, papers and portfolios of drawings long after the hum and roar of Sam's Beemer leaving the garage and careening down Oxford Street.

Sam returned after midnight and, as expected, found Violet already in bed. Whenever she was unhappy, she retreated to the bed with her pile of afghans and quilts. He switched off the Fortinbras CD playing in the boom box and knelt down to stroke her brow with a forefinger, kiss her with lips that stank of beer and cigars, lips cold and damp.

"Hey, you awake?" he whispered.

Violet opened her eyes.

"Geez, you've been crying! Vi, I'm so sorry."

"Let me go, then."

Neither spoke as sounds drifted down from the hall – Max snoring loud enough to wake the dead and Alex screaming at him to shut up, the chimes of the grandfather clock, Elisabet turning the key in the lock and saying good night to her friends.

"Let's just see how it goes, Vi. If you get the fellowship – and I really hope you do – maybe we can work something out. Maybe I can transfer some funds, get some clients to pay their bills, offer my frequent flyer miles."

Sam waited for her response. He didn't expect what

she did now. The precious afghans from her childhood and the comforter rose and Violet patted the bed. He was in her arms, muddy running shoes and all, relieved that Violet Ellison had such a large and forgiving heart.

4

Funny, You Don't Look Like a Martyr...

TWO DOZEN FACES stared at Violet. The eyes were vacant, sometimes macabre, often mocking. She was met with smiles full of sinister intent, smiles of grief, smiles full of pathos. After considering each in turn, Violet took the 'Columbine' mask from the shelf and tried it.

"Can I help you with anything?"

Violet started, looked around the mask and blushed. She didn't know which was more frightening – the 'Alien' mask leering at her from behind a vinyl replica of President Clinton, or the shop assistant's weary 'Generation X' countenance.

"Uh, maybe. My husband and I, we're throwing a party – later, tonight. Dress up," Violet stammered.

"Figures," the young man quipped; "it being Halloween and all."

The Grim Reaper Shop Assistant revealed a mouth full of decaying teeth when he smiled. Violet took a step back just in case he wanted a bite. "Say, that's a nice costume," she remarked, gesturing at his black-on-black clothing; "What are you going as?"

Ignoring her, the shop assistant pulled costumes off racks and held them up for inspection – sorceresses, queens, courtesans. None were to Violet's liking. She begged off, leaving him to frighten another customer while she set out to find the perfect costume.

The theatrical shop on Telegraph Avenue was a two-story curiosity; it was dark, moldy, and stank of patchouli, musk, dried flowers, scented candles. A blue haze of incense hung permanently in the stale air. Reminders of its past as a head shop in the sixties were everywhere – faded 'flower power' posters and peace signs, photographs of the

Grateful Dead and Timothy Leary.

And a smell. Violet couldn't place it, but it was somewhere between patchouli and mildew. Or was it sandalwood?

A metal forest of costume racks was carelessly organized; wooden crates stacked almost to the mildew-stained ceiling lay open and crammed with just about everything from matted wigs, broken prosthetic devices and body parts. There were once-expensive costumes of ruched velvets and satins harvested from the San Francisco Opera, bonnets, fedoras, picture hats and hennins, all preserved with layers of cobwebs.

Nothing caught Violet's fancy until she saw the glint of metal a few feet away. She squeezed through a maze of musty, faded, dusty, garish mermaids, clowns, Abraham Lincolns and George Washingtons, shoved aside animal parts, Charlie's Angels and forgotten movie stars until she reached it – the shimmer of a pile of armor, including a sword.

Trembling, Violet picked up the weapon – a fourteenth century broadsword of tremendous size – and tested its weight. She was barely able to lift it, but managed, and then found a barbute, a helmet, and tried it on. The helmet slid down to her nose.

"Luke, the force is strong.... I am your father!" she breathed in the deepest voice she could muster to her reflection in the mirror.

"Mamma! Mamma, look!"

Violet turned, shoving the helmet up on her brow so she could see. Elisabet, Alex and Max were standing before her wearing vinyl pig heads.

"What do you think, Mom? The three little pigs?" Elisabet asked, her voice muffled in the mask. "That's not a bad idea – but who'll be the Big Bad Wolf?"

"The guy who owns the Soda Company?"

"Funny. If you want to go as the three little pigs, get the rest of the costumes if there are any, and meet me at the counter – the line is starting to grow."

Squealing, the children pulled off the masks and ran to get in line. Violet returned to her inspection of the armor and held it up for size.

"Very pretty – I remember you owned just about every book on Joan of Arc." An English voice. Soft and sensual, enough to send her heart pounding.

A month had passed since she'd seen him. Violet would have dismissed him as just another man, just another face in the crowd, but during that month she found herself thinking about him and wondering who he was; waking in the middle of the night and early morning with that face in her mind's eye. Now that he was standing before her in full battle harness, Violet didn't know what to say.

What did you say to a man in a suit of armor?

Violet removed the barbute and fussed with her hair, elbow-length and for the moment, auburn. "Uh, hi," she stammered, feeling every drop of blood in her body rise to her face while he smiled back.

"Lovely to see you again."

"Y'know, I have been trying to place you and it's driving me crazy. You look like someone I know - I normally remember names and faces."

"You don't remember me? I'm mortally wounded."

"You know what they say – the first thing to go is the mind…" Please say you remember something about me. George?"

"Hmm… that explains the suit of armor. Kill any dragons lately?"

"Pardon?"

"Mom!"

Elisabet's shout was a godsend. The children were at the front of the checkout line. "Must go – my kids."

"Yes, I saw them with you. The little one looks just like you. Your daughter looks like Isobel, well, a brunette model of her; more like Ruth, really – well, what I can remember of your mother."

"Does she?" Violet asked, spinning about. "How do you know —?"

"Mom, c'mon!"

"We never seem to finish a conversation do we? Oh no, Max! Max, stop that right now!" Violet dashed off.

"Wait!" he sputtered, trying to push his way through costumes; "I thought you liked knights on horseback! The armor, all that… right then."

His further pleas dissolved in the dust-filled shafts of light.

VIOLET PUSHED HER way through the tide of costumed guests crowding the living room and wondered how long it would take to repair the damage already done. She carried a fresh store of cold cuts that was descended upon before she had a chance to let go of the platter. Escaping with her life, Violet removed wine glasses from the arms of the coronation chair and asked Marie Antoinette to take her Isadora Duncan interpretive-style dance off the chair's fragile seat. She told Bill Clinton that her CD's were not drink coasters, and fished Cheetos out of Elisabet's aquarium before the sea horses died of toxic shock. And despite all this, Violet was pleased. The annual Peters ADF Halloween bash was officially a bacchanalia three hours into its inauguration and there was no hope in seeing it end. Where there was debauchery and revelry, cash couldn't be far behind.

Violet spotted D'Artagnan, a.k.a. Sam, in the corner of the dining room. They'd made a pact to do something outrageous this year, something they'd laugh about for years to come. Violet knew exactly what would fit the bill. Sam was stocking an ice chest with premium ales and designer water when she entered. He did a double take when he saw her Joan of Arc costume, and smiled.

"Nice! Hey, fantastic job you've done with this party; did better than I could by a long shot. I could use your organizational skills and your artwork in the company."

"Nope; I make it a point not to sleep with co-workers, just fantasize about them."

Sam nuzzled her neck. "I'm thinking of a few situations right now… ever go to a party and wonder if you could sneak away to – you know; find a quiet corner?"

Violet laughed seductively. "Ever throw a party and sneak away to let the guests wonder?" She now went up on tiptoe to offer him a salacious invitation to join her out in the back yard behind the juniper bushes.

Sam glanced around and winked, saying, "Meet me in five minutes!"

Violet pulled Sam down into her arms when he came out to the yard and sprinted to the dark corner away from the house where the juniper bushes grew. She'd taken one of the blankets off the bed and a pillow, brought some food and a bottle of champagne and spread everything like a picnic.

"How much time do we have?" Sam asked between kisses and gropes.

"Everyone in there's so damn drunk. They wouldn't miss you for a second," Violet murmured as she reached into his satin breeches and pulled him down on top of her.

"Damn, Vi! Where'd you learn to do that? Shit! For once you could've chosen something other than Joan of Arc!" Sam laughed as he removed Violet's metal cuirass and tried to unfasten the chain mail shirt. "I hope to God you're not wearing a chastity belt!"

"Why don't you find out for yourself?"

"Mm, you're so soft and warm," he murmured when his hands, and then his tongue, found what they were looking for.

Violet was also regretting her choice of Halloween costumes and pulled at the metal clasps like a deranged stripper until they both fell back onto the wet lawn, laughing hysterically.

"Who's idea was this anyway?" Sam giggled

drunkenly.

"Too bad it wasn't mine."

Sam immediately pulled away and threw his wide-brimmed hat over Violet to cover her naked breasts. He scrambled to his feet to say hello to Marjorie Rotherwell, his biggest client, and owner of a highly successful Berkeley business venture called Rotherwell Baking Company. Marjorie was fourteen years and twenty-eight pounds Sam's senior, a woman who might be Eleanor Roosevelt's love child. Not an attractive woman, Marjorie Rotherwell, but rich and influential and at the present, highly amused.

Marjorie raised a champagne flute to her lips and held it there. An affectation, a means of garnering attention that worked. "I was hoping to talk shop, Sam," she purred, and then looked straight at Violet, who was struggling to cover herself. "But if you haven't got the time because of your secretary here, I won't tell your wife, if you won't."

"I *am* his wife."

Marjorie's eyes widened and then she glanced sideways at Sam, one of those insulting smirks directed at the odd-man out in a three-way-conversation, in this case, Violet, who glanced back and forth between them both to get a clue about what was going on.

"You're Violet?" Marjorie asked, genuinely surprised. "I had no idea. You're younger than I thought – I always imagined, well, it doesn't matter now. I'm Marjorie Rotherwell. I suppose Sam's told you about me. Sam, if you've got a moment?"

"Sure," Sam responded, and throwing Violet a sheepish grin, followed Marjorie into the house.

Violet suppressed a laugh as she watched them disappear into the crowd. Marjorie had her hands all over Sam as soon as she thought they were out of view. Violet had grown used to the women who constantly flirted with her gorgeous husband. Flirting was harmless and it was hysterical when the woman was as unattractive and old as

Marjorie Rotherwell took up the game.

But then she noticed how attentive Sam was and how he brushed hair out of the older woman's eyes and touched her face playfully. *Impossible*, Violet told herself. Sam was just doing his job; he knew how to work people and the Rotherwell account was his most important.

Impossible.

Looking back, Violet saw now how they laughed and brought Carrie and one of Marjorie's co-workers into the conversation. The momentary anxiety fled as quickly as it came. Sam always did get silly and affectionate when drunk. Violet waved at Sam who winked and hailed a greeting, blew a kiss, waved her over. She started to make her way through the pressing crowd when out of the corner of her eye she caught the glint of metal, a shock of bright hair and violet-blue eyes. Wheeling around, Violet searched the crowd and saw nothing. But then over the heads of Napoleon, Ariel the Mermaid, the Transamerica Pyramid and Anne Boleyn (with head tucked in the crook of her arm), Violet again saw a shock of bright hair, the shimmer of a highly-polished gorget in blue-black metal, violet-blue eyes, and a smile. She was remembering now. That smile took her back to her youth…

". . . Here's our little crusader!"

Violet spun full circle upon hearing a familiar voice and accepted hugs from Fred Flintstone and Little Bo Peep. Amalie Peters gave her daughter-in-law the bonus of a kiss and pinch on the cheek.

"Don't you look gorgeous, Sweetie!" Amalie cooed; "Stanley, doesn't she just look yummy? Violet, you never fail to amaze me! Where'd you find the armor?"

Stanley Peters scrutinized Violet, whistling low. "Best legs in chain mail, little girl!" was his verdict on her 'Joan of Arc' costume. Men standing within earshot seconded that opinion with appreciative stares.

"Weight Watchers certainly is working for you. I wish I had your luck!" Amalie continued to gush.

"Luck has nothing to do with it," Violet laughed, grabbing a champagne flute when a tray floated by. "Can't be too heavy when I've got a husband who's used to thin!"

"It shouldn't be about the circumference of one's hips, dear," Amalie said.

Stanley now waved his cigar around the living room and more particularly in the direction of his son. "So this is where my loans have gone to, drunken orgies? I thought he was supposed to advertise beer, not drown in it!"

"Stanley, we talked about this," Amalie sighed, digging perfectly manicured nails into his arm.

"Ouch! Bloody 'ell, woman! What was that for?" Stanley yelped.

"I told you not to start anything," his wife purred indelicately.

"I wasn't starting a thing, I was making an observation. I give my son money to start up a business and I'd like to see his ads on the sides of buses and billboards! I don't want to see a hundred or more drunken sods doing God knows what to whomsoever they please!"

"That's pretty much an advertisement for the beer, isn't it, sweetheart?" Amalie chirped.

"Don't worry, Stan," Violet jumped in, reaching up to kiss her father-in-law's leathery chin. "By the end of the night, Sam'll have enough accounts signed that we can pay back the loan for this house in cash."

"Sam's finally got a handle on things, has he?" Amalie ventured.

"Pretty much."

"Well, he's got a handle on someone," Stanley harrumphed.

"Oh my!" Amalie sighed and then smiled sweetly as she said, "Heard anything from your grandparents, dear?" Violet gently pushed Stan out of the way and stared across the room to where Sam was bobbing for maraschino cherries out of a gigantic martini mixed in a glass Pyrex baking dish with Marjorie, their heads close. Sam and

Marjorie grabbed the same cherry and it looked like Sam was enjoying himself trying to retrieve the fruit off of Marjorie's tonsils. Everyone was laughing when Sam came up victorious and Marjorie dished a bill out of her wallet and tucked it neatly inside Sam's buccaneer shirt.

"Humph! Some bet!" Stanley grumbled.

"Hey, look! Kellie Clark!" Violet exclaimed, eager for a chance to escape. "You remember Kellie – she was with the Weathermen? I let her hide out in my apartment right before Sam came back from England. I wonder what she's up to."

Blowing kisses and making promises to do lunch, Violet beat a hasty retreat to the backyard, taking a seat on the bench swing.

The cold night air was delicious on her feverish cheeks. She removed the cuirass, pauldrons and gorget of her armor, wondering how Joan of Arc could have worn this stuff during a major bout of PMS. Violet stretched her legs and smiled. Stan was right. Nine pounds overweight, but her legs did look great in chain mail.

Impossible...impossible...impossible, the porch swing creaked as she glided back and forth, trying to fight the lump in her throat and blink away the tears.

He loves me... he loves me...

Violet unconsciously wiped her nose on the chain mail shirt and swore softly as the metal links grazed her upper lip, glancing about nervously just in case Sam saw her. She didn't want him to see her crying. He'd probably ask a dozen questions.

"Is that seat taken?"

He came from around the juniper bushes; the flash of his blue-black armor in the party lights caught her attention first. The Blond Man called George strolled across the lawn and stopped before her, smiling down. Violet felt weak at the sight of him, wondering how he could be there when she'd only just thought of him a moment before – and wondering why she'd thought of him.

"Go ahead," Violet invited and watched as he sat on the opposite end of the swing. He moved as easily in the armor as he might in khakis and a tee shirt.

She stared at her hands pressed into her lap, watching as the chain mail links made indentations in her flesh.

When she found the courage to look up, she saw that George was smiling at her.

And then it came rushing in like a tide. Dappled greens and amber filled her mind's eye, bright summer foliage and the tawny, shining, freshly-washed hair of George Knightsbridge standing out amidst the summer colors in her parents' backyard. The eyes so blue they were almost sinful to look at.

"It was April of sixty-nine, George Knightsbridge. That's when I first laid eyes on you. And then in the summer of that year when you came back with Colin and Isobel," Violet spoke up suddenly. "After Mamma died."

"Not quite the summer of love."

A hand was extended and Violet merely stared. If she took it, he'd surely feel how much she was trembling. The hand was withdrawn and shoved back into a gauntlet. After another of those cloying, theatrical silences borne of sexual tension and trepidation, he leaned in and said, smiling, "You pretty much hated me then, Violet. I'm getting a feeling that nothing much has changed."

"I'd blocked out so many memories of that year... well, thank God you're not one of Sam's clients. I was sitting here trying to figure out how not to offend you, just in case."

"Well, feel free..."

"You must think I'm awful to forget you. I don't usually forget names and faces, but that was a year I tried desperately to forget, so..."

"Understandable. I remember the year quite well."

"You were a third wheel."

"Ouch."

"I didn't know you kept in touch with Sam – he

would have said something."

"No, he wouldn't."

"You two never got along, I remember. There was a game of *Risk*."

"Of all the things you remembered…"

"I was still picking up those nasty little wooden cubes a week after the game – and they hurt when you step on them barefoot… so you're a grad student at Cal, or teaching, or —?"

"Teaching. Only for the year."

"It must be weird, coming back to Berkeley after all these years."

"No; weird was running into Sam at Larry Blake's. He was all hail-fellow-well-met when he came up to the bar and we were having a good catch up until I mentioned your name."

"He didn't hit you again, did he?"

"My reflexes have improved, so I had time to duck. No. He looked ill for a moment, and then he invited me to this party. I look at it as a Godsend – having an acquaintance in a strange place. Though I didn't know you and Sam remained friends after all these years."

"No . . . he's my husband."

"Telling hesitation there, Violet."

"Tired, that's all," she said.

"Sam said I'd meet some old acquaintances here tonight, some lovely women."

"Have you?"

"Not until now."

Violet pretended not to be affected by his flirtation and nodded, stared at the juniper bushes. A protracted pause, and then George said, "Nice party."

Her response was a shrug.

"Well, not really – sorry. I don't know anyone but Sam and his folks, and you, and I was so bored until a moment ago." George now turned an ear toward the house, listening. "I thought as much. Nice choice of music.

Fortinbras, is it?"

Violet listened, trying to place the tune. She knew them all. George was staring intently and she ignored him as best she could.

The clouds had dissipated and now Violet could make out his features. There was a definite sensuality about him that made her weak in the knees. His eyes really were an incredible shade of dark violet-blue. She dismissed them as contacts. When he smiled, Violet felt her palms start to sweat, her heart beating.

She didn't like the way he smiled at her. It was too familiar, too sensual. Violet listened to George's stories of England as they gently swayed on the bench, their heels making ruts in the soft ground beneath them.

"I remember this very song, and a tree house," George reminisced. "There was a young girl with enormous green eyes, just like yours, watching me from among the leaves — although wasn't your hair blonde then?"

"Taupe, actually. Somewhere between blonde and brown, it didn't know which way to turn. It eventually settled on the dirtier shade of blonde."

"The auburn color is nice. Suits your beautiful eyes."

"Thanks, I think."

"Your sister Isobel was blonde. She had lovely hair and eyes – not as striking as yours, though —"

"Violet! Vi? Where'd you go?"

Violet reeled guiltily off the swing at Sam's shouts. "Sorry, Saint George. I have to go fight some dragons, and it's past my bedtime," she apologized and would have left if George hadn't taken her hand.

"*Carpe diem*, Violet."

She hesitated. "It's not the day, but my life."

Sam removed his hat in true cavalier fashion as Violet approached, sweeping the ground with it. On any other night she would have eaten it up and laughed, played along, but now she smiled nervously and avoided the kiss he tried to bestow. She threw George a glance in parting and went into the house. Sam watched her leave, heels clipping on the paving stones, and then spun about toward George to demand an explanation.

"Nice party," George said and disappeared out the garden gate.

ALL SOULS DAY dawned cold and clear, damp after a night of rain. Halloween decorations left scattered in the front yard were sodden and bleeding orange and black dye on the sidewalk in fantastic rivulets. Violet kicked away the soft, rotting jack o'lanterns that now looked grotesque on this morning after – like a Christmas tree that loses its glory on December twenty-sixth. She dug the morning paper out from among damp streamers and deflated balloons trapped under the camellia bushes, and as she started back inside, Violet saw Sam and Marjorie at the corner. Sam was carrying a tray of drink cups and a sack of pastries; she was hidden behind an oversized pair of sunglasses and a wool cap. Her plumpness was exaggerated by the pea coat and scarf she was wrapped in. Violet was ready to hail them over but saw that she would have been the third wheel – they were laughing about something and Marjorie was patting Sam's arm and leaning towards him seductively. Violet knew the moves; she'd made them herself. Rather than stay and watch, she went back inside and started cleaning up the aftermath of the party. Moments later, Sam sauntered in, whistling a Fortinbras tune. He bent over and offered a kiss, leaving a scent of Chanel Number 5. Violet smiled absently and kept shoving paper plates and cups into the Hefty sack.

Impossible, she thought. *Impossible*.

5

Come Into the Dark Forest

. . . *RICHARD INSTINCTIVELY ROLLED* out of the way of the powerful hooves of the warhorses as they leapt Deadman's Bottom. The fog had thickened into a curtain impenetrable by the sun; it was impossible to discern who was friend or foe until close enough to taste the other man's sweat. Richard's household guard had reformed and now made a wall around him as the horses were gutted and their murderous cargo were pitched to their deaths. Screaming orders to regroup, Richard and his captains started another push upwards, beyond Deadman's Bottom to where he prayed the king would still be fighting. Richard moved methodically and mechanically, cutting and slashing, gouging and tearing as men came at him. It made no difference who they were, if they were within an arm's length of his mace or sword, they were dead.

The men were tiring, leaning on one another for support, gasping for fresh air and strength. Richard called a halt and told his men to wait. They would have to wait another hour or so, for Violet had logged off and shouted for Elisabet to hurry up and get her coat – they had to go shopping for Thanksgiving dinner.

"The usual this year, Mom? Mom?"

Violet juggled an umbrella and her purse while yanking a cart off the trolley in front of the store and pushed it past the displays of discounted Halloween candy and pumpkins. She shoved it in the direction of the produce department and all the while working out in her mind the scene she'd just written. A whistle brought Violet out of her thoughts and raised her brows at Elisabet in question. The whistle came from a Cal student that had walked by and was craning for a second look at her dark-eyed, dark-haired, stunning daughter, and Violet wondered if she had ever turned heads, or run a few men into trees and lamp posts when she was Elisabet's age.

"The usual this year, Mom?" Elisabet repeated as she weighed yams against sweet potatoes.

"The usual, being?"

"Yams, white potatoes, cornbread stuffing, Dad ruining the holiday by staying at the studio all day or running out of town to make the soda company safe for democracy?"

"Not funny."

"Don't laugh now, Mom, it might hurt…"

"Beth, if I've told you a thousand times,"

"He's still pissed at you, isn't he?"

"Your father?"

"You're being vague on purpose."

"Elisabet, it has nothing to do with – damn! I forgot your grandfather's olives. It wouldn't be Thanksgiving without Stan hogging the olives… hmm, bread."

Violet feigned interest in the loaves of designer bread artfully displayed on faux wood trestles in the isle. Rotherwell Baking wrappers caught her eye. Pale blue tissue with art nouveau lettering and flowering vine border, a medieval wishing well, a fairy maiden in diaphanous gown, gazing longingly into the well. She'd given Sam the idea and Marjorie had gushed for hours, thinking it was all Sam's doing. It was worth the laugh when Marjorie found out that it was Sam's wife who had come up with some of his best artwork for the bread company and several other clients. Seeing the wrapper brought something ugly to mind – the Saturday morning after the Halloween party…

"Is that seat taken?"

Violet, sitting on the porch swing, glanced up sharply at the question and saw Sam standing over her. Wordlessly, she moved aside the textbooks and papers, the manuscript pages and sketchbooks cluttering the bench and Sam settled into the swing, pulling her against him. "Christ, Vi! Geez, I was drunk! How'd I know Marjorie was going to put a price tag on the game?"

"Keep digging that grave..."

"I wasn't thinking – how many times do I have to apologize? Marjorie is my best client, and she's got connections I need to help the agency grow. And, she paid her bill in full."

"You'll be paying for it 'til your dying day, Sam Peters. And I wasn't thinking of the Pillsbury Doughbitch. I was thinking about George. Why on earth did you invite him?"

"I thought seeing an old friend of Isobel's would cheer you up. I guess it didn't work?"

Violet shrugged. "D'you know, one of the last things I remember about George Knightsbridge was the look on his face after we came out of the hallway that night."

"Hallway?"

"The night of my mother's funeral? Remember?"

"That's not something I'm likely to forget. George looked pretty jealous! Little would he know eight years later we'd hook up and I'd give you another memorable first!" Sam reminisced, running a finger lightly, sensually inside Violet's blouse.

"So you still think it was a first, huh?" Violet said.

"Humor me; I've blocked out your college years on purpose."

"Well, make promises and don't keep them, what d'you expect?"

"Know what would be another first?"

"An apology?"

"I was thinking about that fantasy of yours."

Sam had pulled back the collar of her blouse and was nuzzling gently, his lips making a trail down from the neck to the soft, shadowed cleavage between Violet's breasts. Violet responded as she knew she would – the heat of his kisses and familiar, experienced, touch began the roiling, the sense of urgency. Anger was put aside and all that mattered was this moment. Sam had managed to unbutton his jeans and from what Violet could tell, their backyard tryst was already having a favorable effect on him. She leaned against the redwood back of the swing and allowed him to remove her jeans and shirt, felt the exciting sharpness, the bite of the late autumn air on her naked skin. Sam positioned himself exactly where he knew it would be most favorable. And it was. Shuddering in pleasure, Violet pulled him down on top of her, mindless of the dizzying perspective of the lead-colored sky and the walnut and oak trees as they swayed above her, spun about in all directions, the effect of the swing as it rocked, the clumsy pounding against the clapboards of the house.

The touch was not Sam's then. Sam's mouth and tongue were not on her skin and making every erotic nerve stand on end. It was George Knightsbridge. George was running his hands along the contours of her body and kissing her deeply, bringing her to the most exquisite climax.

George… George…

"George! Oh my God, George!"

Sam abruptly stopped and pulled away. Violet opened her eyes and still heaving from her orgasm, saw the hard glare of Sam's eyes. "What the hell was that?" he demanded. Before another word could be spoken, Sam had dressed and had hurled himself off the swing, slammed the back door, leaving Violet to wonder.

That was the first salvo in a war yet declared.

And all because Violet had said another man's name.

And she didn't even know why she said it. Would Sam have reacted differently if she had shouted Robert Redford? Christian Walsh? The question danced in and out of her thoughts as Violet watched Sam leave for one of his business trips, and for the first time in their marriage, was relieved when the Airporter sped off.

"He's been a jerk," Amalie muttered as Violet came back into the house.

"That's an awful thing to say about your own son,"

Violet jibed, starting to clean up the aftermath of Sam's preparations for the trip. He had left a trail of clothing, books and papers that led upstairs to their bedroom.

"Not as bad as what the son told the mother. He told me what this cold war has been about."

Violet turned, her face crimson and purple in turns. She pushed the hair out of her eyes for something to do, hoping Amalie wouldn't see how she trembled. "That's not something I'd discuss with my mother!" she whispered, shutting the bedroom door behind them.

"He's scared, Darling. He doesn't want to lose you. He thinks you're in love with someone else," Amalie answered with a shrug.

"Christian Walsh!" Violet quipped.

"Who?"

"A singer I like. Old rock band from the British Invasion. He's been jealous of Christian Walsh since Isobel gave me the first Fortinbras album back in 1969."

"No, that wasn't the name – Christian Walsh? Really, Violet! You're what, forty-two? Aren't you a bit old for adolescent infatuations?"

"It's not about infatuations. He thinks I'm having an affair with George, that moon-eyed historian from Oxford who used to tag along with Colin and Isobel."

"George Knightsbridge? *George?* Oh dear!"

"As far as I know, and I would definitely know it, I'm not in love with anyone but Sam," Violet responded.

Amalie nodded and patted Violet's face lovingly. "I know. I told Sam it was unthinkable that you would be in love with anyone else. You're Violet. "

What more could be said? Violet didn't doubt that Sam had his own fantasies or thought about other women while having sex. He was smart enough not to get caught...

"Soft drinks," Violet murmured as she rounded the corner in the grocery store and erased the negative thoughts clouding her mind. As she surveyed the gleaming shelf of bright aluminum cans, Violet spotted the Soda Company's signature silver and gold logo. She wondered why this particular soft drink was so important when there were thousands on which to bid.

That's another thing, Violet thought; *Sam's mistress*. Not a woman, but his work. In their almost twenty years of marriage, work had always come first. Of late, there was more work and less time together.

Violet was frightened and wanted to be rescued from whatever the specter was looming on the horizon.

Where was a knight on horseback when you needed one?

Unconsciously, Violet reached into the sweater pocket and felt the smooth relief of the chess piece she'd found several weeks ago.

"Hey! Isn't this the band you like?"

Elisabet's exclamation at a *People* magazine cover brought Violet out of her sulk. There was Fortinbras in 1969, the year they arrived in San Francisco to play at the Fillmore. Standing front and center was Christian Walsh, the lead guitarist and vocalist. Violet did a double take and studied the cover more closely.

"Yeah, I thought it was that English guy in the neighborhood, too," Elisabet said as she shoved the overflowing grocery cart into the checkout stand.

The resemblance to George was striking. Violet smiled to herself thinking, at least George has aged well. There was no telling what Christian Walsh looked like these days.

"Says they're going to be at the Oakland Coliseum in a few weeks. Something about a thirtieth anniversary tour."

"Your father got backstage passes for us," Violet mentioned as she helped unload the groceries on the stand. "Their record company is one of his new clients."

"I suppose he's not as pissed at you as I thought he was. Eventually you'll tell me what it was all about?"

"No."

"I'm going to find out eventually, so you might as well tell me."

"Let's wait until the tension subsides," Violet said, brushing a lock of Elisabet's dark hair out of her face.

A week later the tension still hovered.

Violet shut down the computer earlier than usual that night, deciding the fate of Richard of Gloucester could wait until morning. She left him quarreling with his brother Clarence over the marriage rights to Anne Nevill, the daughter of Warwick the Kingmaker and the richest co-heiress in England. Anne was Clarence's sister-in-law and he didn't want to give up any rights to the legacy he thought was so obviously his.

But Richard's problems were nothing compared to what confronted Violet. The dishes in the sink alone would make the hardest, most seasoned knight weep. She tackled them for no reason other than to keep her hands in warm dishwater on this cold December night, to use the mundane ritual of passing sponge over old china plates a mantra for her thoughts. Violet made a good attempt at the dishes, but the cluttered counter tops, the table piled high with notebooks, history books, art supplies and costume sketches, plates littered with that night's Thanksgiving leftovers, a Barney doll, action figures and Victoria's Secret catalogues, could wait until morning.

And then Violet glanced at the stack of unopened mail growing beside the printer. One of the third class envelopes grabbed her attention. Violet trembled as she opened it, the knot in her stomach tightening. She whispered a prayer, Prayer Number Sixty-five, before reading the polite, personalized letter of rejection from a book publisher that was clipped to the sample chapters from one of her novels:

> *We feel that, although well written and entertaining,*
> *your work does not meet our current publishing*

needs. We wish you the best of luck in placing your material with a publisher and/or market that would best suit this genre.

Violet fed the rejection slip into the garbage disposal.

A carton of milk in one hand and a cherry pie and fork in the other, she went to the front porch to celebrate yet another setback.

Oxford Street was getting ready for Christmas, evidenced by the colored lights already blinking out of synchronization in windows. The piano player three houses down murdered Chopin and the stupid dog across the way barked his brains out. She glanced over to Cedar Street.

There wasn't a blond man under the street lamp tonight.

Once the pie was little more than a cherry stain around her mouth, Violet washed it down with milk straight out of the carton. She next retrieved the bag of leftover Halloween candy she'd hidden in the chest of the deacon's bench and dug through the cellophane-wrapped candy corn, the Starburst fruit chews, to the good stuff – the gold foil-wrapped Rolos and the Three Musketeers bars, scooping her treasures into a mixing bowl and finishing them off with a box of Screaming Yellow Zonkers. No one was awake to see the Practically Perfect Mamma do any of this.

By midnight the candy was gone and Violet had used up the day's quota of self-pity. Stepping over Sam's luggage and garment bag, various rain boots, Legos and Tonka trucks, Violet negotiated the hallway from front door to living room and went in to do the evening ritual of cleaning up and folding laundry.

Framed photographs of her parents, her sister and brother-in-law, now all dead, were dusted and replaced reverentially. Violet glanced at each of their faces and wondered what God's quota was for automobile accidents, plane crashes, and cancer in one family. After polishing the frames, she glanced behind her, wondering if the familiar ghosts were lounging on the sofa, watching and taking notes.

Seize the day, Violet!
What are you waiting for, Violet?
Why are you waiting Violet?
Why do you still love him, Violet?
"I don't know; I wish I knew."

VIOLET? VIOLET, WAKE up. Violet, you've fallen asleep on the sofa again. Violet?"

Violet stirred, shifting, protesting in confused, incomplete, sentences while pulling the comforter around her. The voice was vaguely familiar – English, deep, soft and sensual. It was a lover's voice.

She opened her eyes slowly and blinked at the television, uncertain of her state of consciousness. Christian Walsh filled the screen.

"Hello, Violet; I wondered when you'd wake. How many nights a week do you sleep on the sofa? It can't be all that good for your back."

Violet sat up and rubbed her eyes. No, this had to be a dream. Still, he continued: "I bet you've got plenty of questions. That's easy enough; here, let me buy you a Diet Coke and explain it. Come into the dark forest – sorry! The kitchen."

The television went to snow and white noise.

Violet snapped off the set quickly as if it would bite.

She didn't know how long she sat there. It might have been an hour, it could have been less. Violet looked around the living room, sure of an ambush or death-rendering fright. Everything was the same. The brass rubbing of the Ashmolean Knight, the replica of the Westminster Abbey coronation chair, good, old Parsifal.

Nothing had changed.

But there was light under the kitchen door!

"There it is; on the table – want ice with that?"

It had to be a dream, Violet thought, standing in the doorway of the kitchen. Christian Walsh was pulling clean dishes out of the drainer and setting them on shelves. And while he did this, he sang bits and pieces of *Stairway to Heaven*.

Violet's first instinct was to shriek; but no, this was a dream. Nothing would come out of her throat if she did. Instead, she looked at the table where Christian pointed, for where before a stack of history books had cluttered the tablecloth, there now was a crystal goblet and a porcelain vase filled with exquisite silver roses, yellow and white freesia. Beside them stood a glass bottle of Diet Coke.

"Well, Violet?" Christian asked as he continued to put away dishes. "Don't you have any questions? It's ten minutes to one in the morning and I'm in your kitchen doing the washing up."

It was then Violet noticed the kitchen, from polished floors to shiny, squeaky-clean counter tops. Even the drafting table where the computer and printer sat was better organized than it had been in years.

"What the Hell! What did you do? How'd you do this?"

Christian raised blond brows quizzically. "This?" he gestured around the immaculate kitchen. "This came easy. It's part of the job description," he explained, still putting away dishes. Violet didn't think she had so many. "I make it my business to take care of hard luck cases. Your name came up on my list this month. Ask me something harder, Violet. Aren't you a bit curious – or frightened?"

Violet closed her eyes tightly – so tight, she could see waves of light and spots dancing, the colors purple and red – and opened them.

No, he was still there.

He picked up a box of cereal and studied the nutrition panel, frowning. "The carton is more nutritious," he murmured.

Violet claimed her precious box of Cap'n Crunch

With Crunch Berries before he could dump its contents down the garbage disposal.

"No; I'm asleep," she chattered now; "I'm dreaming, and tomorrow at five-thirty, I'll wake, and you'll be gone, and kitchen will be ratty again, and —"

"Something harder, Violet. You're constantly asking someone to help you – what is it you say?"

Christian turned to face her and for the first time during their bizarre discourse, their eyes met. Violet recognized the look. No one had looked at her like that since her first time with a man.

He took a leather-bound planner out of the breast pocket of his blazer and thumbed through it. "Here it is: 'There's got to be way out of the mess that's become my life,'" Christian read, and smiling, added: "Well, here I am. Ask something truly difficult. I'm as real as you want me. I'm here to help you out of trouble."

"Oh no, I'm asleep," she insisted; "I'll wake up disappointed."

Christian stroked Violet's cheek furtively, then tenderly, as one might a lover's. At first Violet was beguiled, then frightened. She stepped away.

"You don't have to be afraid of me," he whispered. The voice, so sensual, was a caress. "I'm as real to you as all your problems and disappointments. I *am* real, Violet. I'm whatever you want me to be."

Violet thought she understood then. "God?"

Christian smiled, amused. "I wouldn't presume that much. This Armani jacket is as close as one gets to that image."

"Oh geez, you're an angel! Right, right; geez,"

"Angel? Who said anything about angels? You're a smart woman; haven't you figured it out yet? I'm your knight on horseback."

"You expect me to believe —?"

"Well, you can believe whatever you want. That's entirely up to you. You've never been big on anything unconditional – especially faith."

"That's not true. Love. I'm a believer of unconditional love."

"What do you think is being offered? But it's all up to you."

"Are you suggesting —?"

"It's the whole picture, the big picture, I'm talking of. Still, it's up to you." Christian came close again, but this time Violet didn't move.

"Come, follow me to the dark forest, it's just beyond the hill," he whispered. "Go into the forest glen, my love, my love, gaze down into the crystal pool, watch the ripples die, whose face do you see? I wonder if you'll think about me…"

The caress of his hand on her cheek was as heady as lovemaking. She closed her eyes and felt the touch of a kiss on her lips. When she opened her eyes, Max was kneeling over her and grinning, the alarm clock buzzing furiously on the nightstand.

"Dad gone! Daddy! Where Dad?"

VIOLET PACED ANOTHER circle around the bus stop bench and watched another Transbay bus go by, waving it on. Glancing at her watch, she knew she couldn't pass up another one. Just another five minutes, just a minute longer…

"George!" she called, when he appeared at the light across the street. In a moment he had dodged traffic to join her. Violet's heart started pounding, her hands breaking into a sweat. Same blue jeans, same white dress shirt, same Armani jacket, same brown suede boots as Christian wore in the dream. But over them he wore the khaki overcoat, probably cashmere. Violet glanced around self-consciously. One of her neighbors was waiting at the light and watching.

He was smiling down at her, the knee-weakening smile from her dream. "Good morning, Violet Ellison."

"Hi."

"Purple."

"Pardon?" Violet sputtered.

George pointed at her sweater. "I remember your favorite color. Purple. Not many can wear it. But you can – and well."

"Thanks."

He now watched as she rifled through a zippered pouch of compact discs and chose one, handing it to him. "I remember now, and remembered why I tried so hard to forget," she said.

"Fortinbras," George chuckled, but not unkindly. "Dark Forest is your absolute favorite song. And Christian Walsh – well, we won't go into that."

"The tree house in my backyard," Violet murmured, smiling.

"You used to sit up there with a record player and an extension cord long enough to hang someone, and you'd play that song over and over. You used to sit up there and stare at me," he laughed now; "I thought there was something wrong with my face!"

No. There was absolutely nothing wrong with that face.

"You reminded me of someone," she admitted. He did remind her of someone.

"Christian Walsh." They said in unison.

"That was the best summer of my life, sixty-nine. Before —" George stopped abruptly, shoved his hands into his coat pockets, his head bent as if in prayer.

"Before everything started changing," they said in unison, the thought coming to both of their minds in that second.

"You used to tease me about him – and warned me to guard my heart. I remember," Violet said wistfully.

"Yeah, well, it's said that Christian's broken a few hearts in his many, many, many, many, years."

"I wasn't talking about Christian Walsh."

George was about to speak, and then he looked up and pointed. "Here's your bus. Have a nice day, Violet Ellison. I wonder if you'll think about me."

The words struck Violet like a lightning bolt. She whirled about but George was gone, disappearing into the French Hotel. The driver of the Transbay bus growled at Violet to make up her mind.

Once seated on the bus, Violet glanced out the window and was suddenly hurled back to July of 1969, to the overgrown garden behind her parents' house in the Berkeley Hills. She was fifteen and sitting in the tree house, watching her sister Isobel laugh, talk, smoke pot and play Risk with her English lover Colin, and Colin's best friend and cousin, George. It was not so remarkable for what happened that summer night, but for the smile George had offered when he saw Violet above them in her hiding place.

Violet remembered the brilliant color of his eyes in the fading sunlight and how she felt when she went to sleep that summer's night, listening to Dark Forest...

> *Come, follow me to the dark forest, it's just beyond the hill, Go into the forest glen, my love, my love,*
> *Gaze down into the crystal pool, watch the ripples die, whose face do you see? I wonder if you'll think about me...*

6

Have I Gotta Deal For You!

NED PERCY WATCHED as Violet meticulously sorted the mail in two piles, opened it, and made calendar entries. Every morning the ritual was the same. On this particular morning, however, Ned was edgy and twice passed up a thick, square, envelope that Violet picked up and set down in turn.

"Whoops! There's one. We can eat this week." Ned snatched up a check and from the look on his face it was safe to assume they'd be eating well for at least six months. He grinned like a ten-year old with a new mountain bike and leaned in, saying: "So little girl, whaddaya want for Christmas?"

Violet wasn't listening. She picked up the square envelope and waved it. "What's this?" Ned turned the envelope over in his hand and tossed it back.

"An invitation to the annual pediatric AIDS benefit at the Sheraton Palace. Fancy dress ball – dinner, dancing, you know, society shit. Four simultaneous parties – New York, London, San Francisco, L.A., all on MTV, VH1, the Internet. A lot of our clients and their industry friends show up. Looks good on 'Entertainment Tonight' – y'know, the entertainment industry really does give a damn."

"Want an RSVP?"

"Depends on what day of the week it is."

"December sixteenth – weekend after next. Let's see – a Saturday."

"Nope; got plans. Meeghan's in town."

Ned glanced over his expensive wire-rimmed glasses and shot Violet what he thought was a seductive smile. She ignored him and wistfully glanced at the invitation before dumping it into the wastepaper basket. No sooner was it in, than Ned fished it out.

"Why don't you go this year?" he asked.

"Why don't you take Meeghan?"

"If Meeghan could put two words together to make a coherent sentence, I would."

"If Meeghan didn't stand around modeling undies all day, her little brain wouldn't be so cold and she could figure out a 'Dick-and-Jane' book."

"Jealous?"

"Are you kidding? Why do you go out with women like that? Never mind."

"Cuz you're not available."

"Don't push it, Ned."

"I want you to go."

"Me? I'm not an entertainment lawyer," Violet laughed. Then she glanced at the invitation and winced. "Besides, I can't afford the price."

The conversation was picked up again at lunch en route to Caffe Malvina in North Beach.

"The firm will pay," Ned argued. "You know how to charm and schmooze, talk business, work a room. I need the firm represented this year, and you're the best part of the firm."

"Didn't work before, not working now…"

They took Violet's usual table in Caffe Malvina, the table with the wobbly leg, the one stuck behind the door and beside a picture window fronting Washington Square. Violet passed a menu with the bread sticks and shook her head in warning when Ned looked as if he was formulating a new argument.

"What happened to your loyalty, Violet? I'm beginning to think you took this job only to work."

Violet grimaced. "I didn't have a choice. You were the only thing in town."

"I was the best thing in town! So? You gonna win one for Ned?"

"Can you see me at a society ball? I don't fit into that

crowd."

"I'm dead serious, Violet. No better place to pitch a story or treatment. You can get dressed up."

"I haven't got a dress!"

"Maybe I can help you with that, too. But even if I can't, you'll go."

"I won't."

"You will."

"Won't!"

"Violet . . . "

The bread sticks were gone in the fifteen minutes Ned continued to plead his case. Violet studied the plate of ravioli with pesto sauce the server set before her, giving her something to do other than reply to Ned's fervent yet embarrassing pleas. She gave in a little, just enough to shut him up, when the ravioli was gone and she had run out of excuses and resolve.

"It'll be like throwing me into the Coliseum with the lions, Ned; everybody that's anybody in the entertainment industry in the Bay Area will be there, and I'm more interested in getting my histories published."

"I'd rethink that course. The money's better in trade fiction. Get a steamy romance novel published and in grocery store checkout racks, then concentrate on your dead English kings."

Ned's hand was there when she reached for her Diet Coke. The grip was firm, decisive, assured – everything Ned could be, but wasn't. He wasn't gorgeous, but he was handsome. When the light hit him just right, she was reminded of Robert Redford, or rather, Redford's less-attractive younger brother. Looks notwithstanding, Ned had charm and generosity, and when it really mattered, a heart the size of Alaska.

"Don't be afraid of success," he said now. "You'll never break in if you can't be more positive, take risks. Go to that party, and I guarantee invaluable contacts. Go! Have fun!"

It was Violet's turn to spring for frozen yogurt and she invented her next line of attack while watching the vendor swirl two servings of vanilla classic into giant waffle cones.

"Everybody there will know I'm your secretary – and think the worst."

"They'll think my taste in women has improved."

"Thank you, I think! Ned, you know the chances of Sam wanting to go to something like this."

"Go alone, then. The kind of men you need to connect with will be there. You can be the user for a change."

"User?"

"Don't play dumb, Violet. The only reason anyone goes to these things is to make connections – both industrial and physical, and let's face it, your chances of hooking up with the right men are better than mine. Wear the right dress, use the right makeup, do your hair up – damn! I'm getting hot just fantasizing about it!"

"Ned!" Violet laughed nervously, playing just as nervously with a stray lock of hair. "I'm not a naïve waif, but I am married and it wouldn't be right. Besides, the idea of another man… I couldn't. It would kill Sam."

"Like he'd give a rat's ass. It'd probably come as a big relief, or it'd be one hell of a wakeup call – which is what the sonofabitch needs." Ned grumbled, half to himself as they waited at the light and a streetcar lumbered by. He was ready with another cheap shot when he noticed Violet's stricken eyes and ashen pallor. "God, Violet! I am so sorry," he whispered. "C'mon, it was meant as joke… shit, I'm going to pay through the nose for that one."

She wiped the melting yogurt from his Grateful Dead tee shirt. "For the rest of your life, Ned. When's the last time you washed this shirt? Sixty-eight, sixty-nine?"

The walk back to the office was silent. When they were outside Ned's office on Jackson Square, he suddenly turned to Violet and extended his arms in supplication.

"Violet? Whaddaya say, kid? For old times' sake? Puhleeze? How many chances do you have at something this big?"

She started tending the geranium and pansies in the nineteenth-century window boxes on the brick façade. "I'll think about it," she said at last.

"Think about it, Violet; think real hard."

After running a tape, Violet knew she came out a loser in this proposition. The cost of a dress would be nothing compared to getting her hair and nails done, finding accessories, and shoes. She was still regretting her lack of bargaining skills that evening on the walk to the Transbay Terminal.

"I wonder if you'd reconsider that dinner proposal."

Violet didn't bother reaching for her pepper spray or turning around. "You didn't make one. Good night, Ned."

"Gosh, you're right! Well, I am now."

"Maybe another time. I'm really tired, and I've got all this research to do for my thesis. Thanks all the same."
"C'mon, I know Sam's on another one of his search and rescue missions for the agency, the kids are at the Peters' for the weekend."

Violet spun around and offered The Look. The look that warned. The look that bode ill. He knew it and backed away. "Yet another reason I shouldn't work for a friend, especially one that knows me so well."

"Who says former lovers can't be friends?"

"I'm beginning to think that."

"Okay, okay, I'll back off. You're the best damn legal secretary in San Francisco and I don't want you to quit."

"I can't afford to quit. Behave. See you Monday!"

VIOLET WAS INDEED alone. Sam was indeed gone on another gallant quest to save the Soda Company account and the boys were at their grandparents' house until Sunday night, it being the second weekend of the month; Elisabet out with friends or at the studio.

Although Violet cherished rare moments of privacy, the house was unfriendly when empty, and being alone in it always took getting used to. Any minute the family ghosts would spring from the furniture and wallpaper and start asking questions. Rather than answer them, Violet went to bed immediately after making a supper of day-old bread and questionable salami. That night she experienced the most erotic, most disturbing dreams – all of which included George Knightsbridge. The next morning she half-expected to find George sitting at the kitchen table, dressed in Sam's bathrobe and looking 'morning-after' sexy.

No, Barney the Dinosaur had taken Sam's chair.

Saturday morning was spent at the university library gleaning material for her thesis paper. The world and its problems slipped away for a short while, only until a paragraph about the bill of attainder brought against George of Clarence by King Edward the Fourth reminded her of a temporal obligation.

Violet took a break in copying out passages from Gardiner's history of Richard the Third and pulled out a bundle of dog-eared, past-due bills she'd carried around for seven weeks, sorting out which could be paid and which would go with an entreaty for mercy.

A slow, methodical signing of her name to checks in her elegant, italic hand suddenly became a book signing party at Borders Book Store and Cafe. Instead of sitting at a polished oak table in the Doe Library reading room, Violet was settled comfortably on a plush chair in a cheerful, airy, sunlit shop with copies of her popular history of the Wars of the Roses piled neatly before her in two even stacks. The air was intoxicatingly heavy with scents of coffee, new paper, book glue and exotic potpourri. Smiles greeted her as she signed Violet Ellison on an ivory page just inside the cover and below the title, as she listened while bibliophiles offered their own interpretations of the Wars of Roses and asked her about

Anne Nevill being hidden in a London brothel by her brother-in-law Clarence and how Richard of Gloucester searched the entire city of London for her...

"Morning!"

Violet looked up and removed her headphones, not at all surprised to find George Knightsbridge standing over her. The damned light was behind him again, casting a halo in his golden hair. He was dressed in that expensive Armani jacket, blue jeans and white dress shirt, suede boots. But what caught her attention was the book.

In his hands he held a copy of Wickham's *The Mountains and the City*, perhaps the driest text ever written about medieval Tuscany but fascinating all the same. Violet had her own worn, personally-annotated copy and loved it. Her first and most ambitious novel was about fourteenth-century Florence.

"Hello George."

It was a flat response; neither delighted nor disgusted. Wary. George picked up on that immediately. Still, he waited for more.

She was uncomfortable by his presence, the discomfort one felt at the age of sixteen when running into a crush in the hallway between Math and Latin classes. Or when one woke in the morning and labored over conversation with the stranger on the other side of the bed.

"You're stalking me," she quipped.

"You'd like to believe that. I won't flatter you and say that I am – Gardiner!" George took the book out of her hands. "I hate to admit it, but I like him. And Kendall." He winked then and offered that radiant, knee-weakening smile. "Historians aren't supposed to like both; we're supposed to line up in two separate camps. In which camp are you?"

"Neither."

"Liar."

"And you?"

"Oh, I think Dickon of Gloucester was as black as

Gardiner paints him."

Violet was intrigued. "So you take the Tudor apologists' word at face value? The victors of Bosworth, who gave us men like Henry the Eighth and Cardinal Wolsey?"

"Pretty much."

"I guess you're like Pepys, who said all the history he ever learned he got from Shakespeare."

"Not exactly."

"And you believe the Shakespearean portrait of Richard as a slobbering hunchback."

"Blimey! I didn't know he slobbered."

"You need history lessons," Violet chuckled and flipped the pages in her notebook until she found an entry.

"I've had a few. Ten sixty-six and all that. Got a doctorate in history – Roman and Early Christian Britain. Oh, and a masters of fine arts in illustration. I've done a few dust jackets for juvenile books and fantasy novels back in England. You can say you're sorry any time now."

"At the risk of satisfying you, I don't think so."

"You've got such a nice smile. Quite lovely. Ah, there it is! See? That didn't hurt, did it?"

Violet now burst into laughter and pulled out the chair beside her, inviting him to sit. George had leaned over to peruse the stack of history texts surrounding her like a wall, commenting to himself on their merits, when he noticed the small bound notebook she leafed through – a book with a hand-tooled leather cover that was smooth and worn with age. His face turned swiftly ashen, his demeanor sullen.

"Where'd you get this?" he asked quietly, tapping the notebook.

"It was given to me." Violet frowned as he reached for the book. "What?" she demanded, pulling it out of his reach.

"After all this time!" George whispered. "I can't believe she kept it – look on the inside back cover, no, underneath."

Violet did as requested and George fingered the initials crudely tooled underneath the right inside flap. 'G' and 'K' entwined by ivy leaves.

"It's yours?" she asked, now offering the book.

"No. I made this for Bella for her twentieth birthday. I thought maybe…she and Colin were the best, absolutely the best. So unfair it happened…so damned unfair! If they only knew the pain they caused."

"Yeah; I'm beginning to wonder what God's quota is for fiery deaths by automobile and airplane and incurable diseases for one family. Throw in relatives on the Titanic and we've got all the bases covered, don't we?" Violet said bitterly, her voice wavering, ready to break. She expelled a labored sigh and threw her things into her briefcase.

"Violet – Violet, wait!" George shouted as she started out of the library. He caught up with her in the stairwell outside the humanities reading room.

George reached out to prevent her from heading down the stairs and the touch sent a jolt of sexual tension through Violet. She pulled away. Aware of the faux-pas, he stepped back, shoved his hands into his coat pockets and swore softly to himself.

"Look, I shouldn't have said anything. I know it hasn't been long, and God knows the wound hasn't healed."

Five months to the day, Violet ciphered mentally. She'd never spoken of it, never vented her grief. Being the mother of three children had forced her to be stoic in the face of tragedy. She couldn't allow herself the luxury of wallowing in tears or self-pity. The few tears that had been shed were vented in private and infrequently.

But five months was a long time to hold the tears back.

"I didn't see you at the funeral," Violet said, feeling her throat constrict. She coughed to mask the lump starting to grow, blinked to hold back tears.

"I was doing historical research in Greenland."

"Greenland? Don't bother trying to explain. It's okay," she sighed.

"No, it isn't. I haven't been able to talk about it – I haven't wanted to, not until I came to California. It all came back as soon as I saw you at the French Hotel – actually, in front of your house. And when Sam told me about the party, and mentioned you, y'know, everything about that summer came back, the years after… she called me a few weeks before the accident, before I left for Greenland. Out of the blue, really. We hadn't been – well, we talked," George now said, finding a need to explain. "She used to call every week on Friday. Without fail. We talked about what I was doing, what she and Colin were doing. She talked a lot about you."

"I've got to go," she said, heading down the Annex stairs. "I've got to get Christmas shopping done, pick up Sam's shirts at the cleaners, do some grocery shopping, be the perfect soccer mom —"

"Why are you angry?"

"Do you have to ask? I don't want to talk about my practically perfect sister and her charming, erudite, husband who had all the answers and all the numbers. Or don't you remember what a disappointment I was to them?"

"Only because you settled for Sam."

Violet dumped her briefcase on the stairs and crossed arms against her breasts defensively. "If you remember, Isobel was pretty set on getting us together, as were Amalie and Stan, and everyone else. No one bothered at the time to ask me what I felt!"

"I think even then you loved him."

"It seemed like a good idea to everyone that I did."

"Didn't you?"

A moment, then, "Yes," she sighed.

"What about now?"

"He's my husband. The father of my children."

"That sounded forced. Or were you forced to make decisions you weren't ready to make?"

"If you're talking about the circumstances of my marriage you can stop."

"Sorry, I wasn't."

Violet was prepared to offer a defense and then looked away, watching the shadow of tree branches dance on the floor. "Maybe we both should get on with our lives such as they are or aren't."

George expelled a painful sigh and spread his hands in the universal sign of hopelessness then lowered himself on to a step. "They were my dearest and closest friends," he murmured. "But I don't expect you to understand."

Violet recognized the pain in George's voice. "I do." She plopped down on the step below him.

"Here. I'm supposed to give you this. Been carrying it around ever since the Halloween party, trying to find a perfect moment. Colin's mum sent it after the accident. She said you'd know."

From his pocket George had taken a small square of wrinkled, stained tissue paper that he held out at a safe distance. Violet frowned but nevertheless accepted the minuscule parcel that might have been a bit of nothing, a scrap to be tossed into the wastepaper basket.

She gasped and then a hundred or more memories flooded her imperfectly ordered thoughts – of childhood, of playing dolls, of fighting battles against the clothesline dragon with balsa wood swords and paper helmets. Of seeing two lovers in a moon-washed bedroom, of the afternoon at the cemetery, of years of silence and loneliness...

The medal of Saint George of Cappadocia lying in her hands gleamed in the soft winter sunlight and shot rays across her face. Wordlessly she slipped it around her neck and through a film of tears smiled at George Knightsbridge.

"Do you suppose we could be friends now? Could you ever trust me? I made a promise to Bella to make you behave."

"I'd forgotten our promise," she whispered. The promise made that summer's night so long ago, the night she sat in the tree house and listened to *Dark Forest*, the night she'd entered the bedroom and found Isobel with Colin. The promise that if either should die the survivor would wear the medal of Saint George as a shield against the hurts of the world. A dissoluble bond between sisters.

She recounted this to George.

"Violet Ellison, you're the last person in the world who needs a knight on horseback!" George remarked, and touched the medal gently as it dangled from its chain around her neck. "But don't you already have one?" Violet dared to look in his eyes and was going to ask if it was he when George continued, saying happily now, "I remember the suit of armor. It was when we were on holiday between terms. We all three went to Canterbury. I was researching Chaucer for a paper. We stumbled upon an antique shop in Maidstone and there was the absolutely incredible suit of armor. When Isobel saw it, she said that Violet would sell her soul to the Devil for it. 'I've got to get it for her for her birthday. She'll never speak to me again if I don't.' That was in April of sixty-nine. I thought, 'I don't know this girl named Violet, but she must be pretty fabulous.' Now I know."

George smiled down at Violet, a handsome, tawny, god, but more real to her now than before. She bowed her head and watched dust in a silvery mote waltz across the scuffed tops of her burgundy leather clogs. When she glanced at him from under her bangs, Violet saw that his face had grown softer and melancholic, making years melt away.

"Do you know what the last thing I said to her was, George?"

"No."

"Funny thing, I can't remember. It was probably nothing. She divorced me. She went to England to live a storybook life with Colin, sent pretty postcards at Christmas; talked to me on my birthday and holidays as if I was a casual acquaintance from high school, talked to the children and exchanged photographs. Our conversations were always memorable for what wasn't said. To this day, I've tried to remember what I did wrong. What I did to displease her. It couldn't all have been Sam."

George offered a hand to help her off the stairs. They stood holding hands for a while, taking full measure of one another.

"That's quite a bit of nothing – a painful bit of nothing," George whispered.

"We've said enough about it. Let's move on."

"Lead the way."

"Want to get some lunch?" Violet asked after the embarrassing silence had gone on long enough.

"Are you asking me on a date?"

"I'm asking you if you want lunch. Are you hungry?"

"Starving,"

"I've got seven dollars – that'll buy us lunch at Burger King. You can tell me how you got Parsifal here from England."

"Parsifal?" George asked, following her out of the library.

"Parsifal. The suit of armor. It's at home. Well, he had to have a name!"

It made sense, George thought. It made perfect sense. More than the sudden and unfortunate deaths of two people both he and this charming woman named Violet had loved.

7

Nothin' Says 'Sorry' Like Dinner for Two

VIOLET THOUGHT NOTHING of the lights burning in the hallway and kitchen as she dropped her shopping bags by the front door and kicked off her muddy boots. From the trail of luggage and clothing, it looked as if Sam was home. She stepped over the battle-scarred carry-on blocking entry to the living room, removed Sam's rain- soaked trench coat from the coffee table and tossed it over the hall tree. Then she did a double take passing the seldom-used dining room.

The good china and flatware were laid out on a pristine, linen tablecloth. Dinner for two – beef Bourgogne – was prepared. Candlelight softened the partially stained walnut paneling and the heavy Gothic furniture. And in the background, Violet's favorite classical piece, Britten's *Courtly Dances from Gloriana*, played out of the tape deck.

"Consider this an apology."

Sam stood in the doorway with an ice bucket and bottle of Dom Perignon in his arms. "You know… the Halloween party, other times, stuff."

"Ah yes," she said, "stuff."

He glanced at the Christmas parcels topping the Target bags. "Almost through with Christmas shopping, or just getting started?"

"Somewhere in between."

"Interested in dinner, or do you want to write for a while?"

"Not in the mood."

"For dinner, or —"

"Writing."

"Excellent! Is this a date, or —"

Violet tilted her head in that way Sam had always thought beguiling and smiled. "Haven't been on a date in a while."

"Sit. I'll be with you in a minute."

Violet took a seat at the end of the table and ran her hands delicately over her mother's Irish linen tablecloth, remembering the occasion for each stain and the guilty party who'd put them there. There was the merlot stain, her contribution to the family tradition. Isobel got it in her head to fix a black tie dinner, only Colin had man- aged to get their main course, a twenty-pound turkey, stuck on his head and Violet blew wine out her nose from laughing so hard...

"Deep in thought, Vi?" Sam called.

"Huh? Oh, yeah, yeah... school, my writing... you weren't supposed to be home until Wednesday. I assume things went well in Los Angeles?" Violet asked when Sam reentered with the corkscrew. He bent down and offered a lingering kiss. When Violet opened her eyes, she saw a tender smile. It had been months since she'd been on the receiving end of one.

"Better than expected," he said; "six figures to start."

The cork fired out of the champagne bottle and ricocheted off the china cabinet. Sam quickly poured two flutes and then drank from the bottle, passing it to Violet, who drank deep to steel her courage. He sat next to her – not across the table, but beside her.

The prospect of freedom from debt preoccupied Violet for the rest of the evening. She was excited, but cautious. Promises from Hollywood, she knew from experience, were like pie crusts – easily made and quickly broken. She wouldn't think about Alex's braces or tires for the car until she saw the money in the bank.

Dinner was quiet; the conversation, pedestrian. It was safer to discuss Elisabet's latest painting, her eclectic mix of friends, Alex's victory over a video game or Max's rebellion against potty-training than find another avenue to travel upon, one that would perhaps lead them back on course before they strayed too far.

And then there was nothing left to say. While the tape played over and over, Sam drank the rest of the champagne quietly and Violet pushed sticky, creamy, crumbs from the chocolate decadence cheesecake around her plate. Sam at last put down his champagne flute and leaned over.

"You've got great hair; I love it," he murmured, pushing the locks of hair straying from her loose chignon off her face. "What is it about you?"

"You tell me," she murmured, studying the pattern of the crumbs intently.

"Well, let's see… it won't be too hard. You're loving, you're caring, you're forgiving, and you've got a great sense of humor."

"Pretty, I hope?"

"Big, beautiful, gorgeous green eyes; a smile that stops traffic."

"Boundless amount of patience."

"For stupid, uncaring, insensitive men. I could go on for hours, but I have a better idea," Sam whispered. He caressed her long, slender, neck and then kissed it. "Just tell me if you think so, too." He next kissed her mouth. Violet broke away and amidst Sam's pleas, left the dining room. When Sam finally followed, he found Violet in the dark living room, lit only by a fire in the hearth. The laundry had been tossed to the carpet and Violet was curled up on the sofa wrapped in nothing but an afghan throw.

"What is it about you?" Sam whispered huskily when she patted the sofa and then let the throw slide from her naked shoulders.

They made love for hours, moving from under the watchful eyes of the Ashmolean Knight to the behind the curtains of their canopied bed. The sun was a stain of light on the horizon and peering through the clouds when Violet finally moved to her side of the bed.

"Since we've figured out what it is about me, maybe

we should explore the question of us?" Violet murmured.

"There's no question," Sam replied, pulling her close. "I meant what I said earlier. I'm sorry. I'll always regret the hurt I've caused you. You always say the morning gives us chances to get it right, well, I want to get it right and keep it that way."

Violet kissed him passionately then, and she knew he was as good as his word, when later that Sunday, the doorbell rang and she found Marjorie Rotherwell on the porch.

"Oh! I wasn't expecting – is Sam here, uh, Violet?"

"In the back," Violet replied, tightening her grip on her bathrobe collar. "We're kind of busy right now," she said more firmly as Marjorie started to enter.

"He'll want to see me, dear. It's about business."

"It's about eleven-thirty on a Sunday morning. Can this wait?" Violet demanded.

"Excuse me?" Marjorie asked with a fixed smile splitting her face in two. "I don't think you understand."

"The misunderstanding's all yours," Sam replied, joining them at the door. "Back from Portugal, Marjorie?"

"In the flesh. Sam."

My, wasn't there a lot of it, Violet thought.

"We had a ten o'clock yesterday and I waited for three hours. We busted our asses to get the mock ups to you and you didn't show," Sam said quietly. "I hope it wasn't a subtle message?"

"Did you think —? Oh, I knew I should have called. Well, I'm here now, aren't I? I've seen your mock ups of the print ads and I just don't think," Marjorie began, but Sam dismissed her with a wave of the hand.

"I'm free tomorrow during the day if you want to call Carrie and make an appointment," he said.

"Tomorrow evening would be better."

"Violet and I have tickets to a concert in San Jose."

"Tuesday, then."

"Castle Records has me all day, Marjorie."

"What about in the evening?"

"Family stuff."

"Well, let's do this now."

"Not free."

"Hmmm… if it's free time you want, I can give it to you. See you, Sam, tomorrow?"

"Bye, Marjorie."

The door closed. Sam stood with his hand on the doorknob for a moment and casually took the Sunday *Chronicle/Examiner* from the hallway table, flipping through the sections and supplements to the *Sporting Green.*

"If you did that for me," Violet began.

Sam glanced up and shrugged, tossed the paper down. "The client is always supposed to be right, but sometimes you have to set boundaries and draw the line somewhere."

"She'll pull the account, won't she?"

Again, a shrug. "She's only one client," he said and returned to the video game in the living room.

Violet watched intently as he concentrated on the destruction of gargoyles and dragons while trying to reach the next level. "What?" Sam turned to look at her, still working the controls. Violet had slipped down onto the floor cushions next to him.

"As much as I despise that woman and how she treats you, I didn't want you to jeopardize an account for me."

"Getting my priorities lined up, Vi. I need to make room for that fellowship – some creative financing. Rotherwell Bakery isn't my only priority, you know."

"Thank you!" Violet exclaimed tearfully.

"Hey," Sam whispered, "Anything for you. Anything at all."

Violet knew he meant it.

8

Better Go Home Son, An' Make Up Your Mind...

THE LIGHTS WERE up on the stage and Christian Walsh stood center front, a coffee mug in hand, the local morning paper tucked under his arm. He surveyed the venue for that evening's concert and took cautious sips off the mug. The worst thing about touring was the coffee – and maybe the loneliness, but loneliness was something he had gotten used to. The coffee was a different matter altogether.

Concert venues changed nightly, six days out of seven, but they all looked the same after a week, a month on the road. The landscapes of metal and rubber with their acrid, chemical smells, the arc lamps, the scrims and the spotlights, were different only in placement and quantity. The stage, whether raked, polished wood or black vinyl overlay, was the same expanse of emptiness. This was the home Christian Walsh had defined for himself thirty years ago in a dingy Lincoln public house.

A door opened in front, bringing in a pale gold shaft of morning light to blind Christian and make him curse. "Hey!" Kevin Wakefield shouted in greeting.

"Hey yourself, and shut the Goddamn door!" Christian greeted. He sat on the floor and spread the Oakland Tribune, hoping to learn something interesting or new about this venue the band visited every other year, some- thing he could impart to the audience that night.

Like a house cat craving attention, Kevin stretched out in front of him. He removed the A's baseball cap from his tangle of curling black hair and then moaned. "I don't know if it's jet lag, the water, or too much red wine," he said.

"All three, I suppose. You've never travelled well."

"Where'd you go last night? We were invited to Lesh's house for drinks," Kevin queried.

"I was there, but I left. Isn't the same without Jerry – didn't like being paraded about like the eighth wonder of the world, if you must know."

"Can't help it if you are…"

"Don't start."

Kevin grunted and looked at Christian carefully, as if expecting to see something new or different on a face he'd seen for over thirty years. "You're in a better mood than usual."

"I like California – hey! There's a football game at Candlestick Park this Sunday. I've never been to an American football game, have you?"

"We're flying home on Sunday."

"Never been to a football game here in the States. I've heard great things about the Forty-Niners," Christian stated as he scanned the sports page. "What if I flew back after the game? I can meet you back in London."

"I have a better idea," Kevin said, taking the business section of the paper. "Sally, the girls and I will stay in San Francisco with you. We can have Charlie Bonnett change our flight and we can all go home together."

"If it'll make you sleep nights, I'll give you my hotel key – just so you can keep an eye on me," Christian jibed

"Not a bad idea though I don't fancy spending Christmas in Tijuana chasing you down in wedding chapels."

"That never happened. I'm flattered you think the women still fight to get in to my bed."

"Word on the street, mate; word on the street."

Having been whacked with the newspaper good-naturedly, Kevin removed and replaced the baseball cap as he once again stared at the sports arena being transformed into a concert venue. "I expect a right proper showing tonight," Kevin yawned; "last show of this year's tour, and all."

Christian winced as he shifted to make himself comfortable. "Jesus! That hurts like nothing before," he muttered, adding: "We're getting too old for this, Kevin."

"Oh no; not the age thing."

"You have to admit it's getting harder. At least for me it is." "Know what your problem is?"

"No doubt you've got the solution for it." "That's always a possibility."

The large violet-blue eyes peering from behind the newspaper were warning lights to go no further. Still, Kevin ventured forth into dangerous waters.

"It's been years, Chris, and we made a promise. We'll have to talk, eventually." "Now's not the time to discuss it."

Now was the perfect time to discuss it, when they were both in good humor and not exhausted from a performance and Kevin said as much. "We did promise to have this talk one day and it's getting perfectly clear to me."

"Not today, Kev."

Kevin expelled a sigh and gave his attention to the roadies coming on to the stage to set up for that morning's rehearsal. When one of them asked about Christian's schematic for lighting, Kevin turned and saw that Christian was still brooding over the newspaper. Kevin had always been told by the ladies that he was attractive – sexy even – a tall, dark, handsome, kind, with Mediterranean eyes and dimples like lunar craters. But it was Christian women still waited at the stage door to see, sent birthday presents, and named their first-born sons and pet budgies after. Looking at Christian in the flattering soft morning light, it was easy to see why: Tawny hair, brilliant blue eyes, square, strong jaw and soft, sexy voice – Christian had it all.

Kevin muttered something about saving the lights for another time and shooed the roadies off stage. Christian rewarded Kevin's patience with his famous ninety-watt smile, but it was far from sincere. "Better now than never," hinted Kevin.

The newspaper was folded meticulously on Christian's lap. "My objections won't stop you, Kevin. Say what you have to say so we can finish the tour quietly." The voice was tired, edgy.

He'd prepared this speech years ago and now that the opportunity lent itself, Kevin didn't know what to say. "Maybe now isn't the time," he sighed.

"Just whose cage are we rattling here?" Christian asked. "It's been mine for the last thirty-five years."

"Only wondering," Christian said with a wink; "but it's good to know nothing's changed."

Kevin was ready to say that that was the problem – that nothing had changed, that Christian had been rattling a few too many cages of late. The words were forming on Kevin's lips when Christian finally put aside the news-paper and took his acoustical guitar from a roadie that ventured out on to the stage. Standing alone center stage was how the world and Kevin saw Christian. Alone in his own universe, alone with his private muse. A million people loved him, but he was a million miles away.

TEN HOURS LATER, that stage was a flurry of streamlined activity in preparation for the show. Outside, fans queued up at the box office for a last minute chance at good seats. The season ticket holders and lucky few who did have rights to premium seating waltzed smugly past the growing line where Fortinbras tee-shirts stretched across middle-aged bellies, where remembrances of earlier concerts, most particularly, the first American concert at the Fillmore in July of 1969, were discussed. Violet Ellison was one of the privileged few and listened fondly to the stories, eager to share a few of her own.

Since she was fifteen, Violet had wanted to go to a rock concert. Now, at forty-two, she stood at the Coliseum entrance waiting for Sam, a VIP pass around her neck proclaiming that she was someone. Twice a kindly security guard approached her and smiling asked if she needed an escort to her seat, or if she needed help. Of course she needed help – for believing that Sam would ever show up anywhere on time. He'd be late to his own funeral.

She paced another trail and was ready to make a call when she heard the shouts.

"Vi! Violet! *Mizz Ellison!*"

Thornton came out of the white-hot glare of headlights and sprinted from the parking lot, nearly colliding with vehicles and concertgoers to reach Violet.

"Where is he?" Violet hissed.

"He got a call..." Thornton gasped, leaning against a support beam. "He's not coming. Had to take a conference call with New York."

"Soda Company?" Violet hissed.

"No; the communications firm that does the bread TV ads."

"Rotherwell!" Violet spat.

"Yeah," Thornton said, nodding.

Violet fought the tears stinging her eyelids and swallowed the lump rising in her throat. She removed the VIP pass and handed it to Thornton, saying, "Enjoy a bit of rock 'n roll history!"

If she hurried, she could make an exit before the tears were evident. Jostled and pressed, Violet looked for the gates while digging in her coat pocket for a handkerchief. She found a package of Rolos, a package of tissues and the Isle of Lewis chess piece.

"Some help you are!" Violet muttered at her talisman.

"Excuse me, pardon me! Lady!"

Violet was startled by Coliseum executive shoving his way past her to an entrance that was now being un- locked. The chess piece was knocked out of her hand as the executive's entourage came through the burgeoning crowd. Violet watched despondently as it rolled into the darkness. She thought about going after it for only a moment, and then headed for a gate being opened by security guards.

Assuming this was the way out, Violet's path was suddenly blocked by limousines and more security personnel who materialized as if out of nowhere, wearing lemon-colored 'Event Staff ' jackets. Unknowingly she'd stumbled into the band's entourage and was now pushed back to allow them access to the stage entrance.

The band members were escorted from their cars and away from a multitude of autograph-hungry fans. The size and girth of the security guards blocking Violet's path to the parking lot made it impossible to see anyone or anything. She didn't care. Getting a glimpse of Fortinbras wasn't as exciting now as it had been two hours or twenty-seven years ago.

But Christian Walsh had seen her.

He glanced over the heads of roadies clustering about him for last-minute instructions and saw Violet. He rarely noticed anyone while on tour, much less while preparing for a show, but now he stared at the woman standing off to the side and he couldn't look away.

CHRISTIAN WAS THE first one ready to leave after the show, which was unusual. He always lingered backstage or took forever to remove the stage makeup and have a solitary, congratulatory cigarette for another fine performance. He was pacing the parking lot, making rectangles and figure eights in a deliberate pattern, as if searching, when Kevin finally came out.

"There you are! Is this where you've been all this time? C'mon then, Sally's throwing a surprise birthday party for me back at the hotel – Chris?"

Christian ignored Kevin and for the hundredth time surveyed the empty parking lot, staring at programs and beverage containers, the souvenirs of yet another Fortinbras concert skipping and sailing in a breeze across the asphalt. Yards of fluorescent-lit emptiness were all around, but she was nowhere in sight.

"Did you see her?" Christian asked.

"See who?"

Christian saw the amused expression on his friend's face and decided to let it go. Probably just another fan.

As Christian turned to join Kevin, he stepped on something and looked down. A white object gleamed in the light of the street lamp. Christian picked it up and discovered an ivory chess piece, a knight of medieval fashion.

Turning it over in his hands, he studied it carefully and was fascinated by this little treasure.

"Christian, c'mon!"

"In a minute, Kev," Christian called and pocketed the knight on his way to the limousine.

VIOLET WAS MAD.

No a better homonym was furious – or better still, seething. Irate. No, incensed and indignant.

Pissed! That was it.

No, she was frightened. Hadn't Sam brushed Marjorie off when she demanded to talk about the problems with the company's print ads? Sam had placed Violet ahead of business. He'd kept his promise to spend more time with her and now he'd probably lost the best account the agency had, blown off an opportunity of a lifetime.

"What have I done? What have I done?" Violet wailed as she came screeching into the parking lot outside the agency. Odds were Sam was still on the phone with New York doing damage control.

She didn't remember climbing the twenty-seven steps to the agency entrance, but on the way up in the freight elevator she tried heartfelt apologies, promises to make things right – even giving up the chance at the Oxford fellowship – when she finally threw open the doors.

Violet was totally unprepared for what greeted her.

A radio was turned up to deafening and the lights were off, for the exception of the desk lamp behind the screen. Sam was probably drinking himself unconscious. He always got plastered when something went wrong. *Dear God*, she prayed, *let him still have the account!*

Violet's calls were drowned out by the music and she stopped just short of the screen, obscured by the shadows. She was close enough to see Sam on top of Marjorie Rotherwell. All one hundred and eighty-two pounds of her. All of her dimpled, aging, pink flesh and cellulite.

Violet didn't know whether to cry or laugh. The sight of her sweating, glistening Adonis with the washboard stomach and body to die for caught in the lamb shank thighs of an aging whore as he tried to bring her to new heights of ecstasy was comical. Their moans and shrieks were still ringing in her ears when she stood in her bathroom and twisted the wedding band off her finger; they were with her while she pulled the handle and watched the wedding band Sam had purchased at an antique store on Sutter Street swirl its way down the toilet. They followed her around the kitchen while she canvassed for junk food and tossed it all into a plastic garbage bag, while she chopped vegetables for a stir-fry.

"Mom?"

Violet ignored Elisabet, who entered the kitchen fresh from a night class.

"Mamma?"

"What, Elisabet?"

"Oh shit, you're crying! What's happened, Mamma?"

Violet took a cleaver to a pile of mushrooms and started whacking at them, dumping the confetti she'd made into the wok.

Elisabet now reached for a knife and carefully cored bell peppers. "Eventually I'll find out, and eventually I'll have to know. What did he do?"

"Who?"

"C'mon! I'm not stupid! Dad may be everyone's darling boy as Grammy Am says, but one thing I've learned is that he can insensitive and selfish."

Violet mumbled something, and then reached for a tissue to wipe her eyes.

"You did *what?*"

Elisabet took the hot mitt from Violet and grabbed the kettle before it whistled itself off the stove.

"I flushed my wedding ring down the toilet."

"I don't think Dad would get mad about that – he's done worse."

"You have no idea."

They continued to chop vegetables until the wok was almost overflowing. Elisabet glanced at her mother and saw the tears coming faster now.

"I should have known all along, I should have known twenty years ago, I should have, I just should have!" Violet was muttering to herself. After a moment, Elisabet stopped work and placed the knife carefully on the counter.

"I have to know, Mamma. I will find out, so please tell me. Maybe I can help."

When Violet turned to face her and raised her hands in the universal sign of hopelessness, letting them drop to her sides, and as her shoulders slumped with a fresh downpour of tears, Elisabet felt a clammy chill overtake her, then a wave of nausea.

"Anyone but her! I could understand someone like – but her? Why her?" Violet sobbed.

"Oh God, did you catch him with someone? Who? Carrie? Son of a – Marjorie? *Marjorie?*"

Violet stopped wagging her head in response and attended the teapot, taking great care with pouring.

"What are you going to do, Mamma?"

Two cups of tea were placed on the cleanest spot on the kitchen table and for a moment Violet held hers to savor its warmth on this cold December night. "I don't know," she sighed at last.

"Where's he now?"

"With her, I suppose."

"Did they see you?"

"I hope the Hell they did!"

Violet's hands began to shake so hard the tea sloshed angrily out of the mug and burned her. Elisabet grabbed a wet dishcloth from the sink behind them and pressed it gently against her mother's wounded wrist.

"I am so stupid!" Violet hissed and began sobbing. "How could I not have known something was going on – he lost his wedding ring a couple of months ago, he's always on a business trip – why was I so stupid?"

Violet's sobbing was uncontrollable now and as she convulsed with anger, she swept the dishes off the counter so that they shattered in a thousand directions and showered the kitchen floor with porcelain shards. Elisabet dodged a piece of china and stepped back carefully when Violet looked as if she would turn on her.

"What will you do?" she asked.

"I don't know… Christ, how do I explain something like this to the boys? They're too young to understand.

Never mind – you don't! I blame myself!"

She wept silently and soon began to make sniffling, wretched sounds so that Elisabet found she could stand idle no longer and embraced her, whispering consolation, until they heard the drone of Sam's BMW in the garage. Violet broke away and ran, the slam of her bedroom door muffled by the kitchen screen banging shut as Sam entered and found Elisabet sweeping up the shards.

"Whoops," Sam chuckled. "Does your mother know about this?"

"Yes. She got some bad news," Elisabet said, not bothering to look at her father.

"What, did someone else die? Every time she loses a relative we lose another place setting."

"No – Dad, you know there's no one else in her family. Geez."

"What then?"

"She found out something tonight that upset her."

The shards were swept slowly and methodically into a dustpan while Sam hummed a song and helped himself to the tea left on the table.

"Well," he said, between sips, "I'd rather hear it from you – it will be less painful."

Elisabet paused, considering her choice of words. Finally, "Mamma didn't get the fellowship."

"Ouch!" Sam replied, setting down his cup. He headed towards the living room stairs. "Looks like I have to do more damage control."

"More than you'll ever know..." muttered his daughter as she finished cleaning up. As soon as she heard the bedroom door close, Elisabet reached for her mother's address book on the drafting table and flipped through pages, watching the door. She picked up the phone and dialed a number, waiting nervously.

"Uh, hi. Yeah, this is Elisabet Peters. Yeah! Hi, no, everything's fine. Well, maybe not. That's why I'm calling..."

"HEY, YOU AWAKE?"

Sam had taken care to use mouthwash and freshen up before he climbed into bed. Violet caught the lingering scent of Chanel Number Five and Jack Daniels when he bent over to kiss her. She pretended to sleep and it wasn't until he'd switched off the lights that Violet opened her eyes and found him smiling. A loving look she once though reserved only for her.

"Vi, Beth told me what happened."

"Life's full of surprises," she answered, keeping her voice even so that it wouldn't betray her anger.

"I know you were counting on that fellowship – maybe you'll get another chance at it?"

It dawned on Violet what Elisabet had done. *Clever girl!* "Maybe in the spring," she answered, turning away from Sam and pulling the covers close.

"Guess it hasn't been your night. I'm sorry about the

concert. Did you enjoy it?" he murmured, running a hand under her pajama jacket. The touch of his icy hand made Violet go cold for a different reason.

"I gave Thornton our passes and went to a movie," she lied, nevertheless allowing him access to her body. She wouldn't make it difficult for him – not yet.

"A movie?" he laughed as he stripped away her pajama jacket and pulled down the matching shorts. "What'd you go see?"

"*Brief Encounter.*"

His hands were sliding down her stomach and past her waist as he distributed long, lingering, kisses, his hands went into the band of her underwear and encircled her hips, kneading, until he had finally removed the underwear, then he slid the covers off and started a massage he hoped would bring arousal.

"Mm, God, you taste good, you feel so good, Vi! Those passes didn't come cheap. I had to practically prostitute myself for them. You could have met Christian Walsh in the flesh! You missed a great opportunity, Vi."

"Not really. I've loved Christian Walsh since I was fifteen," Violet murmured as she shifted in the bed to ac-commodate him. "He's the only man I've ever loved that hasn't disappointed me. If I finally do get a chance to meet him, who knows? I might be disappointed."

"Let me make it up to you now!"

For the first time in their marriage, Violet pretended to enjoy their coupling. She acquiesced to his sexual demands, even those she wouldn't have countenanced before. After tonight, he'd never call her a prude again. But then, after tonight, he'd be lucky if he got anything from her at all. It had to a mid-life crisis, this sudden un-quenchable sexual hunger of Sam's. There was no other explanation for a man whose appetite was still unsatisfied after being with a woman only hours before.

When he finally rolled to his side of the bed and took as many of the covers with him as possible, Violet resisted the urge to have it out, came to the realization that it wasn't worth the effort. Leaning over, she picked up the Walkman headphones and switched on the player. Christian Walsh's voice lulled her to sleep and dulled the pain just a little.

9

Can't See the Forest for the Christmas Trees

CHRISTIAN WOKE IN a foul humor. His night had been restless and his sleep interspersed with dreams of the woman he'd seen last night at the Coliseum, and, strangely, of chess games, like the one made famous on an episode of *The Prisoner*.

Around nine o'clock, someone knocked on the hotel suite door and Christian shouted at whomever it was to go away. He wanted privacy to ruminate over last night's dreams. From those ruminations came a song – a sensuous, enigmatic, ballad written for a woman he didn't know and despaired of ever seeing again. It became an obsession for days. He joined Kevin and Sally Wakefield and their daughters for meals in the hotel restaurant but made excuses to retire early and then spent all night working on the song. He was still laboring over it on Thursday morning when he heard Kevin's familiar raps on the door, a secret knock known only to them since their adolescent years in Yorkshire. Before Kevin could ask how he was, Christian thrust the sheet music in his face.

"Been working on a song if you must know," Christian said in response to the question forming on Kevin's lip. "I must!" Kevin said, and studied the piece and whistled. "Really – hey! This may top *Dark Forest!*"

"There's still some life left in me," Christian said as he disappeared into the bathroom.

"This I can see! This'll wrap up the new album!"

"But first we have to sell the one we just finished," Christian called over the drone of the shower and invited Kevin to try out the song while he cleaned up. Kevin was still picking out the tune on Christian's cherished Martin guitar fifteen minutes later when Christian returned to scoop up the clothes neatly laid out on the unmade bed and disappeared into the bathroom to dress, then came back, ready to go out. He took his cigarettes off the table and shoved them into a pocket of his new Armani jacket, then searched for his keys in his jeans.

"The other pocket," Kevin offered. "Going out? Want to grab a bite somewhere?"

"No thanks; there's a fantastic book shop in North Beach, d'you remember it? City Lights?"

"More books? How many books can one person read?"

Christian smiled, saying, "I now collect books the way I used to collect women." Kevin grunted and held his tongue. "There's also a huge bookstore on Union Square, lots of stuff, great books for children. D'you want me to pick something up for the girls?"

"Huh? Yeah, yeah, might as well."

Christian checked the collar on his white dress shirt for spots of blood or forgotten shaving cream, then combed his blond hair a fourth time, noting how providential it was the gray was blending nicely. But the hair- line was thinning just above the temples. God, he looked terrible; he really was getting too old for this kind of life…

'I really think this'll put us back on top of the charts, Chris. D'you want to get some people together and lay some tracks down?" Kevin was saying.

"That's not the song I meant." Christian replied, taking the sheet music away. "It's not for recording."
"You're kidding!" Kevin protested.

"Never more serious. See you tonight, then?"

"Oh… *ohhh!* Hey, come clean, then. Who is she?"

"You think I'm fool enough to tell you? See you tonight, Kevin. Lock the door on your way out." Christian said and left to the accompaniment of Kevin's exasperated sighs.

Christian was never happier than when he was on a book-buying excursion. He made a habit of purchasing a new book in every city he stopped in while on tour, and San Francisco was no exception. After hitting Rizzoli's on Sutter Street, he went to Union Square and combed the Borders on Powell, and ended his tour at City Lights on Columbus Street. Weighed down by his purchases, he walked further into North Beach to get lunch.

That Thursday, Christian arrived late at Caffe Malvina, a small place he considered home now. He nodded to the waiter and discovered that his usual place at his usual table was taken. An auburn-haired woman had piled a shopping bag and purse on the only other vacant chair at his table behind the door, the one at the window facing Washington Square and Union Street. He decided not to intrude and took the small table in front of her.

After a brief exchange with the waiter, Christian dumped his shopping bags of books on the floor and glanced around the cafe, searching for the couple from Minnesota he'd met yesterday. They had taken to him like a long-lost son and shared his passion for literature and gardening. And they didn't know and didn't care who he was.

Years of having to dodge admiring fans and boorish journalists in the normal course of a day made him apprehensive of meeting anyone, much less normal people. Strange, how that journey from Lincoln had turned him into a multi-million dollar star that yearned for small luxuries like privacy and anonymous excursions to bookshops when he could get them. All he started out to do was playing his music and earn some money for school. Even today, thirty years from the start of that journey, he still could not enjoy blissful anonymity. He was proof that if one stayed in the business long enough, one became an elder statesman, the object of idolatry, and the object of ridicule. Just a half-hour ago, at City Lights, two women stepped back respectfully when one of them reverently whispered, "My God, that's Christian Walsh!" And then the color rose in their faces when he smiled in greeting and asked how they were getting on. Christian wondered when the candles lit at his feet would finally burn down. This quaint, friendly cafe on Washington Square had been for almost a week the only place in America he'd felt welcome, and all because he was just another hungry tourist in search of supper and an hour's worth of peace...

". . . Sorry it took so long! Be careful! Plate's hot," the waiter chattered as he gently shoved Christian's new purchase, a pristine hardback limited edition of Hardy's *A Laodicean* to one side of the table. "Do you want Parmesan with that?"

"Not with Hardy – Romano or Pecorino usually go best," Christian quipped, his humor lost on the young man.

A plate brimming with ivory laces of fettuccine smothered in fragrant mushrooms was placed before Chris- tian without further attempt at conversation. The sliding plate launched the Hardy novel and projected it noisily onto the floor. All heads turned, and it was then that Christian recognized the woman sitting at his usual table by the window, the one behind door. She was staring as rudely at him as he was at her.

"George?" she asked. The voice was soft, captivating, but not girlish.

Christian smiled shyly as he retrieved the book and dusted it off. "No, not George," he murmured to himself.

I do envy George, though!

She ducked back into the book she'd been devouring. Midway through lunch Christian glanced over and saw that she was staring again. He tried to act and look uninterested, but found himself staring back once too often. Soft features, auburn-colored hair. She had the most extraordinary pair of green eyes Christian had ever seen.

He was bowled over. The light had been dim that night, but Christian remembered her. She was the woman from the Coliseum.

He took a gamble then.

"Excuse me, can I borrow the salt?"

She wheeled abruptly at the sound of his voice. Christian had to repeat the question before the salt shaker exchanged hands, and didn't know whose hand trembled more – hers or his.

Christian picked up a scent – of freesia, something with herbs. Definitely sexy. Her being so close made him nervous in a nice kind of way. He hadn't felt like this in years, this combination of discovery, expectation, dread and infatuation. He wanted it to last forever. A powerful, sweet sensation of physical attraction combined with the mystery of who she was, overwhelmed him.

He immediately noticed the absence of a wedding band, though there was a pale stripe where one might have been. Their eyes met when he glanced up. She looked away, but he could not mistake the brightness of her eyes, or the flicker of interest they held.

Say the word, give me a sign, some hope, Christian thought; *say the word!*

"Sorry I'm not George!" he whispered to her.

She blushed and said it was no problem – he looked like a friend. Picking up her fork, she swirled a length of fettuccine and smiled at him. It was enough to send Christian's spirits into orbit. He was about to invite her over when the great bells of the church across the square boomed, sounding the hour.

"Oh God, Ned's going to kill me!" she exclaimed after a glance at her watch.

"Where are you off to?" Christian wanted to know with amusement. "Look, would you like to join me? I'd be happy if —"

"I can't; I really shouldn't."

"Who's Ned? Boyfriend, or —?"

She was having a terrible time of gathering up her things. Magazines and papers slid out of her backpack, items purchased at an expensive lingerie shop fell from the shopping bag; cosmetics and personal belongings scattered onto the floor. Christian knelt to help her, taking articles at random but tactfully holding the line at the lingerie.

"At least tell me where you work," Christian pleaded, scooping things up and tossing them into her backpack. "Maybe we could get together for a drink, coffee maybe, something? Later? I'd really like to, I mean, if you're not seeing anyone, and you'd like to."

She shook her head and pushed the hair escaping from her chignon out of her eyes. Christian couldn't get over how attractive she was and how attracted he was to her.

"I've got to get back to the office. I am so sorry," she stammered, still trying to gather her things in a cool, un-affected, manner that wasn't working.

"Well, could you give me a telephone number? A name? Can I ring you up?"

She paused and Christian could tell from her face that she was considering the proposal. "I'm really sorry," she said at last.

"Wait! You don't have to go —"

Without another word, she was out the door.

FORTINBRAS!

In Violet's mind they were still twenty-year olds from England making their first appearance on the *Ed Sullivan Show;* she didn't want to think of them as nearing retirement. They were older – a *lot* older.

And she had turned down the offer of a date with Christian Walsh.

Violet turned over in bed to see if Sam was still asleep, and when his nocturnal rumblings and spasms of breathing confirmed this, she took off the headphones, switched off the Walkman and slipped out of bed, pad-ding quietly downstairs. In the living room closet she found an old hope chest behind the unused skis and tennis racquets and dragged it out. Throwing back the lid released a musty smell of lavender and cloves, and a thousand memories – happy ones, for once.

She found an old record album under her high school yearbooks. Bypassing the psychedelic art on the cover, Violet opened the leaf and studied the band photographs inside. A smile now crept to her lips and she laughed softly, remembering the sultry summer nights alone in the tree house and listening to Christian Walsh's plaintive voice, hearing the mysterious, sensual lyrics to *Dark Forest* for the first time.

I called him George!

"WE'RE GOING FOR a world record, right?" Elisabet called out to her mother as she carried more Christmas decorations out of the house and piled them on the lawn. "How many times the human ear can stand *Dark Forest* and *Stairway to Heaven* and *Nights in White Satin?*"

Violet had gone back up the ladder with another string of Christmas lights, singing along with the lyrics to Stairway blaring out of the stereo in the living room.

"Well, I guess it's one way of dealing with it," Elisabet sighed.

"What was that?"

"Have you talked to Dad?" Elisabet wanted to know as Violet came down the ladder.

"I'm not in a mood for endless hours of denial and changing of subject, of turning everything around to my fault and my problem," her mother answered. "Unless you have a better idea, Beth."

"He's my dad and all, but if it were me, I'd give him a choice."

"I'm letting things cool off first, then we'll talk."

Violet positioned the lights against the front yard window and wrapped them around the hedges of juniper and bay, climbing back down to inspect her work.

Handmade angels of wood and tulle floated in the hedges; snowflakes danced from the front porch ceiling; artificial snow piled up in the window and porch corners; a wreath four feet wide beckoned visitors from the mullioned windows.

"Christmas by Costco has arrived at the Peters household," Elisabet commented, and winked at her mother. "Good to see some things are still normal."

"As normal as I can make them right now," Violet responded.

"We need a tree," Elisabet and Alex said in unison.

"That's your father's province," Violet replied.

"Better get the fake one out of the garage," muttered Elisabet.

"Looks like fun. Need any help?"

Violet spun around at the sound of George's voice, flushed with pretty color and asked how he'd been, where he'd been keeping himself. "You startled me," she answered when he asked what the matter was. "For a moment I thought – forget it."

"What?"

"I thought for a moment you were Christian Walsh," Violet admitted shamefully.

"You seem disappointed," he teased.

"Well, the voice."

George now studied the yard and frowned, pointing and asking, "What are those things poking out of the bushes?"

"Angels. They're dancing. Another insult like that and I won't invite you in for coffee."

"So I still look and sound like him, do I? I'm flattered. I hear he aged nicely – *ow!* What was that for?"

George was still rubbing his forearm when Violet led the way into the kitchen. He winked at Elisabet and whispered, "Thanks for the call – sorry I couldn't come sooner."

"Just asking you to help with damage control, Professor Knightsbridge," Elisabet replied.

"Call me George," he answered and both he and Elisabet offered toothy smiles when Violet spun about with brows raised.

"Mom, you didn't tell me you knew Professor Knightsbridge," Elisabet said, starting up the coffee maker and kettle.

"We go back to the dark ages," Violet teased while she opened the cookie jar and found the Tupperware bin of pastries. "I didn't know you were taking history classes."

"Required. He's not as dull as the others, though."

"Oh thank you very much, I think," George quipped. He glanced at Violet and said, "Are you alright? You look wan."

"You know the story – overworked, underpaid. Spending my nights working on papers and novels when I should be sleeping," answered Violet in a light but false tone.

George was about to press the argument when Elisabet shook her head and nodded towards the boys. He looked down and found Max smiling up at him, Alex tugging on his coat.

"Gentlemen!" George greeted, and picked up Max, who started to fret and then giggled when George made a face.

"Do you live in a castle in England?" Alex demanded.

"Do I what?"

"I saw a picture. You were standing in front of a castle," Alex said and picked up the Fortinbras album Violet had taken from the hope chest. He flipped back the cover and pointed to the inner artwork. The band was standing outside Alnwick Castle, circa 1970, judging by the hair and fashion.

"That's my evil twin," George remarked and shrugged when he saw both Elisabet and Violet frowning. "No, that's actually a nice chap called Christian Walsh – your mum has always liked his music. I don't personally live in a castle, but I live near one. It was built in the days of King Richard the Lionheart and I used to play there when I was your age. I found a sword and helmet there – my mum made me give it to a museum."

By the time the muffins and cookies were set out on a platter, juice, tea and coffee poured all around, the boys had been won over by George's charm. He then regaled them with stories of a battle that had taken place there almost five hundred years before.

Around five-thirty Sam burst in from the garage, apologizing and muttering about getting some things and having to go back out again. He stopped dead when he saw George sitting in his chair.

"George! How's it goin'?" Sam greeted, extending a hand. His glance at Violet was one part worry and one part pique.

"Fine, can't complain – yet."

"Haven't seen much of you since you got into town. Loved that suit of armor you wore to the party. If I didn't know better, I'd have sworn Violet had something to do with it," Sam commented, looking first to George and then Violet, waiting for a reaction. When none came, he started piling file folders and art supplies in the briefcase tucked between his legs.

George shrugged, saying, "No, it was a rare moment of daring. Imagine my delight to meet Violet in her Joan of Arc costume."

"I bet!" Sam muttered.

"Hey! Saw your ad for suppositories last night."

"Did you? It's a new account." Sam crowed. "Made a few thou on it. Promised some more, too."

"Amazing how you made something so gross interesting."

"Hey, wanna a beer or something? You're not staying for dinner, are you?" Sam inquired and threw open the refrigerator. "Vi, do we have anything to offer guests?"

"It was your turn to shop," Violet said after accepting a kiss that, George keenly observed, was more perfunctory and sterile than any he had given his wife after their divorce.

"Dad, did you remember the tree?" Elisabet interrupted.

"Tree?" Sam asked and when he saw Violet and Elisabet's faces, knew he was in trouble. "Damn! The Christmas tree! Vi, this is a bad time to get a tree. Maybe next weekend – isn't it early for a tree?"

"Ah yes, it's the little things that get us in trouble with the ladies, right, Sam?" George quipped and enjoyed the discomfort etched on Sam's dark, pretty-boy face.

Elisabet scooped Max off the floor and headed out the door with him. "Maybe December twenty-sixth isn't too early for you? They'll be on sale then!" she grumbled.

"Violet, I've got to move. I have a date," George spoke up, snatching a last cookie and dumping his cup into the sink. "Call me if you need some research materials or help with the dishes."

"Dishes?" Sam grunted, looking at Violet.

"Merely a joke. The sink is so full of dishes – never mind. Nice seeing you again, Sam." "I'll walk you out," Violet offered.

Violet and George were at the front gate when George murmured, "I hope by the time I get home the icicles Sam threw at me will have melted. I'd hate to die of pneumonia."

"You know him as well as I do."

"And that's the problem. See you 'round, Vi."

"Don't call me Vi!" came the playful retort.

When he was halfway down the street and ready to enter the crosswalk at Rose Street, Violet went after him. "There is... something... need to talk about!" Violet was panting and shivering all at once. "George, he's cheated on me."

"I know."

"You knew? You didn't say anything?"

"What could I have said? Isobel told me – you found out you were pregnant, wanted to get married, Sam took off for weeks."

"Not that! Wait – you knew about that?"

"Standing in the middle of the street isn't the place for this conversation, Violet," George said gently. "And I've really stepped in it if, by the look on your face we're talking about something more recent."

"I'm thinking things over, giving myself time to calm down. All good ideas, right? But now, what if... what if someone was attracted to another person, but it seemed impossible... life too complicated, and —"

"Vi!"

Sam was standing at the gate with Max in his arms. Violet threw George a glance that bespoke of hopelessness and then turned back, looking over her shoulder at the man waiting in the street, oblivious of the headlights coming at him. George moved away just in time.

"Nothing's impossible," George whispered and headed home. He wouldn't look back.

Watching Violet with her family brought a tide of painful memories that washed over him and left him drained.

THE KITCHEN THAT had hours before resonated with laughter and the scent of freshly brewed coffee was now silent and dark, save for the cheerful click-clacking of the Kit-Kat clock and the ice-blue glare of the computer monitor, the rapid-fire strokes on the keyboard. Violet didn't bother looking up when Sam entered and started rummaging through cupboards and drawers in search of a snack.

"The boys are in bed," he muttered, bringing the makings of a sandwich with him to the table and pulling out a chair. It was the chair George had sat in. Remembering this, he moved to a different chair. Violet watched him out of the corner of her eye.

"Where's Beth?" she asked.

"Out with her friends."

"I saw some of her paintings – she's got your talent with color and form. We may have a genius in the making." Violet angrily pounded on the space bar.

"Want me to pick up a tree?"

"Sorry about the tree."

She'd believe him if the tone wasn't so disingenuous, or affected. Or if he'd spent time actually combing the tree lots along San Pablo Avenue instead of on top of Marjorie Rotherwell. He tried to lean in for a kiss, and when she purposefully turned to reach for a book, retreated.

"It's just a damn tree!" Sam murmured, as if not wanting the children upstairs to hear. "What do you want from me, Vi?"

"A Christmas tree? Like you promised?"

"What else?"

"Nothing."

"It's something. Lately it's been something."

"I need a dress for the charity ball next Saturday."

Sam leaned back in his chair, and sighing, considered the turkey sandwich before him, paying particular attention to the mustard that oozed over the sides of the bread. Sam always gave minutiae its due whenever avoiding the real issue.

"What charity ball? You didn't tell me."

"Pediatric AIDS benefit at the Sheraton Palace – I told you, wrote it on the calendar. I'm going in Ned's place this year. I need a dress."

"Don't you have a little black dress?" he finally asked.

No, that's your rich girlfriend, and it's a BIG black dress...

Violet said aloud, "Since when do I wear black? You've known me since we were toddlers. Do I wear black?"

"Sorry!" he replied, a little afraid. "That's it?"

"No point in arguing Sam – not over a Christmas tree or a dress. I'll think of something."

Sam now gave the sandwich its due and when he was sopping up the mustard with a crust, he reached over and took her hand.

"What's bothering you, Vi? C'mon, it's me. You've always been able to tell me."

Yes, it is you…

"I have to think about it a while before I can say it — if I tried now, it would all come out wrong," she said at last.

"It's George, isn't it?"

"George? God no! Wrong Ellison sister. He had a crush on Bella, not me. Hated me as much as he hated Colin."

"But he's been showing up like a bad penny. Did you invite him over?"

"He stopped by. Elisabet actually knows him from Cal." Violet paused. "She audits one of his classes."

"So… nothing's going on."

The look on her face was enough to tell him there wasn't — and that he had blundered. "Where's your wedding ring?" he suddenly asked.

Violet glanced at the fingers of her left hand and held them out. "Oh that. I think it went down the garbage disposal. I'm losing weight even in my fingers."

"Maybe I can replace it."

Violet stared daggers at him, offered the most damning look he'd ever seen, and finally logged off and went through her evening ritual of organizing, sorting through notebooks and pages, making entries in a log.

"You've always had nice handwriting," Sam complimented as he watched her sign a field trip permission slip for Alex. Violet shrugged and finished cleaning up the table, ignoring him. He was still at the table when she switched off the computer and the lights. She was halfway to the living room when Sam followed and caught her gently by the arm.

Illuminated by only the flickering glare of the television set that was perpetually on, Sam bent down and gave Violet a gentle kiss. It was warm, sincere, and Violet

was glad that for once she felt nothing.
Absolutely nothing at all.

10

*Dreams Come True, Don't They —
Wait a Minute! This is a Dream?*

VIOLET HAD ONE lunch hour to find a dress for the charity ball.

Christmas shoppers were out in droves that Friday, sparing no quarter in pursuit of gifts worthy of a Christ Child. There wasn't a square inch of sidewalk or pavement free of traffic from Bush and Kearney to Post Street. Violet was caught in the midst of a human cattle drive and was propelled towards Union Square, a park of mani-cured hedges and finely clipped lawns, old men and the homeless encompassed by expensive shops. She was jettisoned toward Stockton Street and from there pushed and jostled to Neiman Marcus, where she paused to admire the Christmas displays before going in. Unwittingly, she passed Christian Walsh and Kevin and Sally Wakefield in a crowd coming out of the store.

The limo's here, let's go," Kevin said to Christian, handing over an armful of shopping bags. "We've got that radio interview in an hour."

"Hunh? What'd you say?" Christian muttered, avoiding the doors that nearly took his head off. He'd just seen Violet and couldn't believe his good fortune.

"Christian? Something wrong?" Sally queried in motherly concern.

"Nothing a shrink or a gun to the head wouldn't cure, Darling," Kevin said to his wife.

"Kevin... don't start."

Avoiding Sally's murderous stare, Kevin took Christian's arm as one might a small child's. "C'mon, there's the limo. We'll go back to the hotel and then the station. Did you get your Christmas shopping done?"

"Yeah; sure."

Christian was still distracted and allowed Kevin to prod him toward the waiting limousine.

Sally looked around Kevin's broad shoulders and picked Violet out of the crowd. She knew Christian, and knew this had to be the root of his preoccupation for the last seventy-two hours. Christian wasn't one for thirty-second infatuations. One night stands, maybe.

Sally now patted Christian's face and whispered, "Humor the handsome brute; he's been an absolute bitch since turning fifty." She then raised a brow toward Violet. "She's very pretty; who is she?"

"Stop the car," Christian ordered as the limousine started to pull into traffic. "Stop the bloody car now!" Kevin groaned and threw Sally a look that was borne of years of frustration.

"Chris, what's wrong?"

"Stop the bloody car!"

Christian got out. "I'll make it back in time for the interview," he said, nearly slamming Kevin's hand in the door.

"Chris —!"

He disappeared into the department store.

"A lady so high," here Christian gestured below his shoulder, for he was well over six feet and Violet was on the petite side, "with auburn hair and wearing a dark blue coat; have you seen her?"

The sales assistant at the perfume counter said she had and directed Christian toward the escalator with a bottle of expensive designer cologne. He declined the offer of a sample and got out of the way of a cloud of something called 'Poison', sprinting towards the escalator, which he climbed two steps at a time.

His palms were sweating and his chest was pounding. Either it was a heart attack or the anticipation of seeing her again.

God, he prayed, *let it be her...*

Christian went up to the sportswear department, saw

her on the escalator going down and tried to get her attention. He tried to get past an elderly woman with enough shopping bags to fill Wembley Stadium and was forced to wait as she unloaded her cargo and got off on the third floor.

She was nowhere on the third floor!

He went down a level, his heart turning somersaults when he spotted her in one of the evening wear salons on the second floor. She was casually browsing clearance and sales racks teeming with gowns. Christian apologized to the sales assistant that approached him and asked if there was something he was interested in. It wouldn't have been in the best of taste to say petite ladies with large green eyes, so Christian shrugged and said he was just looking for now.

He was a clothes rack away when a sales assistant swooped down as if out of nowhere and lured the woman towards the exclusive collections – Armani, Karan, Versace, Escada, Betsey Johnson. From among the beaded and embroidered dresses of status quo black, a medieval-style dress of velvet brocade in a blue-violet colorway was selected. From the look on her face, Christian knew she'd found the perfect dress.

It was perfect.

When she emerged from the fitting room, the sales assistants and customers nearby all voiced admiration for this unique selection, this extraordinary dress. She stood in the mirror and adored her metamorphosis, turning on command, holding up her back, holding in her stomach, smoothing the velvet over her breasts, caressing the wide belled sleeves and letting them fall over her long, elegant hands and fingers.

And then she caught Christian's reflection in the mirror. His apprehension of being turned away melted when she whirled around in a brilliant swirl of color and smiled.

"Hi," he greeted, deciding on something natural and

unpretentious.

"Hi." It came with a pretty blush that spread across her cheeks and throat.

She fidgeted with the off-the-shoulder décolleté, a show of modesty that Christian found beguiling and sensual.

Christian took a step closer, and nodded, running a hand in his hair while he stared appreciatively. "Well! I must say that dress is something. Really, really, something."

"Really? Thanks. Betsey Johnson. I've always dreamed of something like this," she responded, taking a turn.

"Well, dreams do come true... party dress? Of course! That was stupid, sorry."

"For a business function this weekend."

"Listen, um, I really would like to take you to dinner. I wasn't kidding, before, that is... I'm not kidding now. I know we've only just met – in fact, you don't know my name, and I don't know yours, well, maybe you know who I am, but, anyway – bugger! – And if you're not married or seeing anyone, it's as good a place as any to start. So..."

Her eyes were suddenly as large as two moons, though Christian couldn't possible imagine that they could be larger or lovelier. She started to smooth the skirt of the dress nervously, looked at her shoes – why was it that women looked at their shoes when they didn't want to answer?

"Oh, you've got something going on with... Ned! Ned, is it?"

"I can't believe you remembered that!" she laughed.

"Lucky Ned."

"You don't know Ned – Ned!"

She had addressed a businessman in a bad suit that now joined them from the escalator. He was swinging a briefcase and chewing gum, reminding Christian of those insufferable Bond Street-Types back home, the kind that shoved you on the street and went on their merry way without so much as an apology or a by your leave. The type who charmed and won girlfriends away. Christian glowered at the man and summed up his competition, deciding it wasn't much. But he was experiencing something he hadn't felt in years – jealousy.

"I thought we were going to meet at the Dress Barn," the Bad Suit said. "I've been to a hundred stores and called Emma and Annie – wow! Killer dress!"

It took him long enough, Christian thought. He cleared his throat and smiled at them. "Well, got to run... have to buy a present for my best friend's wife. He doesn't know about us, you see, me and his wife."

The joke was lost on the Bad Suit, but the woman stifled a laugh. "Do I know you? I know you, don't I?" The Bad Suit asked, scrutinizing him.

"If you're lucky, you will," said Christian, and looked her straight in the eyes. "Gotta go. Nice meeting you both. Bye."

She actually looked disappointed.

Good!

Christian raised a hand in farewell, and looking at his watch, backed away, but lingered long enough to find out if The Bad Suit Called Ned really was competition, and pretended to be interested in the accessories displayed on a glass counter top.

". . . you don't think it's too much, Ned?" she was asking.

"Too much? With a dress like this you can pretty much get whatever you want! Damn! That guy looked familiar; didn't he look familiar to you? I coulda sworn I've seen him somewhere—"

"That was Christian Walsh, stupid. Fortinbras? I wish I could lose another five pounds by tomorrow."

"Where would you – *hello!* Look at the price of this, and why were you thinking I'd spend the next year's rent on a dress you'll wear once? Put it back – no, don't start!

Christian Walsh, huh?"

She threw The Bad Suit a pained look and went back into the fitting room. Moments later she came out with the dress on its hanger. Alternative dresses were offered, but she refused. This was THE dress, the perfect dress, the only dress. No other would do. After a last caress and a yearning gaze, she relinquished her treasure and thanked the sales assistants before going down the escalator.

Christian, completely captivated by Violet Ellison, walked back to the hotel.

Sally Wakefield poked her head out into the corridor as soon as she heard his door open. "Well?"

"A very deep subject, Sally."

"Did you see her? Did you talk to her?" Sally demanded. She noted the flushed cheeks and smile. The rascal was up to something.

He asked what she was talking about and Sally reminded him that all school day bets were off and he owed her. Twenty-four years of friendship gave her the privilege of his secrets. She wanted all the facts, down and dirty.

Kevin heard the conversation and joined them. "Dinner downstairs tonight? We can talk about your new song," he hinted.

"Actually, no. I'm having dinner at Caffe Malvina."

Christian had decided to stop in at Caffe Malvina around seven that evening. Maybe she'd be there. Maybe she'd stay for dinner and they could see where the rest of the evening might take them.

"I DON'T KNOW why we had to come all the way up here for a drink, Violet; there were at least six decent bars within a block of the office!" Emma Solway grumbled as she dumped her designer daypack on a table. She threw Annie Gordon, Ned's process server and file clerk, a look.

"It's romantic, it's Italian, it's all Violet — and she's up to something," Annie Gordon replied, settling down beside Emma, who was not at all pleased by Caffe Malvina; nor was she pleased by the table Violet insisted they take – a table behind the door, a table with a wobbly leg.

"It's a nice restaurant. You get good service and a view to die for," Violet replied.

"I'll say," Emma and Annie sighed together, admiring the young waiter that approached with two menus. He winked at Violet and complimented her on her appearance. She was looking quite pretty that evening. Emma had noticed that too, had also noticed how preoccupied she was. Every time the door opened she almost leapt out of her chair.

"Ned had a flight to L.A., if that's whom you're waiting for," Emma commented, checking her appearance in a compact mirror. Violet was doing the same, reapplying lipstick for the third time in less than an hour.

"Me? I'm not waiting for anyone in particular," came the guileless reply.

"You expect us to believe that?" Annie demanded. "Every time the door opens you start shaking – oh God, please tell me we're not waiting for Sam; I don't want to be a party to murder, Violet!"

"Let's order a pizza."

"Pizza? That'll take too long, and the last bus to Berkeley is at six-forty-two – hey! Since when did you eat pizza?"

"Yeah," Emma queried, "When?"

"Is this the Spanish Inquisition, or what? Everything I've done tonight has been suspect."

"Violet, you don't usually invite anyone out for dinner and drinks on a Friday night. You're the last one to leave the office, and I know you go straight home," Emma said.

"Maybe I want to be a little more spontaneous – a little more independent."

"I'll say one thing for Sam Peters," Annie quipped,

"he may not know how to keep it in his pants, but his stupidity has done you a world of good!"

"Did you get the jury instructions copied?" Violet asked Emma.

"Let's not talk shop — let's talk you. How are things?"

Emma and Violet had been friends since Violet found her weeping in the reading room of Moffett Library on the university campus three years ago. When offered a handkerchief and then a cup of coffee and a bagel, Emma told Violet she was looking for a job and a place to stay — Emma's stock-broker husband of fifteen years had decided to take most of the savings account and his twenty-year old secretary to Cabo. Violet immediately offered the mother-in-law apartment above the garage and twisted Ned's arm until he gave Emma the position of receptionist at the firm. Emma, who had lived the life of a society maven for most of her adult life, was surprised that anyone would show such kindness, especially to a stranger. Back then she didn't know Violet, and didn't know how much Violet understood her predicament. Now it was Emma's turn to be charitable. When the wine came, Emma poured two glasses and pushed one towards Violet.

"In wine there is truth — so give it to us," Emma said.

"I'm going to wait until after the holidays. Ned said to let it lie, to forgive him." Violet said quietly.

Annie scoffed at this. "I know you've been friends with Ned since the Ice Age, and I know you've known Sam since you were babies, but advice from Ned about Sam? That defies all reason," she said.

"Everyone is giving advice —"

"We're not," Annie and Emma replied in unison. "That's because you know better!"

"Well," Emma sighed; "maybe I don't. Maybe what you need is an opportunity for payback. You need to find another man and have an affair."

"Me? Have an affair?" Violet laughed, and snatched away the last of the bread sticks, chomping down noisily.

"Yeah," Annie said after appraising Violet while she checked her lipstick for the hundredth time; "you're just not the type for affairs."

They talked about failed relationships, broken dreams, the resilience that came with being in their forties, the opportunities afforded them by living in the nineties rather than the fifties, the joys of motherhood, of being single, and the perverse delight they shared in trashing Ned and his hedonistic ways, Sam and his cheating heart, until Emma glanced at her watch and said they had twenty minutes to catch the last bus home. As they were hurrying for the 30 Stockton to the Transbay Terminal, a cab pulled up to Caffe Malvina. Christian Walsh got out and went inside, took his usual table, the table behind the door, the table with the wobbly leg.

He smiled up at the waiter and asked how he was, wanted to know if anyone interesting came in that night.

The waiter shrugged and said, no, just the usual crowd of people, the same people he saw every day...

11

Hey! Somebody Get me a Pumpkin and Three Fat Mice…

"IS THERE ANY way you can change your flight?"

"Can't. I'll lose a big account if I don't do some damage control —"

"Damage control. It's getting old, Sam."

"Yeah, well, if I had you working for me, none of this would have happened."

"How is this my fault?"

"Did I say it was your fault?"

"It pretty much sounded like that —"

"What I meant was that we talked about you joining the firm as the art director and designer last year. I need someone I can depend on."

"Oh sure, I'll just quit the only steady job with the only steady paycheck we've got so you can have one more scapegoat along with the two space cadets from Hell who still read Archie comics! I'm a writer."

"And when was the last time you published something? Other than the church newsletter?"

"Like I haven't been trying." *Bastard!* "Cheap shot, and you know it."

"I shouldn't have brought it up."

"Damn straight."

"Not now, Vi! You've been in a rotten mood for days. Is it that time of month? Have you seen my planner? I thought I just had it."

Violet lowered herself on to the bed and watched Sam throw things into a carry-on bag mindless of order.

This surprised her, considering how meticulous Sam was about everything, from the order of socks in his underwear drawer to his neurotic insistence that the blue sponge be used for dishes, the yellow for wiping counters and floors. She handed him three clean shirts and four ties that were thrown on top of the heap. The carry-on was zipped closed.

"Why so much? If this is just an overnight trip."

"Usually they are, but then again, who knows? I don't know how long this'll take," Sam replied, and leaning over, kissed her brow. "And if you want to keep this house, the car, get braces for Alex, you won't keep it up."

"You – just – got – back – from – Chicago," Violet responded in short, clipped, words. Her voice was even and controlled, a warning he should take note of her mounting unhappiness.

Saturday mornings were for lying in bed together, watching as the room turned a soft, buttery yellow with the rising of the sun, of sharing the children's dreams and nightmares from the night before as they wandered into 'The Big Room' one by one, of playing hide and seek behind the bed curtains, of sword fights with Parsifal (who always won), of walks down to the Produce Market on Shattuck Avenue for Saturday morning treats. All of it seemed to be a lifetime ago. It was like a death in the family – that sensation of boundary to mark what had been and what lie ahead.

Was it possible to break that wall? To still the ticking clock and hold forever the days in March when everything was comfortable? When love felt new and exciting again, and happiness still a possibility?

Violet didn't know if she could. Or even if she wanted to.

Sam bent over to kiss her again. "Why New York?" she demanded, moving out of his arms. "Can't you teleconference or go to the District headquarters in L.A.?"

"Something this explosive requires personal contact."

"So… looks like I'm going to the charity ball alone."

"We can't afford to lose the soda account!"

"But the marriage?"

That came quite unexpectedly for both of them. Hearing the laughter and the squeals of the children downstairs, Violet closed the bedroom door and turned to Sam, who was pacing. She waited, watching his every move, like a peregrine falcon watches its prey from the clouds. She was like that now, ready to swoop down and take him in her talons.

And he knew it.

"What's going on, Vi? I said I was sorry about Halloween, about missing birthdays, anniversaries, the kids' school concerts, what more do you want? For the last month you've been moodier than usual, angry, I just don't know how to react to you these days. Maybe you should see a doctor."

"The problem isn't my head and you know it."

Her eyes were dead on his and cold. Suddenly it occurred to him. *She knows!* Sam raised a hand to brush the locks of straying hair out of her face and stopped when he saw the line of her jaw go steel-like. He kissed her gently on the cheek instead. "I really have to do this, Vi. You've never protested before," Sam said.

"Only because your motives weren't so suspect."

"What's that supposed to mean?"

"You're on the defensive, Sam."

"We can't afford to lose this account! The income isn't there – it isn't where it was promised, things changed, and —"

"Sam, what happened to the six figures from Enigma Films?"

"You know how these things go, Vi."

"You didn't get the contract, did you? You lied about it, didn't you?"

Sam paused, sorting through artwork and copy now. Violet studied his face for an indication of something hidden. He always smiled nervously when he lied.

"These things take time, you know, I was given a promise." A smile crossed his lips and he shrugged.

"What are we going to do? Sam, we've got so many bills."

"Shit! What time is it? I still have to shave and change."

"Sam, I really wanted to go to this party tonight. It's bad enough I don't have a dress."

"So go!"

"I don't want to go alone! I'm sick and tired of doing things alone!"

"So ask George!" he snapped, and disappeared into the bathroom.

"I shouldn't have to go begging for an escort!" she called through the bathroom door.

"Violet, I don't want to fight – not today, not tomorrow, not ever. Why do you always start something just when things are settling?"

Settling? What was settling?

Violet went into the bathroom when she heard the flush. Sam reappeared, closing the French doors to the toilet behind him.

He opened the medicine cabinet now and took out five bottles of various pills, opened each bottle one at a time, took a single pill out and lined it up on the vanity, closed the bottles and replaced them in the cabinet. Next he downed each pill, one at a time, without water.

"One pill makes you larger, one pill makes you small?" Violet quipped.

"What?"

"Nothing… bad joke."

Sam responded by reached for the shaving gel and razor. In the palm of his right hand he made a mountain out of the green gel that oozed from the canister. Violet reached out and took a fingerful of the shaving gel and slowly, erotically, painted his chin with it, following the outline of his face, kissing him while doing so. She took the razor from him and held it ready. The idea of lathering up a man and shaving him had always been sensual and exciting to her. Violet wanted to experience it for the first time. Maybe Sam would find something exciting about it, to feel a woman's hand on his face – to have her sit astride his lap wearing a silk chemise and nothing else…

"Don't bother," he said quietly and took the razor.

"I could manage to live with it if you told me Marjorie Rotherwell was all part of this plan. It would explain quite a lot, and I wouldn't have to wonder every time you came home late, or not at all."

Shit! She knows!

"Marjorie?" he laughed. Again, the smile. "What's Marjorie got to do with this?"

"Is she going with you?"

"Violet, I don't know what you're talking about."

"You haven't answered the question."

"She's not a corporate officer of the soda company. At least, I hope to God she isn't!"

Nothing she could say or do made a difference. Once his tie was straight and the shoes matched his business suit, Sam bussed Violet lightly and started out the door, then paused and returned.

"Forget something?" she asked, holding up his personal organizer.

"Look, Violet, I know the timing on this trip is bad, but sometimes that's the way it has to be," he answered softly. "I should be back by Wednesday."

Again, there was the smile. She nodded. "Better go."

"I'll call – shit! The tree!"

Outside the taxi honked impatiently.

"Better go," she whispered after a last kiss.

AN HOUR LATER, Violet sat on a swing at the park, watching the boys build roads and tunnels in the sandbox, pushing their Thomas the Tank Engine trains through and making the requisite train noises – the beeps and squeaks that became white noise after a while. Her attention was fixed on little Bethany Beaulieu, the neighborhood darling, dressed in a pink princess gown and wearing a pair of sparkly dress-up shoes.

"I can still go to the ball," she murmured to herself. Pushing off, she scooped up Max and settled him into the stroller. "C'mon boys, let's go play Cinderella," she said.

Elisabet dropped her paint brushes when she heard Violet's shouts and the slam of the front door, appeared at the top of the attic steps to find out what the latest crisis was. "Help me find something to wear for tonight," Violet said cheerfully when asked where the fire was.

"Yes, Cinderella, you too shall go to the ball!" Elisabet giggled.

Violet threw open the doors to the closet and sighed. "One problem, though – I don't have anything to wear."

Elisabet echoed that sentiment when, after unloading everything in Violet's walk-in closet on to the bed and sifting through old bridesmaid and prom dresses, it looked hopeless. Violet and Elisabet studied the brightly colored pile of organza, silk and velvet with furrowed brows and arms crossed.

"Well, one thing I know about you, Mamma," Elisabet sighed, "you certainly aren't one of those women who fear color. Hopeless."

"What about this?" Violet held up a prom dress from 1969 and Elisabet remarked that from the brightness of the colors and Peter Max-style pattern, sunglasses would be needed.

"I can't believe I kept this," Violet quipped. "I wore it to a party in the summer of sixty-nine to make an impression on a dark-haired boy who looked like Leonard Whiting."

"Who?" Elisabet asked.

"Romeo. 1968." sighed Violet as she tossed the dress back onto the mountain of clothes.

Violet suddenly spun about, pulling open an already overflowing dresser drawer. She burrowed for a few minutes and then out it came from a garment box – a cocktail dress of iridescent champagne lace, A-line, sleeveless, with a daring oval, Victorian décolleté. It was barely worn and still held the scent of new fabric. A matching slip dress of silk in tie-dye watercolor shades of soft beige, mauve, peach and the palest blue lay beneath it.

"The Dress!" Elisabet squealed happily.

"Took your grandmother three weeks to design and make this and your father came down with a case of the Soda Company flu — so much for my trip to the CLIO Awards. I only wore it for fittings," Violet muttered.

"Yeah, but Dad won some award that year?"

"Rising star or something," said Violet.

"You never wear half of what you've got in here," Elisabet said, poking her head into the dark abyss of the closet.

"No need to. Got a dress code to follow at the office and I have no where to go most of the time."

"I've never understood why Dad doesn't take you to the award dinners and stuff."

Violet used to wonder about that, too; now she knew. She took from the jewelry chest a damascene silver collar studded with pearls, a large pear-shaped aquamarine dangling from it, and held it against the dress. Elisabet breathed approval.

Violet again brightened with revelation. "Where's that velvet swing coat Grammy Am made to go with this dress?"

Elisabet knew. She disappeared and moments later returned with a knee-length coat of silk velvet in a shimmering hue of champagne, with a funnel collar and wide bell sleeves. The sheerest, glittering, hosiery was dug out of another back drawer and soon Violet was admiring herself in the full-length mirror nailed to the closet door.

"Thank God for Weight Watchers!" Violet sighed happily when she slid her hands over her hips and stomach, smoothing the lace gently.

"Y'don't think the neckline's too low?" Elisabet

wondered, reaching out to pull it up another inch, only to have her hand slapped away.

"No!" Violet laughed.

Elisabet stared in amazement. "This is so…"

"So… me."

"Shoes," Elisabet sighed, looking at the boxes on the floor. "You've got every shade of brown, black, but nothing neutral or glamorous!"

"Wait a minute!"

Violet disappeared under the bed and came out with dust bunnies and a shoebox. Under the dusty cover lay a pair of strappy sandals of silver leather wrapped in tissue. "Sam & Libby, I think. Yeah. A Christmas present to me from me," she explained. "I fell in love with them."

Violet slid into the sandals and took a turn in front of the mirror. "Wow!" Elisabet offered.

"Thank you," Violet whispered happily. "Now, call your grandmother – she owes me a favor – and ask if she wants to keep the boys over night, and then we can discuss hair and makeup?"

"I've got nothing going on, Mamma, I can stay home."

"No, Beth – you've given up too much of your time babysitting. Get her on the phone, okay?"

Two hours later, Violet stood at the front hall mirror checking hair and makeup, applying another layer of peach-colored lipstick to an already perfect face with Elisabet and Amalie smiling in approval.

"I don't know why my son prefers a business trip to New York when he could have this arm candy tonight," Amalie sighed, fastening the silver collar around Violet's neck.

"Arm candy? Grammy Am!" Elisabet giggled.

"Look how beautiful your mother is," Amalie said. "There are fools, and then there's Sam." She turned Violet around for a motherly kiss.

Violet blushed, understanding the compliment, then

said: "Okay! Walk me to my pumpkin?"

Elisabet bowed with a flourish as she opened the front door and led the way down the walk to the street, where she opened the door to her father's orange Beemer and handed her mother the keys. "Is midnight okay?" she asked her mother.

"We'll see," Violet answered, turning the key in the ignition. "one never knows about running into princes."

The Beemer roared off towards a BART station with Cinderella inside, singing along to *I Know You're Out There Somewhere.*

12

*Your Name Wouldn't Happen to be
Prince Charming, Would It?*

AT SEVEN-THIRTY, Violet emerged from the BART station outside the Sheraton Palace a hothouse flower. From *décolleté* to strappy sandals, she was a knockout; this wasn't your ordinary work-a-day Violet, but a drop-dead gorgeous Violet. Photographers started to circle when a popular local television personality, Raleigh Dinsdale, arrived simultaneously and in the glare of a dozen strobe flashes he collided with Violet. They laughed at their clumsiness and the paparazzi assumed Violet was his date.

"Guess we should just go along with it," Dinsdale commented with a wink.

"I don't know," Violet laughed.

"C'mon, this could be a lucky break for both of us," he urged.

"Maybe for you," Violet said between her teeth as she reluctantly acquiesced to media demands, striking attitudes and smiling for these total strangers who assumed she was someone – and hoped to God none of it would be aired or printed for her family to see. Five minutes was all Violet had the courage for, however, and she begged off.

"Come inside with me – everyone will think I'm with a gorgeous brunette for a change," Dinsdale insisted. Before Violet could protest, he'd linked his arm with hers and they entered the grand ballroom, a decorating nightmare of late Victorian clutter, replete with potted palms and full-length mirrors in gilt rococo frames, heavy chandeliers of crystal and brass. At least, Violet thought as she glided forward on the news anchor's arm, she wasn't as overdressed as the room.

Violet glanced around and was daunted by the glittering crowd. What if someone recognized her as Violet

Ellison, Legal Secretary? She imagined being tossed out on her bottom until she caught a glimpse of herself in one of the full-length mirrors in the foyer, then looked back and smiled.

Well, she'd look damned spectacular on her way out.

An older gentleman with a bad comb-over approached her with two flutes of champagne, offering one. He announced that he was a programming director for a well-known cable channel; didn't he see her in a 'Showtime' movie? The one that just won six Emmys?

"No, she was in the mini-series that lost – the one with Jane Seymour," Dinsdale quipped. It was clever enough to hold the comb-over's interest and he hovered despite Dinsdale's efforts to make it look as if Violet and he were an item, much to Violet's discomfort. Violet didn't think she could go through with it. What could she say to these industry moguls and hangers-on that would be of interest? They'd heard it all, seen it all. More than likely done it all and with everyone else in the room.

She grabbed a champagne flute from a waiter's tray and went headlong into unfamiliar territory for the first time in her life. Working a crowd soon became as effortless as smiling and soon people wanted to know who she was. Unfortunately, Dinsdale became her shadow and added fuel to their speculation when he lured Violet to the dance floor for almost an hour. By the time that hour was up, she had grown tired of her role as mystery woman. The idea of charming a room full of self-absorbed industry executives was novel when one wasn't actually in the situation. Now it was nothing to get excited over. And Violet lost her allure as soon as younger, more spectacularly endowed women arrived. Soon she was sitting on the grand staircase, watching, a plate of fruit and cheese on her lap. Her fifteen minutes of fame were up and she was hungry for something more substantial than California *haute cuisine*. Twenty minutes later a taxi dropped her off at Caffe Malvina.

The restaurant was quiet that evening, a few customers scattered here and there. Looking around for a place to sit, she saw that her corner table was occupied by Christian Walsh.

He was dining alone and reading a copy of Thomas Hardy's *A Laodicean*. Violet smiled up guiltily at the waiter when he materialized out of nowhere and asked what her pleasure was. Rather than say what was on her mind, Violet ordered her usual – the fettuccine with porcini mushrooms and kept her eyes on Christian Walsh.

Thirty-one years might have passed since her first glimpse of him on the *Ed Sullivan Show*, but the violet-blue eyes were still the same. So was the part in his blond hair, the square face and jaw. So was weakness in Violet's knees, the pounding of her heart at the sight of him. The years in between had improved what Violet found so attractive.

"Here you go, Violet," the waiter chirruped, placing a plate on the table. "Better move the bag; do you want Parmesan with that?"

"Uh, maybe not – sequins taste better with pesto… it was a joke, Enrico." "A very little one. See you 'round, Violet."

The waiter retreated, shaking his head and muttering about 'some people'.

Violet pushed the creamy strands of homemade fettuccine around in circles, listening to her heart beat echo in her ears. Strange, how seeing Christian Walsh made her breath come quicker, make dryness overtake her throat and that long dead feeling of anticipation suddenly spring alive in every pore.

Nonsense, she told herself; it was *who* he was, if it was anything. Don't flatter yourself thinking he'd be interested.

More than anything she wanted to talk to him. He wasn't three feet away, yet she couldn't think of what to do.

And what would he think or say if she asked him to pass the salt?

"Excuse me; may I borrow the salt?"

At first Christian frowned, being taken momentarily from his book. But when he looked up and saw Violet, he nearly knocked over his pot of lukewarm tea and bowl of congealed minestrone to pass the salt shaker.

He'd thought about her; no, he'd been thinking about her all day, dreaming of her all night.

You're too old for adolescent infatuations, Christian, he told himself. He told himself to take a flying leap. "Are you alone?" he ventured. That wasn't quite the greeting he'd planned. When she nodded hesitantly, he suppressed a smile. *What man in his right mind would stand her up?* "Would you like to join me?"

She picked up her plate and utensils and came over.

The reading glasses were ditched into a pocket, the hair smoothed back – the slightly receding hairline hopefully not too obvious.

Now that she was facing him across a table, Violet looked at Christian Walsh and marveled that she didn't faint from embarrassment. *No, Violet,* she thought, *don't act the fool; don't tell him you've listened to his music since you were fifteen – although it's the truth – that you had a crush on him for so many years – that you'd kicked yourself for two days after running out of this very restaurant – after he'd asked you out on a date.*

She smiled. *There!* That was simple enough.

"We didn't get a proper introduction last time. I'm Christian Walsh."

"Hello; pleased."

"So am I. And your name is?"

"Violet Ellison."

"Finally I know your name. Marvelous name… Violet."

His hand was extended and Violet took it. The hand was warm and soft. She let her eyes slide down and noticed the absence of rings on his fingers. That was never a true indication. Sam lost his wedding ring and hers suffered a burial at sea.

"Did you have a concert tonight?" she asked, starting to eat. Friendly, normal banter was always good. Stay away from controversial subjects – politics, religion, sex, whether you would consider having sex with a woman in her forties, are you married...

Christian picked up his fork and tasted the minestrone growing cold and congealing in its bowl. "No, we finished the tour at San Jose. I wanted to see an American football game at Candlestick Park and Kevin's – Kevin Wakefield's wife and girls had never been to San Francisco, well, here we are. We leave for England on Monday."

"Funny," she said with that incredible smile that melted him down to his socks, "I never thought of San Francisco as a vacation spot. Living here, I guess."

"You'd travel halfway 'round the world to spend a week in London, wouldn't you?"

"Well, I'd choose York over London, first."

"Really? York? Why?"

"History. Middleham Castle, Towton, Richard the Third, the abbeys, I like English medieval history."

"Cold as Hell in Yorkshire – I know, I live there."

They laughed. There it was, the safest and surest topic of all. The weather.

Christian couldn't believe he was sitting here with this incredibly splendid woman and conversing so familiarly. He watched with pleasure as she undertook normal things such as unfolding a napkin and brushing away the hair that never seemed to stay out of her eyes, pushing the pearl onions under her crostini. Glancing up at him from under those dark, silky eyelashes.

"You know, I've always wondered about the lyrics in *Dark Forest*," Violet said after a long interval during which they both tried to place the song on the loudspeaker. "Suicide? Lost love?" She stopped when she saw Christian's bewildered expression. "Oh. I bet you get that a lot."

"Uh, no, no; not at all. Well, yes, I do get asked that a lot."

"It beats 'What keeps the band together', I suppose."

"I guess. Transparent tape."

"Pardon?"

"And really strong glue. That's what keeps the band together."

He looked so serious. Violet tried not to laugh and then lost it. Christian felt the red-hot flush of embarrassment, but managed a quick recovery. He leaned back and studied her appearance, nodded approvingly. "Absolute knockout, your ensemble – if you don't mind my saying so."

"Really? Thank you. I really just threw this together. I wanted the purple dress – you know, the one in the store, but —" Violet stopped and glanced down, hoping the dim light would hide her embarrassment. *Why would he care about what she wanted; whether she could afford an expensive dress?*

"You can tell me it's none of my business, but dressed like that, you should be out on a proper gentleman's arm," Christian commented.

"The party turned out to be a bore. And I don't know any proper gentlemen."

"Sorry. Actually, I'm not sorry; seeing how things have turned out. Business function, right?"

"Entertainment industry thing."

Christian grunted. "I was supposed to be at one of those tonight. A lot of overdressed people posturing. You're not in the entertainment industry, are you?"

"Writer. Out of necessity I'm a legal secretary. But writing, writing is what I do. Histories, and I've written a couple of novels."

Violet noticed how his shoulders relaxed at this disclosure.

"Really?" he asked, his voice brighter. "I don't know many writers – well, those living, anyway."

"I've read *Far From the Madding Crowd* maybe four

times," Violet remarked, tapping his book. "Thomas Hardy is good company, I think."

He winked. "Not as good as some people."

"Some people are better than others."

"Oh, I definitely think so," he said and leaned in, saying, "I think we need to celebrate. You see, Violet Ellison, I wondered if I'd ever be fortunate enough to see you again."

Violet wanted to be flippant and remark that his comment was as smooth as a glass slipper and he was certainly as charming as a prince, that she'd best beware of his intentions, but the words wouldn't come. She knew from his eyes that he wasn't being smooth, or charming, or purposefully romantic. He was being himself and quite nervous about it.

"Well, here I am," she replied. *Let him make of it what he would; she wasn't good at playing the flirt, either.*

"Then we celebrate."

A bottle of champagne was ordered and Christian poured two flutes, offering one.

"I don't usually get chances like this – going out, dressing up," she admitted, savoring the dryness of the champagne.

"You're not missing much." Christian scoffed.

"Oh, I don't know; it beats a Saturday night date with a quart of Haagen Daaz," Violet said.

"You? I find that hard to imagine!"

"Y'think? So what's your favorite flavor?"

"Chocolate mint."

"Pecan Praline."

"I'll remember that."

"I top it off with a bowlful of Cap'n Crunch's Crunch Berries."

"Do I want to know what that is?"

"Breakfast cereal."

"Breakfast cereal? Really? Hmm, what you learn about people... I still don't believe you have to stay home nights. I mean, look at you!"

Violet laughed self-consciously. "Go on."

"I'm sorry, I didn't mean to —"

"No really, go on!"

Again they laughed. Christian leaned closer and was ready to touch her face when he remembered the 'three feet of personal space' rule and backed away. He looked head on into her eyes and Violet returned the gaze, not knowing whether to bolt or stay.

She decided to stay.

Without changing expression, Christian said softly: "You've got incredible eyes."

"That's not the best line I've heard."

"So? Top it if you can do me one better."

"You've got a killer smile," she purred.

"Hear that one all the time, but not as well as you did it. Come up with something better."

"Let's see... I've been in love with you since I was fifteen... nope, you've probably heard that dozens of times."

"Yeah, I do get that, along with certain articles of women's clothing. How 'bout, I've been looking for you all my life?"

"Ouch... not exactly original."

"Okay. How about, come to England with me?"

"I'd say that was one I hadn't heard before."

"It's not a line, Violet."

"Get out."

"It's not a line."

"You're not serious!"

"Seriously. I'm serious."

"Well, if I was fifteen..."

"All the more reason. Time waits for no one. We get older, we know what we want."

"You're not serious!"

From his expression and eyes she knew he was. "Seeing anyone? Married, perhaps?" he now asked. Violet hesitated.

"It's pretty much over, I think."

"Too early for an affair, then?"

"Never too early for a friendship."

It was sometime before Christian removed his gaze. "Want dessert?" he murmured, his voice as erotic as a caress.

When they finished dining, Christian suggested a walk through North Beach. The December evening was cold, almost freezing, and the fog had vanished, but there was something about this old neighborhood that begged one to explore. They walked west on Union Street, strolling up to Grant Avenue and down toward the Financial District and Chinatown, through an eclectic neighborhood of shops from vintage records and music, pastry, vintage clothing and books, trendy boutiques, and Italian restaurants. The entire neighborhood smelled deliciously of Italian spices. They paused and window shopped, showing each other their preferences, laughing together and stealing glances they thought weren't noticed. Christian offered his overcoat when Violet shivered from the cold. She couldn't remember the last time a man offered his coat, a chivalrous, charming gesture she often wrote about. The gesture was all the more special because it was his coat. It was warm and it was scented with his cologne.

"So. I read quite a bit. Do I know anything you've written?" he asked after a quiet space of time.

"I'd be surprised if you did. I'm not published yet. In fact, I'm one of the million unpublished writers in the Bay Area – we all waste our Saturdays sitting outside a Starbuck's working on Chapter One, Page One. Some of us with yellow legal pads and pencil, some of us with laptops. We're all waiting to be published and we don't know if it'll happen. But we tell everyone it will, that the deal is almost final."

"It'll happen. *Carpe diem*, Violet!"

Violet glanced at him sharply, warily. It was a look

that sent out warning signals. "Something the matter?" Christian asked gently.

"No; you just sounded like a friend of mine – kinda look like him, too."

"George, is it?"

"God, your memory is good! I better be careful of what I say," Violet laughed.

"I'd never use it against you. What do you write about? What should I look for?" he asked.

"Well, unless you're into medieval history you may find my work boring. Dead English kings and knights on horseback, mostly. I've written a popular history of the Wars of Roses, some papers for historical periodicals. A shrink would say I'm longing for a man to save me from myself – God, I'm babbling; I'd better stop."

"No, I was enjoying it. Charmed completely."

"That's a first! I'm never sure if people really want to hear what I have to say."

They paused in a conversation that was banal yet necessary, each trying to think of what to talk about, if only to keep the interest alive, each not knowing that in the other's mind, there was no chance of it fading.

The leisurely stroll brought them full circle to Washington Square Park. The softly rolling green was deserted save for couples wandering out of the restaurants that encompassed it. Benches marked perimeters and the great basilica raised by the proud Italian-American community that once singularly populated North Beach, that enormous wedding cake of a church called Saint Peter and Paul's, kept vigil over her neighborhood.

Violet and Christian took a bench in front of the basilica. They sat in nervous silence for what seemed an eternity while Christian studied Violet's profile and wondered at his luck in finding a woman like her – someone who laughed at his stupid jokes, someone who listened, someone who didn't seem to care who he was.

Violet scuffed her right foot back and forth against

the grass so that the lamplight danced off the silver sandal and made it seem as if a thousand fireflies danced on it. She sighed and said, "I suppose now this is where you shake my hand and escort me to a waiting taxi?"

"No; this is where I either get to kiss the girl, or get a sod off for coming on too fast."

She waited, staring down at the dew glistening off the fog-damped grass under their feet. Violet felt him lean in closer and sighed – a faltering, anxious sigh.

She thought, *he's going to kiss me. He's going to kiss me and I'm going to be sick to my stomach!*

Her stomach was careening in somersaults and her hands wouldn't stop trembling. Thank God it was as cold as hell; the weather was as good an excuse as any if he asked why she shivered.

"Under the present circumstances, I'd rather not walk away," Christian murmured. "And maybe…" He allayed her present fears by backing away, after touching her cheek with a gentle hand and a wink.

Christian sat quietly and watched the traffic on Union Street for the longest time, as if trying to sort things out. His brows constricted as if something worried him, something dark had crept into his thoughts.

"My grandmother used to bring me here on Sundays," Violet said. "We'd go to the basilica. She'd light a candle for my parents, I'd count the minutes until we could leave – I've never been in a scarier place."

"Really! That big church?" Christian twisted about and pointed at St. Peter and Paul's. "D'you think it's open?"

"I don't know – we can always look."

He was on his feet, hand extended. Violet took it and they strolled across the street. She'd climbed these steps to the church a hundred times or more in her lifetime, inhaled the comforting scents of candle wax and incense, yet she could only think about the hand holding hers.

The doors were locked, but the windows in the doors

were fortunately unglazed or pebbled, so that they could look inside. Violet went up on her toes to see what had fascinated Christian. The nave was dimly lit, the racks of votive candles softly illuminating the many statues and shrines that decorated the nouveau baroque nave.

"I see what you mean, Violet. I'd find it hard to pray with all those saints staring at me!"

"Taking note of all my transgressions and imperfections," she quipped.

Turning, Christian looked down and smiled, brushing a tendril of hair off her forehead. "Nothing I can see," he whispered.

She looked away, smiling, and fumbling for something in her evening bag, took out a coin purse and dropped a coin in the Poor Box outside the doors. "For that kindness, I'll treat you to a cappuccino."

They found an empty table in the corner at Café Roma, away from the college kids and theatre-goers. "Someone's left their crossword puzzle for us to do," Christian said, when Violet returned with two cups of coffee. "Do you like them?"

"They help me think – oh here's an easy one: author of *Adam Bede*. George Eliot."

Christian nodded and carefully wrote the letters in the boxes. "A six letter word for beautiful; hmm… how about Violet?"

Violet glanced at him sideways and smiled, brushed the hair out of her eyes. "That just won you points – how about this one: Edward the Second, Henry the Eighth and George the Third – nope, 'losers' doesn't fit."

"Royal embarrassments – doesn't work."

"Dead English kings? I love dead English kings."

"What about live English musicians?"

"Hhmmm… this could be a trick question. Let's see now. I suppose it would depend on a lot of things, like, tomorrow morning, would he wake up and remember who I was, or even care?"

"I'd remember. I'd especially care." Their eyes met.

"You might be disappointed," she said softly. She kept the gaze, which soon became a stare off.

"Let's just see," Christian whispered, turning her face gently toward his. "Ever think you'll find your knight on horseback?"

"Probably not. I don't know if I'd be happy with my knight. At least in my mind he's exactly what I want him to be."

Her smile gave him courage. "Perhaps, maybe, if you blur the edges, you'll find he's got some redeeming qualities, or he's willing to be whatever you ever wanted."

She closed her eyes as his face come close and took in a heady scent of citrus and musk. Just as their lips met, the bells of Saint Peter and Paul's started to ring the hour – midnight. Violet swore softly and slid out of Christian's arms.

"What's the matter?" he laughed. "D'you turn into a pumpkin now?"

"Or something like it."

"I could give you a lift."

"No!" Violet almost screamed, and then, nervously, "I'm sorry… it'd be an imposition, besides, I live in Berkeley, and my car is parked at the BART station - shit! The last train leaves at midnight!"

"Can we get together tomorrow night?"

"I —"

"I can come to Berkeley. I haven't been there in – bugger, it's been a while."

The bells tolling made it impossible for Violet to think straight, that and Christian's anxious smile. She ran outside on to Columbus Street, looking about frantically.

"Look, there's a taxi," Christian said and he hailed the Yellow Cab over, gallantly helping her into the back seat. The heel of her right sandal was caught in the door frame and the sandal fell outside as she slid over the seat. "I'm at the Huntington," he informed her quickly, afraid the taxi would speed off. Then he leaned down and whispered, "Ring me, Violet – and be sure to ask for Thomas Hardy!"

"Thomas Hardy? Oh!"

The taxi sped off. Violet looked back and smiled at the dejected yet exquisite man watching as she disappeared into traffic on Columbus Street.

Moments later Christian found the sandal in the crosswalk, glittering in the moonlight. He picked it up and murmured, "I don't even want to know…"

As she settled into the backseat, Violet started to giggle. The driver turned and smiled. "Have a good evening, Miss?" he asked.

"One of the best. I'm going to Berkeley – would you mind taking me there please?" Violet stared down at her stockinged foot and laughed now. "I lost my other shoe!"

"So that makes you Cinderella, I guess?"

Yes, Violet thought as she watched the Christmas lights of San Francisco, *it pretty much did.*

13

Don't Think it Was a Dream...

FOR ITS BEING one touted one of the most romantic cities in the world, Christian found nothing romantic about San Francisco. Nor was there anything romantic about counting wallpaper flowers or the number of pastiglia medallions on the ceiling. At least the ribbons of smoke spiraling from his cigarette held some interest, as did the drunken argument being waged in the corridor by two German physicists in town for a convention.

Christian reached over and picked up the travel alarm clock, wondering why it hadn't shattered the night with its annoying "chirrup, chirrup." There was a good reason – it was only three in the morning.

He seized one of the goose down pillows, pummeling it into a shape comfortable for sleeping. Who was he fooling? There'd be no sleeping tonight.

She'd left without giving him a telephone number or address. But she'd given him her name, the lingering scent of her perfume and hope. Things he'd not had from a woman in years.

The encounters he'd had with women lately – usually at bars and supper clubs after a show – were selfish. He, for physical release, she, for the privilege of having had sex with Christian Walsh, rock star. They all seemed to think the coupling would be a mystical, spiritual experience, these nameless, faceless women between the ages of twenty-five and thirty-two, women he barely remembered. He wouldn't dignify the physical aspect of it by calling it 'making love' because there was nothing akin to love about it.

If it happened with Violet Ellison, it would be different; it would have to be special. It couldn't be any other way.

Funny, after all these years of being alone and pretending to like it, how meeting one woman could make reality so ugly and unappealing.

He turned on to his back again and stared at the ceiling, watching tracks of light from automobiles in the street, listening to yet another police siren wail, the argument that found new life in the corridor.

The nightstand light went on and Christian sat up, extinguishing his last cigarette. He got out of bed and scuffed across the carpet to the desk in search of a new packet. Opening the drawer, the telephone directory caught his eye.

The night clerk was not at all surprised when Christian came into the lobby at a quarter to four in the morning and paused by the desk. "Morning, Mister Walsh. Can I get you anything?" he offered cheerfully.

"Yeah... is there a telephone directory for Berkeley?"

"That would be the Oakland telephone book."

"How can I get one?"

The clerk looked under his counter and on the shelves behind him and finally came up with an Oakland directory. A year old, but it would do. Christian walked into the lounge with the book and took over a booth.

Sally Wakefield was seated in the lobby waiting for Kevin and their girls to come down for breakfast when Christian came in at half past eight.

"Morning," he said, dumping himself on the sofa beside her.

"Well, Goldilocks!" Sally queried, ruffling his hair affectionately, "Whose bed have you been sleeping in?"

"No one's, unfortunately. But there was a moment and a lady last night," Christian admitted, surprised he'd done that. But not as surprised as Sally, who now leaned in and kissed him on the cheek.

"So. You're willing to share," she murmured.

"Well, at least with you. In one moment last night, this morning actually, everything became brutally clear."

"Who is she?"

"I've got her name and that's all. Sally, how'd you like to help me find someone?"

Sally looked down and saw a telephone directory in his hands. "Sweetie, anything for you – but let's not tell Kevin! You know how he'll start prying and ruining things."

"Don't tell Kevin what?"

Kevin was there, three-year-old Julia in his arms and ten-year-old Jemma hanging on to a spare hand. Tamsin, a six-year-old clone of Kevin, was tagging along, clutching a Barbie doll.

Sally jumped up, pulling Christian with her. "We're going to surprise you with breakfast, Sweetheart! Guess who's joining us?"

Kevin's eyes widened at this revelation then saw Violet's sandal sticking out of Christian's pocket. He pulled it out and all three girls lunged for it.

"Hey! Where's Cinderella?"

"Kevin," Sally warned.

Christian gently took the shoe from him and exchanged it for the telephone directory. "I don't know; how many Violet Ellisons could there be in the San Francisco Bay Area?"

As they went out into the misty, overcast Sunday morning, Kevin shot a glance at Sally. "How many do we have to find?" he whispered.

IN BERKELEY, VIOLET sat in her living room with telephone in hand. She dialed a number, and then hung up.

This was madness. He'd probably hang up or plead a memory loss if she called to explain her actions last night. Again she pressed the rapid dial and waited for the concierge to answer. Halfway through the third verse of the second playing of *We Wish You a Merry Christmas* Violet decided it truly was madness; it would be the biggest mistake.

"Hello! Hi, how are you... uh, Thomas Hardy's room, please."

Muzak entertained her and then the phone buzzed eight times before a breathless Christian answered. Running for the phone! That was a good sign, wasn't it? Violet hung up, suddenly overwhelmed by cowardice. The last time she'd dated, Richard Nixon was President and the rules had probably changed – more than likely against her.

The rapid dial button was warm from overuse. Violet pressed it again and waited, pacing another circle around the living room, throwing herself into the coronation chair.

"Uh, yeah! Hi, it's me," Violet said to the concierge. "I think we were disconnected. Thomas Hardy's room – again?"

This time Violet sang along with the Christmas Muzak. "Hello?!"

He sounded perturbed.

"Christian, hello. It's Violet. Violet Ellison."

Ten minutes later she hung up and sat quietly in the coronation chair, watching the rain pelt the front windows. The phone's ring propelled her out of the chair. Her heart was pounding like it would burst out of her rib cage when she pressed the 'speak' button.

"Hello! Boy, that was quick!... uh, hi! Grammy Am! No, no, I just thought you were Sam, Sam, yeah, right... uh, how're the kids... they want to stay another night? Y'know, that's not a bad idea. As a matter of fact, I was invited to a last-minute party tonight, some of Sam's less-obnoxious clients. Yeah, I wanted to surprise Sam by schmoozing with them a bit, letting them know he's on top of things. You know, damage control... okay, great. See you tomorrow, then. Love you. Bye."

"*Liar!*" she swore at her reflection in the mirror.

She needed to talk to someone. Walking in a downpour four blocks to George's house seemed at first like a good idea.

"You're not at church," she greeted, following George to the spare bedroom he used for a studio. "Is your marine biologist friend —?"

"Oh no; it turns out she was two hours late and not impressed at all when she did show up at the restaurant. I drowned my wounded male pride in a pint too many at a bar on Union Street. And you?"

"Just as you see me."

"Which is?"

"Just Violet."

"Ah, a woman of mystery," he said, hastily covering the watercolor painting on the easel standing in the center of the floor. "So what's so mysterious?"

"I was going to ask you that."

Violet had stripped away the sheet from the easel and was face to face with herself as Joan of Arc. It had to be her: those were her eyes, her look of indignation. The sword in her hand was a nice touch.

"What was it you said?" George mused, coming to stand beside her. "Never argue with a woman holding a sword?"

"It's good, George. I've tried a self-portrait – I thought it would help work out the grief over Bella and Colin – it didn't – but I've never been able to come as painfully close as this. Do I really look this good?"

"Well, yes, to me you do, and you've ruined my Christmas surprise."

The sheet was replaced and George sat before the drafting table under the western window, picking up a number two pencil to continue the work interrupted by Violet's appearance, a sketch of the view. On the table were various quick-studies, and most of Violet and Isobel.

"I guess... well, hey, my timing's off as usual, huh?" Violet stammered. "Better get going."

"What's the matter? I've got the coffee going if you want to stay."

"It's just, these pictures, it's —"

"It's nothing. You became my muse. It's your eyes, Violet. Two large, lovely windows to another world, to a lost soul. Don't make much of it; next week it'll be the dog next door."

"I wanted to talk to you about Christian Walsh."

"Said to be one of the finest composers and musicians of his time. His time must be coming up."

"He's also got a wonderful sense of humor."

"So I've heard."

"And he almost kissed me last night – and he wants me to go out with him." I came out in a flood. "We met on Thursday at the café and then I saw him again at Neiman Marcus, it was all by accident. And last night at the café again – by accident. Christ, I'm going crazy!"

George put down the pencil and spun about on the stool. "I'd rather not hear it – not now, at least."

"Why?"

"There's a lot of reasons, but mostly it's a sense of *déjà vu*. And don't flatter yourself thinking it's something that it isn't."

"I don't know what to do."

George held her at arm's length for a moment. "Then I hope you never figure it out. It'll be better for all concerned."

When she at last said goodbye, George stood before the easel and stared into Joan of Arc's eyes.

He wasn't a good liar.

DRYING OUT BEFORE a blazing fire, Violet still didn't want to think about Christian. She turned on the television and stared at a Sunday morning news show. The house was too quiet with the boys at their grandparents' house, Elisabet with her friends and Sam still gone. The television went off and Violet sat listening to the neighborhood. Across the street the piano player was still trying to perfect Chopin and the neighbor's dog was barking anew. Violet heaved herself off the sofa and threw open the front door.

KNOCK. IT. *OFF*!"

The momentary quiet was actually refreshing and in that moment Violet decided what she'd do.

"What's the emergency?"

Ned stepped aside to invite Violet in. He was still in bathrobe, tee shirt and pajama bottoms, though it was three in the afternoon. The remnants of breakfast were on the coffee table, the Sunday papers, several case files and a hand-held Dictaphone on the sofa. It was safe to assume Ned had spent Saturday night alone.

Ned's condo in Emeryville was surprisingly different from his office. One could sit on the chairs and dine off the tables. The sense of order in decor and arrangement could be described as anal, so immaculate were the rooms. The miniature watercolors Violet had painted years ago hung in places of honor over the fireplace. Her medieval ladies. A Christmas gift when she couldn't afford to buy something.

Ned shoved aside the newspapers and invited her to sit. "You look like hell, Vi," he said, going into the kitchen to start a fresh pot of coffee. She followed, not bothering with her raincoat and hat.

"I met someone last night. I was with him for most of the evening," she blurted out. Ned turned, brows raised and face white. "Whom did we meet?"

"That's one scoop too many," Violet chided, taking the coffee measure out of his hand. "I don't need another night without sleep." She prepared the coffee and then opened the refrigerator, knowing exactly where the bread and margarine would be. Ned had a peculiar habit of keeping bread in the fridge. She plopped two slices in the toaster and then returned to the refrigerator for milk, fruit, cheese, and what appeared to be the remnants of a roast turkey.

Lost sleep? Ned mused silently.

"A musician, British."

"At the party? I thought it was just a Hollywood

North thing —"

"It's weird. I met him at Caffe Malvina on Thursday afternoon."

"Must be the water in that place," Ned quipped, returning to the living room with the brunch Violet managed to whip up. He made an about face and she caught the teetering carafe and sugar bowl.

"No, we *didn't.*"

"That'd be a first," he muttered under his breath.

She sat on the sofa and curled up, watching the fire in the fireplace and the erratic blinking of the lights on Ned's Christmas tree. She didn't remember him ever having a tree before. While they quietly shared brunch, Violet pulled over Ned's laundry basket and started to fold. It was a means to avoid confrontation and not discuss what she'd come to discuss.

"Did you want to?"

"I don't know. No, that's a half-truth. An unconvincing half-truth. You know what's worse? I didn't bother telling him I'm married with kids."

Ned turned the pages over in a file and then threw it down, sighing. "Revenge isn't always sweet, you know."

"You know more about that than I."

"Good hit. But I know you better than Sam or anyone, and you know me, and you know you've come to the wrong person for advice on taking a lover or having an affair."

Violet put her coffee cup down and punched his shoulder gently. "I came here because I thought you'd understand."

"Violet, you're talking to Ned Percy. Don't ask for my blessing or for me to shake my head and tell you it's wrong. This is just another one of those dragons you so love to fight."

THE NOISE AND warm scent of stale beer hit Violet like a wave as she opened the door to The Nag's Head. A few heads at the bar turned when she entered. She paused, looking around for familiar faces, was relieved to find none.

The bartender asked her pleasure and Violet responded by pointing in the direction of the stage. Christian was jamming with locals in an interesting rendition of *Bohemian Rhapsody* accompanied by drum, tin whistles and Christian's acoustic guitar.

A familiar, yet long-dormant jolt of sexual electricity surged through Violet when her eyes lighted on him. It was that sixth grade crush, the eighth grade first kiss. It was seeing Sam Peters all grown up and through a cloud of margaritas. It was better than all of that.

Violet noted with amusement that after he noticed her Christian tried to act cool and unconcerned but he grinned like a Cheshire cat. When his set was finished, he honored requests for autographs and compliments on his performance and worked the room to get to her.

The look in his eyes told Violet she was forgiven for last night's abrupt departure. They kissed hesitantly, sweet for a first kiss, and Christian took her in his arms and held her close.

"I BET YOU haven't read this one."

Christian glanced over Violet's shoulder and resting his chin against her delightfully perfumed neck, looked at what she was browsing.

"Nope. Can't say that I have. That's right – you like knights on horseback and swordplay of all kinds. Should I invest in a suit of armor?" He jibed and laughed when she blew a kiss and disappeared around the stack.

How could he have been this fortunate? To discover a woman whose idea of an entertaining evening was browsing a bookstore and a late night supper? While they perused the shelves, they discovered bits and pieces of each other and quietly marveled at the discovery. Christian liked splitting apart and going off alone, to look up and find her eyes meeting his at the same time, to smile, and have that smile returned. Even while they browsed magazine racks for late-night reading material he found his gaze returning to Violet and each time it was charged with a jolt of sexual electricity he hoped Violet was experiencing.

How much longer?

Worse still was the anticipation and uncertainty of where the evening would lead – or end.

Their dinner at Starz was quiet, for neither would broach the subject on both of their minds. Both decided silence was the safest measure. Only when the crème brûlée had turned to soup and he was on his fourth cup of coffee did Christian venture into unknown waters unafraid. If he didn't find out now, he never would.

"Tell you what, milady," Christian suggested as he waited for the waiter to leave; "I can find a suit of armor, ride over to your house and take you away from all this – provided you wear one of those nice medieval numbers with the plunging necklines."

"I've got a suit of armor."

"I'm not at all surprised."

"I wish I had a little medieval number with a plunging neckline," she whispered.

"I know of one."

"Do you?"

"It's kind of blue, kind of violet, I know you'd look smashing in it."

"Would you settle for a pair fuzzy slippers and a ratty bath robe?"

"Provided I can help you out of them!"

"Okay… I've got a large bed with curtains, the type they use in castles… just in case you were wondering."

"I was."

Christian's mind danced with the most erotic and sensual images of Violet it had offered yet and it set him into turmoil.

"You wouldn't happen to know where my shoe is?" Violet purred as she toyed with the open collar of his white dress shirt. His breath came rapidly at her most delicate touch. Jesus! What would happen in bed? "So?" she whispered.

Christian's response was a passionate kiss, the photographer laying in wait be damned. "Let's go back to my hotel and get it," he said huskily. "And I hope you don't go running off until at least morning, Cinderella."

14

Time's Up, Cinderella...

"HI! I TOOK the liberty of ordering breakfast in, unless of course..."

Violet self-consciously nodded and finished towel-drying her hair as she came from the bathroom, holding a hotel-issue bathrobe tightly about her. He'd opened the drapes to bring in a pale winter sun that now broke through the morning fog, and while she had been in the shower, had festooned the suite with flowers – multitudes of flowers.

Christian had been up for some time, already dressed and standing at an intimate breakfast table complete with a vase of flowers, champagne and Diet Coke. A new log was burning in the fireplace. All this had been done in the span of an hour.

"Morning," she stammered, more than a little self-conscious. "Sorry – you know, I didn't think – what I mean to say is, I thought —"

"Not to worry... I'm not very good at this."

"Neither am I – obviously."

"Maybe together?"

Christian's smile was as shy as hers. He eagerly held out a chair for her and bussed Violet's brow gently as she sat.

This was the moment she dreaded – the awkward 'morning after' conversation with its particular etiquette; stilted questions and responses exchanged between two strangers who wondered if there would be anything to say, as if this was an end and not a beginning. Of knowing it was right, but yet very, very, wrong in for all the obvious reasons.

"I'm sorry about last night," she mumbled. Her eyes

now involuntarily slid to the sofa where blankets and pillows were neatly stacked at one end. A pair of rumpled pajamas lay on the floor with an empty ashtray and the unopened packet of cigarettes.

"It's okay."

Christian leaned over and stroked her face gently, allaying her fears. A lover's caress; one of understanding and future hope.

"You're probably thinking —"

"Whatever my thoughts are at this moment, it's not what you believe. But I am a strong believer it letting things come at their own time. However long it takes, Violet. I confess I don't know if I'm quite ready, either, and it's not something I want to botch up!"

"Thank you!" came a tearful whisper.

"So it's okay?" Christian queried as he sat across from her.

Violet lifted the cover from her plate and laughed aloud when she saw a Waterford crystal bowl brimful with Cap'n Crunch's Crunch Berries.

"Amazing!" she laughed. "Absolutely okay."

He offered a kiss. "Now it truly is!"

"WHERE'D YOU GET this car?"

This asked while Violet was pushing sixty-five in an easterly direction on the Bay Bridge.

"It was my Dad's. A present from his father for his fortieth birthday."

"Vintage Mustang... sixty-seven, sixty-eight?"

"You're good. Sixty-seven. He drove it only once. Killed in Vietnam during the Tet Offensive."

"Army regular?" Christian asked as he passed the coffee mug again and held it to her lips.

"Mmm, no; reporter for CBS. Radio first, then television. He worked with Walter Cronkite – you know, the glamor boys. My dad was with Edward R. Murrow in London during the Blitz. He interviewed Churchill – twice.

Last time I saw him I was thirteen, no, fourteen, and he was on the evening news. Dad's parents were from Ludlow. He grew up in London, then moved to the States right after my sister Isobel was born."

"A bit more glamorous than an Anglican presbyter."

"Presbyter? A priest?"

"Yeah."

"A priest? You're the son of a priest?"

"Actually, he was the dean of York Minster – Violet! There's a truck – Jesus, woman!"

Christian laughed nervously as she sailed from forty-five to zero and within an eyelash of the bakery truck in front of them. Violet was still staring at him incredulously.

"A priest?"

"You're sure it's okay to do this? Taking the day off?" he asked now. She was still staring.

"You're the son of an Anglican priest?"

"It usually takes this long for it to sink in. So you're sure it's okay to do this?"

Violet nodded like a dumb animal.

He had asked for a tour – not the usual sights, attractions like the cable cars and Fisherman's Wharf, the Transamerica Pyramid and North Beach, but the sights of the Bay Area Violet loved as a girl, her childhood haunts.

"Where do you live now?" Christian hinted as they leaned up against the Mustang and studied the empty lot high in the Berkeley Hills that had once contained her parents' home. The foundation still existed twenty-one years after the fire that had destroyed the large house with bay windows.

"Not far," Violet answered and climbed up on the concrete fortifications to walk along their narrow edges like a tightrope walker. "My sister inherited this, and now it's mine. I don't know why she never sold the lot. Or why I haven't."

"It'd bring something substantial."

"Right now it's a refuge for the homeless," Violet

remarked, jumping down on to a soft tuft of grass where the great Tudor fireplace used to stand and picking up the litter from an illegal campsite.

"Build a castle on it, Violet."

"We were going – never mind."

"Ghosts coming back, are they? I know what that's all about."

"Eventually I'll do something with the land, at least before the city takes it away."

She was walking along the former kitchen wall and Christian was at the end of the concrete to catch her when she hopped down onto the grass.

"Eventually you'll tell me, right?" he asked with a smile.

"Eventually, but I asked you first. Tell me about being a cathedral brat." Violet shifted in Christian's arms and giggled when he kissed her neck.

"I'm starved; do you want lunch or something?" he asked.

"That's a cop-out! Was it really that bad?"

Now he lifted her chin and kissed her, saying, "Let's not talk about it right now. Maybe later," he murmured.

"I'm sorry... I shouldn't have pushed you," Violet apologized but her fears of losing him for a small infraction dissipated when he suddenly grinned and tickled her with a day-old beard.

"It was a bloody, awful mess," he finally admitted. He slipped a gentle hand under her sweater as they kissed and was relieved when she melted at his touch. Violet became increasingly responsive as their kisses became deeper and more intimate, but Christian resisted the temptation to take it further. It would be when she was ready. She would tell him and she would lead the way.

Soon, he thought, *very soon...*

"SO IT WAS BLOODY awful, huh?"

Christian nodded and at her suggestion grabbed a six-pack of Diet Coke and some bottled water from the grocery shelves. Little by little, she was breaking down the wall. Violet let him commandeer the shopping cart while she browsed the shelves of bread, holding up loaves of savory sourdough with walnuts and a plain baguette for inspection.

"Sourdough with walnuts! Let's try that." He scooped up a second loaf and lobbed it expertly into the basket, then steered the cart toward the dairy case. "Y'know, it could have been worse," Christian explained as they shopped for a picnic lunch, the location as yet undecided. "Do you like pears or apples? Or is that like comparing apples and oranges? Better still; let's try this kiwi. D'you like kiwi?... I eventually abandoned York and the church, much to my dad's disappointment. And my mum's. It's still a sticky wicket for her. But London was where all the action was. Dad wanted me to be a lawyer or take up the dog collar. I come from a family of priests and politicians. One brother saves the soul of another."

They'd reached the dairy case finally and Christian now agonized over his choices. "Can't imagine what it would've been like to live that kind of life. The life of a priest. I was a chorister, though. What kind of cheese do you like? Do you like cheese?"

"Yeah, I like cheese – get the Monterey Jack, it's California. Oh, some of the Blue Castello. Let me guess – Canterbury."

"No, York, and then Westminster Abbey."

"You must have been adorable, white starched ruff, red cassock and cotta."

"I'm not now?"

Their conversation continued at Mortar Rock Park in the Berkeley Hills, their lunch spread out on the only picnic table in the small recreational area, a conversation punctuated by the sounds of traffic and city noise.

Christian admired the neighborhood, the manicured yards with lawns and flowers, relating anecdotes of his gardening triumphs and failures – speaking like a father of the roses he tended in his London garden, of the horse he bred at his home in Wensleydale, how excited he was at finding a first edition of Joyce's Ulysses and how he couldn't defeat the Warlord of the Ice Kingdom in the latest video game he'd purchased. This man, who played a wicked guitar riff, penned some of the most sensual, and enduring love ballads ever written, was to Violet nothing more than normal.

For most of their meal they dined quietly, the brief silences between them avenues by which they explored their private yet mutual thought – the frightening yet exciting direction in which they traveled, silences broken by hesitant questions, followed by diffident answers.

"So why didn't you remarry? A guy like you?"

"Someday," he sighed, searching the horizon for nothing in particular, "someday when you've got the time, I'll tell you – and if you want to hear." Again there was silence fraught with emotional and sexual tension. "What about you?"

Violet was plucking the petals from a rose that had dropped on the ground and now she concentrated of them, admiring their various stages of decay, how some were still smooth and leathery, others as fragile as rice paper.

"Just one bad relationship after another," she admitted after a silence that was frightening for both. "Coming out of a real downer, if you must know."

"What did you do when your mother and father died?" he now asked.

"I lived with my sister – she was only twenty-one. Came back to America from Oxford to take care of me. Gave up a Rhodes scholarship for me. She took on an enormous responsibility. I made it easier for her by staying out of trouble, waiting until I was out of high school to go through an adolescent rebellion. I think she was grateful, but she never said. But I did make all the wrong choices, do the wrong things – with the wrong people. We never got to mend our broken fences, bridges, whatever."

Christian glanced at her from over the mouth of his water bottle. "When did she die?"

"She died with her husband in a car accident this year. In Northamptonshire on the A34."

"You're alone then? No one else?"

Violet shrugged and opened a bottle for herself. Drinking, she said: "I've got a family, but even in a family you can be so alone that you want to die. I've gotten used to it."

"Sorry, Violet."

"It wasn't your fault, was it?" she answered with a sad, soft, smile. "I loved my sister and brother-in-law to the point of insanity – and they did drive me crazy. They told me to get a sensible education and get a sensible job that pays the bills. So I got a sensible education, sensible job, fell into a sensible life. Fell in and out of sensible relationships. None of it was. Never did anything I wanted, only what was safe. Except I wrote, I wrote every day, about everything on my mind. I still do that. I tried to please in other ways. I designed costumes and helped my grandmother with her dressmaking business, dabbled with illustration, but I always turn back to writing because that is where my passion and talent truly lie."

"My parents had such expectations, and I botched everything. My mother asks if I'm a bit old to still be play-ing rock n' roll, and sometimes I think that myself – especially after a late concert, or when I wake up the next morning aching from the theatrics. There's no amount of working out or pain killers that scares away the aging process." he explained good-naturedly, looking in his pockets for the cigarettes he placed on the bench between them. "Honestly? I'm going all hot and cold over my future. There are days when it's all I'll ever want, and some days, mostly of late, when I don't know. I just don't, bloody know. And I feel guilty because I know I'll be letting the lads down either way. I just don't know."

"I've seen you on stage, Christian. I don't think you'd be happier with any other life."

Christian glanced over and saw how intently she studied him and smiled. "Until last night, I didn't think so. I'd like to think that now, at the end of a tour, there's someone to look forward to."

"If that's what you want."

"Why shouldn't it be what we want?"

"It's late. I should get you back to the hotel or Kevin will have my hide."

Christian cupped her face in his hands and gave Violet a timorous kiss. "Tell me why it shouldn't be?"

"WHAT TIME'S YOUR flight?" she asked when the hotel carhop took the keys from Christian and sped off to park the Mustang.

"Six-thirty, seven, I forget," he finally answered.

Christian took her hand and led her across the street to the steps of Grace Cathedral. They sat under the bronze copies of Lorenzo Ghiberti's medieval doors from the Baptistery in Florence, called 'The Doors of Paradise'. Together they silently watched tourists climb the newly constructed steps and bypass construction workers as they carried lumber to and from the Cathedral School for Boys, also under construction. Christian drew her close, leaning her head on his shoulders.

"That sigh speaks volumes," he chuckled, squeezing her gently.

"I wish."

"Do you wish it could be later?"

"Yes."

"Maybe next time. C'mon," he whispered and drew her up.

They went into the cathedral and strolled the nave amid ribbons of sunlight tinted by stained glass windows.

Violet automatically walked toward the Chapel of the

Nativity and Christian followed a few steps behind.

"Would you come to London with me? Tonight?"

She stopped and wheeled about. "I'm sorry; what?"

"Come to London with me, Violet."

The voice was calm and serious, the face soft and earnest.

"When?"

"Tonight."

"Chris, I can't just pick up and leave; I've got a job. Ned would kill me."

"Who is this Ned?" laughed Christian.

"You don't want to know. I wish I could go with you, but right now…"

"I'm sorry, I didn't mean – well, think about it."

"Maybe."

His hands were in his coat pockets and he looked a little shamefaced, as if he'd done something wrong.

"I'll think about it." Violet said and watched as his chest and shoulders slackened in relief.

"I'll have our manager make the arrangements."

"You won't be disappointed if I decided not to go?"

"Of course I will. But at least I'll have a reason to come back to California."

Out on the steps again, Christian rested his head in Violet's lap and watched the clouds float above them. Con- versation was becoming difficult now, with his departure hours away. Violet was relieved when a German couple came up and asked in broken English if she would oblige them with taking a picture. Violet pointed the Polaroid camera in their direction and shot. Moments later the couple from Bonn returned the favor by taking a snapshot of Violet and Christian, offering the compliment 'nice couple' before they departed. Now Violet sat in the quiet shade and watched the picture develop before her eyes.

"We can do this, Violet. There's a way. I know it."

Violet nodded and then gave the photograph to

Christian. Her hands were shaking so hard that Christian steadied them with his. She slid her hands out and entwined their fingers in a movement that was purely sensual. She took his sweet, melancholic face in her hands and marveled that this man was hers for the asking...

RICHARD OF GLOUCESTER rode a glistening white steed through the gates of Westminster, ignoring the shouts of Edward and those family members concerned enough with his state of mind to conclude that he'd lost his senses.

He rode at a break-neck speed into London, to a Chepeside neighborhood where the houses leaned together and blocked out the daylight. Master Whitlock kept a house and shop there. A tailor's shop where there was a fair young seamstress called Anne. Not his Anne, not Anne Nevill. For weeks he'd been searching for his Anne in every great house and every place unimaginable in London. Clarence swore before Edward and the Privy Council that she ran away to avoid Richard's suit for her hand, but Richard knew his double-dealing, traitorous brother had something to do with it.

No, this fair young Anne was a past love, the mother of his young son. He'd taken up with her when Anne Nevill was lost to him in her father's quarrel with the King that had turned their world upside down. Mistress Anne Whitlock plied a fair needle and offered Richard more than fine doublets or cloaks. She had given her body to him, had shared a bed with him when they were both virgins. Now she was a confidante, a comfort in these dark days of January.

Anne Whitlock saw him riding fast and hard and knew why he'd come. Tonight she'd share her bed and later, she'd hold him in her arms and listen to him speak lovingly of his little cousin, the Nevill heiress, his friend from childhood. It was unfair to her, but for at least a night, the first and greatest nobleman in the realm, Richard of Gloucester, would be hers alone.

She ran to him and allowed Richard to lift her into the saddle without pausing a moment, so familiar was she with his cadence. Richard kissed her deep and hard with the promise of greater pleasures to come and they rode off as the telephone rang and startled Violet from a nap.

The late afternoon sun shot dusty shafts of sunlight into the hotel room. Christian lifted his head from Violet's breast to answer the call.

"Yeah!... right, I'll be ready... no, that won't be necessary, I can get a ride... yeah, Kevin. Bye." Hanging up, Christian shifted in Violet's arms and kissed Violet, who was curled up like a kitten while they shared the sofa. He took the history book, a biography of Edward the Fourth, purchased during their afternoon canvass of bookshops, out of Violet's hands and replaced it with her boots.

"Gotta go?" she asked, pouting.

"Gotta."

"I've decided," Violet called through the bathroom door. When the water stopped, she reached in with eyes averted and handed Christian a towel as he stepped out of the shower. Christian winked when he opened the door and accepted the cup of coffee Violet now offered. Violet's level of comfort with him at that moment surprised her. Until then, she'd only seen his bare feet when he accepted her dare to test the icy waters of San Francisco Bay at Baker Beach. Now he was wrapped in a hotel-issue towel and Violet was weak not just at the knees, but all over. Whatever one might derogatorily think of men in their middle years, it couldn't be said of Christian Walsh. There wasn't a spare ounce of fat on his lean, powerful frame and the sight of him made Violet wish she'd shared that shower.

He dabbed shaving cream on her nose playfully. "What's the verdict?"

"Christian."

"Ah, the voice. You're not coming with me, are you?"

The disappointment in his voice reminded Violet of her morning jousts with Sam.

"At least not tonight."

"But eventually you will join me in England?"

When she didn't answer, he wrapped her in his arms. "Don't be afraid, Violet." "I will come — but when the time's right. I'm so scared, Chris."

"Don't be!" His whisper was as sensual and evocative as a kiss.

"Aren't you afraid, just a little?"

Christian admitted he was.

"COME WITH ME to the boarding gate, at least."

Violet turned off the ignition and avoided his eyes, which were fixed on her. Christian had shoved on a pair of Ray Bans and turned up the collar of his coat, giving him the look of an espionage agent. He fished around in his overcoat and brought out an envelope, a note card, pressing it into her hand.

"May I open it now?" she asked.

The card was purchased at the bookstore where they'd found the history books now weighing down Violet's backpack. Depicted on the card was Edward Coley Burne-Jones' *Love Among the Ruins*. Violet had mentioned over coffee that Coley Burne-Jones was one of her favorite painters. Enclosed were a brass bookmark of the Ashmolean Knight and the Polaroid snapshot of them. Christian had written his telephone number in the card. He also took from his carry-on airline tickets that he tucked silently into the backpack.

"This is just crazy — wonderful crazy," Christian said as they walked through the international terminal to the British Airways gate. "You'll be here if I call?"

"Where else would I be?" she laughed self-derisively.

"But I can ring you up?"

"Of course."

"We'll have lots to talk about."

They said goodbye with a passionate kiss. Violet clung to him, taking in everything about him to remember.

"See you soon," Violet replied tearfully, breaking away.

"Violet!" Christian shouted after her.

She was gone, lost in the crowd of travelers.

15

Fa la, la, la, la, la, la... Nuts

PARSIFAL WAS WEARING a string of blinking Christmas lights, several ornaments and a Santa cap. The imitation Douglas fir had been dragged out of the garage after a six-year exile and now stood ready for decoration, Alex and Max staring in wonder at its naked glory. Alex, too young to remember the tree, touched it carefully, expecting the needles to come away and a sweet, pungent scent of pine cling to his hand. Nothing of the sort happened. One of the branches came off in his hand, a metal rod with vinyl bristles glued and stapled to it.

"You can't grow trees from boxes!" he declared.

"But boxes come from trees, Alex." Elisabet teased.

"Why not?"

"Because!"

Elisabet sighed for the hundredth time and shot him death ray reserved for younger siblings. "Alex, you're not listening! The Christmas tree didn't grow in this box. We got this tree at the hardware store when you were hatched and this year we're using it! Now shut up you and hand me the box of ornaments!"

Alex would not be mollified. "But last year Dad took us to the mountains and we cut the tree and brought it back!"

"That was last year," Elisabet sighed. "You whine like a two-year old, Alex. This year we're using a fake tree. It looks better than a real tree, anyway."

She stepped back and nodded. It was green, full, symmetrical. It looked real; with a spritz of pine-scented air freshener, it would smell real, too.

"But I want to go to the mountains! Dad said when he got back we'd go to the mountains!" Alex continued to whine.

"We're not going to the mountains this year!" Elisabet hissed and shoved him out of the way.

"*Why?!*"

"Because your father won't be back from New York until Christmas Eve and then it'll be too late. Alex, that's the end of it —no! I said that's the end of it!"

Violet had come downstairs, still dressed in the jeans and a brown tweed sweater she'd worn home from the airport. She took the tree lights from a box and undertook the annual ritual of untangling them.

This, year nothing had been spared in decking the halls. It was, as Elisabet moaned, an obscene medieval Christmas tableau. Thousands of tiny firefly lights glimmered and twinkled annoyingly off the ceiling, the mantle, the moldings around the doors and stairways. Heavy candles scented with bayberry and festooned with garland were planted on every available table and space. An evergreen garland was draped, thrown, wound and stretched from wall to wall, intertwined with metallic ribbon. The children's homemade decorations were displayed with the same honor as those purchased at five-and-dime stores and Day After sales. The Ashmolean Knight looked less sinister with purple foil garland and lights twinkling around his frame.

Now Violet quietly set up the Nativity scene in the center of the mantle and stepped back to admire her work, hugging the sweater against her body.

"How was Saturday night?" Elisabet wanted to know.

The question made Violet blanch. "What about Saturday night?" Her question came not as an inquiry but a demand, as defensive as it was angry.

"The fancy society ball, Mom. Was it okay? Enjoy yourself?"

"Oh that. It was a God-awful bore."

Elisabet watched as her mother's face lost its color and she suddenly looked ill. Then her inquisitive eyes slid down to the man's brown tweed sweater enveloping her mother's dwindling frame so that Violet looked lost, almost like a girl.

"Have you lost more weight, Mamma?"

"No."

"You look... smaller. Is that Dad's?" "What?"

"The sweater. I haven't seen it before."

"Bought it yesterday – Banana Republic."

Again the response was unnecessarily defensive and terse.

"Yeah, it looks very... Banana," Elisabet replied, nodding. It looked very expensive and was scented with a man's cologne. Her father didn't wear cologne of any kind. Seventeen unopened bottles of aftershave and cologne sat on the top shelf of the bathroom closet. Elisabet continued to study her mother.

"Did I sprout a wart, or a third eye?" Violet wanted to know and made a great deal out of redistributing the foil tinsel around the Ashmolean Knight.

"You were so happy yesterday."

"Ran into an old friend last night. Just made me feel worse about everything."

"Sorry, Mamma."

"Don't be."

As Elisabet started clearing away empty ornament boxes and bags, she noticed the letter on the coffee table. "Wow! I didn't know – you really did lose the fellowship. Oh shit, Mom. Now I understand the bad mood and all."

Violet shrugged, guessing it was as good an excuse as any for her current state of emotion. She'd been turned down for the fellowship, shot out of the water by a twenty-year old gamer nerd who had an interesting spin on Edward the Second's true nature and personality. He'd seen *Braveheart* thirty-one times by his own admission.

But she could still go to England...

"Can we bake cookies?" Elisabet ventured timidly,

afraid to disturb her mother's thoughts. As expected, Violet whirled about looking puzzled. "Cookies, Mom? It wouldn't be Christmas without you burning two batches." Violet smiled then and everything was back to normal.

"Finally, the good mood," Elisabet mentioned as they iced the last batch.

"Sorry if that's a problem," Violet laughed.

"No, really! Whenever Christmas comes round, or when Dad goes on one of his extended trips to save... whatever it is that needs saving, you turn into a different person."

"Is that good or bad?"

"Well... good."

Violet turned to her left, relieved at having felt Max's gentle hand on her thigh. It gave her respite from this conversation traveling into dangerous waters. She offered the little boy a choo-choo train iced with cherry frosting and decorated with M&M's. A smile as genuine and loving as she had ever hoped for was her reward. Violet swung Max into her arms and returned his favor with a shower of kisses that made him squeal happily. That gave Max courage to lobby for a snowman dusted with green sugar crystals. He was compensated for his effort by getting not only the snowman, but an iced star. Violet looked over Max's head and saw Elisabet smiling. She released Max and gave Elisabet a hug.

They embraced wordlessly until the telephone rang and Violet let it ring. She didn't want to talk to Sam, if that's who it was.

And if it was Christian...

"Aren't you gonna get that?" Elisabet asked, wriggling free.

"They'll call back if it's important."

"Mamma."

"It's okay, Beth. Don't worry."

The familiar smile was reassuring. *All evenings should be like this*, she thought as the mood brightened and her mother turned on the CD player and danced back to the table to one of Fortinbras' fast songs.

Violet suddenly and unexpectedly hugged her again, whispering an embarrassing childhood endearment that made both laugh.

All evenings should be like this, Violet thought as she smiled at her eldest son, who refused to be outdone by his little brother or big sister either in affectionate offerings or sweet remunerations. She suddenly felt as if wrapped in a protective, silken cocoon. No one could hurt her nor steal this happiness pervading her entire being. The kitchen smelled delightfully of boiled icing and burnt cookies. Fortinbras was replaced with Christmas music on the CD player. For the first time ever it really was Christmas in the Ellison-Peters house.

"When we're done here I'll let you play *Sword of Vermillion*," Violet murmured low to Alex and a smile crossed his lips.

"That's Dad's game," he giggled.

"Dad isn't here to know, is he? So as long as we don't erase his game, I don't mind if you don't."

In a rare show of affection, Alex swung arms around his mother and embraced her tightly before running off to set up the video game.

"Dad is going to kill you if you let him play it," Elisabet drawled with a sideways grin; "that's his thinking game."

"So? Changing the subject, what would you think of my going to England for a few weeks, may be a month or two?"

"Dad would never let that happen. I told him you didn't get the fellowship."

"There's some grant money. I made an application and it's as good as mine."

"No there isn't."

"How do you know? Reading my mail or something? That's a very Sam-like thing."

"I know you're lying because you won't look at me. You're asking me to lie to Dad, to conspire."

"I won't let you do that – won't get you in trouble. Think of it as a well-deserved retreat. We'll still go to Disneyland in the spring like we always do, or we can stay up on the Coast. Would you be okay with that?"

Elisabet carefully iced an angel cookie and, "That's a helluva long way to get away from Dad."

"Well, it's a first step."

"So," Elisabet sighed, "you're going to file for divorce?"

"I don't know – that's why I need to get away." Violet said, adding, "I would never leave you or the boys. We're going to make a new life together. But that's not what I'm asking. I need time to make the plans for us."

"Sure. The boys are in day care and school and I can make sure my classes are in sync with their schedules. I guess it would be one heckuva long trip to save the soda company – or something like it. Kids with parents in the military and CEOs of big corporations deal with worse, I guess." Elisabet handed her mother the angel cookie. "Honestly, Mom, I don't know how you've done it all these years."

"Thank you, Beth."

Elisabet shrugged, licking her fingers. "I want you to be happy – and I know you haven't been in a long time."

Violet caressed the wool enveloping her like a security blanket. Christian's favorite sweater relinquished the moment she said she was cold while they walked on Baker Beach. How could one day change everything? Make everything so clear, yet so confusing?

Maybe, she thought, *this was a wake-up call.*

"HELLO?"

Violet grabbed the phone from under the blankets and answered on the fourth ring.

"Hi, did I wake you?"

Sam's voice somehow surprised her. He rarely called at night while on business trips. Calls home were relegated to six in the morning when the rates were cheapest.

"No, I was editing." She sighed, pushing aside the manuscript pages scattered over the bedspread.

"The book you're never finished with?"

"Only one of many."

They engaged in one of their usual pedestrian conversations. Sam grudgingly divulged news of his trip and developments on the health of the agency, none of which interested Violet. She casually mentioned her meeting Christian Walsh. Why lie or hide anything? He didn't have to know where they met – or how. Or how she was thinking of him at that moment while Sam lectured strangely about the irresponsible use of the credit cards. She picked away at the chenille bedspread until the center of a rose was naked and smooth to the touch and there was a pile of ivory velvet beside her.

While he droned on and on, Violet's thoughts wandered to the night before. She had come so close to giving herself completely to Christian; why had she backed down? Why was she so frightened when she knew the marriage was doomed, knew Sam would never change, and she'd never be happy if she kept going on as if everything was alright That was it! Change. Change was good, but it was frightening...

"Vi? Are you there?"

Sam's voice brought her to the here and now. Sighing, she said, "Yeah. So when are you coming home?"

Now there was the most protracted of pauses. Violet turned her attention to the typed pages in her lap and started drawing figures in the margins as she waited – little figure eights, snowmen, stars, daggers.

"That's why I'm calling, Vi. Things are – well, they're really bad."

She was sketching a portrait bust of a medieval lady now. "How bad are they?" she asked.

Cut to the chase, damn it!

"Bad."

"Bad as in a few phone calls would put Band-Aid on it? Or bad as in we could lose the agency, the house, my '67 Mustang and Alex won't get braces?"

Sam exhaled a sigh that sounded like a hurricane through the receiver. "Well, Alex still has a few years before that would be a problem."

Now Violet drew snakes – big, writhing, venomous snakes.

"Looks like I should keep my straight job, eh, Sam?" Violet asked, knowing full well what the answer would be. Whenever a door opened for her, another slammed in her face, a window fell shut. She glanced down at the page that was slowly filling up like an illuminated manuscript with phantasmagorical scribbles and wrote the words 'Christian Walsh' six or seven times while Sam explained the predicament. She wasn't listening and didn't really care. Her interest only piqued when Sam mentioned something about staying until mid-January.

"It doesn't surprise me," she said.

"Look, Vi,"

There it was, the phrase that heralded an excuse. '*Look, Vi...*' Violet cut him off. "I don't want to fight, Sam; I'll tell the kids you called."

"I'll call you Christmas Day." He sounded desperate, almost pathetic now. "Will you be at Mom and Dad's, or at home?"

"Oh, with any luck at all I'll be in London with Christian Walsh," she said airily.

Again a protracted pause. "Vi, that was a joke, right? The bit about Christian Walsh? Vi? Vi, are you still there?"

"Worried, Sam?"

"Was that a joke? Tell you what, I'll try to get home Christmas Day. I can't promise anything—"

"I'm tired, Sam. I'll talk to you in the morning."

The telephone was switched off and thrown under

the bed. Reaching under Sam's pillows, Violet found the remote control and shot it at the television set. The glare of the screen reflected something on top of the bedspread. The card from Christian. She studied it for a moment, opened it, and then replaced it.

The card was still lying on the bedspread when she returned from work the next evening. Tossing her purse and shopping bag of Christmas presents in a corner, Violet nearly sat on it and the mail she'd dumped on the bed when she plopped down to kick off her shoes. Pulling out bills and drug store advertisements, she held up the card, flipped it open and stared at it for the longest time. Then she picked up the telephone and started to dial.

The doorbell rang downstairs just as the connection was made.

"Grammy Am!"

Alex's squeal reached all the way upstairs to Violet's bedroom. "Mamma! Mamma! Grammy Am!"

The rings were answered by a sleepy Christian when Violet slammed the receiver down and turned to say hello to her mother-in-law.

"Hey! What brings you over?" Violet asked breathlessly as she succumbed to a hug.

"I have a dinner date with Gloria Atwater at Chez Panisse but I wanted to come by and ask you something, well, get your opinion," Amalie greeted, placing Max on the bed.

"Well, if it's the dress and shoes, Grammy Am, they're killer."

"Thank you, darling! I'll take every compliment I can get these days," Amalie crowed. "No, I wanted to ask if you'd come to a dinner party Thursday night. It's George's birthday. I know you don't really care for him, but with just a few days from Christmas and with a birthday, I couldn't stand to think of him being alone."

"Pretty!" Max shouted all of a sudden. "Ohhh, love!"

Violet turned to see what Max was laughing about

and suddenly felt a nausea, the bottom of her stomach dropping out. Max was holding Christian's card and waving it, Christian's neat, small hand visible. She calmly leaned over and wrestled it out of the little boy's grasp. Max began to fret and howl.

"Goodness, it's just a greeting card," Amalie laughed.

"It has sentimental value – a note from Sam," Violet replied and tucked the card into the *Book of Common Prayer* sitting on the nightstand.

"Sam?" Amalie asked, her eyes bugging out. "*My* son? I can't remember when he even sent his father a birthday card."

Violet avoided Amalie's quizzical look. "So you know why I want to keep it. He's making up for lost opportunities, I suppose and I'm not going to argue with that."

Damn, she was getting good at lying.

"Anyway, are you game for a dinner party?"

"Sure, why not? No one should be alone on their birthday."

Amalie reached out to ruffle Max's curly hair and nodded. "And you would know, wouldn't you dear?" She whispered to Violet.

VIOLET WAS THE last to arrive at her in-laws' house in the Richmond District, catapulting herself off the 36 Geary and down Eighteenth Avenue to the Peters' townhouse at the end of the block. She could hear the music and laughter as she sprinted in heels, dodging a couple as they walked their collies, side-stepping a pickup game in a driveway, tossing the basketball back to the players. She had barely time to catch her breath and press the buzzer when then screen door flew open and Stan waved her inside with a cigar.

"Here you are! Looking lovely as always," Stan greeted. "Had to stay late at the office, no doubt – here, let me take your coat and bag."

"Thanks," Violet answered and slid out of her coat, taking a glass of champagne from a tray on the coffee table and then claiming a corner of the sofa that wasn't piled with coats and foil-wrapped bottles. She glanced around and noted that there wasn't a person in the room she recognized and was contented to sit there by herself, watching George and Sam's parents mingle with the guests for the entire evening, and wondering where Sam was, wishing she could be with Christian, when she saw Marjorie Rotherwell enter with an older man.

"What's *she* doing here?"

The question was directed at Amalie, who'd passed by with a plate of canapés.

"What, darling? Oh, her. A favor to Sam – he called and asked if we would invite her, something about it being good for business. She wanted to finally meet the handsome professor. I'm talking about George."

"One stud isn't enough?" Violet groused.

"Hmm, what's that?"

Violet smiled sweetly when Amalie offered a devilled egg. She plopped the whole thing in her mouth.

"Finally! Hello, lovely lady!"

George's greeting and hug surprised Violet, who almost choked on the egg, which shot out and spattered over Marjorie's dress.

"You could just say hello," George teased.

Violet ignored him and offered Marjorie a napkin, never taking her eyes from the older woman for a moment. "Doctor Knightsbridge, you should be more careful when you come on to the ladies," Marjorie tittered.

"Missus Rotherwell," said Violet when she'd caught her breath and turning said, "George, there are circles in hell for people like you."

"Don't mind her, Marjorie – we've known each other since she was fifteen, and she pretends to hate me," George said.

"If you've known me that long, you know it isn't

pretense," Violet fired back, batting her eyelashes. George and Violet exchanged simpers.

Marjorie's arm slid through George's and one of her impeccably manicured hands rested on the sleeve of his sweater. The movement was possessive, as was her glance at him. The look she had for Violet was steel-edged.

"Missus Rotherwell," Violet purred, taking a sip of champagne, "does my husband know you plan to cheat on him with my friend George? My father's dead, so I guess there aren't any more men in my life I have to worry about."

The hand on George's arm stiffened and Marjorie's eyes narrowed for a moment. Violet half expected her to hiss and protract her claws.

"What about Christian Walsh?" he quipped.

The attempt at wit stung Violet. For the rest of the evening she was careful to avoid both of them and tried to ignore the sense of betrayal. If this was a set up, it was cruel. That stayed with Violet all the way home that night and into the next day when she took the children for their weekly field trip to the public library. Seated at a corner table in the Children's Room with history texts and notebooks piled around her like a barricade, she worked on her thesis and read to the boys when they ran over with their treasures pulled off the shelves. Max and Alex had run off to find another book when the elevator doors slid open and George appeared.

He placed a single white rose on one of the book stacks and pulled up a chair, sitting quietly with hands folded in his lap and watching her take copious, meticulous notes that a Benedictine monk would envy.

"I'm sorry. I don't know why I said it."

Violet glanced over at him and said nothing, moving her copy of Ross' *Edward IV* from under his elbow. "I only wonder if the comment was three quarters merlot and one quarter humor." Violet said. "Have a good time with Marjorie?"

"You're jealous!"

"No — you're blocking my light — just tired of the Pillsbury Doughbitch encroaching on my life and friends. Moving in on my husband was bad enough, but my friends, too? If she wants me out of the way why doesn't she throw me in front of a bus?"

"That's melodramatic even for you, Violet."

"You're blocking my light."

"So, what I take from this is that it's not all right for Marjorie Rotherwell to sleep with your husband, or your friends, but it's all right for you to sleep with Christian Walsh?"

"Who said I slept with him?"

Violet was glaring at George now and he moved his chair back.

"Well, I just —"

"Don't assume."

The history text was slammed to a close and thumped noisily on the table, garnering disapproving looks from the librarian at her desk and several parents.

"But you would if you had a chance."

"Why do you care?"

"The tone of voice suggests I hit a very exposed nerve. Let me tell you from experience that getting revenge in someone else's bed is never a good idea for all concerned. As a friend, an old friend, I'm telling you this."

"Your concern is touching. Why you care, I don't know."

"I'll tell you if you give me a moment and not bite my head off —"

"Mamma! Cat in the Hat!" Alex shouted as he ran to her from the playroom, waving a well-worn copy of Dr. Seuss, with Max in toe. "Read it to me!" Alex demanded.

"Let's wait until we get home," Violet suggested, putting a finger to her lips for silence.

Alex insisted, however, and Max took up the plea. With Alex at her elbow and Max in her lap, Violet opened the book. "*The sun did not shine. It was too wet to play. So we sat in the house all that cold, cold, wet day…*"

George scribbled a note and tucked it into the pocket of Violet's sweater coat before leaving.

Elisabet found the note on the kitchen floor that evening while Violet and she played *Mousetrap* with the boys.

"'Don't confuse revenge for love; infatuation isn't a bandage. George.' What the hell? Oh. Sorry. Mom's eyes only."

Violet snatched the note away and then watched as Alex rolled the dice and chortled as he turned the crank.

The cage fell on Violet's red mouse.

"*Mousetrap!*" the boys shouted.

16

Be Careful What You Wish For

THE COUNCIL CHAMBER was packed with a vicious crowd that afternoon. Richard was keenly aware that many of the lords were George of Clarence's men; knew he couldn't count on a single man hiding the Whyte Boare of Gloucester under their Black Bull of Clarence. He glanced now at the King, who was in easy conversation with Will Hastings, the Chancellor of the Realm, both of them lounging by a window overlooking Shene's water gate and acting as if this Privy Council session was nothing of great import. For Richard, it was as important as the air he breathed.

Clarence at last entered the chamber and glanced around just as his younger brother had, but offered easy smiles of greeting and exchanged banter just as easily. Richard was now beginning to regret for the first time how much he had inherited from his father. He had received all of the duke of York's sobriety and very little of his Nevill mother's charm.

Clarence sat down without courtesy to Edward and cleared his throat. All eyes turned to him as he hoped they would, and the King at last noticed his irksome brother.

Chairs scraped across the flagstones and papers scudded softly before each council member. The King shuffled his stack purposefully and watched as Chancellor Rotherham placed the petitions for Richard's marriage to Anne Nevill and settlement of her portion of the Warwick lands and estates before Richard. He had barely given them notice when Violet glanced up from her lunch time reading and research to frown at Emma, who appeared at the top of the stairs and dropped stack of photocopies on her counter, and ran back down to answer the doorbell.

"Probably another box of See's Candy!" Emma

wailed; "My hips can't take it! Where the Hell is Ned? He was supposed to be here an hour ago!"

"Don't know, Em…"

Ned promised they'd go home early after the Christmas party, but here it was four-thirty and there was no hope of Violet going home before six. Her desk was unusually cluttered with third and fourth drafts of one-paragraph letters. To add insult to injury, Ned had started a trial that week.

"Here are the exhibits and the jury instructions," Emma whined, returning with a box of copies fresh from the vendor. "Please tell me I can go now; I've got Christmas shopping that needs to get done."

She set the box on the floor behind Violet's chair and noticed the Polaroid of Christian and Violet halfway obscured in Violet's organizer lying open on the desk. Violet wasn't quick enough in hiding the photograph. "You can go now," she hinted.

"Nice guy! Relative?"

"Friend."

"Friend? Violet, you're the type that doesn't have men for friends, except Ned – but Ned defies explanation. And maybe that strange guy named George – he's an artist, so I'll forgive him. Hey, you know, he kinda looks like he could be George's brother. Is he?"

"Friend, Emma."

"Please tell me this is George's long-lost, nicer, older, but handsome brother – a sexy, older brother!"

"Okay."

The Polaroid was moved to the safety of a desk drawer that was locked.

"I don't believe you," Emma whispered on her way down.

The intercom buzzed as Violet was at the end of one particularly difficult section of the transcript. "Go away!" she snapped.

"Uh, Violet? There's someone here to see you,"

Emma announced in a diffident voice, which was unusual for her.

"I'm almost done with this motion, Em! Then we can go for a Christmas drink and shop!"

"George's brother is here."

"What?"

Behind her were soft footsteps, growing closer. Emma's voice pierced the dictation still running in Violet's ear. "Excuse me; excuse me! Hell-*ohhh*! You just can't barge upstairs without being announced! Mizz Ellison is busy right now —"

"Excuse me, Miss; I've got a Diet Coke here. Would you sign for it?"

Christian stood on the landing with a carton of Diet Coke in his arms, a clumsily wrapped purple ribbon adorning the holiday-decorated cardboard. Violet, never taking her eyes from him, waved off Emma behind him, saying, "It's okay; he's a friend."

"I came to collect my sweater. My mum gave it to me, and it's kind of special," Christian continued as he came up and set the carton on the counter.

"Oh geez, I'm sorry," Violet answered when she found her voice, when her heart stopped pounding in her throat; "it's at home."

"Looks like I'll have to settle for a kiss."

It had only been a week since seeing him off at the airport. They were the longest, loneliest days in Violet's life, made worse by the arguments she was losing with herself about the sanity of this.

"What are you doing here?" she laughed between sloppy, noisy kisses.

"Now what do you think?"

"No, really! England's a long, long, way away."

"Don't I know it!" he replied with a put-on sigh, and then drawing her closer, whispered: "Too far from you!"

"Don't I know it!" she replied and hugged him tighter now, suddenly afraid.

Christian laughed softly and swung her up into his arms, let her slide down for a long, passionate, kiss. "I forgot to give you a Christmas present," he said.

"It's so nice to see you," she murmured in his ear.

"And you – look at you!"

Christian stepped back to admire Violet's appearance. Violet, for her part, self-consciously ran a hand along the back of her hair – which had been bobbed to five-inch layers the night before in a pageboy. She had defied the professional dress code and chose to wear a fisherman-knit cardigan with a pair of leggings, boots, wooly socks and a sheer, chiffon mini-skirt.

"It's kinda, well, it's an emancipation proclamation," Violet answered nervously. "A bit much?"

"No! It's all you. I love it! Listen, I've got a red-eye back to London. Dinner, movie, something else?" he asked.

"Sure. Who's buyin'?"

Ned's voice startled Violet so that she propelled herself away from Christian. Ned came around the partition, enjoying their embarrassment. From the look on his face, he'd been there a while. He dropped a file on the credenza and with a broad smile, waited.

"Ned! This is Christian Walsh. Christian, Ned, Ned – Percy! My boss."

"And do you know who you are?" Ned teased and winked at Christian. "Actually, Mr. Walsh, her second oldest living friend."

Both men acknowledged one another with short nods.

Ned already didn't like Christian Walsh no matter how many people in the recording industry thought he was decent and a gentleman. He had Violet's attention and that was unacceptable. Christian recognized the jealousy and tightened his grip on Violet's waist. Ned glanced at Violet, who was being devoured by the singer's eyes and wondered how long it would take Walsh to unwrap this

Christmas package he so obviously thought was his.

"So... what are you kids up to?" Ned queried, feigning disinterest. He cared; he wanted to know what was going on.

"Better let you go, Violet. See you at the Huntington?" Christian hinted. When Violet blushed and nodded, he kissed her cheek and went downstairs. Ned waited for the doorbell to jangle and the door to slam shut before returning to his office.

He was at the computer working on his closing argument when he heard the familiar knock. "Yeah, Violet! C'mon in."

She entered with a stack of documents piled on a stack of case files. Ned glanced up and smiled warmly. She looked more melancholic than usual, softer; he hadn't seen her more beautiful and now he knew why. And he hated Christian Walsh for it.

"You look different. Have you lost more weight?"

"Very funny, Ned."

"No, really! You look – different. Kinda reminds me of you junior year of college."

"Enough about the hair."

"I'm not complaining. It's about time the real Violet, the Violet of past, came out from under all that gabardine. You were never one to bow to conformity. That soccer mom gig never suited you. This look – well, sexy's one word. Violet's another."

"Thanks, I think. I'm going now. You can survive 'til Tuesday, I suppose?"

"Saved my butt again, Vi; couldn't live without you."

"So you've said time and again, but you always manage."

Violet placed the documents before him for signature. She found his pen and handed that over, too. Ned started signing, the only sound in the office the soft scratching across the paper.

"Did you sign the contracts I put on your desk last

night? The lawyers for Nick Andrews' record company have called twice. I used the excuse you were in trial. God knows how long I'll be able to keep that up."

Ned started burrowing. "You put something on this desk?"

"I know, how foolish of me; I wasn't thinking," Violet apologized, pulling the folder of contracts out from under a pile. She waved it in his face. "I'll get Emma to notarize them. You know what else would be nice? The responses to discovery requests in the Peterman file."

"Jesus, I forgot about – can you get an extension? Another two weeks?"

"Ned, they're already a month and a half late. They're threatening a motion to compel and big, ugly, nasty, sanctions, all of which you can't afford right now, what with the talk-show host's contract still up in the air, and employee taxes overdue, and —"

"Violet, I can't do anything about it right now!"

She leaned on the desk and faced him, taking a bulldog stance.

"Look, I can't afford losing this job, and you're going to be slapped with malpractice and suspension if you keep this up!"

"You've stepped over the line, Violet."

"I'll keep going if it keeps my job and Emma's job, and Annie's!"

"All it will take is another word!"

"Get the dictionary."

"So help me, Violet!"

Ned caved, backing away from the desk, and then Violet eased up. From downstairs came the sounds of early evening – of Emma closing up for the night, the distant wail of an emergency vehicle siren, the chimes in the office across the alley, a conversation behind them in Gold Street.

"The saints work such miracles every day. Let's see if I can do them one better," she said quietly, breaking the nerve-wracking silence.

"You're a saint, Vi."

"That's Violet!"

Violet retrieved the documents from him and went to the door, only to be called back. She turned, bemused, and Ned smiled. She was a goddess, this Violet; not a saint. "When you told me a British musician, I wasn't thinking Christian Walsh," he mentioned and Violet gave him the 'whatever-do-you-mean' look. She knew. She was closing up like a walnut. Just like when Sam Peters became more than a childhood playmate.

Then Violet started to clean. She always cleaned when searching for the right opening, or confession. She started moving files back onto their shelves, filing documents in their file jackets, stacking up law books that had long gathered dust on his sofa with the dry-cleaning still hermetically sealed in plastic. Ned assisted.

"Am I obligated under my employment to respond?" she said, forcing joviality.

"No. But I'm asking as a friend who cares."

"Don't ask."

Violet handed over a file box bulging with medical record copies and piled it with notebooks, pointing him in the direction of the closet at the back of the office.

"For what it's worth – if things really are that bad with Sam – well, at least I'm a known quantity," Ned was saying. "You know the risks with me, Violet. Other than what you intimately know of Christian Walsh – and I'm not saying that's a bad thing – you don't know more than that. So, and I know I'm probably shooting myself in the foot."

For the longest time Violet stacked volumes of the Code of Civil Procedure on the coffee table. "Again, am I obligated under my employment to respond?" she asked.

"It hasn't before."

"Your aim's pretty good."

THE HOTEL ROOM was once again decorated with flowers. A candelabrum that might have been pilfered from Grace Cathedral took up most of the space on the small table now laid with supper. Christian had persuaded the hotel chef to conjure up a romantic meal at short notice, and he managed to work magic, offering braised chicken breasts with artichoke hearts in a lemon sauce and fettuccine with porcini mushrooms. The chef held the line at Christian's request for Cap'n Crunch's Crunch Berries.

Studying his work, Christian rubbed the back of his neck nervously and nodded. So far, so good.

He checked his appearance. For once he wore a suit – navy pinstripe from one of London's most fashionable tailors – and a tie. Dressing well always made a good impression.

And then the doorbell rang. His mouth went dry and his palms beaded with sweat. When it rang the second time, Christian took a drink straight from the champagne bottle and strode coolly across the hotel suite to answer it. Six hours of rehearsed conversation and a crash course on medieval history were replaced by "Hello! I've missed you."

"Hi!" Violet greeted, and stepped inside the threshold.

"Glad you could make it," Christian replied and took her coat and purse, which he threw on a chair. He turned to her and grinned nervously, ambivalent about the roller coaster ride of emotion he was going on while taking in those large, lovely eyes and trying to think of what next to say.

"I managed to get the same room, can you believe it?"

"I can," she said with a smile and sideways glance after taking in the flowers, champagne and supper. "Mm! Is that chicken with artichokes, I smell?"

"Then I'm glad I chose it," Christian said as he led her to the table.

"I can't believe you remembered. You must've written it down."

"Don't worry, in ten years when we're an old married couple, I'll forget our anniversary, your lingerie size, where I left the kids."

"Very funny. The table looks nice – so do you."

Christian smoothed the lapels of his navy pinstripe, saying: "Thanks! Thanks very much. I wanted you to see that aging rockers aren't all leather trousers and tie-dye tee shirts."

"Yeah, you really should say something to Kevin."

Their laughter was uneasy, somewhat forced. Christian could only gaze at her and drink in her loveliness. Violet's eyes slid to the table again. He pulled out a chair, asking, "This is okay, isn't it? If you want to eat out."

"You've gone to a lot of trouble. I wouldn't dream of offending you."

Christian didn't taste a thing. He was so engrossed in their conversation that he barely remembered eating, looked down and saw his plate was empty. While she had spoken of her job and problems with her writing, the frustrating efforts at historical research in a limited venue, the day's many fiascoes, he had listened attentively and memorized every expression, every strand of hair, and the soft, clear voice that captivated. Even when Violet rose and walked to the window to admire the view beyond Nob Hill, Christian discovered new and exciting aspects to memorize – that charming new 'look' she wore proudly, but was still uncomfortable with, the graceful movement of her head and hands while she spoke, and her clumsy yet endearing steps.

He felt light-headed and tranquil, glanced at the cooler and saw that the champagne bottle was still full.

As he snuffed the candles and left the table, Christian's thoughts were suddenly in York, in the Minster. There he remembered a girl behind the choir screen, waiting in the dark. The scent of the cool stone and candle tallow came back, the face softly lit by tapers and moonlight. But when he looked down, it was Violet beside him at the window.

"Would you like to dance?" Christian suggested as he picked up the remote control and shot it at the stereo system. *Nights in White Satin* drifted out and Violet laughed as she eased into his arms.

"Interesting choice," she murmured in his ear.

"I thought *Dark Forest* might be too obvious; besides, making love to a woman while listening to your own voice – too weird."

She laughed again and let him lead, airily following. "Vanity doesn't figure in your gene pool."

"You're priceless, d'you know that?"

"This is free, too."

He felt her breath on his cheek, and then her brief yet tender kiss, like a soothing balm, while they drifted slowly and sensually across the floor.

"I'm so very glad you're here," he whispered.

His lips moved from her hair to her ear, to her neck. Christian felt her sigh, a tremble, when she murmured, "I just don't know if it's right."

"All in time, Violet."

Violet wrapped her arms around Christian and kissed him hard. When she opened her eyes, she felt the flutter of his lashes on her cheek as he drew her even closer.

"Sleep in my arms, tonight, just for a little while?" he whispered; "Just until it's time to go?"

He watched as her throat constricted, how the breath drew inward and made the pulsing of her veins under the translucent skin on her breast apparent, the silver chain of her religious medal bobbing and weaving.

"I'm… I'm not ready yet, not for that. Christian, it's been so long since – I'm not comfortable with a lot of things – myself, for one, my… I'm not comfortable – so," she stammered, looking away so that he couldn't see the tears starting to well.

"Not that," he whispered, turning her face so that he could see her eyes. "I just want to be with you. Hold you."

Nodding, Violet sat on the floor beside the fireplace, bringing overstuffed cushions with her. She watched as Christian extinguished the lights so that only the street lamps, the fire in the hearth and the moon illuminated the suite. Christian sat beside her on the rug, eased her gently into his arms so that her head rested in his lap. While they kissed, he unbuttoned the soft woolen sweater and slid the satin chemise off her shoulders. His lips followed the softly highlighted contours of her throat down to her breasts.

"I don't want to disappoint," Violet gasped while his lips explored, his breath and the hearth fire warm on her naked skin.

"I don't think right now that's that a problem!" he laughed.

No, he thought as she began to respond both tenderly and ardently, it would be no problem at all...

NEVER HAD HE taken a woman to his bed and not consummated their union at the same time. Yet it was as satisfying as the climax and afterglow, these few hours in Violet's arms. Her kisses were passionate and her caresses telling, promising. Christian restrained himself, allowed himself only a glimpse and a taste of her body, knowing it made Violet relax and offer more of herself. For the first time in his life, he had wanted to wait, and knew it would be worth the waiting.

"I've got nothing going on after the holidays," Christian said, turning in Violet's arms. "I could come back for a day or two, before the studio sessions and tour preparations."

Violet was looking out the window, catching a glimpse of the sky just starting to turn, watching as the fog wrapped itself around the spires of the cathedral and danced in wisps across a sky mottled by clouds. A lone gull was like her heart at that moment – swirling in all directions, not knowing where to turn, but knowing precisely where it ought to be, knowing it couldn't be there, knowing where it shouldn't be.

"So?" he asked, nuzzling her so that his day-old beard tickled and made her laugh, much to Christian's satisfaction.

"It might be difficult – my work schedule and all. Ned's in trial."

"Ned *is* a trial. Tell you what, milady; I'll order up some coffee and an extremely early, extremely fattening and decadent breakfast and you think about it while you get ready to go," Christian said, kissing her.

"And if I wanted to stay?"

"Don't tempt me woman! I've already missed a flight!"

"Chris! You should have told me!"

"It's nothing – I can get a flight in the morning."

"Kevin's going to kill you," she giggled en route to the bathroom.

"So?" he asked when she came from the shower freshly-bathed and glowing, that smile of shyness just as beguiling and endearing as it had been on that first morning together.

"Give me a call when you get into town," she answered.

"Okay! It's a date," he pronounced happily and from behind his back produced a garment box wrapped in holiday foil. "Promise you'll wear this."

At Christian's urging, Violet tore at the bright green and red paper and burrowed under layers of tissue. His smile only increased in diameter when he saw Violet's face as she beheld The Dress.

"I couldn't!" she stammered.

"Well, it's not my size or color – besides, I couldn't imagine a dress like that going to waste."

"Still."

"Are you going to turn down a Christmas present from a friend?"

"It's just,"

"It's just a dress and one that looks magnificent on you."

"No one's ever... thank you!" Violet whispered tearfully and The Dress was crushed in their embrace.

"I do believe that that is the problem, Violet. No one's ever..." Christian replied between kisses.

"THERE YOU ARE! What time did you get in?"

Violet jumped guiltily away from the stove when she heard Amalie's cheerful voice and managed a smile and a kiss. Then she glanced up at the Kit Kat clock above the door. It wouldn't do to tell her an hour ago, or expect her to believe midnight when her hair was still wet and the after-bath toiletries were still fresh. The grandfather clock in the hallway struck seven.

She avoided the issue altogether and poured a cup of last night's coffee when Amalie glanced at the clock and then at her. Again, Violet managed a smile. Her plan of sitting down at the computer and diving into the morning's work before suffering an interrogation fell through when Amalie offered to start a fresh pot of coffee and make breakfast – her famous Saturday morning whole grain pancakes. She noticed Amalie's hawk-like glance sliding to the box on the floor.

"Was it a Christmas party last night?" Amalie wanted to know.

"Party? Oh, yeah... turned out that way. Boy, was I embarrassed," Violet rambled as she did her best to hide the exquisite violet blue dress from her mother-in-law's scrutiny. "I didn't bring a thing; forgot how many of my friends were landed gentry. I came off looking like a poor waif – which isn't far from the truth."

"Well? Aren't you going to show me what you got?" Amalie laughed and reached for the box Violet was trying unsuccessfully trying to shove under the table. Her eyes bugged out at one glimpse of the evening dress and would have read the card lying between the layers of lavender and blue tissue had Violet not snatched it away.

"It's nothing," Violet protested; "Emma was feeling sorry for me – not having a decent outfit for the charity ball. She thought if Sam got home in time for New Year's, maybe."

"That's odd… because Emma called last night and wanted to know what you wanted for Christmas," Amalie remarked. Their eyes met and Violet was the first to look away.

"Funny," Violet replied with a shrug.

"Funny."

"I can get Beth to watch the boys if you want to go Christmas shopping with me. Only one day left!" Violet suggested with forced cheerfulness.

"Would that I could, Sweetie. My plate's pretty full, too."

"I suppose I should call the airline and find out what flight Sam'll be on," Violet now chattered as she booted up the computer and watched the screen expectantly as if a cartoon or movie would appear, wishing they had a more up-to-date computer system so she could go online and browse the Fortinbras web site, or send e-mail…

"He didn't call last night, if that's what you're wondering," Amalie mentioned and looked Violet straight in the eyes. For once Violet didn't waiver or feel cowed into a confession. The inevitable confrontation was again put on hold when Elisabet entered the kitchen with Max in her arms.

"See? There's Mommy," Elisabet cooed at her little brother and eagerly handed him off. "Morning; you owe me big time for a diaper change," she greeted Violet and exchanged kisses. "George called this morning, right before you came in. Something about the Christmas pageant and party at Alex's school tonight and were you going to help with decorations and angel costumes – be an angel?"

"Shit! I knew I forgot something," Violet swore.

"Oh, and Ned called last night," Elisabet added. "He wants to know if he can stop by with some jury instructions that need correction. By the way, do I get paid extra for being your secretary?"

Amalie thumped the bowl hard with the spoon and blended the pancake batter noisily at this, grumbled aloud, "It's Saturday – and Christmas Eve! I thought Sam was the only fool to work on Saturday – and Christmas Eve!"

"It's just Ned, Grammy Am," Violet replied, shrugging. "Ned's like a piece of furniture around here."

"Living room or bedroom?"

"Grammy Am!" Elisabet giggled, looking to her mother.

And then it hit Violet – Amalie thought that Ned and she – oh, it was too good to be true! Disappearing into her coffee cup, Violet was glad Amalie was off the scent for a while.

The telephone rang and Elisabet lunged for it, rambling about Sam promising to call.

Her face went through a myriad of expressions and then she handed the receiver to Violet. "It's for you – another British guy – Kevin? Says you're a friend, says somebody's missing in action? Please tell me why are all your friends British – and weird?"

Violet ignored Amalie's radar-like glance and took the call in the hallway.

VIOLET'S EYES LIGHTED on him as soon as she entered the gaudily decorated assembly room. A hundred and twenty people were mingling, dining, touring the art displays or taking part in the carnival games, people she'd known all her life, yet Violet found George Knightsbridge first. Assenting to the boys' demands to get in line for the carnival games set up at the end of the room, she told

Elisabet to keep an eye on them and would be only a moment, beating a path around the fourteen-foot Christmas tree George and she had decorated that afternoon to invade the sanctuary he'd made for himself in a corner of the room.

"You're blocking my light," he greeted, not bothering to look up from his work. George was intently sketching the gothic-arched windows across the hall.

"Bah humbug," quipped Violet, dragging up a chair and sitting beside him, helping herself to the two-liter bottle of Diet Coke at George's feet.

"You didn't show up for dinner last night; two Cornish game hens and an opportunity to commit adultery gone to waste."

"Nah, most of the people in this room already think we did it – they're just trying to figure out where and how many times."

"I'm just disappointed it isn't me...get your shopping done?"

Violet nodded and watched as Alex, the least athletic of boys, managed to toss five beanbags in succession into the center of eight brightly painted rings. His reward was an action figure that immediately was coveted by the other boys circling him.

"Mamma!" Alex shouted happily, running at her; "Look! Darth Vader! It's what I wanted for Christmas!"

"Wow!" George exclaimed with enough enthusiasm to satisfy the clutch of seven year-olds. "You've made Father Christmas' job easier!"

"Huh?" Alex asked.

"Santa, Sweetie," Violet added. "Say hello to Professor Knightsbridge."

"It's just old George," Alex muttered, grinning and shook George's hand. He asked if George could take Darth Vader in a fight.

"If I had a really good light saber, yeah, I suppose," George replied after he'd thought about it. "There are other people I'd rather beat up, though."

"What kind of a thing is that to say?" Violet chuckled when the boys ran off.

"Just voicing my thoughts at the moment."

"Do I want to know who's on the hit list?"

"I think you can guess."

"That was a perfect idea, though, putting all those Star Wars toys in the bag. At least I know Alex will get something on his Christmas list. What he'd really like is his father home."

"And what would Violet like?"

"It doesn't matter. It never has."

"Why not?"

"Someone once said to me if you don't get what you want, it's because you didn't pray hard enough, or you've broken too many rules."

"How many do you intend to break?" George wanted to know.

"As many as I need to in order to find the answer," she answered.

"So you can die like Isobel?"

"You're a bastard, d'you know that?"

"I love you too, Violet."

"Let's not bring Isobel into this. I've never liked being compared to her. I was always in her damn shadow – excuse me, but I'm terribly sorry I am not a Rhodes scholar! I'm Violet! Warts and all. And I'm particularly tired of you comparing me and my life to her! We're not alike!"

"Yes you are; God help you, but you are, even in this—"

She at last met his eyes. Those honest, violet-blue eyes that were now full of pain. "I'm not Isobel!" she whispered angrily and left.

He cornered her at the buffet table.

"Go away, George," Violet sniped, pretending to take interest in the roast beef platter and the artfully arranged crudities. "Unless you've got an apology, go away!"

"I've done nothing that needs an apology. What I've stated is the truth. Don't ruin your life for one moment of what you think is happiness. I saw Isobel do it so many times when she felt betrayed or wronged, when life wasn't as perfect as she thought it should be. If you're that unhappy, wait until the time's convenient for all concerned and then make your move —"

She wheeled about and George took a step back, never having seen her so angry. Her eyes blazed and he swallowed hard, waiting for the attack.

"Convenient? All my life all I've ever done was what was convenient for others, what was logical, what was sensible, what was proper! I got a sensible education, got a sensible job, fell in love with the boy next door and married him, got into what everyone swore would be a sensible marriage! I did what was logical and what every-one told me I had to do to be happy, and I am bloody, fucking, miserable! Who's it supposed to be convenient for, George?"

"Violet, don't walk away!"

"You're driving me crazy!"

Her shout was heard above the laughter and Christmas music. In order to avoid further embarrassment and scrutiny, Violet ran out to the corridor and threw herself down on the ancient bench outside the Principal's Office. She ignored the sound of the footsteps, the groan of the wood as George sat down. Without turning, Violet said tearfully, "I don't know if I'll ever see him again! I'm scared to death of what could happen, but more of what might not! Tell me why I should wait when it's mine for the asking? For the first time in my life, George, there's a man who looks at me and sees Violet. His face lights up when he sees me, and I make him happy just being there! He listens to every word I say, whether it's important or not, whether it makes sense or it's bullshit. For the very first time in my life, I mean more to a man than himself!

So please don't ask me to not make a mistake. It might be a mistake if I turn him away. And whether or not you believe it, I'm big enough to take whatever comes."

"No, you're not." George whispered when she left him.

17

Once You Start Running From Your Life, Keep Running

WILL WALSH WAS the current proprietor of Ye Old Stare Inne, having inherited the public house in Stonegate from his uncle Hugh. He knew exactly who would come in and when, which stall or bench they would take. He knew their drink, their supper. It even came as no surprise when a blue Range Rover drove up at eight o'clock on Christmas Eve.

"Will, he's back!" a waitress announced, peering out the window to Stonegate. Will looked round the bar and squinted, then came to the other side and cleared frost off the pane for a look. "I'll be damned!" he swore softly, a smile lighting his ruddy, handsome face.

He'd never understood why his little brother still drove the battered Range Rover. With his money, Christian could buy a Rolls, even a Bentley. But he still drove the Rover bought with his first pay from his first record.

Back then, it was held together by rust and paint. Nothing really had changed save the coat of metallic blue paint slapped on the chassis now and then. And when asked why he kept it, Christian replied that it was the first and last place he'd gotten a decent cuddle.

Christian came in shaking snow and ice from his coat, and from the instantaneous softening of the lines around his mouth, looked glad to be in this place where he had spent a good deal of his adolescence. The stained walls, the faded wallpaper, and the smooth, worn, oak stalls hadn't changed in over sixty years.

There were a few who recognized him, for he was Dean Gwillam Walsh's boy that used to sing in the choir at York Minster and on school holidays scrub the floors and wait tables for his uncle Hugh. He had given his first performance in this very pub and a faded newspaper clipping memorializing the event hung beside other family photos, including an autographed eight-by-ten glossy of Fortinbras.

"Christian! Didn't expect you 'til tomorrow! Just come in from London?" Will greeted. An affectionate hug came with it.

"No, been at the Priory."

"Goin' to keep that old abbey, then?"

"Yeah."

That one word spoke volumes. Will noted his preoccupation. Christian was ready to confess a sin. From the trouble reading out of those blue eyes, Will knew already it was bad and that he'd already spoken to their mother. It was remarkable how two grown men could be cowed into complete obedience by a frail woman in her eighty-eighth year.

Will certainly remembered. What man growing up in that life could not?

He remembered the highly polished oak floor of the second landing, as clear as pier glass. The ebony-encased clock ticking his life away. And then, *"Young man! Come and answer for yourself!"*

The dreaded sixteen stairs. That was the distance from the haven of the second floor landing to Kathryn Walsh's sitting room. Will imagined there'd been nothing different in Christian's recent audience – except now there'd be an unlit cigarette in his hand and the confrontation had taken place in Kathryn's rooms in Low Petergate rather than the Dean's lodgings in the Minster close. He only wondered why Christian would need to confess his sins after so many years of getting away with murder.

"Here, Chris," a fellow offered, giving Christian his usual place in a booth facing Stonegate. Will slid in beside him, motioning for the waitress to bring drinks.

They consumed their beers in silence. Sips more

tentative and suitable to a hot cup of tea barely skimmed the top of Christian's glass. Will studied Christian while he drank and he waited. Eventually he'd come clean; Christian could never hide a secret.

"I'm having Christmas and New Year's at the Priory. Are you coming?" Christian spoke up suddenly.

"Who's coming?"

"The band, their families, my studio friends. Missus Burnes is laying on a Christmas feast not to be believed. She's in an excellent mood and we wouldn't want to disappoint her," Christian explained, grabbing one of the meat pies the waitress brought and finishing it in three bites. He certainly was troubled, for Christian never ate pub food – especially Will's.

"It'll be a change from cold goose and congealed gravy with Mum and her housekeeper. So the tour was better this year?" Will was fishing and coming up with an empty hook, hoping to find a topic Christian and he could both enjoy. He'd always been proud of his little brother's success and fame.

"There were high points." Christian smiled and decided not to keep it a secret. "I met a woman, Will."

"Don't you always! I always envied your luck!"

"She's not a groupie, or anyone like that." Christian's voice was combative, though it didn't seem to bother Will, who knew from prior confessions that his little brother's life was far from sex, drugs and wild parties, and never had been even though he let on that it was just to keep a private life private.

"Bugger! You look serious."

"I know what I want now; things have changed."

"Can't blame me for wondering. Not with your track record."

"She's keeping something from me."

Will grunted and said quite candidly, "If she's not talkin', she's married."

"I don't think she'd —"

"The only thing a woman would keep from you is her true age, her real weight, and if she was married!"

"How'd you become an expert on the subject?"

"It's not a matter of expertise, little brother, but putting two and three together and finding out they don't make four. If she's married, that would complicate matters wouldn't it? And our dear mother would drop dead of shame. Especially after that story of you and the bishop of Lincoln's wife showed up in the *Daily Mirror!* God help you, but there's lots of unmarried women around; you don't need to play in another man's yard!"

"You know that was all a lie, don't you? Some jealous girl getting even for something I didn't do? Or for doing what she wanted?" Christian immediately went on the defensive and Will only guessed how miserable that audience with their mother must have been. "I've done complicated before," Christian snapped. "Violet isn't complicated. At least to me she isn't."

"Pretty name. Women are complicated. Don't fool yourself. My God, Chris! After that trouble with Sarah!"

"It just happened. I didn't expect it – or want it! But now that I've been with her – y'know Will? When the time is right, she'll answer my questions. She'll want to tell me because she loves me. I'm sure of that much."

Will sniffed. He shook his head mournfully at his little brother. Some things never changed. Christian's bad record with women was one of them.

Christian took the cigarettes out of his coat pocket and chose one, then suddenly crumbled it, letting the fine paper and tobacco drift into an ashtray. "I'll find a way. I knew when I saw her in San Francisco. I just knew! She's a writer, you know; she's got a degree in history and trying to finish a master's degree, I think; she loves the middle ages."

"Well, that would account for her liking you."

Christian ignored the jibe and continued. "She's pretty, funny, sexy, oh, God! Where to begin?"

"You're far gone, that's for certain! And certainly she's not what we're used to."

"I'm pretty sure about how I feel. But I want to give her time to think about everything, and when she's ready, make up her mind."

Will shrugged. He'd never had a dark moment in twenty-seven years of marriage to his wife. Christian, on the other hand, had always been the fair-haired child, his mother's pet, even with that mess about Sarah.

"Yeah, just give it time. She'll come round."

"I can wait. I've waited this long," Christian murmured.

Will raised his glass in tribute and drank, then left to take care of patrons. Christian stared out the window into Stonegate and watched a pretty young woman with dark hair cross the street and go into a bookstore. He smiled to himself, knowing that until he saw Violet Ellison again, he'd be looking for her in every woman he met.

WHEN CHRISTIAN RETURNED to his medieval abbey in Wensleydale northwest of York, Mrs. Burnes had already opened the living quarters and was putting away his things, getting ready for Christian's annual Christmas and New Year's celebrations.

Deirdre Burnes of Hampstead, London, was a large woman with a nasty disposition. For nearly thirty-five years she'd been in service to the Walsh family and that longevity gave her license to say whatever came to mind, no matter how it came out or whom it offended. She was rehearsing her evening litany – complaints ranging from Christian's sloppiness and lack of consideration to his failure to separate dirty from clean laundry in the luggage (*That's what laundry bags are for, Mister Christian!*) – when she heard the key in the lock.

"'Evening, Missus Burnes."

The keys fell into the glass bowl on the mantle beside the pictures of Kevin Wakefield's little girls and Will's three boys.

"That it is, Mister Christian."

The coat was dropped in the chair. "Is there anything to eat?"

"A salad, some chicken. Mister Christian, I don't know how many times I've asked you to use the laundry bags I pack. I know it would make my life easier," Mrs. Burnes muttered.

Christian kissed her forehead on his way out of the living room, saying: "My job in life is to make yours difficult."

Mrs. Burnes' neatly plucked brows rose as she held up by two fingers a ladies' scarf made of silk in shades of blue with an arabesque pattern. It was scented with a light, flowery perfume.

"Perhaps you're not telling me something, Mister Christian?" she asked, holding the scarf by a crooked finger.

"There it is! I'll have to call Violet and tell her it's here. It's her favorite. Thanks for finding it, Missus Burnes." Whistling a few bars from the song he was working on, Christian skipped upstairs and locked himself in the library.

He always locked himself in the library when at home. What he did there, Mrs. Burnes didn't care to know. At least he was out of her hair and a good thing too on this Christmas Eve, with a feast to be laid tomorrow.

Halfway through rolling out pie crusts, Mrs. Burnes remembered a telephone call she had to make and picked up the kitchen phone. She was surprised that Christian was on at such a late hour and talking to a woman – an American woman, at that. From what snatches of conversation she got, he was pouring out his heart.

So that's what it was, she thought, replacing the receiver and smiling to herself. *Mister Christian was in love.*

VIOLET SWITCHED OFF the phone and pitched it under

Sam's pillows, then guiltily retrieved it, tossing it under the bed. Four calls in two days. This latest call had roused her from a fitful sleep. Hearing his voice through the receiver, a million miles away, but close and against the pillow, it was too much to bear. Throwing off the covers and mindless of the unusual, bone-chilling cold, Violet slid out of bed and padded softly down the hall to the children's rooms. Whenever her heart was in turmoil, the children by their existence reminded her of what was good in the world.

Max protested and kicked off his blankets when Violet whispered 'I love you' in his tiny ear. She had to pry the crumbling gingerbread man out of Alex's hand and remove the headphones to the Gameboy from his curly head. For a moment Violet's heart skipped a beat when she glanced down at her eldest son. God help him, but he was mirror image of his beautiful father. At least she had that much of Sam.

"Something wrong?" Elisabet yawned when Violet looked in on her.

"Can't sleep," Violet confessed.

"Mm.... Christmas Eve. I remember all the years I couldn't sleep, the excitement, waiting to see the presents downstairs," Elisabet recounted as Violet smoothed the hair off her brow. "Mamma, are we ever going to have a Christmas with Dad home?"

"That's up to your father, Beth."

"That Dad on the phone?"

"No."

The next morning when the phone rang, Elisabet again asked if it was her father as she started piling muffins on a tray for Christmas brunch.

"That was a friend of Aunt Bella's," Violet answered and was glad Elisabet had turned to get the orange juice from the refrigerator. She wouldn't be able to see her mother's guilty, lying face.

"I think this is it," Elisabet mused now, studying the

tray. She blew her mother a kiss as they headed out of the kitchen, and then looked back, asking: "Something wrong, Mom?"

Amalie was taking another tour of the living room when they entered. Stanley had already claimed possession of the remote control and Sam's recliner, the boys seated on his lap, out of striking distance of the Christmas tree that magically had sprouted presents over night, from stairwell to front door, myriads of brightly-wrapped parcels, bundles and shapes, and one unwieldy package that Alex was coveting with his large, brown, eyes. All that was missing was Sam.

"Where's Sam?" Amalie asked.

"Still in New York. The soda company contract is on life support," Violet answered very business-like, and set her tray piled high with blueberry and cranberry muffins, scrambled eggs and sausages on the already burdened coffee table.

"Again?" Stanley harrumphed.

"He's there doing damage control."

"A cardiac surgeon could learn a thing or to about damage control from Sam," came the snipe between puffs on a cigar.

"Stanley! Put that thing out!" Amalie demanded, and then more quietly to Violet, "Are you going to lose the agency?"

"He says there's a possibility, Grammy Am."

"And you believed him?" Stanley Peters now sniffed from behind the remote control.

"Stanley!" Amalie snapped.

"He hasn't given me a reason not to," Violet answered with a noncommittal shrug. Stanley harrumphed again and continued to channel surf.

"I do believe that is a genetic defect," Amalie mused, watching the screen change as quickly as the blink of an eye. She now watched Violet busy herself with brunch and straighten an already immaculate living room, even seeing to the arrangement of 'blinky' lights hanging off that poor suit of armor she loved so dearly.

"What do you think?" Amalie asked gently, helping redecorate the tree with tinsel Max had clumped on one branch.

"We can survive. I still have my job with Ned."

"Violet, eventually you'll have to do something," Amalie murmured as she pulled her daughter-in-law toward the staircase and away from the others. "I know he's my son, Darling, but it's not doing either of you any good."

"You're not saying I'm not the right wife for him?" Violet answered defensively, hoping Amalie wouldn't see her relief.

"Doorbell!" Alex shouted, anticipating the obnoxious buzz from the front porch. "*Now* can we open our presents?"

Violet was surprised when the doorbell rang a second time. If it were Ned, he'd ring, knock and then enter. Elisabet glanced at her mother and answered the third ring.

"Hi, Elisabet! Happy Christmas," George greeted, passing over four clumsily wrapped presents. He looked over Elisabet's dark head to smile at Violet.

"Hello!" Violet greeted and as she took his coat whispered, "I'm glad you don't hold a grudge."

"Anger should always be fleeting," George said. "Besides, it wasn't my place to pry. And I can't think of better punishment than to suffer the disapproving looks and embarrassing questions of your friends and family, wondering who I am, and what business I have sleeping with their Violet, and knowing they've got the wrong guy!"

Amalie's high color was higher as George came forward and offered a handshake and kiss with his dazzling smile, asked how she was getting on. Had she heard from their friends in Ludlow? Amalie flushed prettily as he made a to-do over the antique cross she'd purchased in Venice.

Stan barely moved from the recliner, but moved his unlit cigar from one side of his mouth to the other in order to mutter something akin to 'hello'. The football game was getting started and nothing perturbed Stanley Peters more than interrupting his game.

"Dallas, Washington game?" George asked.

Now Stanley grinned and patted the hassock.

Amalie decided to help Violet with a fresh pot of coffee. "Violet! Please tell me you're not having an affair with him!"

"I'm not."

"It's just — it wouldn't be the answer to your problems."

Violet none-too-gently shoved the coffee carafe into Amalie's waiting hands. "It's Christmas, Amalie. Can we for once try not to solve poor little Violet's marital woes and forget about the peripatetic ad man? Just for twenty-four hours? You can hammer away at me tomorrow morning."

"I put my foot in that, didn't I?"

"A bit."

Violet now embraced the older woman and planted a kiss on her flushed cheek. "I love you, Amalie. You're one of the best things that happened to me. And I know you don't want to hear this, but I find it hard to believe that a man as unkind and selfish as Sam could have come from two people as loving and generous as you and Stan. And that is one of the reasons why it's been so hard for me."

"Oh Violet!"

"Promise me, Grammy Am, that if it all does hit the fan in one explosion, you'll still love me?" Amalie nodded and said they'd better get back before the tears and maudlin promises started flowing.

Again, the doorbell, this time followed by a knock. Ned entered with Emma, Emma's son Mason and Annie. Ned's arms were piled with gifts. He shouted greetings over the roar of the football game and allowed Violet to remove his coat, then took one look at the living room in its garish glory and whistled.

"Well, at least it doesn't look like a Frank Kapra film," he cracked and Violet threw him The Look in jest. "I'm just saying that it looks like the set of costume flick. Always wondered why this house looks like a Franco Zeffirelli set, and then I remember it's Violet's." He added his gifts to the obscenely abundant pile already under the tree. "Hey! Look at the haul Santa brought! I know this wasn't done on Violet's salary!"

"*Ned!*" five adults and Elisabet hissed.

Ned barely acknowledged George but wondered who he was and why he was there. After introductions, he still wondered. What annoyed him was how George's eyes never left Violet and followed her out of the room. George's charm also annoyed. Violet's family were caught in his spell and the boys listened rapturously while George played a video game with them and regaled them with stories of medieval battles and knights in armor.

"Are you making a hobby of collecting handsome, blond Englishmen?" Ned murmured good-naturedly. "You need to get out more, Violet; at least try Italian. This blonde British god thing is getting old."

Violet gave Ned The Look That Said Die.

After Christmas brunch, the children were put out of their misery when Violet borrowed Parsifal's Santa cap and pulled it down around her ears, sitting in a traditional spot at the foot of the tree. That was too much for Alex.

"Dad is supposed to be Santa's helper!" he protested.

"Alex, your Dad is in New York and can't do it this year. Why not let Mommy? She'll do a great job," Stanley explained, drawing the bewildered child into his arms, knowing Alex didn't like wrinkles in familiar and comfortable routines.

"But Dad – !"

Now Alex started to cry. Violet corked the tears by dragging out the largest of the presents and sliding it over to him. Unwrapped, it was a mountain bike. Alex forgot his unhappiness and now fended off his little brother for possession of this, the greatest of treasures. He soon forgot his father's absence.

The presents were distributed and opened in an orgy of paper tearing, the minutes punctuated by laughter and squeals of delight.

"Hey, you missed one," Elisabet mentioned, pointing to a small present still hiding under the tree. Violet reached back and pulled it out, surprised it had her name on it. The handwriting was vaguely familiar.

"Who's it for?" Ned asked. He crawled over and tried to take it away, but Violet fended him off with a playful slap.

"Get off! It's to me," she laughed, and carefully opened the package.

She started to tremble when she saw it was a jeweler's case from London. The smooth, polished, walnut case itself was expensive. She sprang the catch and there on the ruby-colored velvet was a large silver medallion – a knight on horseback. Violet recognized the figure as Saint Michael, the great wings and halo hammered so that they truly sparkled. A dragon lay under the horse's hooves. The medallion was suspended from a heavy gold chain.

"Who's it from?" George insisted, leaning forward.

"You didn't bring it?" Violet asked.

"Not me."

"Ned?" Violet queried, a nervous smile parting her lips.

"Innocent. I don't have good taste. You've told me that at least a hundred times," Ned confessed and their eyes met.

He knew from whom it came.

Further inside the case was a handwritten note – from Christian. He must have dropped the gift on her desk when he was in town Friday last. Violet thought it was from Ned and thought nothing more, depositing it under the tree after returning from the Huntington Hotel yesterday morning. Strange he never said a word. Violet tried mightily to suppress a smile.

Watching how she blushed, Amalie said: "Probably it's from Sam," knowing full well it wasn't. In eighteen years, Sam had never given Violet a present whether it was for an anniversary or Christmas; she didn't think he'd start a trend now.

Violet turned the awkward moment around by slipping the jeweler's case into the pocket of her oversized sweater and suggesting that everyone come outside to watch Alex try out his mountain bike.

"Had I known it would win brownie points, I'd have bought a suit of armor and a pony years ago!" Ned whispered on his way out.

"No comment," said George in passing.

Annie pulled Violet out of the kitchen doorway and back into the kitchen after everyone had gone into the yard. "Something you'd like to share?" she queried.

"No," Violet replied simply.

"It's not George, it's not Ned – who the Hell is it?" Annie demanded.

"Christian Walsh," Violet confessed after a moment's hesitation.

"Christian Walsh? You're not fifteen, Violet. C'mon who is it? I bet it is George!"

"Whatever," Violet answered, heading outside when she saw the boys start to argue over the bike.

THE MEDALLION HUNG round her neck and lay in the hollow between her breasts. Violet lay deathly still in the bed with the curtains drawn. The medallion was like a white-hot coal searing her skin. She reached under the shirt and felt its warmth, the smoothness of the engraved back, the bas-relief of the knight on horseback.

Violet slid out of bed and removed the medallion. It then was tucked inside the jeweler's case hidden in her lingerie drawer, only to be removed again moments later and replaced around her neck. The ritual would be repeated three more times before she fell into an exhausted and troubled sleep.

18

Tell Me What's Bothering You

KEVIN AND SALLY Wakefield always enjoyed the holidays at Christian's country home situated in an idyllic expanse of meadow and moor. Or as Kevin put it, in the middle of bloody nowhere.

They both thought he was mad when he bought this monstrous pile of stones and dry rot. Christian spent years turning it into a sanctuary from the stress and madness of the music industry. Kevin and Sally were among the privileged few granted asylum here.

"Not one word to him," Sally warned as they walked up the driveway.

"We're going to have to talk," insisted Kevin; "I don't like not knowing."

"You've been the guardian of his secrets since childhood. Don't you think it's about time Christian kept something of his life to himself?"

"Not if it concerns the future of the band and our future!"

Sally threw him a pained look, the kind that meant a heated debate before falling asleep, and led the way into the living quarters by a late Gothic gate house and cloister, up a flight of stairs. Christian had turned the refectory into the kitchen and the rooms above into a living room. On the eastern side of the cloister was the library and music studio, affectionately and derisively called 'the sanctuary' by those refused admittance. Here also were guest rooms, and, in the tower, Christian's bedroom and adjoining study.

"Mister Christian's on the telephone," Mrs. Burnes announced when she entered the small parlor with a fresh pot of coffee and a new tin of biscuits; "he said he'd be only a moment. Do you want more coffee, Missus Wakefield?"

"A bit, please."

"Is he talking to Charlie Bonnett?" Kevin wanted to know. Charlie was the band's tour manager.

"No, California – a Miss Ellison, I think." Mrs. Burnes crept closer and whispered, "Every night now for a week! He calls her at the same time. He almost missed a radio interview because he insisted on making the call."

"Darling..." Sally warned, patting Kevin's knee solicitously as Mrs. Burnes trundled out.

By that evening's festivities Kevin's mood hadn't improved. He watched as Christian mingled and laughed with his family and North Country friends, talked shop with the record company executives and constantly saw that everyone's glass was fully charged and their plates teeming with Mrs. Burnes' celebrated pastries. He looked happy and so relaxed that Kevin wanted to punch his handsome face in. Playing hide the sausage and God knew what else halfway around the world while he kept the band on tenterhooks, wondering if they had a contract or tour!

"Why the long face?" Christian wanted to know when he passed Kevin en route to the kitchen.

"The end of the year always reminds me of blown opportunities," Kevin answered curtly before going to look for Sally. He also noticed how Christian glanced at his watch continually and finally picked up a phone.

"Hi, Violet, it's me. Happy New Year – Christ, this isn't the message I want to leave on a bloody machine. I'll call you later – love you. Bye!"

Kevin decided he needed a drink more than his wife's company.

AFTER THE NEW Year was toasted, Christian took his favorite Arabian and the dogs for exercise on the Priory grounds. Kevin was leaning up against the Range Rover when he returned an hour later.

"Nice night for a ride if you want to catch your death

of cold," Kevin greeted.

"It's invigorating; helps me think. Helps my creativity. Why are you still up? You've got a wife to cuddle up to on cold nights."

"Wanted to talk to you."

Kevin fell in step behind the large dogs and followed Christian into the stables beyond the courtyard.

Noting Kevin's atypical silence, Christian said with a smile: "I'm waiting, Kev. The look on your face tells me this isn't going to be pretty and you're not about to take prisoners."

"I got a call from Charlie Bonnett an hour ago." Kevin had decided to jump right in without his usual prologue of how they'd been friends since childhood. "He said he got the distinct impression from you that you were having second thoughts about the European tour in March."

"He wasn't far off."

"What's going on?"

"The signs have been there. If you knew me as well as you tell others and the press, you'd have figured it out!" The subject and conversation were annoying Christian who now banged harness and saddle onto hooks angrily. He started pitching hay into the stalls for something other to do than belt Kevin.

"We've worked so hard for this!"

"I'd be the first to admit that."

"I can't believe you're ready to chuck it all! Is it Violet?"

The pitchfork dived into a stack of bales like a javelin. Kevin took a step back just in case. "No! Why must your solution for any of my problems always be a woman?"

"History speaks for itself, Chris."

"Says the man who makes paying alimony a pastime. You ought to be grateful. My lousy love life has produced ten platinum disks!"

"And made life miserable for the rest of us."

Christian stopped, unable to believe what he'd just heard. "That came from way down deep. I've always told you what I think; why not do the same instead of hiding it?" he demanded quietly.

"Jesus! Do you have to ask?" Kevin swore. "We've been friends since we were kids. Fortinbras is our dream! All those afternoons at the Inne, the rides down to Birmingham and London, going over to Ireland in search of gigs."

"Dreams die," Christian answered softly.

"You owe this much to me. All I ask is one more year."

"The truth is, I don't know if I have that much, or anything, left in me. For the band, at least. Two week vacations here and there aren't enough anymore, Kev."

It came out all at once. Kevin felt it rise in his chest and in those few minutes vented nearly thirty years of frustration.

He recounted the winter of Christian's nineteenth birthday and the late night wedding at York Minster – done in secrecy to avoid Gwillam and Kathryn Walsh's assured objections. There was the frightening ride in the ambulance and the death of Christian's baby so soon after her birth. And there was Christian's twenty-first birthday party when Sarah walked out and never came back. Through all of it, Kevin stood by Christian and saw him through the blackest of times.

Through this soliloquy Christian sat as still and cold as stone. There was nothing he could say in his defense. Not that it was necessary. He'd pretended for years that it had never happened. But not even Kevin knew how it started, that ill-fated love with Sarah. He'd keep that secret close. Maybe, Christian thought, there'd come a time when he could share it.

Sarah!

Christian thought of her and at last saw a face. The girl in the cathedral by the choir screen, waiting in secret for him. She'd always been the faceless specter threatening from the shadows. That significant loss of love and this woman now in his thoughts, the woman he had hoped one day to meet and despaired that he ever would, the woman he now was sure was his, had inspired his most haunting and sensual love ballads and she never knew it. His sweet, beautiful Violet...

Kevin had paused and now sighed, bringing Christian back to the Priory stables. ". . . say the word. We go on or we end it."

"She committed suicide."

"What?"

"She committed suicide a week after leaving me. Found her in an east end flat. She was with that bass player we met at the Isle of Wight Festival. You know, the one who auditioned for the band. They shot up heroin and played Russian Roulette."

It was the first time Kevin had heard that, and he was not so much surprised by the revelation, but Christian's admission.

"Chris, I'm sorry."

"I never knew how many bad habits she had until the end."

"I just assumed."

"It's always been easy to make me the villain. No one bothered to ask."

"Let's give it a rest for now, Chris. Then we'll talk."

"No; we've said all there is to say. You've only stated the very obvious truth. I signed a contract for the tour. I signed contracts for the television show and commercials. I've got obligations to fulfill. After the tour, well, we'll all have to sit down and talk about things. If Violet decides she wants to be a part of my life, that's the way it's going to be. The band will have to understand – and so will you."

"Christian, wait!"

Christian didn't turn, but kept walking towards the

house.

THE DRESS LAY on the bed, a luxurious river of violet blue cut velvet and silver trim. She ran a hand over it lovingly before discarding her bathrobe and sliding The Dress over her head. It was cool to the touch, the silk lining like Christian's caress on her skin.

From under the bed Violet found her silver sandals and laughed softly to herself as she slipped them over her feet. Tonight there'd be no leaving them on the sidewalk outside a café in North Beach.

She reached for the champagne flute on the nightstand and took a sip, savoring the dryness and bubbles.

On the television, Dick Clark was getting ready to drop the ball on the Big Apple. She switched off the set and went downstairs to the living room with the bottle and flute.

The decorative candles were lit and the room shone with a soft ocher patina. Now the stereo went on – *Nights in White Satin*. Violet swayed gently with the music, remembering.

And then the telephone rang. Just as he promised.

"Hello?" Violet's voice was soft, alluring.

"Hi! What're you doing up so late? I thought you were always asleep by midnight."

Sam's voice was jarring. It was sometime before she said, "Uh, hi! Happy New Year."

"Is it? You don't sound pleased to hear from me." Violet's eyes darted frantically to the grandfather clock. Five minutes to midnight. "Violet? Hey, are you there?"

"What? No, I'm still here. I thought I heard one of the boys."

"So how was Christmas?"

"Fine. I had friends over, you know, Ned, Annie, Emma, Carrie and Thornton – couldn't leave them out – and George. I invited George since he had nowhere to go, oh, and your parents."

The minute hand was sailing round the clock face too rapidly for Violet. She took a gulp of champagne and nearly choked as the bubbles went up her nose. The spray went down the bodice of her dress and now she reached for her discarded bathrobe, mopping delicately as she listened with no interest at all to Sam's recounting of his holiday in business meetings.

Outside, the bells and whistles of the San Francisco Bay Area proclaimed the New Year.

MEET ME AT the airport next Friday.

Violet glanced up at the board and studied the electronic schedule for arrivals. A careful reading propelled her toward the new terminal, still unfinished after eighteen years of construction. She hurried through corridors and crowds, mindless of tender greetings and tearful good-byes playing out around her. The stink of diesel, new paint and new polyester carpeting only made her sharpened senses more intense. Oh Lord, she prayed, let me not be sick to my stomach, not in front of him.

The twenty-minute wait was unbearable. Then she saw the plane. First a silver speck in the sky and then slowly, a shimmering, metallic bird. It soared on to the runway and coasted to a halt. The accordion ramp from cabin to terminal snaked out and minutes passed before the first passengers disembarked. Violet waited, her heart pounding unmercifully. The sweat formed on her hands and her mouth was suddenly dry and then full of bile.

He appeared out of a crowd and looked tired but tan. *Tan?*

"Hi! Where are the kids? Geez, Violet! What'd you do to your hair? What're you wearing?"

Sam offered a kiss and draped an arm casually about her shoulders. What did she expect for a greeting after a five-week separation that still had no acceptable rationalization?

"I got tired of the Soccer Mom look. And it's a school day." Violet answered, suddenly uncomfortable with his unaccustomed intimacy in public. She expected the negative reaction to her new hair and new look. Gone were the khakis and loafers, the pastel oxford cloth blouses and neat sweaters that spoke of money where there was none, the look Sam had always preferred, now replaced by a medieval-looking tunic of her own design and an oversized cardigan, complimented by leggings, scrunched-down socks and Doc Martins.

Sam's complaints reminded her of Christian's reaction and how much he liked the look. Christian had added with embarrassment that she was already a knockout as far as he was concerned, but the new look only enhanced what was already perfect. Violet had laughed and told him to stop before he stepped into something and kissed him...

"Don't you think it's a bit young for you? Geez, you remind me of my parents in the sixties – they didn't know their places either!" Sam continued to whine.

"Now just where is my place with you exactly?" she asked. Violet ran a hand through her bobbed hair and said flippantly it would be easier to color the gray now that it was short; the clothing wouldn't have any bearing on his revered status in the community. She smiled back at a man admiring her legs as he walked by.

Sam offered one of his theatrical, labored sighs that meant disapproval and offered her his carry-on. He caught the glint of silver around her neck and looked down, dragging Christian's medallion out with a finger.

"That's very pretty. Christmas present?" he wanted to know.

"Yeah," Violet stammered. She forgot she was still wearing it and tucked it into her sweater. "Remind me to thank Mom."

"Mom?"

"Sure," he answered, studying the medallion closer

now. It was already scented by her perfume and skin, a sign that she had never removed it and had become her talisman. That was a good sign. "I gave her a call after I talked to you last Monday. I knew we didn't leave things smoothly, so I asked her to pick something out for Christmas. Something medieval, you know, that crap you like so much."

Crap?

"Amalie's one in a million," Violet replied, throwing Sam's carry-on into the trunk of her Mustang. Too bad she couldn't throw him in next to the battered luggage.

"Yeah, she said it was between a biography of Richard the Third or that – thing." Sam made a circular motion with his finger and then touched the medallion again, this time carefully, as if it was still molten silver.

Lying bastard!

"Hey, nice tan!" she complimented as they screeched out of the airport garage.

VIOLET STEPPED OVER the boxes of Christmas decorations and switched on the lights, grabbing the mail scattered in the hallway, especially a thick envelope from the State Department. She tucked it into the current issue of *Writers Digest* before Sam could see it.

"I'll fix something for dinner," she offered while Sam grumbled his way upstairs to unpack. A half-hour later they sat in the kitchen, dining on two-week old leftovers from Christmas dinner. Sam found a bottle of champagne in the cupboard above the refrigerator. "Excuse the pun, but your hair kind of grows on me; and your legs definitely do justice to those tights," he complimented and chuckled, hoping she would too. For the last hour Violet had been silent and entertained herself by pushing the food back and forth on her plate as if it was a redevelopment project.

"A person's hair shouldn't have any bearing on the content or worth of their heart or soul," she murmured.

He made a rumbling sound – a laugh being suppressed or disapproval – it didn't matter to Violet. Then he said the comment sounded like it belonged in one of her romantic stories. She took her plate to the sink and did something unconscionable – scraped the untouched meal down into the garbage disposal.

"Violet? Violet! *Violet!*"

She switched off the garbage disposal when she realized Sam was behind her. Turning, Violet forced a smile and slid passed him to the living room where she started on the laundry. Sam followed and armed with the remote control, stretched out on the sofa with his head in Violet's lap to watch TV.

It was a less than satisfactory homecoming.

THE CALL CAME at six the next morning. Violet was surprised by how well she received news she had anticipated. In fact, she was relieved. When Sam turned over in bed to ask who it was Violet said, "Nobody."

She was surprised that her only reaction was perturbation. This was something she'd expected. No, she hoped for it. Still, she said nothing to anyone and even when Sam returned with the children at ten-thirty that morning Violet kept quiet.

"What's bothering you?" Elisabet wanted to know as Violet sat for a portrait. Violet was strangely silent and circumspect. Violet glanced up at her daughter standing at the easel with paintbrush raised and ready and said it was nothing.

Sam slid his arms around Violet while she washed dishes that night. The fact that she was washing dishes wasn't as surprising as how she tensed as he explored under her blouse and unhooked her bra. Whenever he was gone for more than a week she always wanted it as soon as he was in the door. And she always wanted it bad. He was more than willing to accommodate her right there in the kitchen. But so far she hadn't asked.

"Violet, how many times —? The blue sponge is for the dishes; the yellow for the floors," he murmured in her ear.

"Over a hundred problems we could discuss and you go for sponges," she answered, continuing to wash with the wrong sponge, letting the soft yellow celluloid pass gently over the raised pattern of roses on her English bone china. At that moment she had no capacity for anything else. The mundane, simple ritual of washing the dishes by hand and rinsing them, placing them in a drainer, was all she wanted.

Sam had unbuttoned her blouse and was nuzzling her neck.

Violet suddenly turned off the tap and picked up the small wastebasket and carried it out to the porch. When she didn't return, Sam went looking and found her sitting alone on the porch swing. The night was nearly freezing, yet there she sat, staring up at the brilliant sky. He was ready to say something, to remind her of a joke, something that would make her smile at him, when he noticed the tears. Violet rarely cried. She sat on the bench and swayed back and forth, staring up, the tears making bright ribbons on her face. Sam shoved his hands into his pockets and went back inside.

Sam was still trying to figure Violet out a week later. He'd even gone so far as to cook up another one of his famous gourmet dinners. This time he enlisted help from the children, hoping for a united front. "Know what's bothering Mamma?" he asked Elisabet as they set the dining room table.

"Nothing more than the usual – the job, the writing."

"Finish the sentence, Beth."

Elisabet's eyes met her father's then quickly averted her glance to Max, who had decided to bring his Matchbox cars into the dining room and on to the good china laid out for five.

"The writing, the job, the usual."

"C'mon, she's had setbacks before and never acted like this."

"The writing, the job, the usual, Dad?"

"It's another guy, isn't it?"

Beth gaped like a fish out of water as she swallowed her response. Besides, she was saved by the slam of the front door and the jingle of keys thrown onto the coffee table.

"Oh look, Mamma's home!" she chirruped brightly.

For the first time in a year the Ellison-Peters family sat down as one and broke bread. Elisabet glanced from her mother's face to her father's and wondered why Sam bothered. They didn't need ice from the dispenser in the refrigerator door for their fruit punch – there was enough of it in this very room to keep Antarctica frozen for a millennium.

Mercifully, the telephone rang while Elisabet and Sam cleared the table. Violet leisurely took the call. Fifteen minutes later she entered the kitchen and watched Sam and Elisabet's mini food fight before speaking up.

"Hey! What's up?" Sam laughed, daubing her nose with mashed potatoes.

"D'you remember Rachel Grant? From my history honors class at Cal?" Violet opened, nonchalantly switching off the computer and printer she'd only just switched on and organized and reorganized papers and books into symmetrical piles.

"The one who was found naked with my best man at our wedding reception?"

"The same."

"She's in town to host a seminar on thirteenth-century polemics."

"Gag me," Elisabet murmured and was relieved when her mother smiled and winked, when her father made faces at her over her mother's head.

"I'm going over to the City to see her, meet for a drink, discussion, talk about old times."

"Want a ride?"

"Ride? No; I'll take my car."

"Want me to wait up?"

"It's up to you; but you know how we get when we start talking. I'll be late. See you in a bit – oh! If George calls, tell him I can't make his study group tonight. Tell him a friend came into town," Violet said and scooping up her purse and keys kissed Elisabet good night on her way out the back door.

Forty-five minutes later, Christian opened the hotel suite door and smiled in greeting. "Shall we take that first step?" Violet whispered tremulously after a kiss.

He smiled and said he'd like nothing better than for her to lead the way.

19

I'm Sorry; Shall I Scream Louder So You Can Hear Me?

VIOLET GROPED CLUMSILY for the telephone when it rang and jarred her out of a delicious sleep. She knocked it off the nightstand, and swearing, pushed it under the bed and the tangle of clothes. Turning, Violet clutched the blankets against her naked body for warmth and modesty, remembering where she was. She knew for certain when glancing toward the bathroom light she saw Christian beside her, resting on an elbow. He'd been there for some time, watching her sleep. An unlit cigarette was in his hand.

"Hi," he greeted with a kiss.

"What time is it?" she purred sleepily.

"A little past two. Are you hungry?"

"Not particularly. Two, you said? I'd better be going."

"Please stay. I don't know when I'll be in town again."

"I have to go."

Christian kissed her to halt any further argument. He slid his hands under the warm blankets perfumed by her sweet and heady scent of freesia, a scent that would now bind her to him and the memory of this, their first time making love, to take her in his arms.

There had been nothing like it. To possess this woman and marvel at her glorious body was surely Heaven's gift to him. To experience the climax he'd dreamt of since first setting eyes on her and not be disappointed.

Christian could only stare in wonder as she slept, one knee drawn up and a hand tucked under her cheek, the curve of her hip and the full breasts. She'd protested and giggled that her body was nothing he'd want; she was over forty and gravity had started its cruel journey – and she still had ten pounds to goal. Nothing he'd want? She was everything he'd ever dreamt of.

Now his gentle hands wandered over the exciting, sensual contours of her body. Still unfamiliar but wholly intimate. It had been years since a woman made him so excited, made him feel eager and alive. He had a plane to catch soon, but Violet's body was tempting him to miss the flight. When their lips met he knew he'd be swept away and eagerly awaited the moment. Her kisses were at first timorous, petal-like in softness but they quickly gave way to an urgency Christian recognized and welcomed.

"So you'll stay?" he murmured in her ear and then let his kisses wander. He didn't remember the answer, for she had managed to get him out of his bathrobe and under the covers where it was warm and inviting.

He did remember the alarm going off at five-thirty and hearing Violet swear softly as she slid out of bed.

Christian claimed her pillow and took in the scent of perfume left there. The shower went on and for the better part of an hour he drifted in and out of sleep, listened as Violet got ready to leave. He'd eventually have to get up and leave for the airport but it wasn't something he was looking forward to. To do that, he'd have to leave this bed and San Francisco. And her.

Violet returned from the bathroom dressed and brushing her hair. She sat on the bed and reached under for her shoes, which she retrieved with the telephone. The blue-gray light of dawn shone into the window and affected a halo round her face and hair.

"I owe you an apology," Christian said.

"For what?" she laughed.

"I should have expected your response. It was too much to ask," he said, kissing her. "I have a habit of sabotaging things, having everything blow up in my face."

"You're being silly," Violet said, leaning over to return the kiss. "If anything, I owe you."

"Isn't it a bit early to be playing the debting game?

Who owes whom?" he laughed. "So can I be smug and gloat and know you chose me over him?"

"What?" Violet asked, her heart catching in her throat.

"The other guy. The bloke who was stupid enough to lose you."

Tell him the truth. Now.

Violet was about to speak and hesitated, then looked him straight in the eyes. "I've loved you for the longest time and didn't even know you. I knew him for a lifetime. Strange how it all works out."

"Strange," he murmured, bringing her close. "So you'll think about it?"

"Yes."

"You know where to find me," he murmured in her ear. Picking up her coat and purse, she blew a kiss and was gone.

SAM WAS WAITING on the porch with the morning paper and a bag crammed with pastries when she drove up at seven-thirty.

"How's Rachel?" He smiled at the blank look that suddenly clouded her face and threw an arm around her affectionately. "Rachel, Vi. You know, the only woman I know that likes fat, loud, best men. You look wasted. How much wine did you drink?"

"Wine?"

"You're wasted. Why don't you call in sick today?"

Sam came with her upstairs and watched amusedly as she changed clothes for work. During an unimaginative conversation about matters domestic and inconsequential, it never dawned on him that Violet would do the unthinkable – to take a lover, have an affair, and share her body with another.

But that evening George knew at once from the look on her face. He stepped aside to let her in and led the way into the living that overlooked San Francisco Bay.

"So?" he asked.

Violet threw herself into the overstuffed chair and held her hand out for Bede, George's overweight and overbearing Russian Blue that now purred upon recognition. Bede climbed into her lap and made himself at home, demanding a back rub. Violet obliged the cat absently as she watched a freighter move lazily through the Golden Gate.

"He wants me to come to England. He wants me to marry him," she said at last.

George handed her the highball of gin and tonic he'd been nursing and sat on the floor in front of her. "It doesn't surprise me."

"I don't know," she sighed; "I just don't want to think about it."

"Well, that's a lie." George lifted her chin with a finger and raised his brows in question. "To marry Christian and ride off on a white charger into an English sunset, you'd have to get a divorce first. I'm sure you're aware of that?"

"I haven't told him yet – I haven't told Christian about anyone."

"It might be a good idea to come clean with everyone, Violet."

"That would be easy. When have I done anything that's easy?" She scooted off the sofa and crossed to the bar, pouring herself a vodka. After a shot, and then another, said: "George, I'm feeling guilty about what I did, but I'm also feeling – happy, like I have something to look forward to, something I haven't felt in a while, and I also feel like it's not the wisest thing I've ever done."

"Tell him how you feel."

"I don't know…"

"Well, if it's obvious to me, it should be obvious to everyone concerned. Don't make the mistake I did."

Violet turned and smiled, truly surprised. "You? You've got to be kidding! C'mon, confession's good for the soul. Anyway, it would help me feel better."

"I... Violet, I don't think it would be a good idea right now. Maybe when you've thought it over a day, about you and Christian."

"You opened the door, George."

"I said I didn't want to talk about it. It's still too painful, too soon."

His voice had taken on a hard, cold edge, like the glass table Violet leaned against. George was avoiding her, avoiding the subject, by picking up the mid-term papers he'd been grading until her arrival. His pen scratched angrily across the title page of one and when he looked up, Violet saw it in his eyes. She gasped involuntarily and set her glass down.

"Oh Jesus, George! Oh, no."

"Violet, what did I say?"

"It was Isobel! Oh my God."

"It wouldn't do us any good to dredge up the past, Violet."

"If you had told me years ago, I would have understood. Now at least I know why you keep asking me not to make the same mistakes! My God, my sister!"

"Violet, I don't want to talk about it."

"Tell me about you and Isobel, and why."

"That's none of your concern."

"I think it is."

"Look, you came here wanting absolution or understanding for jumping into the sack with a man you barely know."

"Well, with what I know about you and Isobel, that makes us both members of that exclusive circle of Hell reserved for adulterers and you've got no right to judge. Just give me an answer."

George rose and went to the door, opening it. Violet didn't need a prompting look or word and grabbed her purse.

"I'll call you tomorrow; maybe we can talk," he

muttered.

"I always thought there was someone else; I didn't imagine it you. You were the good friend. You were the big brother —"

"Wait! You can stay. Sit down."

He wanted to reach for the bottle of gin sitting on the table behind them, to make the moment theatrical and dramatic as he poured a good, stiff, drink and swallowed it so that the gin would burn his throat and numb his senses. Instead, George sat beside Violet on the sofa and looked her straight in the eyes.

"All I'll tell you is that during our time at Oxford I loved her. I worshipped her and I knew she'd never give me the time of day so long as Colin was in the picture. Colin and I were best friends and cousins and it wasn't my place to touch another man's lover. But I did."

"How did it happen? Colin and Isobel were the disgustingly perfect couple. They were one word, one entity. What did you do?"

"What do you mean? What did I do? These things have two players, if you haven't already figured it out. It just happened," George murmured. "And those were the best years of my life."

"It was when Bella went to England after Granny Mowbray died, wasn't it?" Violet mused.

"Before. Long before. You know the rest," George said relaxing into the sofa. He watched the skyline of Berkeley below him, the flight of a blue jay as it skipped from cedar to eucalyptus to pine. Night was coming on fast; the winter sky was purple and blue with salmon ribbons of light stretching across the silhouette of the Golden Gate Bridge.

He was lost in another winter's twilight, one where he woke and saw a blonde goddess beside him, the gold hair spilling over his chest and face as she greeted him with a kiss. Eyes that were soft and loving, eyes that in days past had diverted to him whenever he walked into a room, watched him while he played poker with Colin, while his wife went on endlessly about some acquisition in an antique store, watched as he got in his car and drove off or boarded a plane to somewhere.

He never expected that an argument with Colin would drive her into his welcome arms. Nor did he think the guilt would follow him.

"It was hard enough to leave her, but the accident," George whispered.

"It wasn't an accident. The most perfect of couples were arguing about getting a divorce when Isobel crossed the barrier on purpose, went head on into a beer truck. Six eyewitnesses confirmed it."

George did grab for the bottle of gin now and couldn't pour a drink his hands were shaking so hard. Violet was there and took the bottle from him, topping off his highball.

"I guess death is the best way to avoid an issue," she continued. "Bella always got out of any trouble she caused and no one ever knew she was the cause of it! She had a flair for the dramatic, even though I was the actor and artist in the family. She made everyone pay for her mistakes, made everyone feel guilty about their sins when there was nothing to feel guilty about. She encouraged me to stay in a marriage that was slowly disintegrating and forgive Sam for all his trespasses – I guess that's the pot calling the kettle black. I stopped loving my perfect hypocrite of a sister long ago. It was all pretense. But the anger and sorrow at her death is very real and comes from guilt." Violet sniped and when she saw George's stricken face, took back her words and embraced him. "And now forgive me."

"It's the truth."

"I shouldn't have asked," she whispered. "That was the only sin I never confessed."

"Compared to the multitude on my shoulders, it's very little."

He brushed aside her wispy bangs and then touched her nose playfully, much like Christian had done on two occasions. So much so, Violet's heart ached.

"What sins could you possibly have committed?" he teased; "Saint Violet, patron saint of the working woman, the put-upon housewife, the betrayed lover?"

"The sin of last night."

"I know exactly what you're going through. I've no right to say this, not with my track record. I ruined my marriage, and I ruined Colin and Isobel's."

"My situation isn't like yours. I can't remember a day in all our years together that Sam said 'I love you' and meant it. Whenever we're out to together, his eyes are always on the leggiest, blondest, woman in the room or on the street, and not on me, openly comparing me to them, belittling my achievements, ignoring my pleas for understanding, ignoring my loneliness and unhappiness."

Violet suppressed a sob and moved away so that George couldn't see her tears. He gently turned her face towards his and kissed her cheek. "Give it time. It will come to you in the middle of the night, or on a walk with the kids, or sitting on the 'F' bus. I hope whatever your answer might be, it's the right one, and you won't be torn apart, or made sorry."

Bede now interrupted the serious interval by rubbing against George's leg. The clock was striking five.

"Do you want dinner or something? I could grill two steaks, throw a salad together?" he offered Violet, dumping the cat onto the sofa.

"Sure. Let me call Sam and tell him I won't be home for dinner."

"Oh Lord, you don't think he suspects me?"

"You? Yes."

George heaved himself out of the chair and pulled Violet up with him. "Then all the more reason to stay for dinner – share a last meal with a condemned man!" he jested weakly, and then, more seriously and turning her face gently towards his, said, "Just be sure, Violet darling; just be very sure of what you're getting yourself into when you do make that decision."

She smiled then and reached up on tiptoe to kiss his cheek, saying she was lucky to have a friend like him. "I only wish you didn't look so much like Christian," Violet remarked wistfully as she followed him to the kitchen; "it only makes it harder."

IT CAME TO Violet as she was pulling into the parking lot outside of the agency studio. It was as clear as the bright blue sky that Sunday afternoon. It was most definitely clear when Sam pushed his chair out from behind the partition when Violet's angry heels clipped against the cement floor.

"This is a surprise!" Sam greeted.

Violet removed the rose-patterned paper napkin from the paper plate of the same design that filled her hands. A slice of birthday cake, candles still impaled on the shimmering white icing, was plopped on the ad copy before Sam.

"Hey!" Sam exclaimed, "What the hell?"

"So was Elisabet's twentieth birthday party. It was a bigger surprise when you didn't show up."

"Her birthday? Shit! I knew there was something —"

"Disappointing me at every turn is something I've gotten use to, but don't make it a habit with the kids; you want to stay in their good graces."

Turning on her heels, Violet was gone. She was revving up the engine when Sam skipped down the stairs three at a time and fell against the car panting for breath.

"I'm sorry, I forgot!" he gasped. "I'll make it up to her – I had a meeting with the Rotherwell people, and the soda company."

She wanted to ask if the hotel in Cancun had bothered to send back his car keys and organizer but Violet merely smiled. She'd keep that secret a while longer.

"When you finish here it'd be nice to see you at

home; your parents want to talk to you about that latest loan – the one you didn't bother telling me about."

The one you used to bankroll your holiday in Cancun with Marjorie and that model for the Soda Company ads!

That was the first salvo in the war. Sam's attempts at family outings and intimate suppers all fell flat. It all came to a nasty boil a day later and even then Sam didn't quite get it.

Violet woke and saw Sam smiling at her, the smile a prelude to his body's needs. They made love as they had on so many other mornings, but Violet, as soon as Sam was in the shower, crawled out of bed and was immediately sick to her stomach.

A sensation of drowning had started to overwhelm her several days before and then the need to escape, a desperate need to be with Christian replaced all other thoughts. Only the job and the children had kept her feet soundly planted on reality's *terra firma*.

Until that morning.

"You okay, Vi?" Sam asked, coming out of the shower and finding Violet huddled over the toilet bowl. For the first time in months he was solicitous and carried Violet back to bed, wrapping her in her favorite robe and even putting a Fortinbras CD in the boom box. Hearing Christian's voice only made her feel worse.

"Jesus!" Sam now swore softly when he saw how ashen her usually glowing complexion had become; "Vi, you're not pregnant again, are you?"

"No!" she snapped. "It's nerves – just nerves. I need to get away. I need to be alone for a while."

"I can take the kids to my mother's —"

"I mean for a while."

"How long is a while?"

The thought came as easily as the words. Violet now turned over in bed and said to Sam: "I can still go to England for the winter term."

"You didn't get the Fellowship."

"I received a grant."

Sam's perfectly groomed brows rose into perfect arches. He said he didn't have time to discuss it – maybe that afternoon.

That afternoon, Violet had the plan neatly laid.

"So who's offering this grant? George?" he asked for the ninth time in an hour. His chopping at the semi-frozen ground with a spade had only made the flower bed a muddy soup, his late afternoon efforts at domesticity a ploy to win Violet's attention failing miserably.

"What does it matter?" Violet asked wearily; "What matters is that someone thought enough of my talent to allow me to go to Oxford for the winter term."

"It's too convenient, too strange coming right now," Sam argued as he threw the spade into the bed intended for freesia and hyacinth.

"Why?" demanded Violet, planting bulbs in a haphazard, angry manner.

"Listen, Vi, you've been acting strange ever since I got home. You said nothing's bothering you, but damned if there isn't something. Talk to me!"

Would it do any good?

Expelling a sigh that joined the late afternoon mist, Violet said, "Why can't you just let it be and accept it? I'm going to England and that's that."

He followed her inside and to the kitchen where she started washing dishes. A favorite pastime when the heart and mind were trouble, he mused, and then sighed, "But it's twelve weeks! Twelve, damn, weeks! You could stand twelve weeks without the kids?"

The expression on Violet's face told him that that was the silliest question he'd asked in a lifetime, given the fact that the large house was echoing with Max and Alex's shouting, the sound effects from video games, and Elisabet's boom box, and they'd just tripped over Tonka trucks and baseball gloves on the way inside.

"Don't you think I deserve this chance? That I've

worked my ass off for it?" she asked quietly.

"A trip to Los Angeles or New York, yes."

"You should let me go. Let me go."

Sam hadn't caught the enormity of her words. "Can we discuss this in the morning? I've been in the studio all day mixing soundtracks and —"

"It can't wait. Tomorrow. Tomorrow I'm going."

Sam still didn't have a grasp on the situation by next morning as he watched Violet pack.

Her methodical placement of lingerie and clothes, the careful selection of toiletries and cosmetics belied the anxiety tearing her apart.

"What's really going on, Violet? There's something you're not telling me."

"I've called a cab; you don't have to take me to the airport," Violet answered as she brushed past him to get more toiletries out of the bathroom.

"This is about Cancun, isn't it? It won't happen again. It was dumb, stupid, so —"

Violet tried to suppress a smile. "When were you in Cancun?" she lied, her voice as guileless as she could make it without laughing out loud.

"When the hotel called after I got home, I just figured you knew. You were so quiet, I just assumed."

"It's about a lot more than Cancun."

"I told you it was a stupid mistake."

"One of many. What happens when the novelty of Marjorie Rotherwell wears off or she gets bored with your moves and wants another boy toy? Do you hook up with Carrie? Another client?"

"I told you, Vi —"

"My name is Violet Joan Ellison! My name is Violet! Stop calling me Vi!" she began to sob. Sam tried to take her in his arms for a comforting embrace but she pulled away and sat on the bed, twisting and knotting a silk scarf until it was pleated beyond repair. "In the twenty years we've been together, when did you ever think to call me by my name?"

"But I thought it was cute."

"I'm a grown woman and I'm tired of being cute!"

With the mascara running down in inky tracks across her cheeks, her nose as bright as a cherry, Sam didn't think 'cute' was appropriate either. "Is that what all this is about? Okay, Violet."

"It's about more than a name. When was the last time you woke up in the morning and really thought, 'What can I do to make Violet, anybody, happy?' Have you ever, in any moment of your life, thought about someone other than yourself?"

Sam and Violet now stared each other down. Sam took a step forward to embrace her but knew it was a mistake as soon as she slammed the suitcase closed.

"What if we started over, Violet? What if I spent more time with you, the kids – if I stop hammering you about the weight? Look, you're not that overweight."

She slammed the bathroom door behind her and was in there such a long time that Sam hoped he'd remember to put the razor blades away. When Violet reemerged her appearance was refreshed and she seemed calmer.

"At least you can listen to me now," Sam demanded.

"I have to go."

"Who is he?"

"He?"

"Well, it's got to be another man, that's the only reason I can think of."

You're that sure of your animal magnetism, she thought. *Too bad a soul didn't go with the perfect veneer.*

"Is it George?"

Violet almost laughed. "George? He was Isobel's lover, not mine."

"Is there someone else? At least tell me."

Violet reached for her coat and umbrella. "I'll be staying in London the next few days, then I go to Oxford. I'll call when I get there."

"Vi!"

She turned and said quietly, "Didn't I just tell you? Don't call me Vi."

The children were sprawled across the living room, engrossed in their respective activities. Elisabet took the suitcase and carry on from her mother when she appeared on the stairs.

"The Airporter is outside," she said, not looking at her father's ashen face, but meeting her mother's gaze head-on. "Don't worry, Mom. We've got this under control."

"Okay!" Violet said, kneeling down to hug the boys. "I've marked up the calendar so you can see when I'm coming home. I've got to go now; give Mamma a kiss and a hug?"

"Do you have to go to the soda company, Mamma?" Alex asked.

"No, I'm actually going to school."

"You have to bring me back something," Alex pronounced. "When are you coming back?"

"Right before your birthday – or sooner," Violet answered and wrapped him in her arms for a suffocating hug. "I love you so much!"

"Mamma let go!"

"Are you okay?" Elisabet whispered now, concerned. Tears started to pool in Violet's eyes and she looked too pale. "You *are* coming back, aren't you?"

"I'm never going to leave you!" Violet sobbed into her daughter's hair.

Outside the taxi honked and after another round of kisses and hugs and promises of letters, e-mail and telephone calls, Violet rode off.

"Som'ting wrong, miss?" the taxi driver wanted to know when he glanced in the rear view mirror and saw Violet huddled over and sobbing miserably. "Do you want to go back?"

"No," Violet answered, reaching for the box of tissues that was offered; "everything's okay." How could she tell a complete stranger that it wasn't?

20

Toto, I Don't Believe I'm in Berkeley Anymore

VIOLET HAD NEVER so much as set a foot outside the United States; now she found herself standing amazed in Heathrow Airport. Why she should be more impressed by the size of an airport and less by what she had done had not registered.

Dragging her suitcase in the artful manner of an experienced traveler, Violet passed safely through customs and was welcomed to England.

Now that she was here, what next?

"My God!" Violet exclaimed when she saw it; "A McDonald's!"

Her stomach full of Chicken McNuggets and fries, she set off on her adventure. It hadn't occurred to her to get a hotel room. Getting on that Virgin Atlantic flight to London had been the only concern. Now that she was in London, the adrenaline surge had slowed and reality was taking its place.

She would have to make the call. Violet whispered Prayer Number 57, for guidance, and as an extra measure, Prayer Number 59, for quiet confidence, and dialed up the number, getting a business-like woman on the second ring. At first her heart stopped, her mind conjuring a freshly-aproned, perfectly-coiffed English housewife in her mid-forties, the type of housewife that once graced the television airwaves in America. A woman in crisply starched gingham and pearls. A Donna Reed or June Cleaver. The woman sounded friendly and knowledgeable, too knowledgeable.

Why would Christian settle for a wife like that?
What if Christian had been lying about being divorced?
And wasn't that calling the kettle black?

"And who shall I say called, Miss?" the perfect

housewife asked kindly.

Give a pseudonym and get on the first plane out of Heathrow, the voice inside Violet's head warned, that warm, soft, male voice.

Christian's voice. George's voice.

"Violet Ellison, Ma'am."

There was a pause and then: "Oh! Miss *Ellison!* Yes, well, that's a name I've heard a lot of these past few weeks. My, you do have a lovely voice; mind you, he said you did! Oh my dear, I am sorry, but Mister Christian isn't in town right at the moment," the woman replied and then identified herself as Mrs. Burnes, his housekeeper.

The lump started to grow in Violet's throat. Watching the departure monitors flicker above her was tempting.

Get on a plane, Violet; go back to California!

"He shouldn't be later than Wednesday of next week, and I can leave a message at his hotel," Mrs. Burnes offered. "My dear?... Miss Ellison? Are you still there?"

Violet swallowed the lump and dried her tears with the back of her hand. "Yeah! Yes, that would be fine, Missus Burnes."

A promise was made by Violet to call as soon as she found a place to stay. Mrs. Burnes would be sure to give the message to him when he called. He had a habit of calling her during her favorite television show while he was out of town, you see. There was a repeat of *Coronation Street* that evening, and more than like Mr. Christian would call just as the story was getting good.

The conversation ended with Violet and Mrs. Burnes the best of friends. Had Violet known Mrs. Burnes at all, she would have known how large an obstacle it was she'd overcome.

GIVEN THE CHOICE of staying in a sterile, cookie-cutter airport hotel, or a four-star establishment beyond her means, Violet opted for travelling further afield and found a room in a small bed and breakfast in Westminster, one of those Georgian town houses you knew would smell of carnations and roses, of freshly-baked bread and new paint the moment you saw it. And it was everything Violet hoped it would be, this little place tucked neatly beside the Abbey.

She was appraised with motherly concern by the blue-rinse proprietress who brought out photographs of her seven grandchildren when Violet mentioned calling home to speak with her children.

"Business trip all this way? Still, there's nothing like an adventure to make the job interesting, eh, Miss?"

Violet only smiled and wondered if anyone could see the scarlet letter burning on her chest, that enormous 'A' Hester Prynne made so fashionable. Would these Londoners be so quick to help if they knew she'd left her husband and kids to spend a few weeks with a man she barely knew?

Violet knew she'd done the right thing when she woke the next morning, safe in the warm cocoon of a comforting but unfamiliar featherbed with goose down coverlets. Watercolor light shone through gossamer curtains, and strange yet delicious smells of breakfast came up the stairs from the kitchen. Somewhere in the boarding house a maid was singing opera (or at least trying to) while scrubbing out a bathroom. The tune from *La Traviata* ended with the metallic clang of a brush into a pail.

It was right coming to London. Last night while she dined alone at a cafe near Covent Garden (and not for a moment wondering where Christian was or if he'd be glad to see her), she enjoyed her independence and now recalled snatches of polite conversation with the waitress, a woman near her age. Was she on vacation? Yes, sort of, from America. Traveling with her husband or boyfriend? No, alone, thank you. Alone? How wonderful to have someone so understanding!

Yes, it would have been wonderful. Had that truly been the case, Violet doubted she'd have come so far to get away.

"Oh, Violet!" she sighed at the reflection in the steamed-over mirror. "What have you done?" Rubbing away the moisture, Violet expected to see a crone scowling back at her. All she saw was a tired woman in her forties.

A woman tired and scared.

Oh, Violet; what have you done?

"Goin' out for the day, Miss?"

Violet smiled in response to the proprietress' question and she stopped by the desk. "Thought I'd get some work done today. Could you point me in the direction of the nearest library?" she asked.

The proprietress did one better and offered a map of London and directions to a local cafe she swore was better than most of the four-star restaurants in the district.

Violet took the Underground to Tottenham Hill Road Station. The British Museum, British Library and London University were all here and she spent most of the day wandering in and out of collections in search of material for her story of Richard and Anne.

Not surprisingly, she found herself uninterested in the task, even with a copy of Harleian 433 before her – volumes of Parliamentary rolls and extant documents of the Yorkist period in fifteenth-century England. These were documents she'd dreamt about for years, and now they were as uninteresting as the bespectacled old gentleman sitting across the table and making doe eyes at her. He cleared his throat and announced it was indeed a wonder that such a pretty little thing like her would be interested in history. Violet told him to get stuffed.

Dinner at an Italian restaurant and then back to the hotel in Westminster. Violet's second day in England had passed as uneventful as the first. There were no calls or messages for her at the desk. Before going to bed she called home and to her surprise, Amalie answered. Sam had gone on a trip to Los Angeles – the soda company. The children were still at school and day care, Amalie said;

she was on her way to pick up Max just as the phone rang

"You don't sound like a woman glad to be in England and at her life's work, Darling," Amalie commented.

"Just tired, Grammy Am," Violet admitted and was glad to have finally told the truth about something.

In the background Violet heard the grandfather clock in the living room strike three and knew the children would be home in an hour.

"Darling... is it really the term at Oxford? Is that why you left so unexpectedly? Or is it something else?" Amalie ventured. When the silence grew telling, she added, "Or is it someone else?"

Again there was a silence, and then Violet whimpered: "Please don't turn on me, don't hate me! Sam's been having an affair with one of his clients and I found out. I needed to get away."

"Sweetheart, don't cry! Didn't I already say I wouldn't? Violet, I know how it's been. For years I kept my mouth shut, hoping things would work themselves out. But I've watched you suffer in silence for too long, and I know Sam's many sins. I just assumed you knew because you didn't say a word. I only wonder if you can forgive us for our – complicity. When Sam called and told me what you did, I was so glad for you! We gave him the talking-to of his life yesterday, and for once he took it like a man. God, the mistakes I've made with that boy! Violet, if this is the only way it can get through to him, so be it!"

"I needed to be as far away from Sam as I could get, but the children, no, I won't take too long. Just as I promised, twelve weeks and no more."

"Don't worry about them, Angel. You're no good to them if you're not to yourself. Sometimes it takes going away in order to look at things in a new light. And whatever it really is, you don't have to keep it from me."

"You're Sam's mother —"

"When have I ever betrayed you?"

"Never!"

"Don't stay away too long. Sam's patience is short, but you know that."

"I love you, Grammy Am! You've always been there for me, when Mamma and Dad died, when Isobel —"

"You're my child as much as Sam, Darling. And I made a promise to Ruth and Michael that I'd always look after you."

"I love you!"

"I love you. Now, get to bed. I'll tell the children you called."

"I've sent postcards, and some packages," Violet volunteered.

"Good night, Sweetie. Call me tomorrow, okay?"

Violet stayed late in bed the next morning. The night's dreams were of Sam, Ned, George, and strangely, her long-dead father. But none of Christian – not the dreams she'd had of him before coming to England, dreams that left her exhausted and petulant.

What if Christian wasn't even in the country? More importantly, what if he really didn't care? Things said in the heat of passion were quickly forgotten by morning's first light. She knew the truth in that, having lived twenty years with Sam Peters, seventeen of them in wedded combat.

Groaning, Violet turned over in bed and pulled aside the organza curtains to see what kind of day was ahead of her.

Outside the sky couldn't make up its mind to turn cloudless or overshadow London with rain. A troupe of schoolchildren were chattering en route to the Abbey and downstairs she heard the doorbell and the cheerful voice of the proprietress with a gentleman.

Then the telephone suddenly rang.

Christian was standing with his back to her when Violet came down fifteen minutes later. He turned, hearing the footsteps. In two strides he was across the lobby and she was in his arms. His passionate kiss was the final confirmation that she had indeed done the right thing.

"I CAN'T BELIEVE you've never been to London."

"Never been to a lot of places. Christian, I've never been out of the States."

"You mean to tell me you just got on a plane? Just like that?"

"Pretty much."

"What did Ned say?"

"He threatened to fire me – but then he loaned me the money for the trip."

"Unwilling accomplice, no doubt?"

"He did offer to drive me to the airport and said to send back Dewar's if I managed to get to Scotland. The look on his face was priceless."

"Guess you had to be there."

"It was a declaration of independence."

"More like a declaration of war!"

Violet slipped an arm through his and delighted at how Christian pulled her closer as they strolled through the Abbey chapter house and past a tour group. Her heart was ready to burst. The last three hours had been a soothing balm after forty-eight hours of not knowing her fate. She had made up her mind to tell Christian about Sam and the kids as soon as they went back to the boarding house that night. Surely he'd understand her reticence in telling him straight out. She'd planned the entire confession. Everything else he knew or would know.

"If I promise not to mention marriage or commitment, will you stay a while?" Christian asked after a time.

"How long is a while?"

"However long it takes for you to make up your mind about what you want," he said, kissing her hair. "And to tell me that you love me."

"You're charming and persistent," she laughed. "But all I can give you is twelve weeks."

Christian steered her towards Saint Edward's Chapel. "Consider this the siege of a castle – okay, okay! Not another word."

As they walked through the high nave and into the chapel of Edward the Confessor, Violet regaled him with news of her successful research at the British Library.

"You're a rare woman, Violet Ellison. I admire a lady who can talk about the vagrancies of historical fact in one breath and then scream like a fishwife at a football game in another. A woman who can so excite me!" He smiled and drew her into his arms. "But let's get our priorities straight here. Have you come to England to solve medieval mysteries or make love to me?"

"One more than the other," she whispered seductively after they'd kissed. "You'll have to guess which one."

IT WAS PAST midnight by the time they got on the Underground and headed for Christian's house in the southwest of London. He lived in an expensive neighborhood full of Georgian and Victorian houses that reeked of privilege and old money. Everything was neat and clean, reminiscent of a Disney movie set.

"There's a town above Berkeley called Kensington. In the hills," Violet mentioned as they climbed the stairs at the Gloucester Road station on the South Kensington – Knightsbridge border.

"I don't live in Kensington exactly, I've got a house in Knightsbridge. Raphael Street. Here, it's this way."

Violet froze and suppressed a giggle. Christian immediately hugged her and wanted to know what was so funny. They had shared a bottle of Bordeaux at dinner and were a little drunk.

"Do you have a friend named George?" she demanded, and burst out laughing.

"Lots of friends, but no one named George. Don't you have a friend named George? Violet my sweet love,

England is the country of Saint George!"

"And that's the joke! Oh God, Chris, sometime when I'm not so drunk, I'll tell you. But you wouldn't believe me if I did!"

Mrs. Burnes came from her rooms as soon as she heard the key turn in the lock and heard Christian's soft laughter, the surprising sound of a woman's voice, low, soft and pleasant. She folded her plump hands across her mid-section and smiled at Violet when they came upstairs – not a forced, polite smile out of respect for her employer's guest – but a genuine smile. If the Right Reverend Gwillam Walsh, Dean of York Minster, were alive, he'd take Christian aside and tell him that for once he'd done something right.

She had expected another of Christian's casual girlfriends – high maintenance and little substance – women who looked good but couldn't join three words together to make a coherent sentence. Mrs. Burnes knew what they wanted from Christian, and in her continued examination of the woman standing nervously on the second floor landing, knew this one didn't expect much but managed to get all. She was pretty sure this one was giving Christian a challenge he'd never come up against before.

Violet's casual appearance in blue jeans, jacket and sweater was how she expected Violet Ellison of Berkeley, California to look. And she was quite pretty – prettier than Christian let on during interrogations.

"Mister Christian, is this Miss Ellison?"

"Missus Burnes! You didn't have to wait up. Yes, Missus Burnes, this is Violet; Violet, Missus Deidre Burnes."

"Did you dine out with Miss Ellison?" Mrs. Burnes demanded, erasing the smile from her lips and remembering her role as drill sergeant.

"She wanted to try English food so I took her to Veronica's," he admitted sheepishly.

"Veronica's!" The tone made Violet smile, knowing it was immediate disapproval of his actions. "I made a perfectly decent roast of beef with parsleyed potatoes, just as you requested for the lady —"

"Why don't you show Violet upstairs and help her get settled?" Christian hinted with a wink. "We'll worry about the rest of her things in the morning."

He came up an hour later and found Violet relaxing on one of the large window seats fronting Hyde Park and the Serpentine. She turned when the door closed and smiled, then resumed her vigil on a sleeping London.

Christian removed his coat and tossed it on a chair, then started up a fire in the hearth, moving about the room as if it were a typical evening at home. He half expected to start a conversation about how his day went and listen as Violet in her turn recounted wifely appointments with the butcher and greengrocer or share gossip from the Ladies Auxiliary meeting at Saint Peter's. It was natural if not right to have Violet in this room.

His Victorian bedroom was scented with her toiletries and warm from the bath she'd just taken. Violet wore his thick, comfortable bathrobe and had claimed the attention of Tristan, his ancient Labrador. The dog's large graying head was contently situated in her lap and adoring her, lapping up the soft praises Violet offered while she stroked his muzzle and lovingly scraped her fingers across his back. Christian had never seen him so calm.

Christian didn't remove his eyes from Violet while getting ready for bed; he was worried that if he blinked she'd be gone and he'd wake up in another sweat, aching for her body. He was aching for her now and had been since that morning when she came down the boarding house stairs and into his arms.

"Tristan, come!"

Reluctantly the Labrador turned in the direction of the voice and had second thoughts about heeding the call.

After a second, sharper, command, the dog came at

his master's bidding and lumbered out of the bedroom.

Violet had stretched out on the window seat and exposed one of her shapely legs, which she drew up seductively as she settled into the pillows. Christian tried not to stare too obviously.

"Missus Burnes doesn't know what to make of you," he chuckled.

"That makes two of us."

"You've confounded her, Darling. Very few people have ever done that."

"She loves you like a son."

"Well, I do know that she likes you. Our conversation consisted of what would best please Miss Ellison and how I'm not to scare you off. How atypical you were of my usual guests. It's true; you're not the usual kind of guest here."

Violet leaned over seductively, and winking, said: "Blondes in their twenties?"

The robe had slipped from a shoulder and Christian tried again not to stare. "Not at all; never," he chuckled. "Why settle for blonde school girls when I have you?"

He was poking about in the fireplace again, his back turned, and when he caught a scent of freesia, Christian looked up and found her kneeling beside him.

Violet gently inclined her mouth towards his, placing a hand on his face, letting it slide slowly and sensually into his open shirt. She then unfastened each remaining button one at a time while she kissed him long and hard, excited by the warm mint taste of his mouth, just by the touch of him.

He eased back onto the carpet, bringing her along. Violet kissed his neck and shoulders as she pulled away the shirt and while doing this allowed her hands freedom to explore. He gasped, then moaned, her gentle touch sending fire through his body. He'd waited so long for her and now didn't know if he could hold out, wait until she was ready. The bathrobe slipped from her shoulders and fell to her waist. Christian reached up and tugged until it dropped in a soft heap around them. He let his hands test the smoothness of her skin and discover again the marvelous contours now enhanced by the light of the fireplace.

She arched her back and shuddered with delight as Christian encouraged her.

Violet was more than ready; she'd planned this seduction on the flight. For nine hours she devised a fantasy too imaginative and erotic for even her most erotic of stories. She must have looked feverish, however, for the elderly man seated next to her kept asking if she was all right.

The urgency was now too great. Violet had driven Christian into a frenzy. She was on top of him, guiding him, kissing him, exploring his body with her mouth and tongue. At the moment of their union Christian could hold out no longer. He was overtaken and she laughed softly when he was done, gently smoothing back his hair and wrapping her arms around his sweating, relaxed body.

"Not having you, and not knowing," he murmured. Violet laughed again, exhilarated by his desire.

"I don't think it was fair for you, though."

"It was my turn to seduce," she teased, willing to admit that for once she was glad to have made love to a man, knowing that for the first time it was appreciated. For the first time in years she had found pleasure in a man's body and enjoyed bringing him to climax.

"I think you liked taking charge – *ow!* Is that a shoe I'm lying on?" Christian laughed, and pulled out one of his boots from underneath his back. Violet, feeling self-conscious with the lights still on, jumped into bed and snatched up the pillows and blankets before Christian could claim them.

"I've always wanted to do that!" she laughed.

"A private joke?" Christian asked when he dove in beside her.

"Someday I'll tell you."

"Excellent! I like to hear how awful past lovers were!"

"I do like being in charge – well, the taste of it. I am, as Louisa May Alcott, wrote, embracing my liberty... Chris? Christian, what are you doing?"

"Mind your business, milady. I'm in charge now!"

Violet started laughing as Christian, easing down under the luxurious mountain of blankets and comforters, began tickling her, and then gasped when she felt his lips on her. "Oh, I definitely think you're pretty much in charge now," she said breathlessly.

For the first time in years, Violet didn't restrain herself, didn't force herself to keep silent for fear the children would hear, didn't worry about a knock on the door, a telephone ringing. She sank into the featherbed and groped for the covers, still trembling from the intensity of what she'd just experienced when Christian wrapped them in the down comforters.

"So, in answer to your question about twenty-something blondes, why indeed settle for less?" Christian whispered, exhausted and at last ready for sleep. Violet cradled him in her arms and listened contentedly to the even rise and fall of his breathing.

"I've got a computer you can use – and I'll respect your hour just before dawn," Christian said all of sudden in a dreamy, sleep-induced voice.

"What?" she asked, kissing his hair.

"For your writing, Darling... on the desk across the room."

"Christian, I don't want to tie up your life. You've got the tour, and the sessions and I don't know —"

"The tour is not until the end of March... I can't think of anything better than to come home from the studio tomorrow... find you here. Violet, you won't jeopardize anything. You need this time away, and I need you here."

FEAR OVERWHELMED VIOLET when she woke the next morning. That and silence. There was no coffee grinder going off at five-thirty, no television set blaring on with the forced happy music of cartoons, no demands made on her before she had a chance to gain full consciousness.

The silence of the morning was a new revelation.

Not all men snored.

She woke beside Christian that morning and from under the tangle of thinning, silky, blond hair, saw his face close to hers. He was just beginning to show his age, but here was the sweetness and melancholia that had captured her so many years before. Violet watched Christian sleep, noting how his face softened and was child-like. She imagined how he might have appeared forty years before. Was this the face his mother kissed every night? Gone were the lines, the hard edges stress and responsibility etched into the still fine skin.

She kissed Christian and slipped out of bed, stirring the embers glowing in the fireplace before padding softly across the bedroom to the desk where a laptop computer sat. She switched on the desk lamp and gently opened the computer, cringing at its loud bells and whistles. Christian stirred slightly in the bed, undisturbed.

She took a deep breath and settled in to write.

"WANT TO COME TO the studio with me?"

Violet looked up from proofreading that morning's work and smiled, shaking her head. "You don't mind, do you? I'm really into this research at the British Library. I just can't believe the wealth of material available to me. You just don't know," Violet gushed excitedly. "I mean, to have all this knowledge at my fingertips, knowledge I've been dreaming about, wanting to devour word by word, to have the books – I actually found Harleian 433! Can you believe it? The papers, the paintings, to smell the smells, feel the stones —" she stopped when she saw that he smiled broadly. "I'm doing it again, aren't I? You think I'm crazy."

Christian leaned in and kissed her gently. "No, just incredibly happy."

Mrs. Burnes coughed and offered servings of fresh fruit, then topped off Christian's cup.

"Can we meet for lunch?" Christian asked Violet, taking a last gulp of coffee.

Mrs. Burnes continued shuffling in and out during this domestic conversation which included plans for a drive up to York (*not again, Mister Christian!*) and deciding where to have dinner, making arrangements to bring Violet's things from the bed and breakfast in Westminster. They acted like an old married couple, she thought amusedly.

She'd been a witness to many mornings such as these with Mr. Christian and his girlfriends, but this morning had been different. It was apparent Mr. Christian wanted Miss Ellison to stay and he never looked more serious about a woman. The housekeeper tried not to smile as they exchanged compliments and hinted at last night's intimacies and being all too adorable about it.

The blast of a car horn outside made Mrs. Burnes curse and she slammed down the coffee pot. "I don't know why that boy doesn't come to the door!" she now swore and Violet looked at Christian with raised brows.

"Wait a moment – doorbell," he said, casually picking up another muffin.

Sure enough, there was the doorbell, and off Mrs. Burnes went to answer it. Kevin Wakefield soon entered the dining room with the put-upon housekeeper right behind him. She was still berating Kevin for his lack of manners when it came to car horns.

"Come on, Chris, let's go. You're late – *hello!*" Kevin took off his sunglasses and offered his most charming smile when he noticed who was sitting across the breakfast table. "At least now I know why Christian dropped everything in the middle of a television taping yesterday.

Welcome to London, Miss Ellison."

"Call me Violet," she said, offering a hand.

Kevin leaned over and gave her a kiss on the cheek instead, whispering: "I'll call you a lifesaver!" He then glanced at Christian. He was beaming like a bridegroom the morning after and wouldn't take his eyes from her, though it was easy to see why. Violet Ellison looked positively delicious in the morning. Christian looked positively shagged out.

"C'mon, let's go," Kevin barked good-naturedly. Christian obediently grabbed coat and briefcase, and then as usual searched for his keys.

"In the other pocket," Kevin and Violet said in unison.

"Gotta run," Christian murmured pecking Violet on the mouth. "See you? Dinner at Aubergne de Provence?" "It's a date," Violet whispered and blushed under Kevin's amused scrutiny.

"See you later, Violet," Kevin said and planted a kiss on her cheek before they left.

"Well aren't you the most popular girl at the ball!" Mrs. Burnes chuckled and was amazed when Violet suddenly darted from the living room.

"Chris!"

Violet was at the door, clutching his bathrobe round her. The pale morning light made her breathtaking. Even Kevin had to stare.

"Did I forget something?" Christian murmured, removing his sunglasses and leaning in to plant yet another kiss on her delectable mouth.

Panic set in now and Violet shook her head. *No, Violet; don't tell him about Sam and the kids on the doorstep. That's not the way. Tonight...*

"See you later?" she whispered.

"Gotta go," he laughed, running a hand lightly over her exposed shoulder.

"Y'know what scares me?" asked Kevin as they drove

261 - *Ellen L. Ekstrom*

off.

"Any number of things, Kev…"

"She fits. She really fits in. It looked so natural, you two sitting there."

"I know," Christian said softly. He looked back and waved to Violet, who was standing at the window. Tonight when he returned she'd be waiting for him.

21

Sorry Darling, You Can't Pay for Your Sins With a Credit Card

NED HATED BASKETBALL; he hated it as much as he hated wrestling, and for as long as he could remember he hated basketball. It had nothing to do with his middling height, it was the moronic nature of it, the players' astronomical salaries, the interminable season.

So why then was he watching basketball?

Six case files were open on the coffee table, a dictaphone in his grasp. The fire in the hearth was still blazing and had been alight since five that morning when he woke and decided to get some work done on his most troublesome files. Outside, the February sky was still gray, still dismal. It had rained for six weeks without any sign of a let up. The weather suited his mood.

Getting up to find a cold beer, Ned knocked one of the files onto the carpet. Several pages of handwritten notes slid out of the folder and he picked them up without paying attention, assuming they were deposition notes or research, placing the bowl of popcorn on top of them. It was then Ned recognized Violet's beautiful cursive hand.

Damn her!

He'd never been so angry or so afraid as when Violet called and announced she'd be taking a leave of absence. She was going to England. Ned didn't need to know why. They argued for an hour, with Ned threatening to fire her no less than six times. It didn't faze Violet, who reminded him of favors owed and all the times she'd pulled his bacon out of the fire, the hours of unpaid overtime. She needed to escape, she needed a rest. Twelve weeks at most. Twelve weeks to sort things out and get a much-deserved rest. Twelve weeks to get her sanity back. To get her head on straight. Unpaid.

He finally backed down and offered a ride to the airport after giving her the money for the trip. He owed her so much. It was the least he could do. Besides, if it was the first kick at Sam Ellison's balls, he was glad to do it. But here it was a month later and there wasn't even a postcard. He'd even gone as far as ask that elusive Englishman, George Knightsbridge, what the Hell was going on, only to get nothing. George was as tight-lipped as ever, those blue eyes only stared back, mocking him.

The revenge on everyone must be pretty sweet, Ned thought as he picked up the phone and pressed a rapid dial key.

"Yeah, hi, Sam; it's Ned. I was wondering, any word from Violet?. . . No, can't say that I have; that's why I called – Oxford? Don't know about that... I thought she was going to see her Mowbray cousins or something; I didn't know about going up to Oxford, to tell you the truth. She'd have said something... Sam, Sam, if I knew why she went I'd tell you. Look, I didn't call to argue. How are the kids?... What'd you just say? I can't believe you just said that! Sam, Violet's hurting right now and I know, and you know, that this is something... excuse me, but I couldn't give a damn about your feelings! This isn't about our feelings, but it's our problem. Yeah! It's our problem!" Ned held the phone away from his ear while Sam continued to shout. "Gotta go, Sam; a pleasure as always. Give my love to the kids. Call me if you hear anything." He switched off the phone and picked up a case file.

Damn her! How could she have done it?

He'd be counting the minutes now until she was home.

VIOLET PUT THE telephone receiver back in its cradle and returned to the desk. She'd never lied to the children before. Now she was lying on a daily basis and that greatest of sins weighed heavily on her.

Why had Mamma gone so suddenly? She had an

opportunity to undertake research, to study about castles and knights in shining armor in England, an opportunity that wouldn't come again for a long time. It would be a few more weeks before she was finished. Then she'd be home with presents and photographs and lots of stories to tell. Maybe she'd be able to bring back a sword or a helmet.

That satisfied even Alex.

Oh, the stories Violet could tell...

Mrs. Burnes knocked, and smiling, came in with a tray of dinner, setting it beside the laptop. "Really, Missus Burnes, you didn't have to," Violet thanked her.

"You've been so busy all day, Miss. Did you enjoy your trip to the Abbey?"

"Yes, thank you. I found Anne Nevill's tomb."

"Anne Nevill!" Mrs. Burnes exclaimed, straightening up from the fireplace grating where she tried to stoke the flames into something more substantial than a yellow glow. "Now she was a pathetic queen. I like her story though. Her brute of a father, her tragic sister, her proud, weak mother. And her rotten brother-in-law George of Clarence! Nasty man! Nastier than all of them! Deserved that butt of malmsey, that one! All in all, Anne was the strongest in spirit. And I've always believed she truly liked Richard. I don't think they loved one another as you and Mister Christian, but they were friends and shields for one another against a terrible time. Richard took one too many wrong turns in his life. But isn't it like men to muck things up? Ruin what they have? Play their cards wrong?"

"History buff, Missus Burnes?"

"Not at all, Miss Ellison. Just paid attention to my history teacher – he looked like Laurence Olivier."

"Lucky you!"

"Girls don't have that romance these days! And I do like Anne's story."

"So do I, Missus Burnes. We don't have your medieval history in America. And there's something about the Wars of Roses that is just so —"

"You Americans! There's a lot more to England than medieval gore."

"And a lot more to America than cowboys and Indians."

"Match and set. Someone's always writing a book about the Wars of Roses, though I don't know why; there's so much more to write about."

"This one is about the period between 1468 and 1472. Of Anne and Richard. When I'm finished with the novel I'm going to tackle a history text on the subject. I only wish I had the money to bring my – I suppose since I didn't get the fellowship I can at least study and get a paper done as if I did."

"Don't tell Mister Christian that's the reason you came." Violet blushed and Mrs. Burnes suppressed a smile. "He's your knight in shining armor, isn't he?" the housekeeper giggled.

"He'd like to think that!" Violet laughed.

"Oh, how lovely! What pretty things!" the housekeeper said quite plainly. She had been tidying the nightstands and discovered a photograph of the children on top of Violet's prayer book. "Your niece and nephews, Miss?"

Violet casually took the photograph Mrs. Burnes now waved, being extremely careful not to reveal anything in her movements. Mrs. Burnes was waiting for an answer, obviously, and started to hum one of Christian's tunes as she neatened the photocopied articles and photographs on the table.

"No, Missus Burnes," Violet finally sighed, and adding quite calmly, said, "they're mine."

"I should hope so! That little one is your spitting image down to the eyes. No wonder you've been so despondent, Miss; I'd long for these little ones, too. Maybe we could arrange to have them come for a week —"

"He doesn't know about them, Missus Burnes."

Violet regretted divulging this the moment she saw Mrs. Burnes' eyes blaze. "Is there a Mister Ellison, then?"

She couldn't avoid a direct examination. "Not Ellison, but Peters —"

"Oh, well then! You're divorced! Well, so's Mister Christian. Now that was a nasty break up. But I don't suppose he's told you a thing. So secretive, that one!"

"We're not divorced. But he was having an affair, and I've decided to end it. I needed to get away."

It took a while, but Mrs. Burnes finally nodded and took the photograph back and replaced it in Violet's prayer book, not on top where she'd found it.

"You can only run so far, Miss," Mrs. Burnes said quietly. "He'll have to be told. It's not fair keeping it from him."

"I was going to tell him, but I know what men are like. Once they know you've got kids."

The comment stung as if it had been directed at Mrs. Burnes personally. "Well, you really don't know Mister Christian, do you? Of all the shallow, selfish, women I've seen him with, I thought you were none of them – until now! How could you, Miss?"

Muttering, Mrs. Burnes picked up the sack of dirty laundry and stormed out.

"Missus Burnes!"

Mrs. Burnes didn't heed Violet's pleas that now echoed through the house as Violet followed her. There was laundry to be done and she slammed the door to the washroom in Violet's face.

"You don't understand," Violet said when she found Mrs. Burnes in the kitchen pounding fresh dough into equal, symmetrical loaves.

A round of dough was slammed against the floured board and then dishwater red hands began pummeling it. "Don't I? I understand you've run from a nasty dragon. Oh, I see he's very definitely rescued you from a nasty dragon, hasn't he?" Mrs. Burnes hissed. "And when the

time's right and you've given Mister Peters enough punishment, you'll run back and leave Mister Christian
wondering what the number was of the train that hit him!
How could you, Miss? How could you be so deceitful?"

"Hear me out, Missus Burnes! You don't know what
it was like —"

"What makes you think I'd believe anything you'd tell
me? Why don't you just go back to California and save him
the trouble of finding out?"

Violet began to weep and say that it wasn't like that at
all. If she only knew the half of what her life had been,
Mrs. Burnes would change her opinion.

Mrs. Burnes made no move to comfort her. She had
donned her business-like façade, the one frequently worn
to make Christian's life miserable. At times like those, the
mien was put on. Violet couldn't hope for such charity
now. The coldness in those steel-colored eyes was real.

"You can't say anything to him! I'll tell him," Violet
pleaded.

"You'd be doing us all a great favor if you went
home!" Mrs. Burnes hissed and she left Violet crying in the
pantry. Only Tristan came to see what was amiss, pushing
his soft, graying muzzle into the hands that now hid her
face. He licked the salt tears and then curled up at her feet.
An hour later he was still there when Violet, at last weary
of feeling sorry for herself, decided to go for a walk. Mrs.
Burnes watched her leave. Gray eyes peered out from the
reading glasses and quickly returned to the *Times*
crossword.

Violet didn't return home until after dark. Mrs.
Burnes still wasn't talking, and so Violet made herself a
sandwich and went upstairs. It reminded Violet of those
times where she'd disappointed her mother and father.
Why, at the age of forty-two, she felt she needed anyone's
approval, much less a judgmental, cantankerous
housekeeper's, wasn't really clear, unless it was because
that housekeeper was in Christian Walsh's employment.

That evening when Christian returned home, Violet was in the shower. She'd been there a while, standing under the stream and letting the hot water pound her, letting Mrs. Burnes' judgment on her pound in her brain.

What if she was right?

She heard the bathroom door open and saw his silhouette against the opaque shower doors, watched him move silently back and forth in his nightly ritual of preparing for bed. It was quiet and, unlike everything Sam did, failed to call attention to himself. She could hear Christian humming a song, something he'd been working on for days now. His other obsession, Christian once teased. And when she had asked what the other was, he had kissed her.

"How was your day?"

Christian had joined her in the shower, taking the soap from her and working it into a lather. He stood behind her and let the rich, perfumed suds slide down her shoulders and arms to her wrists and hands. She reached up to caress him and Christian kissed her neck, smoothed the lather across her breasts and down the alluring contours of her abdomen and hips. Violet turned in his arms when she felt his breath quicken, the heat of his body against hers, his caresses and exploration becoming more ardent. Violet raised her mouth to his. Christian's kisses were hard and urgent, but unlike that first night in London, he was deliberately slow and gentle in rousing her, knowing what the result would be.

The fire started to rise in Violet as Christian gave her a torpid and sensual massage, moving deliberately from her face to her ankles. Soon his mouth replaced his hands, his lips and breath warm and exciting as they retraced his path. She couldn't relax. Violet begged for him, but Christian held back until his own climax was imminent and they shared an orgasm so violent yet exquisite that it would haunt their memories for days and months to come.

"So how was your day?" he asked breathlessly.

"Oh, it was pretty routine," Violet gasped; "until now."

He laughed and brushed the water from her eyes, then reached around her to turn off the shower. "Chris, d'you ever think you've done me a favor?"

"I thought I just did!"

"No! I mean, giving me the plane tickets?"

He wrapped her in a towel and then gently dried her face.

"If I remember, I did some pretty impressive groveling to get you here. You're doing me a favor, Darling." Then he kissed her and said, "I love you, Violet." Her melancholic smile prompted him to lift her face towards his. "I'll do whatever it takes," he whispered.

Violet woke just after midnight and turned in bed, finding herself alone. At first she panicked, then lay down against Christian's still-warm pillow on his still-warm side of the bed. When the clock downstairs struck one she got out of bed and went looking for him.

He was in the studio. Usually the door was locked, but Violet turned the latch and found it open. She looked in and found Christian at the piano, working on a new tune. He didn't hear her come in.

Music and words came together in pieces, minuscule montages that formed a romantic, enigmatic love ballad when all combined. It began with a vision of a sunrise in a city of gold far away, of a woman in his arms, of violets growing in gentle pastures, of a woman called Violet.

Christian finished for the night, looking exhausted but elated. He was surprised as he turned and found Violet standing in the corner. Wordlessly she came to his welcome arms and he held her tighter, feeling her tears stinging his face.

"Darling? Is everything okay?"

"Just hold me," Violet whispered.

CHRISTIAN WATCHED VIOLET make a trail of peas and carrots from the mountain of mashed potatoes, then barely acknowledge Mrs. Burnes when she came in and asked if there was anything else. Christian waited and then shook his head, his eyes on Violet. He suggested Mrs. Burnes go out for a movie or something.

"Did you two have a fight?" Christian wanted to know when the housekeeper was as last gone.

"No," Violet lied and smiled prettily, resuming her construction project on the Wedgwood china.

"Look, I know she's a bit much to take most days."

"It's nothing, Chris."

"Well, something's not right," Christian grumbled; "I'm used to Missus Burnes' nasty mood swings, but this?" He shook his head and then went to find the dog for a walk.

The impasse only lasted two days. Mrs. Burnes went out to the garden in search of the cat and found Violet on her hands and knees before the herbs, weeding carefully. The cat, a stray that followed Violet home, was perched on the bricks watching with interest. The morning mist danced round them and settled heavily in the yew trees.

"A nice crop, Missus Burnes," Violet greeted.

Mrs. Burnes lowered her bulk on to the grass and began to delicately pick at the dandelions that had encroached upon the basil and rosemary. They worked together silently until Mrs. Burnes cleared her throat.

"It wasn't my business to tell you yours, Miss," Mrs. Burnes said hesitantly. "I don't know what your situation is like. I only know what a world of good you've done for Mister Christian. I'm sorry, Miss. I didn't want to upset you. I like you. Christian is more like a son to me than my own boys."

They were carefully plucking savory basil leaves and placing them in the wicker basket the cat was trying mightily to bat about with her paws. Violet chased her away and started on the rosemary.

"Go on, Missus Burnes," Violet said when she looked up to wipe the dirt from her nose and saw Mrs. Burnes studying her carefully. "Get it over with."

"I don't think you came here because you love Christian – oh, I think you have some affection, but not the kind of love – well, let me put it to you this way: what happens Miss, when there's nothing more to be said, or when Mister Christian has to go away for another nine, ten months, on tour? Do you go back home and pick up the pieces? Or do you run to another in hopes he'll save you from the dragon?"

"Missus Burnes, I've been fighting dragons and tilting with windmills all my life. I came to England to be with Christian, not to get even. In fact, I didn't know if he would even care if I showed up on his doorstep." Violet hugged herself and ran her hands lovingly over the soft merino wool of Christian's sweater that topped her dress. "The morning he showed up at my bed and breakfast and the look in his eyes when I came down, Missus Burnes, no man has ever looked at me like that. Not even Sam Peters. I wanted that moment to last forever."

"For God's sake, child, you have to tell him, then! You have to make up your mind! No sense dragging it out! This isn't a bloody soap opera! You'll have to come clean with everyone!"

Violet nodded and promised she would.

MRS. BURNES SET a fresh pot of tea in front of Violet and sat in Mr. Christian's place at the table. She poured out the tea for herself and studied her tablemate over the rim of her china cup. "What is it, Missus Burnes?" Violet sighed in singsong.

"Listen to you, little miss!" Mrs. Burnes sighed in mock exasperation. "Aren't we beginning to sound like Mister Christian!"

"I know you want to say something."

"Did you tell him?"

"Tell him what?"

"About the little ones and Mister Peters."

"He started talking about going to York before starting the tour and wanting to give me a Valentine's Day present."

"Coward! It'll only get worse."

Violet absently stirred the sugar cube around in her cup, mindless that the coffee had already gone cold. "I'll call Sam and break the news as gently as I can, and then I'll tell Chris I've made up my mind. Before his birthday next week."

"Birthday! My God, I almost forgot! Well, if you're still in town next week, that is, if he doesn't drag you up to York again, I know a certain young man who hasn't had a decent birthday party in years. Might appreciate it, coming from a certain young lady; might make bad news less."

"Surprise, maybe?"

"Ho!" Mrs. Burnes guffawed. "If that doesn't turn his hair white, I don't know what would! What a way to start your fifties, eh?"

"Conspiring against me, ladies?"

Christian had come in, briefcase and coat in hand, the ubiquitous packet of unopened cigarettes dangling precariously out of a pocket. He leaned over for his cup of coffee and a kiss from Violet, lingering on the kiss. "Oh, enough of that, now!" snapped Mrs. Burnes as she heaved herself up and went about clearing dishes. "It's not like you two haven't been at it all morning – or all night. Eventually you'll both have to get some sleep – I know I'd like to! And at your age, Mister Christian, you ought to be slowin' down!"

Christian glanced at the beloved old housekeeper lumbering out and then at Violet. "I suppose you'll come 'round to sharing the secret," Christian remarked as he leaned down to kiss her again. "But I can think of a dozen ways to make you talk!"

Maybe we could talk now?" Violet hinted.

Christian raised his brows in concern when he saw how worried she looked. She motioned to his chair at the dining room table and he obediently took it. And when she started twisting the linen napkin until it was in knots, he started to feel something he hadn't in a long time – dread and anticipation of the worst.

"You're not leaving me?" he demanded softly.

"No!"

"You're pregnant! Darling, if that's a concern, well, I couldn't be happier —"

"Chris,"

"I know we've only got a few weeks together, and I shouldn't have brought up marriage last night; let's take each day as it comes and not worry about the rest of the world."

"You need to know something, Christian." The car honk outside preempted any further conversation and Violet looked hopelessly at him.

"This can keep 'til later, right? As long as it won't rock my world in a bad way, we can talk later. God, you gave me such a fright! Bye, Darling. Love ya!"

Rock his world? Violet knew it would be worse than the San Francisco Earthquakes of 1906 and Loma Prieta all in one.

22

Happy Birthday, Part One

"WHAT THE HELL was I thinking?" Violet shouted at the top of her lungs; "I was a fool to come here; ever think I could do this!"

Taking the map of London from the passenger seat, Violet glanced at the spidery traces of lines that depicted streets and stopped just in time to avoid hitting a scarlet double-decker bus. A symphony of horns greeted her at every intersection.

"What's the matter with you people?" she shouted in exasperation; "Why can't you bloody drive on the bloody right side of the bloody road?"

"Why don't I pick you up at the studio?" she'd offered that morning. Christian was delighted and took her up on the suggestion. They could go to dinner afterwards, maybe a show.

What Christian didn't know was that Violet had spent the last week planning a surprise birthday party.

She knew she was on the M-something going towards Soho and Old Compton Street. Christian wrote the address of the recording studio down but Violet couldn't find it in the pile of notes, books and articles on the passenger seat. She resorted to asking for directions from a kindly-looking Bobby. An hour and forty-five minutes after leaving the house, Violet pulled up to the studio and spent another fifteen minutes trying to park the Range Rover.

"Violet Ellison...to see... Mister Walsh. Expecting me—" she sputtered at the receptionist as soon as she found the right floor and studio.

Christian, Kevin, Steve and Harry were wired up and wearing cans, going through what seemed the hundredth take on one of Christian's songs. That surge of adrenaline and excitement still coursed through Violet whenever she saw him after even the shortest of separations. Now, as he frowned while trying to make it through his guitar solo without a mistake, he was precious. For a man just turning fifty, Christian still looked sensational. His shirt was open at the neck and a small red mark at his throat was visible: not a cut from shaving, but a testimony of last evening's activities. Draped around his open collar was the tie she'd bought on one of her shopping forays.

When the song was finished the band members howled with laughter. Violet didn't know what was so funny, but it had something to do with Christian. "Hey!" Kevin greeted when he saw Violet up in the booth and motioned for her to come down. Harry and Steve offered kisses in greeting and proposed another game of poker on Wednesday night – provided that she lose this time around.

"You made it," Christian greeted with a kiss.

"So did your car. I went ahead and made reservations at Clarke's. Ready? You can drive," Violet quipped, handing him the car keys. "Damn!" she then swore suddenly as they drove away.

"Something wrong?"

"I left my purse at home."

Christian chuckled and Violet wanted to know why that was funny. "You said, 'I left my purse at home'. I like the sound of it."

"Can we go back for it? I'll only be a minute."

They were back at the house in much less time than it took Violet to drive to the studio. As she hoped, Christian came in with her. He said nothing about the dark hallway when they entered and then nearly died of fright when Violet switched on the lights and they were hit with a wave of balloons and smiling faces, the shouts of *Happy Birthday!*

"Happy birthday, Love!" Violet whispered when Christian caught his breath and his composure.

"That's another thing I like the sound of... Love," he

murmured.

Sally Wakefield claimed Violet's attention toward the end of the evening. Violet had finally taken her shoes off and was curled up on the sofa relaxing, watching Christian and his friends enjoy themselves.

"All by your lonesome?" Sally asked. "You do look tired, Violet."

"I've been feeling off – worn down, I guess. Fighting a cold."

"Please tell me this is forever," Sally begged, offering a sandwich from her plate.

"I wish I could," Violet admitted.

"All I've heard from everyone this evening is how happy and relaxed Christian is. And it's true! It's tantamount to Jesus healing the paralytic, or something! It's truly amazing. You've done in a few weeks what Kevin has tried to do in a lifetime of friendship. And I heard about that Valentine's trip down into Wiltshire – a picnic at Stonehenge! Pricelessly romantic! With Kevin I'm lucky to get a half dozen roses and decent box of chocolates."

Violet wasn't paying attention. She was watching Christian, who had turned in his conversation with one of the recording studio executives and was once more looking for her. They exchanged smiles and Christian went back to talking shop. Moments later he was searching her out again.

Sally nudged her playfully. "Now you see? A hundred women could be in this room and he'd still only have eyes for one."

"I don't flatter myself."

"Oh, I think that admiration is mutual, Sweetie," Sally teased, noting how Violet refused to take her eyes from Christian. "I've never seen two people more in love with each other."

"It's that transparent? Now I have to summon the courage to tell him," Violet murmured as if to herself. "Summon courage?" Sally laughed.

"Yeah – I've always had a problem with telling people how I feel. But I think he knows – at least he will after he sees the present I've given him."

"Good Lord, you didn't spring for that Arabian he's been talking about for years, did you?" Sally laughed.

"A horse? Oh no, something a bit more domestic. I made him a shirt. We went to Jermyn Street, and well, the idea just came to me."

"You made him a shirt?"

"If you knew how much trouble it was getting him out from under my feet to do it – I just hope he likes it. It's impossible to buy something for a man who has everything."

"Everything including you," Sally said, kissing Violet's cheek. "You're priceless, d'you know that? No one will ever be able to compete with that!"

Violet glanced up at Sally from the rim of her wine glass. "That's inferring someone will come along and take my place."

"I didn't mean that – Violet, forgive me. Christ, Kevin's making eyes like he wants to go. Let's make a date for lunch and I'll give you the best apology ever. It's just with Christian's record…"

Sally was saved from digging her grave by the arrival of Kevin with their coats and her purse.

Violet made the lunch date and after bestowing kisses on both Sally and Kevin, walked them to the door. She turned and smiled at Mrs. Burnes who stood at her elbow. "A successful party, Missus Burnes?"

"Better than most," the housekeeper sniffed. "At least as Mister Christian gets older the guests do too. They're not so much inclined to break up musical instruments and throw things on to the carpet like they used to."

Smiling and speechless, Violet took the tray Mrs. Burnes held and started picking up. It was hard to imagine Christian a boy of twenty-one breaking up furniture in a drunken, drug-induced frenzy. But the thought did make her laugh. She was still giggling at the thought when the last of the guests finally said good night and she stood alone at the kitchen sink washing the good crystal by hand.

"Oh now, Miss! You don't have to go to this trouble," Mrs. Burnes chided when she came in with the remnants of the birthday cake. Violet snatched up the cake and passed a fork to her, settling down at the table.

"I kind of enjoy it. I don't wash dishes for fun at home. There, I wash dishes to keep my hands warm. The heater's always on the fritz and the house is so drafty," Violet confessed. "I wash the dishes to forget a lot of things."

"Isn't it amazing how the most mundane of rituals makes us feel better?" Missus Burnes asked, scooping the best of the frosting off the top, but tactfully saving a rose for Violet.

"Missus Burnes," Violet began, "maybe I'm crazy to ask this, but what's this secret Christian has? Everyone looks at me like, 'poor dear! The next victim!'"

"Mister Christian's got more secrets than Victoria, my dear, and they're best left in the past. Besides, why should you worry now? That man's absolutely in love with you and has been since the concert."

Violet cut another slice of cake and dove in. "The concert? He told you?"

"It's all he could talk about. So... if I were you, and I'm not, but I do know Mister Christian pretty well, maybe it's time to share some of your secrets?"

Nodding, Violet finished off the cake and licked the icing from her fingers. She was in one sticky situation.

VIOLET DIDN'T GO up to bed until after two. Christian was still awake, the bed littered with music manuscript paper and notepads of lyrics. His eyes automatically went to the door when it opened and old Tristan bounded in, a new sprightliness in his gait, followed by Violet. She brought with her the sharp night air, a freshness that told him she'd been out walking the dog. He did notice how her eyes were red-rimmed; not from saying up late or taking in too much champagne, but unhappiness.

"Did you like the party?" she asked, starting to undress, purposefully avoiding his gaze.

"Absolutely wonderful, Darling. I still can't believe you did all that for me."

"It's my way of thanking you for all you've done for me." Violet leaned across the bed to kiss him and then reached for her pajamas, disappearing into the bathroom.

"How on earth did you get my mother to come down from York?" he called.

"That was Kevin's hand in the conspiracy. He told your mother you had a proper lady friend and that she had to meet me, because there was no way she'd believe it otherwise!"

Violet returned and from the closet took a garment box. "I hope you didn't think I forgot."

He opened the package with all the excitement of a six-year old and whistled low when he held up the dress shirt. It was made of fine oxford cloth, fine violet stripes on an eggshell ground. "Where'd you get this? Hackett's? Jermyn Street?" he exclaimed. "I bet it put you back a penny or two."

"No; I made it."

"You made it?" His amazement was genuine. "How?"

"I used a technique tried and true for years," Violet confessed. "I waited until you were asleep and then I went down to the living room and used Missus Burnes' ancient machine. It was a challenge, because I've got a machine at home that's computerized and does everything but launch missiles – I bought the fabric at Liberty… so it's okay? You like it?"

"Come here," Christian whispered. He drew Violet into his arms and held her for the longest time. When he released her and she slipped in to bed beside him, the lights went out.

"Violet?"

He'd felt the little body nestled against his, so soft and warm, go rigid. An arm tightened around his shoulders and he next felt the warmth of tears on his tee shirt.

"Darling, don't cry!" he whispered, kissing her brow, her damp eyelids, her chin, and finally, her mouth.

Her response was muffled by the tee shirt and blankets, but it was unmistakable. Christian held her tighter and drew in his breath.

"God, Violet! I've always known... I love you, too! I love you so much; if you only knew how long I've waited."

"The middle of March."

"What?" he asked, smoothing back the hair from her wet cheeks.

"I have to go in the middle of March; I promised only twelve weeks. Every day I look at the calendar —"

"Then we tear up the calendar," Christian laughed.

VIOLET WAS REMOVING the thermometer from under her tongue when Christian came into the bedroom in search of his car keys. He paused and squinted at the read-out. "One hundred and two! Are you sure you don't want to see a doctor?"

"It's just a touch of flu," Violet rasped, trying to swallow a sip of water. "I didn't get a flu shot this year, and there were at least four people at the party coughing up their guts."

"You're staying in bed, milady."

"Christian! The show! I want to go to the show. Tony Carlisle is like Jay Leno!" she whined.

That evening Fortinbras was making an appearance on one of Britain's most popular talk shows. Christian could talk of nothing else for a week and to prove he wore his heart on his sleeve, he'd donned the shirt she'd made, as well as a tie she'd found at Harrods's the day after his birthday when he said he had to have something to go with the shirt. This was the shirt he'd worn for a publicity photo, for the new album cover. A week had passed since his birthday and the novelty had yet to wear thin. Violet amusedly thought she'd have to wait for him to fall asleep before sneaking the shirt down to the laundry.

"Let me come?" Violet croaked, luring him gently closer by grabbing on to the tie, and when he was within striking distance, gave him such a kiss that Christian had second thoughts about going over to the studio early, didn't care if he'd catch her godforsaken virus.

"A thousand times no and then some," he said between kisses. "I want you to still be alive and with me when I'm presented to the Queen. You see, my pathetic love, tonight we're going to announce our inclusion on the list for Queen's Honours."

"Knighthood?" Violet gasped.

"Looks like you got your knight on horseback, Darling!"

He was out again after a quick kiss and Violet was glad of that, for he would have seen her tears and he would have asked why. And there was no way Violet could tell him the truth now. She knew Christian now considered her an extension of himself. He only wanted to be in her company, to listen to her, to watch her perform menial, daily tasks as if they were marvels of natural science, to laugh with her and make love, to fall asleep in her arms.

But for how long? What would happen when he knew she'd been lying to him all this time?

What was it Granny Mowbray used to say?

Once you start running from your life, you have to keep running. Eventually it will all catch up with you.

"It's almost eight! Turn the channel!" Violet called as she came from the kitchen with an enormous bowl of popcorn and a six-pack of sodas, a box of tissues and an aspirin bottle. Jemma Wakefield leapt to her feet and grabbed the remote control from Julia, clicking so expertly that Sally commented it was an art she'd learned from her father.

"Violet, we can watch it upstairs – I don't like that green tinge around your eyes and mouth," Sally teased when Violet plopped down on the sofa.

"I'm not dying – yet. I've been upstairs all day, so indulge me – oh look! Photos of the boys – really, really old photos! My God! Please tell me Christian still doesn't have that shirt – I'll find it and burn it!"

Stills of the band were superimposed over the show titles and Sally roared with laughter as various shots of Kevin, from his Edwardian – Carnaby Street days, to his hippie gear, to the disco era, were shown to the whole of England.

"Is Daddy going to make an ass of himself?" Tamsin wanted to know.

"Tamsin! What did Daddy say about using filthy language?" Jemma chided, and tossing back her ponytails, offered to help Mrs. Burnes with the tray of fruit juice and snack foods, dividing the cookies equally between her sisters and herself.

"You've been a positive influence on her, Violet," Sally giggled as she watched her eldest daughter mimic Violet's moves and tone of voice, her interaction with the younger girls.

"I love children," Violet responded.

"Are you going to marry Christian, Violet?" Tamsin demanded. "If you marry Christian, you can have babies of your own. Daddy says when you get your mess sorted out at home, you're going to come back to London and marry Christian. Daddy says Christian can't live without you – says he's soddy over you."

Not knowing what to say, Violet let her eyes slide from Sally to Mrs. Burnes and waited for the slow burn rising in her cheeks to subside before responding. Fortunately, Sally jumped in. "Sometimes people have secrets they don't want to share with new friends – not yet, at least. And sometimes people listen to conversations when they should be in bed asleep! Now, both of you, no more tonight, and no telling tales out of school – or Daddy will have a talk with you when he gets home," Sally gently scolded.

"Thank you!" Violet whispered, passing a cup of coffee.

"It's back on!" Jemma shouted.

London Tonight was one of the most popular shows in England, as evidenced by the packed house. The camera panned an audience full of Fortinbras' fans spanning two generations and Sally swore she'd never seen anything like it. Tony Carlisle, a handsome, graying, man in his fifties, came out after the studio band's introduction and pronounced he would go home – Fortinbras was all anyone there wanted to see that night. He went on to say that the phones had been ringing off the hook for tickets to the show, especially since Christian Walsh was in the house. No one had the bloody right to look that good and be that old.

The women in the audience went into a frenzy and Mrs. Burnes nudged Violet. "Doesn't it make you proud?" she murmured to Violet.

"Doesn't it make you jealous?" Sally muttered. "The idea of those women all over my Kevin – and knowing he'd enjoy every bloody minute of it!"

After forty-five minutes of banter, jokes, starlets plugging their latest flicks and politicians expounding on what's good for the United Kingdom, Fortinbras at last made its appearance to a thunderous ovation.

"I knew it! Daddy looks like a fool!" Jemma moaned.

"Where did he get those leather pants?" Sally wailed.

"Harry," Violet and Mrs. Burnes said in unison.

Violet expected to hear Dark Forest, but Kevin, with much bravado, announced they were going to debut Christian's latest song, *A Knight on Horseback*.

"Well we know who he wrote that for, don't we?"

Mrs. Burnes chuckled, nudging Violet.

"He wrote a song for you?" exclaimed Sally.

"Quiet, please!" Jemma instructed.

When the song ended, the audience was stunned into silence and then it suddenly erupted into an ovation Sally swore she'd never witnessed in her life with the band, not since *Dark Forest* was performed at the Prince of Wales' concert in 1969.

The camera zoomed in on Christian as he took his bows, and then switched to Kevin, Harry and Steve as they alternately beamed with pride and satisfaction. Kevin caught a rose thrown by one brave woman in the front row and tucked it behind his ear, to which Jemma replied that she wanted to die right there; she'd never be able to show her face at school ever again. He was still wearing the rose when they sat down to chat with Tony Carlisle.

The interview was predictable, including Kevin's mention of their inclusion on the Honors list, and after the audience acknowledged Fortinbras' collective elevation to knighthood, Tony Carlisle turned to Christian.

Then it all started going bad for Violet.

"You've been seen around town with a very striking, very lovely, young woman, Christian. There's speculation that she's the one. Any truth to the rumor?"

The camera zoomed in on Christian and he shrugged.

Don't say a word, Christian; please don't say a word!

"She's a friend, a very good friend," Christian said, a nervous smile on his lips.

No, Christian! You promised!

"I hear she's more than that. Care to fill us in?"

"Well, she's from California – visiting England, you know. She's an historian – doing research on medieval England at the University here, and at Oxford. We met in San Francisco."

"Romantic city, San Francisco," the host teased.

"Yeah... well, yeah."

"Care to tell us how you met?"

Please Christian, don't! You made a promise…

"It's a priceless story," Kevin offered.

Christian recounted his meeting with Violet and then ended by announcing proudly that she'd sewn the shirt he was wearing, which drew a round of applause. The host replied that the women in the audience were all going out after the show to kill themselves now that it was apparent Christian Walsh, the British music industry's most eligible bachelor, was finally off the market.

Tony asked Christian to tell her name. After encouragement from the band and the audience, the camera once again zoomed in on Christian and stayed there when he said:

"Violet Ellison. She's absolutely marvelous, she's absolutely wonderful, everything to me. I'm besotted, absolutely, besotted. Love's wonderful, isn't it?"

That was all Violet needed to hear. She excused herself and went outside to the herb garden where Mrs. Burnes found her a half-hour later.

"Sally and the girls left just now. I told them it was the flu." Mrs. Burnes said, coming up.

"How long d'you think it'll be before it gets back to the States?" Violet said after a time.

"It may not. I know Fortinbras is still news in America, but not that big. Not like their early years."

"Not that big? Missus Burnes, every time they announce a concert in the Pink Section of the Chronicle, you can't get tickets a half-hour later!"

"That's as may be, but the boys won six awards at the British Music Awards last year and that barely made it into the *Times*. Everyone was more concerned about one particular little diva from America showing up in a skin-tight dress that barely covered her bum, and how she could barely make it through her tired one little hit."

"The one who tried to stick her tongue down Christian's throat backstage?" Violet drawled and that set them both to laughter. "God, Missus Burnes, I hope you're right. I'm just mad at Christian for breaking his promise. We agreed to keep me out of the press."

"Looks like the time has come to come clean, Sweetie. Now come inside before the paparazzi show up at the door."

When Violet turned a ghastly shade of green, Missus Burnes looped her arm through Violet's and said she was teasing.

The paparazzi weren't on the doorstep by morning – they followed Christian from the studio. Violet watched him from the bedroom window as he bantered and posed, then told the blokes that he had to go upstairs and do some explaining. Christian was still in a good mood when he entered the bedroom and said he was no doubt in a lot of trouble.

Turning, Violet said he had no idea how much and how high he'd stepped into it.

23

Lovely Carol, What Do We Have Behind Door Number Two?

ELISABET WOKE TO find Max curled up in her bed. Since Mamma's departure this had become a habit – annoying for Elisabet, but she understood all too well what he was going through. Elisabet felt the desperation and fear she knew her brothers felt – wondering if Mamma would ever come back. True, she said only twelve weeks, but how often did a mother suddenly pick up and go half way around the world to study something she could do in the comfort of her living room? Elisabet now drew Max close and Max protested sleepily, his thumb finding its way to his rosebud mouth.

Poor little Max! What would he do when he discovered the trouble started with his birth? It wasn't his fault, of course, but Elisabet marked the change from the day Mamma bought the pregnancy test kit and watched as the stick turned blue. Everyone else in the family was excited that Mamma was pregnant again – even Mamma, though she was thirty-nine when Max arrived. Dad, however, tried to pretend that nothing was going on, that it wasn't important. And when Max was born, he didn't think it was important enough to leave the studio to greet his youngest and last-born into the world.

Elisabet remembered the argument Dad had with Grammy Am. She'd never heard her grandmother raise her voice to Dad, not even when he was being the biggest jerk, but that night she called her son the worst names mentionable… Elisabet now squeezed Max so tightly that he squealed like a little piglet and squirmed out of her arms.

Even though it was Saturday she dragged herself out of bed as the grandfather clock chimed seven, going downstairs to start breakfast. That was nothing new. Not finding the television on and her mother asleep on the sofa was uncomfortably new.

Once the coffee was started, Elisabet went into the living room and switched on the television. She folded the laundry and then picked up after her brothers and father – toys, clothes, shoes, the contents of Sam's briefcase scattered from one end of the living room to the other.

"Mamma?" Alex was in the doorway. His expectant face grew dark when he saw it was only his sister. "It's just *you*. When's she coming home?" he demanded, following her into the kitchen.

"Look at the calendar – she said twelve weeks. Sometime in mid-March."

"She's dead! She died in a car crash like Auntie Bella!"

"No she isn't. I talked to her last night."

"Your mother called? Why didn't you wake me?"

Sam had shuffled in, yawning and making his lion noises to the delight of the little boys. He paused by the stove where Elisabet now stirred a pot of sticky, lumpy, oatmeal – the way Violet liked it – and took a slice of bacon directly from the frying pan, plopping it into his mouth. The grease splattered on to Elisabet's smiley-face tee shirt. She said nothing of his *faux pas* and accepted the good morning kiss he offered. He looked terrible, smelled terrible, and bravely Elisabet so informed her father.

"Your mother's gonna kill you for eating this shit," Sam joked, taking the last of the bacon in a paper towel.

Elisabet said nothing and sent Alex to watch TV and released Max from the high chair with a sippy cup of juice, and then resumed washing the dishes. Sam frowned. Why was it the women in this family resorted to washing dishes by hand whenever they were angry? The dishwasher had been empty for weeks, but every dish in the house was clean. And then she said and did something completely out of character for her, but reminded Sam painfully of Violet.

Elisabet turned on him angrily, trembling. "Okay, I can't keep quiet any longer. Have you always been in denial?" she demanded.

"Hey now, I'm not the one who ran off to England."

"No, but name a month of the year you haven't been running off to save this fucking account, or that, or lying to Mom about money, or meeting with that fat, stupid, whore of a cow."

"Now hold on, young lady!"

"No. She knows about you and Marjorie. I know about you and Marjorie. Your mother and father know! So why don't you come clean?"

"Is that why she's been — is that why she's gone?" Sam asked, his tone sincerely one of discovery.

"Why can't you apologize and give her the respect and attention she deserves?"

"Apology?" Sam squealed. "Who's been moping around since her sister died?"

"I can't believe I just heard that," Elisabet said, taking a sponge to the table. The blue sponge. "Maybe that's why she's gone to meet that musician she's always been in love with!"

"Oh, c'mon now, Beth! Where do you get this stuff? One of your mother's stories?"

"She meets Christian Walsh at Christmas, she disappears to England, put two and two together, Dad. It doesn't make sixteen! Call it revenge sex!"

"You don't believe that," Sam scoffed, but his stomach was in knots.

"I believe what's out there. Maybe you would too if you didn't have your nose in your ad copy."

"Don't start!"

"Well if you don't believe me, ask George! He knows more about Mamma than you do! And he cares more about her! She left because of you! Because you're never here! You're always gone on a business trip somewhere, and there's always something wrong with an account! You make her stay here and you suffocate her, find excuses to shoot her dreams out of the sky! You never listen to her!"

Sam tried to embrace her but Elisabet backed away, another trait learned from her mother. He took a deep breath and composed himself. "She's doing research on her medieval stuff in England," Sam replied quietly, evenly. "She's coming back. Your mother isn't the kind to run away from things."

Elisabet threw the sponge in the sink and then smiled down at Max, who had returned with his empty cup. She scooped him up saying, "C'mon. I'll take you guys to the park."

The playground was several blocks away at Oxford School. It was a meeting place for most of the children and parents in the neighborhood. Elisabet had played there with her brothers for as long as she could remember and kept the weekly outing in the schedule. Mrs. Tremble was there with her daughter Mrs. Newsome and the Newsome's obnoxious twins, The Five-Year-Olds, as were the Chamberlain kids with their au pair and Alex's best friend Justin. Justin and Alex immediately ran to claim spots on the brightly-colored play structure while Elisabet settled on a bench to read. Max immediately tried to bury her feet in the cold, damp, sand.

"Hello, Beth."

Mrs. Tremble was smiling down at her. It would be impolite to turn the neighborhood gargoyle away and Elisabet knew it wasn't the best course to take right now, not with the entire neighborhood speculating about what has happening at 1540 Oxford Street. She smiled hello and hoped that would be the end of it.

"How are The Five-Year-Olds?" Elisabet wanted to know. She really didn't, but it would keep the conversation off the Ellison-Peters children.

"Fine, thanks," Mrs. Tremble answered, inviting herself to sit down. "Look at those two boys! Max and Alex are sure shooting up. Tall like their dad and handsome. I always wondered why he wasn't a model or actor. How's Sam doing?"

"The usual."

"Hear from your mother? She's doing a school term abroad, I hear."

"Yeah. The chance came and she took it."

"Beth! Beth!"

Elisabet looked toward the street and saw a tall blond man coming towards her. *George!* Elisabet waved George over, her eyes registering thanks and relief.

"Beth," George greeted and then smiled inquisitively at Mrs. Tremble.

"Missus Tremble, this is George Knightsbridge." Elisabet introduced and looked up at George, shielding her eyes from the bright morning sun behind him. "George is a friend of the family's. Visiting history professor at Cal. Roman Britain, Celtic."

Mrs. Tremble simpered as George gallantly took her hand and lingered over it, offering a kiss. "A professor? So young," she said.

"I started when I was twelve," George explained and winked at Elisabet.

The Five-Year-Olds were causing a disturbance in the sand box and Mrs. Tremble excused herself to help her daughter cart them home. George took her place on the bench.

"Thank you!" Elisabet whispered.

"You're welcome."

George watched Alex as he tried to swing Max's enormous teddy bear. Max was piling sand on the stuffed toy. "Where is she really, George?" Elisabet asked, not taking her eyes from her brothers.

"Doing research —"

"Don't pile on the bullshit, George," Elisabet sighed. "I know about my dad and the Rotherwell bitch, I know Mamma met Christian Walsh."

"Ouch, you certainly inherited your mother's flair for bluntness."

"If I see a duck, I call it a duck." Elisabet frowned

and then glanced at George. "If she was going to have an affair, why couldn't it have been you?"

"Pardon?"

"Every time I'm out with the boys or with my friends, people stare and I know what they're thinking and saying. It would have been easier if she'd decided to sleep with you instead of running away to the other side of the world."

"Me? Why do you think there's anything between your mother and me?"

"I see it in her eyes. It's the look she used to give to Dad."

"No, Beth. We're friends from a lifetime ago. She's a little sister to me. I was in love with Isobel and Isobel hurt me terribly. Seems like the women in your family have a way of tearing out men's hearts."

Elisabet was about to speak when she realized what he had said. She turned to face him with wide, respectful eyes, seeing him in a new light. "I guess I wasn't imagining things. Auntie Bella was a bitch to everyone, especially Mamma. Blonde syndrome, I guess! It goes with being blonde and beautiful."

George laughed uneasily. "I guess."

"You would know."

Elisabet shoved her hands in her pockets and watched the flight of two sea gulls as they descended on the park. "I know Dad's hurt her but I'm angry because she's hurting everyone else."

"And you don't think your mother's hurting? She's been hurting far longer than the few weeks you have. Let go of your anger Beth. Forgive her and love her."

Elisabet choked back her tears and nodded. She wanted to be held and to be comforted. In the last six weeks her father hadn't offered as much as a hug.

And now George offered. But she didn't accept his embrace for he was as much a stranger as a friend. She did accept his handkerchief, however. Then she cried long and hard. George let her get it out and then said: "It won't be long, Beth. But remember. Forgive her and love her."

SAM WAS ASLEEP on top of the laundry on the sofa when Elisabet returned from grocery shopping later that afternoon. He stirred from his nap and wanted to know what was up. More and more time was spent sleeping on the sofa those days. Less working in the studio and even less doing housework. Carrie and Thornton were always at the door wondering when Sam was coming back and to ask his approval or advice on an account.

"Where are the boys?" Elisabet asked with motherly concern.

"Max went down kicking and screaming for a nap and Alex is asleep on your bed."

She started cleaning the living room, removing articles of clothing from Parsifal and rearranging the photographs on the mantle, picking up newspapers and coloring books, muttering under her breath as Violet often did when the chore was left to her.

"You've turned into an old woman, Beth," Sam laughed. Elisabet didn't find that funny in the least and Sam was saved from his daughter's wrath by the doorbell.

"It's Carrie or Thornton. Those space cadets probably blew up the studio," Elisabet muttered on her way out to the hall. She was back moments later with her arms full of packages and mail. "Mom's got a registered letter from a publisher, and here is some stuff from her. I bet this one's for Alex... Alex! Alex, come 'ere! Alex! There's a birthday present from Mamma!" Elisabet shouted and got out of the way as Alex thundered into the living room from upstairs. Sam placed the letter from the publisher on the mantle and glanced at the letter from Violet that he'd received. Curious, as Violet seldom wrote a postcard. It was thick and scented with her trademark freesia. He tossed it on the coffee table and then knelt down to see what it was that had come all the way from

England.

Both boys had 'Oxford University' tee shirts. There was a sweatshirt jacket from Oxford for Sam, and a poster for Elisabet. Max received a huge plush dog wearing the Union Jack. Alex had a play set of Britain's Knights, complete with castle, horses and artillery. Elisabet moaned that she'd be stepping on the tiny, little swords and cannon balls for years, and went into the kitchen to start dinner. Secretly, she rejoiced that her mother had not forgotten and then scolded herself for thinking she would.

Dinner was laid on TV trays in the living room, a sacrilege in the Violet Ellison Book of Etiquette, but Sam again said that Violet wasn't around to see it and they could always hide the evidence if she should come home unexpectedly.

Sam commandeered the remote control and channel surfed in search of basketball scores when Elisabet demanded he keep it on Channel Four so she could watch the weekend installment of *Entertainment Tonight.* It was the usual ménage of stories on the usual superstars and industry flavors of the month, until an item on the awards recently heaped on the legendary British rock band, Fortinbras.

"Can we watch something else?" Elisabet demanded, feeling uneasy as the commercials rolled and tried to take the remote control from her father, who seemed to be interested.

And then Elisabet's heart started to pound in her chest so violently that she thought it would explode and rocket out of the cavity like an alien fetus.

"...Violet Ellison. She's absolutely marvelous; she's everything to me. Besotted, absolutely besotted." Christian Walsh was saying in the videotape of an interview held yesterday.

There was the handsome, aging blond rocker sitting on a talk show host's sofa confessing his love for Violet Ellison.

The clip cut away to a tape of Christian performing, then one of Christian, surrounded by event staff and security guards, leaving a concert venue with her mother, who looked happy – happier than Elisabet had seen her in years.

Elisabet pried the remote control from her father's hand and snapped the 'off ' button. The boys protested, but she shouted at them to go to their room and then turned to her father.

"It's okay, Beth," Sam said quietly, his eyes still riveted to the black screen.

"Wasn't far from the truth, was I?" she muttered.

"Did you know?"

"I had a suspicion. We all did. George, Grammy Am, even Ned."

"Did she tell you to keep it a secret?"

"No!"

"Don't lie for her, Elisabet."

"Dad, I said no. But put two and two together. After the charity ball she acted so strange, especially whenever she listened to their music."

"Do you know how they met?"

"No."

"The concert!"

"Maybe you should have gone with her to the concert."

"Bastard!" Sam hissed, pushing away his T.V. tray so violently Elisabet had to grab the dishes.

"You don't know if it's serious —"

"She's not getting away with this!"

Elisabet heard her father repeat this to his mother later that night and it surprised her that her grandmother would defend her daughter-in-law so passionately.

"You can't threaten to take away the children from her, Sam! Be reasonable! For God's sake, listen to yourself! Do you think you're not at fault here?" Grammy Am argued.

"She lied to me! She lied to the kids! What kind of mother does that, for Chrissake?" Sam shouted back.

"Please tell me it's the pot calling the kettle black, because that's what it is, Sam. Don't try to use this to justify or explain away your infidelities. No, damn it! You don't think your father and I knew about the women? How long did you expect Violet to stay silent and put up with your nonsense?"

"She's deserted the kids, Mom! Do you think a judge will ignore that?"

"She took a twelve-week vacation! And maybe she really is doing research. You know Violet."

"No, I don't!"

"Well, whose fault is that? Now I suggest that when she gets home you two sit down and talk – and for once in your life, listen to her."

"I don't want to talk. I don't want her near the kids!"

"You're not serious!"

"The Hell I'm not! It's called desertion, Mother! You can call it a vacation and she can call it twelve-weeks screwing Christian Walsh, but it all comes down to abandoning her kids!"

Elisabet had heard enough. Choking back her tears, she went to the living room closet and dug Violet's cell phone out of the hope chest. Pressing a rapid-dial number, she counted the seconds until Ned answered and then asked if he could get a message to Violet.

24

But I Thought You Wanted a Knight on Horseback…

CHRISTIAN SCRIBBLED NED Percy's telephone number on the back of an envelope and stuffed it into his jacket pocket, scooped up his keys in a single movement.

"Missus Burnes! Missus Burnes!"

The housekeeper peered around the living room door and scowled in question.

"Are the bags in the car?" Christian demanded.

"All of them – though why you should need so many."

"Right. We'll see you on Sunday."

Saying goodbye, he slammed the front door. That telephone call bothered him more than he let on. Any call from California meant the twelve weeks were almost gone and Violet's departure was certain. He didn't want to think about it.

His black mood abated, however, when he walked through the library reading room and through a forest of carrels, knowing exactly where she'd be. Christian came upstairs and first saw the boots, one crossed over the other, the socks and leggings, then the gigantic fisherman sweater pulled over a lacy tee shirt and those incredible, shapely legs.

He came around the carrel and gently removed the headphones from the short yet sexy hair, whispering, "Don't you get tired of that song?"

She glanced up and smiled. "It's your song."

"No, it's *your* song. Let's go for a drive," he said now and helped her gather books and papers.

"Where?"

"You'll see."

They drove out of London and north through the Midlands. "Are we there yet?" Violet asked when they stopped at Leicester for dinner.

"Not quite."

"Well, where exactly are you taking me?" she wanted to know when he slid into the bed of their room at the White Hart in Lincoln.

"You'll see in the morning," Christian laughed and switched off the lights. "Come here!"

They were up well before dawn and on the road again, taking the A6108 north and just as the sun started to rise, Christian pulled over to the side of the road.

"Wake up, Darling; we're here. Violet? Sweetheart?"

Violet woke from her catnap in the passenger seat and started to protest, saying the morning was too cold and he was acting too strange, but then she saw it – the massive keep of a castle in ruins.

"Middleham!" she exclaimed.

"Since you're researching Richard and Anne, what better place to come than their home? Breath the air, touch the stones. I know the curator. You're about to get a private tour."

"Chris!" she squealed happily.

The look on her face told Christian he'd receive a thank you of the best possible kind for this gesture and he took her down to the castle.

Violet wandered the ancient stronghold of the mighty Nevills, as excited as a child on Christmas morning. This was the place Richard of Gloucester called home; for it was here he spent critical years of his youth under the tutelage of Richard Nevill, earl of Warwick. And it was here that he first made the acquaintance of his wife, Warwick's daughter, Anne. It was here he came after the battles of Barnet and Tewksbury to be the King's lieutenant and Lord of the North. It was his greatest success, befriending the heretofore unruly northern shires of England and making it secure for the Crown. That affinity would help and hinder him.

Violet stood in awe in the middle of the roofless great

hall, watched as birds and clouds floated above them, climbed stairs carpeted by mossy grass to rooms that now harbored birds and small animals, rooms long since vanished, and touched the stones that once held life, wondered what they might have looked like on a typical weekday morning.

"Did you remember your camera?" Violet asked, coming back to the twentieth century when he asked if it would do. Christian had indeed remembered, and he immediately pulled it out, demanding a photograph. Violet spent most of the roll on Christian.

"What d'you think? Think it's on the market, milady?" Christian teased, coming up behind her.

"I wish!"

"It's in need of some paint, a roof."

"A real fixer-upper!"

He leaned against the tower wall and pulled her towards him for a kiss. "Ever make love in a castle, milady?" he whispered.

"Here?" Her eyes were wide and the darkest, prettiest shade of green. It might have been freezing and snow lay on the ground in insurmountable drifts, but the sky had turned a brilliant shade of sapphire and the clouds had long since evaporated, the sun was starting to warm the stone. There wasn't a living soul for miles. Christian knew Violet was game when she pulled him into a vestibule and started unbuttoning her sweater, guided his hands under the soft wool.

"Jesus, Violet! What are you doing to me?" he gasped after they kissed.

They drove to the Priory that night and spent the hours until dawn making love, both afraid to hold back, knowing the twelve weeks were now only a handful of days. On the way back to London, Christian wrote another song for Violet, scribbling lyrics on an envelope at their rest stops and hiding it when Violet wanted to know what he was up to. By the time they arrived in London the song was done.

And then it all blew up in Christian's face.

Christian had been content for the first time in years. Tranquil was a better word. Around his table were his friends and the people he most loved. That evening not even Mrs. Burnes' grumbling could move him to distraction.

Across the table, Kevin had as usual claimed Violet for conversation. From what snatches he heard, they were arguing about medieval military tactics, something he knew Kevin had no idea of, and wouldn't waste a quid bet- ting on chances of Violet's making a fool of him. Sally and Will's wife Martha were exchanging photographs of children and dogs. Steve's adolescent-appearing girl friend was now asking him how long he and Violet had been married and Christian smiled. Earlier in the evening Will had remarked that Violet and he looked and acted like a couple that had been together for ages.

"Like you and Martha?" Christian complimented.

Very little could perturb him now. He wanted time to stop right there and stay in that moment for all eternity, but Mrs. Burnes came into the dining room looking as if her liver were acting up. Instead of going directly to Christian, she approached Violet, who was inches away from him, reaching into her bottomless apron pocket for a slip of paper. She unfolded it and gave it to Violet. At that moment Christian remembered the call from Ned Percy and his stomach took a dive. Jesus, he'd forgotten about the publishing offer! They'd given her a week to accept it. He'd have to do some clever lying to get out of this one.

And then in a voice surely meant for Violet's ears alone Mrs. Burnes said: "Oh my dear, I hope this doesn't ruin your holiday, but you got a call from California. Sam Peters called; then your daughter, and then Ned Percy. I hope nothing's wrong?"

Hearing this, Christian took a pull from his whiskey neat and avoided both Mrs. Burnes' nervous smile and

Violet's ashen face as they pressed by on their way to the kitchen.

Daughter?

Sam Peters?

Who the hell was Sam Peters?

He pretended not to care or pay attention as Violet got ready for bed. It was a small pleasure, watching as she undressed and slipped into her pajamas and her soft, perfumed bathrobe, as she brushed out her hair and then talked to the dogs. He picked up the music manuscript pages from the bed spread and now pretended to be interested in this latest gift to Violet.

Sooner or later, she'd have to confess her sin of omission. He'd forgive her, that was granted, but she'd have to know how much her secrecy hurt him. Christian wondered how much more was being held back.

Rather than slip into bed beside him and use his shoulder as a backrest as she usually did, Violet switched on the computer and opened a folder of notes.

"That's a pretty impressive contract for a first outing."

Christian referred to the publishing contract Ned Percy had faxed from San Francisco only minutes ago.

Strangely, Violet didn't seem as impressed as he was. She was distracted and Christian didn't want to ask why, not yet.

"I've gotten offers before, and had them blow up in my face. Time will tell; though I trust Ned's judgment."

"Trust is a good thing."

She turned, curious by the tone of his voice. He glanced over the music sheets and smiled. Violet recognized the smile as one usually offered to a victim before the kill.

"I've always thought so," she said.

"Have you?"

"I trust you, silly!"

"How old is your daughter?"

The soft clicking of the keys answered him first.

"Violet?"

Violet, without turning said, "She just had her twentieth birthday."

"Look like you?"

"Uh, no; no, she looks like her father – dark, dark eyes, very tall."

"I see."

Again, the clickety-click of keys pressed against the laptop keyboard.

"Does she know where you are?"

"Huh? Oh, she knows I'm in London."

"Okay." The voice was like a public defender's on cross-examination. It was making Violet sweat. Behind her she heard the crumpling of paper and Tristan's soft thumping of his tail on the bedspread. A match was struck and then the unmistakable scent of a newly lit cigarette, as intoxicating as it was annoying.

"Violet, were you ever going to tell me?"

"Lots of times, and then there was always something I'm sorry, Chris!"

"Anything else I should know about?"

"She's got two little brothers, eight and three, no, his birthday's in August, he's two."

Christian put down the glass of water before he spilled it and nodded, saying: "dark like their father, no doubt?"

"Except Max, the two-year-old, he looks the most like me."

"And what about their father? Would that be Sam Peters?"

"What about him?"

"Are you still with him?"

"I'm filing for divorce when I get back."

"I see."

"No, you don't see. Chris, I didn't keep it from you deliberately. Things moved way too fast, and I just thought give it time."

"Actions speak louder than words. Isn't that the way it goes?"

It was some time before she answered him. The voice was controlled and quiet – the voice Christian hated in a woman. The voice that meant a fight was coming. So far, their quarrels had been minor and usually brought on by his petulance. Now he anticipated a battle royal.

"I can't just drop everything and move out. I've thought of it, but I have the children to think of."

"Isn't that what you've done? Move out, I mean?"

She wheeled sharply on the chair and saw that he was staring at the fire in the hearth, his cigarette burning down to nothing between the first and second fingers of his right hand. Tristan had pressed his muzzle into his drawn-up knee, begging for attention.

"I told them I'm studying in England. It's not far from the truth, given all the time I've put into research. Ned gave me a loan —"

"Well, at least that's a half-truth!" This said bitterly. Christian crushed the cigarette in an ashtray and then pounded the pillows – most notably, her pillows – into comfortable shapes behind him. "I understand now why it took so long for you to tell me you loved me."

"I do love you, Christian!"

"Do you?"

His voice was cold now, uncharacteristically mocking. Violet wanted to retreat but instead she met the battle. "I wrote to Sam a few days ago to tell him about wanting to file and about us. I talked to him tonight – he didn't read the letter. He saw your interview with Tony Carlisle —"

"Don't blame this on me!"

"I'm not! Of course it's not your fault. But he went ballistic on me. He wouldn't listen."

Christian chuckled and Violet thought she heard relief. "Can you blame him? I can understand your lying to me, you barely know me, but a man you been with for, I assume, years."

"I assume you disapprove of everything I've done?" Violet's voice had risen and now it took on an icy quality that frightened even her.

"Only what you've done to your children – and to me."

"Is there any way I could be forgiven?"

"I'll have to think about it, Violet. You've thrown too much at me in one night that it's all too much to comprehend. I mean, if you're willing to leave a man you've been with for years, what chance in Hell do I have, a man you've known a few months?"

The clatter of the keyboard started up again, punctuated by the irritating ticking of the carriage clock on the mantle. Christian was still trying to get comfortable in bed.

"Anything else you'd like to say?" Christian suddenly demanded.

"Maybe we should think about a cooling down period," she said after reflection. "You know, we've been in each other's company non-stop for almost three months."

"That's never been a problem for me. You still love him, don't you?"

"I never said —"

"It's quite apparent by all you've done and what you haven't said. You've got to make up your mind. You know mine. I've never held anything back and I don't intend to."

"You're not being fair!"

Christian swung out of bed and left the bedroom. The door slam meant the conversation was far from over. She knew where he'd be. Again, the studio door was unlocked and he expected her, looked up as she entered.

"Why is it that whenever a man wants a straight answer he's not being fair?" Christian's voice was cold, but not hard.

"You're asking so much of me right now. I don't

want to make another mistake —"

"All this is a mistake? Thanks."

"I didn't say that! And I'm afraid – very, very, afraid, that if I make promises and I can't keep them, I'll lose you. Chris, my life is in turmoil right now – everything but this," Violet gestured around her. "With the children, Sam, a long-distance relationship is all I can offer for the immediate future."

Christian stopped running scales on the guitar. "I've heard that so many times before from women I never got close to loving, and I'd rather not hear it now from you. What assurance do I have that you won't go back to him?"

"If you only knew —"

"I know I need you, Violet. When I wake up in the morning, you don't know the excitement and happiness I feel, seeing you there beside me."

"If you really loved me."

"Jesus, Violet! It's pretty obvious!"

"Don't you know what this is doing to me?" Violet cried.

"I do, because I know what it's doing to me! I'm afraid that if you leave you won't come back."

"Maybe," she said, taking an enormous chance, "you're afraid that if I leave, you'll fall out of love. You know. Out of sight. Out of mind."

"All you have to do is pick up the phone and tell him it's over. We can send for the kids."

"I don't think —"

"What's there to think about, Violet? Make a new start here!"

"Listen to yourself, Chris! Do you think Sam would allow me to bring the children here? He's already threatened to take them away from me! They're his kids, and they do love him."

"I'll love them, too. They're a part of you."

Violet studied the highly polished piano top and saw her reflection – monstrously distorted, aged, an old crone,

one of Macbeth's three sisters at the cauldron.

Well, she had stirred the pot, hadn't she?

"Maybe in a few weeks, months, when things are settled at home."

Christian exploded now. Sheets of music flew about and the piano rang with a dissonant chord. Tristan woke from his nap under the piano bench.

"Maybe? Christ, Violet! What the bloody hell does that mean?" he shouted. "Either you do or you don't! There's no halfway with me!"

Christian now rose and Violet thought that was the end of their quarrel, that he would mutter one of his sweet apologies and welcome her to his arms. Instead, he walked to the door and before leaving, said: "With me there's no halfway, Violet!"

VIOLET SLEPT ALONE for the remainder of the night. Christian had already left for the studio and came home after seven. Their dinner was quiet and cordial, if not strained. As Violet rose to leave and go to bed, Christian took her hand. His look was as neutral as he could affect, but she could read the pain in those violet-blue eyes.

"I made the arrangements. Your flight to San Francisco is at ten tomorrow morning." "Thank you," she whispered tearfully.

Again, she slept alone.

THEY SAT IN Christian's Range Rover in Raphael Street for the longest time, Mrs. Burnes watching from behind the lace curtains. Christian started up the car and then reached into his coat pocket, drawing out a medieval ivory chess piece. The knight he'd found at the Arena in October. He'd thought of it as a talisman of good luck, that somehow it brought Violet to him.

"Here. It's something. I've been carrying it around for months," he murmured, and pressed it into her hand. "Make of it what you will."

The shock of seeing the little knight again, and not their leave-taking, broke down the last of Violet's composure. Everything had started to turn for the better after she'd found it in the Transbay Terminal. Now, everything had come full circle.

It was left there. No tender farewells, no promises. They parted at Heathrow where Christian didn't say 'for however long it takes', but a sterile 'good bye'. Never once had he said good-bye. It was always 'see you'.

As soon as Violet saw the skyline of San Francisco she started to ache. The pain in Christian's eyes as she left him at Heathrow was the last thing she'd see before falling asleep for many nights to come.

She had to pick up the pieces, push on toward a resolution, clean up the mess that had become her life and a think of a hundred more metaphors that prompted walking away from a man who truly loved her.

25

Gimme Another Answer, I Didn't Like the First One

"HOW DO I look?"

Elisabet rolled her large brown eyes at her father. "For the millionth time, Dad, fine!"

"You sure?"

Sam sounded nervous. He stared at his reflection in the shaving mirror, nothing how the stress of the last ten and a half weeks had aged him. Well, he sighed, Violet had always been attracted to older men.

Elisabet watched contemptuously as her father got ready for the homecoming as if it were a first date. For the first time in weeks, Dad had shaved and paid careful, almost narcissistic, attention to his appearance. He was even wearing a shirt Mamma made him for their tenth wedding anniversary. That had been seven years ago and this was the first time he took it out of the box.

"Whaddya think?" Sam asked, holding up a tie Mamma gave him for Groundhog Day. A silly present, a joke. *Who would give a man a present for Groundhog Day?*

Mamma would, if she loved him.

"D'you think I should go with a tie?" he asked.

"Strangle yourself with it," Elisabet muttered.

"Huh? What'd you say?"

"Lose the tie, Dad; you're trying too hard," Elisabet sighed. "She'll get suspicious – I'm suspicious!"

Sam laughed and bussed Elisabet's cheek, left the scent of aftershave in her nostrils. "Last time I ask for fashion advice from you," he joked. "Now that your Mom's coming home, I won't need to, will I?"

"The only advice I'll give is to find a good lawyer!" Elisabet muttered under her breath.

"She's here!" Alex shrieked with joy.

A car pulled up outside, then a car door slam and

Violet's thanks to the driver. Just the sound of her voice, that soft, yet low, voice gave Elisabet chills. Elisabet was suddenly afraid, and wanted to hide in her room until the storm blew over.

"Mamma! Mamma!" Alex and Max were shrieking.

"Okay, let's go," Sam said. Taking a deep breath and a shot of mouthwash straight from the bottle, he went downstairs.

EVERYTHING WAS UNREAL. The only reality to Violet was the town house in Knightsbridge, the all-day drives up to York, dinner parties with the Wakefields, going to the theater in London, the nights and mornings in Christian's arms. That was reality. Not unpacking her suitcases after a night of troubled sleep and avoiding Sam's curious gaze.

"Congratulations on the book deal," Sam said. "I know you've been working your ass off for it – which book is it?"

"The novel."

Sam frowned. "Which?"

"The one about fourteenth century Italy – the one with all the sex and gory battles."

"Well, that oughta sell... not the history of Richard the Third, huh? Too bad; I thought the history was better."

"You actually read my history of the Wars of Roses?"

"Yeah, it was just sitting there. I didn't get most of it, but it was a good read. I guess that's important. I'm happy for you, Vi."

"Thanks. I'm not getting my hopes up, though. Not until I see the book in the window of Alexander Book Company."

"That's safe, I guess."

"I guess."

Violet purposefully avoided Sam's hand as she walked past him to get to the closet and hung up her coat and some sweaters. She moved about the bedroom, making a ritual of unpacking and restoring, pausing here and there to comment about something that was out of place or broken.

"Maybe you should tell me what the last ten and a half weeks was really all about?" he asked when the silence became intolerable.

She finally had the courage to meet his gaze. "Research. Didn't I tell you that?"

"Cut the crap, Vi!"

"Salvation and self-preservation. The preservation of my sanity."

"You could have done that in a hotel room on Nob Hill."

"You would've said we couldn't afford it."

"You could have talked to me."

"That's novel. The idea of talking to you about anything and knowing for certain that you were listening. You could've done a hundred things to prevent my going – and you should have started twenty years ago." Violet replied. That came out quietly and unexpectedly. But Sam was cognizant enough of the problem to respond.

"I can't offer you an excuse. Just believe what I tell you now, Violet. I'm sorry. I wasn't thinking."

When do you think, Sam?

"Too little, too late."

"So everything I've done justifies running off?"

Violet started to clean up the bedroom. Nothing had changed since her departure. Ten and a half weeks of dust and clutter decorated the room. It was Miss Haversham's ballroom, complete with cobwebs. The robotic motions of organizing gave her an opportunity to organize her thoughts.

"No," she said matter-of-factly.

"Did you just agree with me?" Sam asked, a tone of amazement raising his voice an octave.

"No. What I meant was that you have no reason to

escape and I did." Violet explained. "You have a safety valve against the stress of the day. Whenever it gets to be too much, there's always the soda company account to take you away from the kids and me. And if you need quick release, there's always Marjorie with her enormous accommodations. Your lap dog Violet is here waiting for you when you get back."

"I told you Marjorie and I were over and done. Shit, I ended it when you left. Would it make you happy to know I lost the account?"

"Noble of you but stupid. Why don't you sue her for sexual harassment?"

"You're kidding."

"You could give the case to Ned and then I would have steady employment for a few more months because the litigation alone would drag out for at least a year. Then you could run off on another quest to save the soda company."

"It's not like I didn't earn the trip to Cancun or the other trips. They were business-related and necessary to get accounts."

"True, and I get to stay here and deal with small children and overdue bills, a heating system that never works. And when I'm not folding laundry, or working at the office, going to school concerts and birthday parties that you conveniently forget, I get an hour or two to write."

"I'm sorry! How many times do I need to say it?"

"So if you want to know why I left it comes down to my deserving the time off. I needed time away to think, to do research, to figure it all out. To figure you and me into the big picture. To figure out if love ever had anything to do with it."

Sam laughed now. "Is this what it was all about? Getting revenge?"

"That would've been too easy. I'm seizing the day. I'm filing the papers."

Sam came around the bed and took her hands. Violet knew he'd suggest sex; it had always been the perfect bandage for their marital ills. Gently he pressed her to sit and then helped fold the lingerie being taken out of a suitcase. New things, silk, in provocative colors. From the flicker of his eyes and the color rising in his face, the quickening of his breath, Violet knew he was thinking about how seductive and exciting she'd look in them. Lingerie had always been a favorite turn-on. Would it be the same now, knowing someone else had had that plea-sure? Another man had held her body in his arms?

And she had enjoyed it.

Violet got off the bed and went into the bathroom with her cosmetic case, opening her drawers on the left and methodically placing tubes of lipstick and compacts of eye shadows in their rightful places. She paused and then closed the drawers on the vanity quietly, as if trying the wood runners to see if they ran smoothly.

"Are you serious about divorce?" Sam asked, his voice uneven.

Violet turned sharply and frowned at him. "You can accuse me of child abandonment, threaten me with a court order taking them away from me, and expect me not to be serious? I'm a bitch, but I'm no fool."

Sam ran his hands through his perfectly groomed hair and rather than stay to argue his case, went downstairs. Soon she could hear him chopping wood in the backyard. Hopefully it wasn't the coronation chair he was breaking up for firewood.

Lunch was over and the children occupied elsewhere when Sam finally came inside. He stood behind Violet as she hammered away at the keyboard, making lives and distant lands appear out of nowhere as she wrote. It really was amazing how she did that so effortlessly, he remarked and it surprised her as compliments from Sam came so rarely, and that he should try to be friendly now.

"Want to go for a walk?" he suggested.

They chose a path well-worn and well-traveled by their feet: up into the Berkeley hills along narrow, tree-shrouded streets lined with mansions they once dreamt of affording, following familiar routes in silence. Once in a while Violet would ask about domestic matters and Sam would grunt in the affirmative or say he didn't know. They wound up in Indian Rock Park.

The granite formations and trails winding through the monolith reminded Violet of afternoons riding with Christian along the North Yorkshire moors with a gentle rain beating against her face as she rode behind him; feeling his strong, muscular back against her cheek, his taut, sinewy stomach beneath her hands, feeling the rhythm of the horse as they galloped to Jervaulx Abbey where she wrote in a leather-bound journal Christian had given her for Valentine's Day and he would scribble lyrics on a crumpled notepad, where they would have a picnic lunch no matter the weather and just enjoy the silence of one another's company…

". . .So I asked the studio head to reconsider the artwork for the two sheet and he gave me some more time. The campaign for the Soda Company kicked off and the revenues are starting to make up for the loss of Rotherwell's. Looks like Alex is going to get braces after all, and maybe we can get you a new car. Do you want to take a trip somewhere? Just you and me? Go to Paris, maybe?" Sam was chattering away. Violet paused in her walk and looked at him as if seeing him for the first time, a stranger on Market Street, just another guy in line at Starbucks.

Sam pulled Violet close as they sat atop what Violet had always called the 'Queen's Bench' and stared at Berkeley below them. He rested his chin on her shoulder and listened to the steady rise and fall of her breathing, inhaled her familiar perfume.

"I should have brought you here more often," he murmured. "Want to come back tonight?"

Violet shook her head. "It's over," she replied.

ELISABET HEARD THE front door open, her parents' voices and then the jangle of keys. Dad's Beemer was soon roaring out of the garage. Looking over the hallway balustrade, Elisabet saw her mother standing at the window, her arms crossed defensively, watching the street. She wanted to go downstairs and ask what had happened, but it was all too obvious.

This wasn't the homecoming she wanted. Mamma had come home changed. She was quiet, diamond-edged, nervous. Elisabet didn't need an explanation; it fell out of Mamma's purse when she put it on top of the refrigerator to keep it away from Max, who was searching for treats. Scooping up keys, cosmetics from a leather pouch, tampons and breath mints, Elisabet paused when she saw the note cards. Pretty things, with pictures of England on them, but inside where she ought not to have looked was a man's writing. Lines of love poetry and promises of undying affection, almost Victorian and certainly corny. There were photographs of Mamma with Christian Walsh. Flipping over one of the photos, she saw the inscription: *I'll love you always. Christian.*

And then there was the magazine cover. A British tabloid, really, with her mother and Christian's faces prominent among those of the Royals. Christian had scribbled a note on that, too. Another proclamation of love.

"What're you doing?"

The question made her jump, squeal in fright. Elisabet panted for breath and dared look at her mother. Violet quietly took the magazine from her and claimed the photographs. Not a word was spoken; it wasn't necessary.

But Elisabet would never forget the look on her mother's face. She looked like the lion at the Oakland Zoo – sad, trapped, fierce.

"It fell – stuff fell out – uh, I guess you found your

prince," Elisabet confessed.

"There's nothing to find," Violet replied quietly. She looked at Elisabet while flipping on the computer and then as quickly as she had appeared she was gone down the hall, muttering something about finding her notes. Later that night, Elisabet returned to the kitchen and was surprised to find it dark. She hadn't heard her mother come upstairs. As she walked back to her room, Elisabet paused in horror when she heard the sound – an ugly, retching, noise like an animal in pain. Her mother was curled up in the coronation chair in the dark living room.

"Mamma?"

When Violet didn't move, Elisabet reached up and switched on the little lamp above the mantle. Violet shifted as if in pain, avoiding the light. Elisabet said nothing and handed her the box of tissues, saw the ivory chess piece in her mother's right hand.

A knight on horseback.

Elisabet threw herself into her mother's arms, whispering, "It's okay... it's okay. I love you!"

THE SKY WAS sharply black and speckled with a million stars, the air, biting and cold, fresh. Violet kicked the garbage can into place at the curb and leaned on the fence to take account of Oxford Street before going in and calling it a night.

The piano player was getting close to mastering Chopin but the neighbor's dog still had its vocal cords. Looking south, Violet saw him under the street lamp and suddenly felt afraid. A moment later he walked up the street.

She trembled as they stared through one another like lovers meeting after a painful separation; two people, while not having shared the most intimate of love, who knew each other completely.

"Go ahead, say it," Violet finally spoke up.

"A little early for the cans, isn't it?" he greeted.

"Too tired to write," she finally answered.

George nodded. "How was the vacation?"

"Good of you to call it that. Want some coffee, tea?"

"Sure. Sam's gone, I take it?"

Violet nodded and gestured towards the house. She said nothing until they were in the kitchen. Cups were taken from the shelf, placed on a pristine, white tablecloth on a table strangely devoid of notebooks, toys, dirty dishes and papers. The sugar bowl and creamer were set carefully beside two teacups and saucers. George knew her careful, deliberate, actions were just buying time.

"Gone in a door slam and a screech of tires," Violet said at last. "That was the hardest thing I've ever done, George. But I needed to do it."

George shrugged and offered to start the kettle, then reached into a cupboard for the bread and jam. "Leaving England was the hardest thing you'll ever do. Don't kid yourself."

Violet nearly collided with him as she reached for the teacups. They stared each other down until George backed away first. He watched the angry flip of her skirt as she walked across the kitchen for the hundredth time.

"D'you think it was easy?" she demanded.

"No, especially for everyone concerned."

"Please don't lecture me about morals, and obligations, and what good mothers don't do. Everyone from Elisabet to Sam, to Amalie, to Annie has given me an opinion on the subject whether I've wanted to hear it or not. I hoped that you would understand and for once not throw in a penny."

"Had no intention of doing that," George replied, defensive.

"Ah, but it's coming!" Violet responded and sat down at the table, pouring a cup of tea. Only the tremor of her hand betrayed her feelings. "Damn it to hell, what have I done?" Violet suddenly cursed, and got up to retrieve the sugar.

He placed a hand on her shoulder and caressed soft wool when she passed him again and felt the unmistakable shiver of sexual attraction. The warmth. Violet's shoulders dropped suddenly and she went into a spasm of gut-wrenching sobs. George stepped away, shocked, and watched impotently as she vented grief. She looked so young and small then, and George remembered the girl of fifteen sitting in a tree house, sobbing uncontrollably as *Dark Forest* played on a phonograph. Violet looked so helpless and alone now that George swore softly and gathered her in his arms.

"Don't cry! Please, don't! Things will turn round, they always do!" George whispered as he kissed her hair and her forehead, and smoothed back the locks obscuring her large and lovely eyes.

George now bent down, his face close. Just visible were her parted lips, the smooth unlined skin around them, the curve of her cheek. The perfume she wore had always been heady; now it was like an aphrodisiac. He kissed her and met with no opposition, was surprised that she kissed him back, and felt her tears on his face. Her large, luminous eyes were all that George could see when he opened his and in that moment knew it had been a mistake.

"I'm such a damn, bloody, fool!" George muttered. "I'm sorry, Violet!"

Without another word he was gone.

"GEORGE?"

Annie repeated herself a third time, her pitch rising successively. Violet scowled and motioned toward the boys playing with Emma's son Mason at the computer. "Why don't you guys go outside while we get lunch ready?" Annie suggested.

"Ned I'd understand, but George?" Emma stated. "And here we thought to comfort you, yet another single woman out there to fend for herself."

"Violet doesn't need anyone's help!" Annie remarked.

Violet angrily slapped cold cuts on slices of wheat bread and squeezed mustard onto each in a smiley face pattern, covering up the artwork with a lettuce leaf and second slice of bread. The truth of the matter was that she didn't need anyone, not even Annie and Emma.

"Boys, c'mon; enough of the computer. You heard Annie. Outside," Violet said. "Take your sandwiches outside – you can sit at the picnic table and have lunch." Once the boys were out of the kitchen she moved about cleaning up.

"It'll be so great to have you back at work," Emma said, hoping to change the dark mood that had fallen upon them. "We've gone through one temp after another – no sooner do I train a girl on our archaic computer system than she leaves for a better job. And Ned's humor will improve. He goes around like a big, lovesick, dog or something."

Annie jabbed Emma in the side and gave her a warning look. "How's the book coming?" Annie asked, joining Violet at the sink to wash dishes.

"I'm looking at the last galleys. The cover's been a bitch – eventually they'll realize it's not a book that needs Fabio and a half-dressed supermodel on the cover."

"You should do the cover. Your work is good."

"Do something like an empty helmet with a rose crushed beneath it," Emma pondered. "You know, in shadows?"

"Sort of like me?" Violet mused.

"Violet, that isn't what I meant."

"I know, Em. It just struck me, though. I go from one tragedy or soap opera to the next without missing a heartbeat," Violet replied, smiling. Both Emma and Annie now hugged Violet and whispered support, promises that life would get better. "I'll get through this storm – a bit damper than usual, but I will," Violet said. "And speaking of storms, better get the boys, it's starting to pour."

An hour later, Violet sat in the living room at the neo-gothic window, watching the rain come down in buckets on Oxford Street.

Oxford! Maybe it would have been better for all concerned if she had really gone to Oxford.

Settling in on the sofa for once devoid of laundry, Violet spread out the pages of the galley and studied them, marked lines and paragraphs with a blue pencil. The sound of the rain and the grandfather clock ticking became a mantra, and Violet moved to their respective beats, making marks, turning pages until she was jarred out of her deep concentration by the ring of the telephone.

"Hello?"

"Hi, it's me."

Violet's heart skipped two beats. "Hi!"

"How are things?"

"Fine – listen, I should have said something, should have made it clear —"

"Um, I'm at the airport. Getting ready to take a flight out. There's so much I want to say, wanted to say. I love you. I always have. I always will, but I know with your life – shit! They're calling my flight. Gotta run. Take care of yourself, Violet."

"George, wait! George, don't – *George!*"

She was answered by the hum of a dial tone.

A VASE FULL of freesia and white roses stood in the middle of Violet's desk, which looked as if she'd never left. Moving aside the law books that had lain open for weeks, Violet placed the bundle of telephone messages in her hand on the cleanest spot and then dumped her shoes and purse into the empty file cabinet drawer behind her. The closing of the drawer brought Ned out of his office.

When their eyes met Violet came around the partition and wordlessly embraced him. "Welcome home, Vi," Ned whispered, planting a kiss on her ear.

"That's Violet!" she teased and wiped back a tear.

Emma was there next with another bouquet of flowers. Violet gasped at the beauty and size of it. "You didn't!" exclaimed Violet happily.

"I didn't. They just came."

The pounding of Violet's heart should have been apparent to Emma and Ned, who now urged her open the card. She'd waited for a phone call, a fax, a card. As soon as she got on the plane she vowed she'd take care of business and then call him when she had the courage and he had the patience to listen.

But now...

Her face went to stone and the card was torn into four equal pieces and dropped into the wastepaper basket with the expensive sheath of white roses and daffodils.

"Geez, look at this mess! At least you were right about needing me back, Ned," Violet chattered nervously as she settled in to work as if never having been gone. The Dictaphone was clicked on and the earphones were plugged in. The familiar, comforting clickety-click of the keyboard told Ned that all was well. It would never be the same again, but all was well.

At noon he came out and stood at the counter, watching as Violet fielded two calls and managed to keep her hands on the keyboard, check a cite in the Code. She glanced up and smiled, told him to wait.

"Lunch?" he asked, when she hung up the phone. "Want to go to Caffe Malvina?"

"Your deposition in New York is going. I'll make the flight arrangements after lunch," Violet replied, handing off a pink telephone message. "Could we go somewhere else for lunch?"

"Sure; there's a new Asian place on Washington, a little cafe."

"My treat. I owe you for some Chinese food."

"Good; and then as soon as you get the check from the publisher, you can take me to Starz."

"Another restaurant I'm tired of."

"Is there any place in San Francisco Christian Walsh's feet didn't touch?"

Violet was going to tell Ned to go to Hell, but she'd been saying too much of that of late and instead, she kissed his cheek, murmuring, "I hate to say it, Edmund, but it feels good to be back."

"So how's the publishing coming?" Ned asked as he helped her with her coat. When he reached down to get the eyeglass case she'd dropped, he noticed the flowers sticking up from the wastepaper basket and the name on a scrap of card.

George?

26

Happy Birthday - Part Two

VIOLET WOKE AROUND five o'clock just as the sky was turning. It was going to be a blistering summer morning if the clouds lowering over Berkeley dissipated and let the sun burn through. July was her not her favorite month for that reason; hot weather only made her temper worse, and of late, she'd been the victim of a very nasty disposition.

She rolled over and tossed the alarm clock on to the floor, then burrowed deeper into the pillows, unconsciously reaching out to embrace the man she wanted so badly. In a delicious state of semi-consciousness she willed Christian Walsh into her bed, seeing his blonde head upon the pillows, feeling his arms around her, his lips on her bare skin.

But she was alone.

She had been alone for months now.

The sinking in the pit of her stomach woke Violet. Around her were familiar bed linens, clothes, photographs and cherished belongings, each taking on strange aspects in the blue-gray light and she took comfort in seeing them.

She was alone now. She had been alone since the night she returned from England when Sam walked out, still in a state of enormous denial. Three days later he moved his things to a Russian Hill condo. He was gone and that was that.

George, too. George had made himself scarce since her return, using his doctoral thesis research as an excuse to stay away, his trips to Greenland and other far-flung places keeping them as far apart as possible.

She was totally alone.

It was safe to say she'd made the biggest mistake of her life and she was paying dearly for it.

The downward spiral started on her birthday in

May…

"Violet! Sam's on three."

Violet pounded the button on her phone and cradled the receiver against her chin, not missing a comma in the dictation pouring out of the machine.

"Yeah, Sam… thank you. Forty-three's not as bad as forty. Are you taking the kids this weekend?"

Violet glanced up when she felt Ned's presence and waved him away, taking the papers out of his hand. While she listened to the countless reasons why Sam couldn't take the kids on his weekend, she checked the papers for signatures and tossed them into her 'Out' basket, handing off a fresh sheath of documents for signature.

Ned stood at the counter and eavesdropped. "That's the third time he's called this week," he chuckled when she finally hung up.

"So?"

"So what's the problem now?"

Violet gave him a pained look. "It's my birthday, Ned."

Coloring with embarrassment, Ned observed the abundance of balloons and flowers round her workstation. "Anything from London?" he inquired.

"Not funny."

An hour later Ned came out of his office and leaned on the walnut partition for some time before speaking.

"Listen, can I take you out for your birthday? You, me, Emma, Annie, the kids?" Violet's brows arched in amusement and she smiled in assent. "What would you like for your birthday, Vi?" Ned asked gently, and Violet knew he was serious.

Looking at him dead on, she said, "I want to turn back the clock and correct mistakes. I want the pain to go away."

"Not even with the largest bottle of aspirin, Vi. But I can promise you something in blue, or with sequins, or how about a pony?"

"A pony with sequins? That'll work."

Ned arrived at Violet's at a quarter to eight that night, surprising Elisabet with his polished appearance and the scent of Violet's favorite men's cologne.

"A little overboard even for you, eh, Edmund?" she quipped.

Ned decided to let her have her little joke and watched as she made the boys stand still while inspecting their appearance for the umpteenth time. He marveled that two women so different as Elisabet and Violet could be so alike in so many ways.

The doorbell rang and Violet shouted that it would be Annie. Sure enough, Annie came in with a date and shouted up the stairs for Violet to get her butt in gear.

Again the doorbell rang.

"That'll be Emma!" Violet shouted as she ran downstairs fighting with her earrings. Ned whistled in approval for she'd decided to wear something chic, short and black for a change. Violet was horrified when she opened the door and discovered Sam instead.

Sam smiled sheepishly and offered a single red rose. "Happy birthday," he greeted.

"Not bad after twenty-plus years of forgetting," Ned murmured none too softly.

"Ned!" Elisabet hissed, aiming a sharp elbow into his solar plexus. By now the boys were all over Sam and demanding he join them for Violet's birthday dinner, inviting him inside.

"That's okay. I can give as good as I get," Sam replied, brushing past Ned and intentionally jostling him. His gaze was all for Violet, however, and he was still smiling, still waiting. "I just came by to get the stuff I left in the garage. Is this a bad time?"

"Yes," Ned and Violet answered.

"We're on the way to dinner," Violet explained as Sam tried to lure her into the hallway. She was saved by a car horn. "Hey you guys! Here's Emma – and look, she's got the Cherokee!" Ned shouted. Violet steered Max and Alex toward the porch and Emma's Jeep, bypassing Sam's obstructing arm.

Sam wasn't put off. "Can I come by later?"

"Only if it's to pick up the rest of your things."

He nodded and roughhoused with the boys one last time before they went with Elisabet to the limousine.

Violet would be in a better mood when he came by again – birthdays always put her in a nasty temper. Still smiling like the Cheshire cat, Sam stood on the porch and tried to get another glimpse of Violet. She did look great in that dress.

"Now's not the time to start a trend, Sam," Ned muttered as he locked the door behind them. "By the way, she prefers white roses. Nice talkin' to you."

"My side of the bed's not even cold yet," Sam fired back. "Fast work, Ned. I'd be surprised if you pulled it off, though. You both have a lot of baggage since your college days together. And who knows? Maybe that British rocker's still in the picture."

Ned merely smiled at this and decided that though it would be the most perfect of birthday gifts to Violet, he'd refrain from punching out Sam's lights.

The Jeep was turning on University Avenue by the time Sam left the porch. He dropped the perfect red rose on the rattan settee and walked down to where his ancient Beemer was parked in its usual place under the acacia trees, ignoring the constant ringing of the telephone in the living room.

AN ANGEL FOOD cake ablaze with what seemed to be a thousand candles was placed before Violet as the waiter and Violet's family and friends sang *Happy Birthday*.

"Okay, Violet! Make a wish before Max does the deed!" Ned instructed, struggling to keep Max in his chair and away from the candles. Violet did as she was told and closing her eyes formed a thought. When she opened them, part of her wish had come true – for surrounding her were the people she loved: her family and closest friends.

She extinguished the candles in two breaths and accepted the congratulations that came with her achievement.

What achievement? Forty-three and I still can't get it right, still mucking up my life!

She turned then and saw him.

The bright blond hair and violet-blue eyes, the knee-weakening smile. Violet's heart started to race as she watched him cross the restaurant.

No, it wasn't him; just someone who looked like him.

"CHRIS? CHRISTIAN, WE'VE got five minutes before the next set."

Christian ignored Kevin's pleas and waved him off as he pondered a moment before adding something more to the greeting card, studied it carefully, and then slipped it into an envelope. "Could you see that it gets posted?" he asked a stage hand passing by and handed off the card.

"Couldn't that wait?" Kevin groused.

"Yesterday was Violet's birthday."

"C'mon, we're down to the wire."

Roadies were wiring him up; someone took the fountain pen out of his hand and replaced it with his Martin acoustic. The stage hand came around again and Christian noticed the card in his back pocket. "I want that posted," Christian ordered.

The stage hand nodded and started moving a crate, oblivious to the activity picking up and the greeting card that fell on to the floor to be kicked under a console.

"Are we ready?" Kevin demanded.

"Sure," Christian muttered and was following Kevin and Steve back out to the stage when Charlie Bonnett, the tour manager, suddenly blocked his path. Standing next to Charlie was an exquisitely beautiful young woman.

Christian noticed the eyes first. They were the darkest blue but so similar to Violet's.

"Christian? I'd like you to meet Elise Maesbury. Elise just wrapped shooting the new James Bond movie with Pierce Brosnan here in Paris," Charlie introduced.

"A pleasure," Christian muttered before he took a last drink from the water bottle.

Before he was nudged on to the stage Christian studied this girl named Elise Maesbury more closely. Yes, they were Violet's eyes.

IN THE MIDST of the dark stage a lone spot light burned down on Christian. He leaned into the microphone and said in flawless French, "This is for my beautiful Violet." It was emotion-charged and barely a whisper.

There was silence, now followed by the deep, plaintive chords of an acoustical guitar. Christian took a breath and sang The Castle, the song he'd written for Violet en route from Middleham to London. He didn't remember finishing, nor the rapt attention of the audience, nor later, its thunderous applause. He did see the girl named Elise standing in the wings with Charlie.

Yes, they were Violet's eyes.

He was still pondering those eyes when he heard Kevin's shouts from the corridor, heard Harry say they were going to dinner without him if he didn't get a move on. Christian reached for his gear bag and switched off the dressing room light, went into the silent, empty, corridor that led to the stage.

"Hello."

Christian spun around at the sound of her voice, surprised to find her there. She came out of the corridor, moving like a sylph, like one of those vamps in a Humphrey Bogart movie. He took the unlit cigarette out of his mouth and pocketed the lighter, taking the exquisitely manicured hand that was extended towards him.

"Hi," he greeted, his brows rising and falling in perplexity. *Elaine? Eleanor? Ellen?*

"Elise Maesbury," she offered; "we met before the second set?"

"Yeah; yeah. Hello! Thanks for coming. Did you like the show?"

"It was fun. You're pretty good for a – sorry! Didn't mean that, really," Elise apologized, blushing on cue.

"Don't bother. I've gotten used to it."

"That one solo – what was it? Such a romantic song."

Elise of the exquisitely manicured hands, the porcelain skin and magnificent eyes studied him now, like a scientist marveling over a find. She was nodding her head, the perfect head tipped to the left while doing so. Violet often did that. In Violet, the act was charming, in Elise, well, he didn't know. But he knew he didn't like Elise's attempt at it.

"An experiment," Christian finally said.

"Excuse me?" she asked, baffled.

"The song. It was an experiment." Now it was his turn to blush.

Out with it, man! Tell her it was written for the woman you're hopelessly in love with.

"Y'know," she said smiling, coming closer so that he could see how flawless her perfect skin was, "you're quite the looker for – damn! I'm doing it again!"

"For an old bugger? Don't apologize," Christian laughed softly, never taking his eyes from hers. "Besides, I hear some women like older men."

"You heard right."

"Did I?"

The smallest amount of space lay open between them. Christian didn't have to look too far down into Elise's startling eyes, for she was tall, willowy, like a gazelle, like all the clichés one could use for a gorgeous super model or starlet.

"Look, have you got plans?" he asked; "Would you

like to grab a bite to eat?"

"I'd love to."

Christian smiled and Elise smiled back.

Oh yes, they were Violet's eyes.

VIOLET, RESTING HER chin on her folded hands, studied the remnants of her birthday cake in the blue glow of the computer screen. The whipped cream frosting still held its shape, though one of the blush-colored roses was losing its battle with gravity. She prodded the rose towards the top of the cake and then anchored it with one of the candles. There'd been enough candles on the cake to burn down San Francisco again, she mused. One candle for every year, one candle for every joy.

The grandfather clock struck twelve. Violet placed a mixing bowl over the cake and tucked it away in the refrigerator behind the doggy bags from the restaurant. There was nothing else she wanted to do that night; she was too tired and too melancholic. On her travels through the house making sure all were tucked in and all was locked up, Violet passed the cell phone peeking out of her back pack at least five times before picking it up.

The 'chirrup-chirrup' was answered when almost a minute had passed. "Hello, Walsh residence! Missus Burnes, here!"

Mrs. Burnes sounded as if she'd been running from out of doors. In the background, Violet heard the music to a television show, probably *Coronation Street*. Violet could picture her leaning against the hall tree. Behind her would be the Laura Ashley wallpaper that Christian detested.

"Missus Burnes? Hello, it's Violet... Violet Ellison?"

"What a delightful surprise! How are you, Dearie? How are the children?"

"They're fine. Missus Burnes, is he at home?"

"Oh my dear, he's still on tour."

"I forgot. Well, could you tell him I called?"

"I'll tell him."

"Promise me?"

"Promises are meant to be broken, Dearie. I'll leave a message at his hotel in Paris. He should be there until tomorrow."

"How is he?"

"Busy, Miss. You know Christian."

No, Violet thought; but I thought I did.

"I was wondering if you had his number in Paris," Violet gamboled, taking a breath and waiting.

"Just a minute," Mrs. Burnes said at last and went to find her address book.

The number was exchanged and after a number of forced pleasantries, Violet was glad to hang up. She spent a good fifteen minutes staring at the birthday cake before picking up the phone again.

The hotel room telephone was answered by Kevin Wakefield, who at first was put off to be roused out of a perfectly contented sleep, and then cheered considerably when it realized who it was.

"Let me talk to Chris if he's there," Violet begged after a few minutes of banter and teasing.

"Can't do that. He's not here."

"Morning walk?"

"Not exactly, luv."

"C'mon, Kev, tell him to get out of the shower. It's me on the phone!"

The pause should have warned her. Violet started to feel queasy. That horrible sensation one feels when getting bad news.

"Out with it, man!" she jested, in perfect mimicry of Christian, though her throat was ready to constrict with tears.

"You don't want the details."

No she didn't; and swallowing the lump in her throat, Violet jested that that was more information than she needed. "Tell him I called, would you?" she was finally able ask.

"I'll do that. Violet, he did try to ring you up before the second set last night."

"That's more than I deserved, I guess."

"Hey, it was great talking to you. I'll tell Sally you called. Take care now."

"Right."

His tone and the words made it perfectly clear to Violet her telephone call would not be returned. Switching off the phone, Violet returned to the kitchen and took the birthday cake out of the refrigerator.

The first thing to go was the rose.

27

Twists of Fate and Other Ways to Prove Life Sucks

THE DREAM WAS always the same – a dream that materialized in the quiet hours before dawn when Violet was semi-conscious. It was a dream that took on frightening aspects of reality, but a dream, nevertheless.

Violet was curled up on a high, broad, window seat embraced by gothic arches in a large room, the room part of a castle by the sea. Apropos for castle bed chambers, the room was lavishly appointed from tester bed with curtains, to carved oak wardrobes and high-backed chairs of state. As always, Violet watched the fading horizon until daylight turned to purple dusk.

Then the torchlight appeared in the distance, like a hundred fireflies, amber sparks dancing off pennons and battle harness. As the light continued to waver and gambol, the dark shapes took human form and the approach- ing army was more familiar. Violet knew the tall, blond, lord astride the gray percheron who rode at the army's fore.

Then came the labored footsteps from below, the hollow, metallic, clink of mailed boots on the stone case-ment. Violet would turn as the door opened.

He was weary, begrimed with dirt and blood, but whole all the same. His face, though lined and showing all of his forty-plus years, fulfilled the promise of youth and his hair, now dusted with gray, was thinning.

Violet would melt into his arms. Their lovemaking would be sweet, ethereal and her lover, a knight in glisten-ing, dew-kissed armor, was tall, blond and faceless.

It had been the same for years, this dream from her

adolescence. As she aged, so did her lover. That morning, however, when Violet, in her dream, opened her eyes after a long, passionate, kiss, she looked into Christian's eyes. Standing at the foot of the tester bed, watching them as they came to climax, was George.

Violet woke gasping for breath, clutching at the pillows and trembling. Hurling herself on the empty side of the bed, she lay there until the panic subsided and the doorbell rang. Glancing over at the alarm clock, she saw that it was ten o'clock, was more alarmed that she'd slept so late on a Saturday, her weekend with the children.

Elisabet was dragging a large package through the hallway and into the living room when Violet scrambled downstairs.

"It's from George," Elisabet responded to her mother's question. To the second question she replied, "I let you sleep in. God knows you need it. D'you want some coffee? A diet coke? I don't know how to make coffee, but I can open a can at least."

That Violet needed sleep was an understatement. The last three months had been pure hell – trying hold down a job, care for the children, proofread galleys and decide on a dust jacket design for the book. The publisher had decided to push up the release date of her historical novel and wanted it out by Christmas. Their non-fiction department had also expressed an interest in her popular history of the Wars of Roses and Violet found herself too busy to cope with any of it for the first time in her life.

"Where do you want it? And what the Hell is it?" Elisabet asked, shoving the cumbersome parcel up against the coronation chair.

"I didn't think he'd finish it," Violet murmured in response. Gingerly, she unloosed the silk ribbon holding the foil wrapping together and as she did so, George's gift was revealed. By this time, the boys had heard the commotion and wandered into the living room to see what it was. Max, holding an empty cereal bowl and spoon sticky with oatmeal, rushed at it, held back by his sister before he could damage it.

"Mamma!" Max crowed, pointing with the spoon. "See, Biff? Mamma! Sooward. I want a sooward! It's Mamma!"

"Wow! It sure is," Elisabet whistled low.

Violet had no immediate response to the watercolor portrait of herself as Joan of Arc. She ran a hand through her hair and then puffed out a sigh in bewilderment.

George didn't seem surprised when she arrived at his university office an hour later. "I wanted to thank you," she said quietly when asked how she was getting on.

"It was supposed to be for Christmas, but I guess it'll do as a graduation present," George said, and hooking his toe on the chair beside his desk, pulled it out, inviting her to join him. He pushed the thermos of coffee in her direction, too.

"That won't be until next May if I can finish the units."

"You didn't say how you were, Violet."

"I'll let you know in another month – another year," she replied, shrugging and with a forced laugh. "You look great."

"Do I?" George replied and smiled at her. "And you? You've made yourself pretty scarce," he said, returning to the papers on his obscenely-cluttered desk, scribbling here, marking notes in margins, there.

"Gladstone wants to release *Longing* during the holiday season, it's been taking up most of my waking hours, well, that and the children, the job."

George nodded, shuffled papers and dug through a desk drawer for a highlighter. Violet watched him as carefully as a mouse watches a cat from its mouse hole, afraid to say anything or move for fear he would pounce.

"Strange… how things turn out," he sighed all of a sudden and looking up, dazzled her with a smile. "We bare our souls to one another and now we've nothing left to say."

"It's a wonderful portrait, George. I love it. I'm going to ask Stan to make a special frame for it – something with a gothic arch, trefoils, the whole medieval thing," Violet babbled, avoiding his eyes.

"I loved doing it. I wouldn't have done it for anyone else."

"You know," Violet said, shifting in her chair so that she could whisper, and George's office mate wouldn't hear, "sometimes I think I fell in love with the wrong blond Englishman."

George guffawed at this, saying: "No, it's Christian Walsh, it's always been Christian Walsh, and will be Christian Walsh, Walsh without end, Amen."

"You can be such a prick," Violet sighed, and tried not to smile.

George reached out to brush the hair out of her eyes and then kissed her cheek. "And now, something more serious – I suppose I ought to tell you now, so when I ask for a ride to the airport, you won't kill me. My fellowship was only for the academic year – they offered to renew it, but I should get back to England. I'm going home next week. Got some family business to take care of."

"Your parents aren't sick or anything?"

"No; it's a family anniversary. I made a promise to come home, so… I'll be back in the winter; I promised to give a week-long series of lectures here, and then I want to be here when the book comes out."

She knew what he meant. It had been a year since the accident. He spoke of other business, matters vague and secretive and then finally expelled an irresolute sigh, saying, "Violet, when you came back from England, well, a lot of what I said was cruel."

"It's okay, I deserved it," she whispered.

"I just wanted you to know – look, we've done each other enough damage, and I know you're busy with the children, your job, book coming out and all, so."

"George, there's so much I have to tell you. I think I understand now."

"No you don't, not really," he said softly. "I don't think you will, not right now."

"Are we friends, George?"

"Till the sun dies, and the moon dissolves into the stars."

Violet caught her breath at this. One of the lines from *Dark Forest.* "Not one of his better lyrics. But he was so young then," she murmured.

"Weren't we all?"

THEY SHARED BRUNCH after this, saying very little and promising silently to let the past go. George finally said it was what he was going to do once he returned to England and told Violet she'd be better off letting go of the re- cent past, to get on with her life, to step past that invisible barrier that marked passages in one's life. There was so much to look forward to. The dark ages were over and the renaissance was just beginning, he said as they parted.

Violet knew exactly what he meant the next morning, but the past lurched at her, like a shard of glass twinkling in the sunlight to catch her attention.

She attended church for the first time since returning home and stayed long after the smell of candles and in- cense had died. Alone in the nave, she knelt in her usual place in her usual pew, the one behind the great carved oak pillar, and struggled for prayers, but none came.

The afternoon sun shot brilliant ribbons of transparent color from the rose window behind her, a ray striking the religious medal dangling round her neck, a white-hot flash that seemed made of liquid fire. For a moment the light was blinding and when she looked up she thought Christian was standing on the chancel steps. When Violet looked again, he was gone.

That shard of glass in the sunlight was like a dagger on Monday next, when she took an industry magazine out of Ned's office to read during lunch. The summer film season was at its peak, but what got her attention was a photograph of a popular new British actress.

Violet's heart seemed to stop beating and all the air had been sucked out of her lungs. She'd seen the girl on Masterpiece Theatre only last week. Now she saw her in a photograph with Christian at a gala for the British music industry.

Despite Christian's many protests to Violet that he couldn't dance, he looked like he managed pretty well with this starlet old enough to be his daughter. There were photos of Christian and this girl named Elise Maesbury cuddling in an Italian bistro. They'd gone there, too, many times. Christian had a thing for Italian restaurants, didn't he?

Without saying a word, she left the office.

Two hours later Violet was sitting in a booth at The Nag's Head, still holding the magazine open to the photograph. This was the booth she'd shared with Christian on two occasions. If she leaned back, she could still catch his scent in the worn leather back of the seat. She was starting to feel relaxed, and hopefully soon she'd be numb. If she was numb, Christian could stab her again and she'd not feel a thing – no, wait. Christian didn't hurt her. She had screwed him.

Still not numb...

She heard the now-familiar soft scuff of penny loafers on the floor but didn't bother looking up when the footsteps ended before her. Everything was a blur, soft and dreamlike, but she was still conscious. Still aware of Christian and his pretty blond...

Violet reached for the drink and frowned when she saw it was down to half-melted ice and a lime wedge. How many did that make? Four, six? Not enough, that was certain.

"I didn't know you were in the habit of three martini lunches – *whoa!* Make that gin and tonics."

Her eyes darted upward, startled and angry at the

sound of his voice. He had the nerve to come here! "Emma said you were on your lunch hour," Ned said. "If you didn't want to be found out you shouldn't have told anyone where you were going." He noticed the magazine and gently lifted it out of her hands. "Ouch!"

"They're engaged. The wedding's in February. Valentine's Day. We went to Stonehenge and had a picnic on Valentine's Day!"

"Impossible!"

"Doesn't look like it."

"Look, this is the BMI gala. Looks like a publicity opportunity for both."

"Go away, Ned!"

"Most men don't fly halfway round the world to deliver a Christmas present. Violet, I know what I know. I know he's a pretty decent guy. He must be to capture your attention."

"Didn't I ask you to leave?"

"I know what I know. Let me stay."

"As long as you don't gloat."

Ned eased into the booth beside her. He was alarmed, then, when Violet started to cry and reached out to him for comfort. He held Violet in his arms until her misery left her exhausted.

"I thought I was past all this," she sighed. "I'm forty-three years old! Somehow it isn't supposed to be like this!"

"What makes you think it gets easier as one grows older?" Ned asked, leaning over to take away the drink that was just placed in front of her. "In my experience, it's harder to take every time it happens, the break up, that is – if this is what it is. It's also more wonderful falling in love again. And making up. Remember?"

"Spare me."

"Okay. The pictures upset you. But they're only pictures. It could be anything. Do you think he's the type for twenty-one year old girls?"

Violet smiled and then laughed. "You are."

"I'm not the guilty party here. What about Christian?"

Violet shook her head. "Once, in London, a young girl asked if he was the father of Christian Walsh. 'You know', she said, 'The guy who wrote *Dark Forest*.' Took a while for him to get over that! All night he kept asking if he really looked 'that old'. Poor, sweet, fool."

She explained the sudden end of it, the scene at the London flat, the frightening, sterile silence at Heathrow, saying: "I could have gotten used to his attention. I enjoyed it, never having that kind before."

"I guess you could."

"It would be nice."

"Yeah, I wasn't too romantic was I?"

"Pizza and beer in the front seat of your Renault Dauphin would turn any girl's head. Turned mine." Violet stared at the coffee cup in her hands for the longest time and then looked at Ned and whispered, "I just don't want to be alone!"

WITHIN THE SEMI-darkness of the bedroom, behind the protective cocoon of the bed curtains, she was wrapped in a love she'd experienced before but was in some aspects new and more exciting. The same love that overwhelmed her in London, the love that woke her at the Priory in Yorkshire. And when it drifted away to a warm afterglow it left Violet in tears. She saw first Ned, then Christian leaning over her in the bed and smiling tenderly. Again she was swept away, but this time Ned had claimed her body. She was back in the apartment on Spruce Street, The Moody Blues played on the old record player and the bedroom was filled with incense. The fire surged through her body and she cried out as she never had before while Ned wrapped her in his arms and swore that he loved her, that he'd never leave her.

George was watching her watch him from the tree house now. He reached up and let Violet slide seductively into his arms and when their lips finally met it was like an explosion of such powerful sexual electricity that it almost tore them apart.

Christian came to her now and they lay first in the soft mossy grass at Middleham Castle and then in the large bed in York. He had thrown off the covers so that she could possess his body with her mouth and hands, letting her take her time and explore anew what she had already enjoyed. He tumbled her onto her back when he was ready and gently pressed her against the featherbed, coming into her so gently that Violet wanted to weep from the rapture he caused. When she reached up to kiss him, Violet found she was alone.

The grandfather clock downstairs struck three in the morning and sitting beside her was Elisabet, a look of concern etched on her smooth face.

"Ned! Ned, she's awake finally!"

The bedroom door opened and Ned came in with a glass of orange juice.

"Hey," he whispered, taking Elisabet's place. "The next time you want to drink your lunch, make it Diet Coke. Here."

"But I thought. . ."

"Drink your juice like a good girl."

"The magazine —"

"The magazine is in the garbage can downstairs," Elisabet said as she fed Violet the juice. "Ned brought you home. You came home blasted, Mom. What were you thinking? You don't drink, Mamma."

"She won't after this, Beth," Ned intervened; "Here, let her sleep again."

"My head!" Violet wailed.

"You deserve it." Elisabet glared at her mother and handed over the aspirin and a fresh glass of juice. "Get some rest."

Downstairs in the kitchen Elisabet started a fresh pot of coffee and sat at the kitchen table opposite Ned. "You don't look so great yourself," she offered.

"Be thankful it was booze this time and not booze and pills, or just pills," he murmured and when Elisabet threw him a frown, said, "Nothing." Ned flushed, deciding it was best to spare Elisabet that memory.

THE SOUND OF the toilet flushing down the hall sounded like an atomic blast in Violet's hung-over ears. She groped for the alarm clock and squinted at the numerals. Swearing, she staggered out of bed. Elisabet came around the corner and shook her head.

"You're wasted," she said and offered her mother a sterile, cold, kiss for the morning.

"I'd start to feel better if I knew what the Hell I'd done."

"Tied on a really big one."

Ned was asleep on the sofa and woke when Violet slammed into the coffee table. "Morning, Violet," he yawned.

"What the hell happened yesterday?" she demanded, shoving over the laundry to sit beside him.

"You did a striptease at The Nag's Head and they had to call Vice."

"Ned!"

"Okay. I found you at The Nag's Head. You had that magazine in one hand and a gin and tonic in the other. You couldn't even stand up. I brought you home. Thank you for not puking in my back seat."

"Ah, the good old days," Violet muttered.

"You kept babbled about George and Christian – how the Hell does your fruity friend George figure in all of this?"

Violet waved him off and told him it was none of his damn business as she walked into the kitchen. She found the magazine peeking out of the wastepaper basket under the computer table. The oatmeal was bubbling in the pot when she'd finally made up her mind to place the call to London.

"Hello?"

Christian's voice was sleepy and unmistakable.

"Hi. It's me. Violet."

The silence on the other end was so complete Violet could hear Christian's dog at his elbow. "Uh yeah, hi... hi – uh."

His voice sounded raw and congested.

"Maybe I called at a bad time."

"Violet? Violet, how are you? It's been a while."

"How are you, Christian?"

"God the flu, addually. Had to cancel three ciddies. We pick up next week if I surbive this."

"God, I'm so sorry! My timing's always been bad. Look, I just wanted to hear your voice. To say hello."

"It's been a while... look, maybe. . ."

Violet's courage was faltering and her voice was now thick with emotion, her eyes burning with hot, salty tears. "Well, I'll let you go. Call me sometime, okay? Oh, and congratulations on your engagement."

"Yeah, right. Right. Uh, sure. Wait, Violet!"

She hung up and made more than she should have of stirring the oatmeal scorching on the stove, the acrid, stench filling the kitchen with a fine blue smoke.

"Wrong number," she said to the inquisitive Elisabet.

CHRISTIAN REPLACED THE telephone in its cradle and stroked Tristan's soft muzzle and neck when he edged close to the bed. He picked up the cigarettes on the night stand and lit one, taking a single drag and then put it out when he began to cough. Now Christian patted the bed, summoning Tristan to take up the empty side on his right, which they did eagerly.

He took from the night stand drawer a photograph of Violet and studied it as if for the first time, remembering that Thursday afternoon in December when he first saw her in the Caffe Malvina. The evening in York when he got the call from Mrs. Burnes to come as quickly as he could to London. That bitterly cold morning in London when she came downstairs and into his arms.

The next morning he drove to Middleham.

As before, he arrived when the castle ruins were at their romantic best, with the sun dappling the ancient stone and gently countryside.

The pain came back with the memories.

"Lord, I am such a damn fool!" he whispered into the sharp, cold air.

VIOLET WAS IN the loft and working on research for a particularly nasty contract dispute between a local talk-show host and the employer television station when Ned finally arrived around noon the next day. For once he was in a suit without the benefit of a deposition or court appearance and he stood at the counter signing documents for an unreasonably long time. He wanted just to be near her, to see her smile or hear one of her biting yet endearing insults.

Violet at last glanced up from the law book opened before her and stopped the irritating tap of her pencil against the desk.

"It's okay, Ned. I swear. It's absolutely okay."

Not exactly what Ned wanted to hear, but he was satisfied for the moment. He reached into his pocket and took out a worn guidebook of Middleham Castle, a *Pickwick Portfolio* issued in the fifties, presenting it silently.

"Geez, Ned!" Violet exclaimed softly. She was genuinely pleased. "Thanks!"

"I thought you might like it; found it in a second-hand shop. It literally fell at my feet – fell out from behind some large, dusty volumes."

"This is really great. Really."

"Um, if ever you want to talk – whatever."

"Understood."

"I can't stand what you're going through."

"That makes two of us. But it's just another soap

opera. Give it another day or two. All will be right in Ned's world soon enough," Violet quipped. Ned turned to leave and Violet called him back, offering a pen and a settlement conference statement for signature. "If I haven't said it, it's because I didn't think it needed to be said. All the same, thanks," she said, taking back the document.

Ned was relieved the matter resolved itself civilly. He left Violet to pour over the guidebook, not knowing what turmoil it caused.

28

Thank You for Asking, But Misery Suits Me Just Fine...

THE CORRIDOR FROM dressing rooms to stadium exit was finally clear of fans, hangers-on and paparazzi. Christian was the last to leave as usual, taking his time to remove stage makeup and change his clothes, to have a cigarette. The roadies had already packed up the vans. Elise was probably waiting outside.

Christian put out the cigarette and left the dressing room. His footsteps echoed eerily through the empty corridor.

"Great show, Mr. Walsh," a stage hand said in passing.

"Thanks," he replied, shifting his bag off the sore shoulder to the less painful one. He passed a telephone on his way to the parking lot and then wheeled about.

What could it hurt? Christian dialed a number now etched in his memory and waited. There was no answer.

He'd try again when he got back to the hotel.

Twenty-seven cities in thirty-two days. The concerts varied from city to city, along with the quality of the performance. He remembered the concert at the Verona Arena when he'd sung the wrong lyrics to a song he'd written over twenty years ago. They all had a good laugh about that, but inwardly Christian was perturbed. Always a perfectionist, he'd never allow that from anyone else.

And then there was the party in Rome. It was reminiscent of certain parties in San Francisco during the summer of sixty-nine where the food, the drink and the women were questionable. Christian wasn't a prude, but he was appalled. What kind of life was this for a man nearing fifty?

Back at the hotel, he dialed Violet's number again and again there was no answer.

By the time the band returned to London in late November, Christian had made a decision that came as a surprise to everyone but Kevin.

"What do you mean? No tour next year?" Harry asked. Steve shoved Christian's annoying big dogs out of his way and repeated the question. The band was having dinner at Christian's house in Knightsbridge and the matter came up in the course of conversation.

"No tour next year. This is it for me. For a while."

"Chris, we need to promote the new album," Harry spoke up.

"That's what television is for, and the radio. It doesn't hurt not to tour. Look, how can people miss us if we're never gone?"

Christian was adamant. Only Kevin, through the two hours of discussion and argument, understood Christian's reasons. It was finally decided to take the next two years off to concentrate on another album or work on solo projects. The compromise was less than satisfactory to all, but it was nothing to break up over.

Kevin entered the living room in search of his coat and found Christian alone, working. He had been sullen since the Copenhagen concert and looked more tired than usual. He watched as Christian scribbled lyrics and crumple up the sheet, then scribble some more, toss the page onto the growing heap.

"Why don't you go to California?"

Christian glanced up at Kevin with raised brows. He knew perfectly well what Kevin meant. He just didn't want to acknowledge the problem.

"I'm engaged."

"You're bloody miserable, that's what you are."
"Right."

"C'mon, Chris! Lie to me, lie to Elise, lie to Violet – but don't lie to yourself. And you're a bit of a prick if you can't forgive Violet."

"She left me. The thought never came into my mind

to leave her – or lie to her."

"You pushed her away. Didn't it occur to you that her back was up against the wall? Or was it so familiar a situation that it made you uncomfortable?"

"Want a lift? I'm going to the Maesburys. Elise is expecting me in an hour. It's on your way home."

"Going to pick out china and flatware patterns, then?"

"Christ, Kevin! Will you grow up?"

"Only when you admit you've made a mistake. We all know. You can't hide it. Go to California. It's really simple, Guv. Go to her house in Berkeley. Stand outside the door – or do it on your knees, if that's what it takes – you say quietly and slowly – especially slowly, because women never believe what they're hearing when you give them the truth – you say to her, 'Violet, you're the only one that matters. I can't live without you. I got it all wrong. I'm sorry, Darling. I love you.' And you do that until she says yes or until you freeze your ass off, or the police take you away for being a public nuisance. See how easy that was?"

Christian tried very hard not to laugh. "Things will get better," he assured, though wondering himself. He avoided Kevin's sympathetic stare. "We make our choices and – whatever."

"How do you know? Oh here. I picked this up at Waterstone's. It was on the counter."

Christian took the postcard Kevin offered and turning it over saw it was an advertisement for a book by an American author named Violet Ellison.

On his way to dinner that evening Christian stopped by Waterstone's on Charing Cross Road. Elise screwed up her mouth petulantly when he pulled into a parking space.

"This isn't Clarke's," she sighed.

"You're right. I can see public school did you a world of good," he quipped, hoping for a smile or a laugh. He received a glacial stare for his attempt at humor. Violet would have fired one back – and it would be something more biting, daring another salvo.

"We've got dinner reservations for eight o'clock, Darling," Elise reminded him.

"This'll only take a moment."

"I've heard that before!" she grumbled, following him into the bookstore.

The atmosphere was reserved and quiet, almost like a library. Christian knew what he had come for but decided to browse a while, declaring in excited whispers at each treasure found, and then pausing almost in reverence before the new acquisitions displayed in the center of the first floor.

"I know you love books, but I didn't think you went for this sort," Elise sniffed, glancing at the copy of Violet's book he now held in his hands as if it was the Sacramentary. She scooped up a John Grisham novel and waved it. "Now this is excellent reading. D'you know they're making a movie of *Rainmaker*?"

Christian wasn't interested. He was thumbing through the book and smiling, making remarks about it as if it was already familiar, saying, "Yeah, she mentioned that – Christ, she put that morning under the yew tree in! She teased me about adding it in one of her stories, though I didn't think . . . wow!"

Elise caught a glimpse of the photograph on the back of the dust jacket. "Pretty, I guess. Violet Ellison," she pronounced, then giggled.

"What's so funny?" Christian wanted to know.

"Surely that's not her real name!" Elise continued to giggle. "It sounds so —"

"So Violet," he remarked.

"Do you know her?" Elise said, her voice rising.

"She's a friend from another life time," came the answer. Christian was glad that it came so easily. "I'm glad things are finally looking up for her."

Elise didn't want to hear any more. She was appalled when, rather than put the book down and leave, Christian said he was buying a copy. He was still holding on to it when they arrived at Clarke's for dinner.

For Violet, things did improve.

The first week in December Violet and the children passed a bookstore where in the main display case was Violet's book and Violet's face for all the world to see.

Alex saw the display first and darted towards it, pressing his nose against the glass. The larger-than-life photo- graph was more than flattering; Violet thought it was one of her best. It had been taken in February when Chris- tian was still very much a part of her life.

"Mommy!" Max crowed, pointing.

"Let's go in." Violet suggested.

Max was prodded off the table where his mother's poster and two dozen copies of her book took the center display. A few patrons had discovered it and were glancing at the dust jacket notes. One woman picked up a copy and brought it to the cashier.

"Hey, that's you!" one man exclaimed when he saw Violet and did a double take.

Elisabet grabbed a copy of the book, running her hands over the dust jacket lovingly. "Can I buy a copy?"

"Beth, I've got a box of them in the kitchen!"

"But it'd be so cool to buy one! You'll get the money back, won't you? For Grammy Am?"

"Go ahead." Violet laughed, and hugged Max and Alex, who didn't seem to notice or care that their mother was a celebrity. Elisabet marched up to the cashier and proudly pointed out her mother standing by the door with her brothers. Violet dug her hands into her pockets and shrugged when she was acclaimed by the store clerk; fame was a new experience.

So was sitting at a felt-covered table at Michelsen's Book Store and Cafe with a stack of her books in front of her and pen in hand.

One at a time strangers and acquaintances stepped up and smiled nervously, asking Violet for an autographed copy of her first novel, *Longing,* a saga of fourteenth-century Italy and the wrong choices made by two people.

Time-warp to the twentieth century, Violet thought as she signed her name for the hundredth time, and it was the story of Violet Ellison and Christian Walsh.

She had earlier delighted the crowd by reading one of her favorite passages from the book, a wedding scene, and now people were candidly sharing their favorite scenes and paragraphs, marveling that she could have found time to write at all, what with a full-time job and kids. Violet wondered that herself.

"So it came out. Do you know how many have sold?"

Violet glanced up, a little surprised to find Sam smiling down at her. She managed a smile of her own. They rarely spoke those days, and saw each other for five minutes while transporting the children from her house to Sam's car.

"Too early to tell. What shall I write?"

"How about, 'to Sam, I loved you once'."

"True enough," Violet answered, writing.

"If I said anything now it wouldn't count for much."

Violet signaled to the book shop owner that she wanted a break and slid away from the table to find a fresh cup of coffee.

"It wouldn't have meant anything before. What aren't you trying to say, Sam? Anything you want I should know about?" Violet responded, handing Sam a cup and offering to pour.

"Just to see you. And to ask you to forgive me."

Violet smiled then. "Ask. It won't do any good."

Sam looked around nervously, then touched her arm gently, afraid. "Violet, let's make a clean start. I know I was a real asshole, but sometimes —"

She gently shrugged him off, moving over to sample the pastries and crudities on the buffet table. Quietly, she turned to face Sam and he caught his breath. She was different now, prettier, calm. It was true that age improved women despite what he had always believed and what society fed him.

"No. I like my life now."

"Friends, then?"

She stared at the hand extended, ignored it.

"Look, I made some stupid mistakes and I want to make it up to you!"

"I like things the way they are, Sam. Still, you can hang around and maybe we can go for dinner after the store closes."

"Is there someone else?" he hinted. Violet hedged. "No."

"Liar. It's that British musician still."

"I don't have time for entanglements. Or getting hurt again. I've got to get back," she answered and returned to the table for more autographs.

THE MICROWAVE BELL startled Violet out of her concentration. Pushing away from the computer, she leaned over and opened the oven, taking out her dinner. No matter that it was 12:30 a.m. Dinner was dinner, at any hour. She took a few minutes to wolf down the pre-packaged entree and turned on the radio.

"… Here's a new song from the legendary band, Fortinbras, from their new CD."

Christian's voice – a sad, soft tenor – filled the kitchen. The phrase 'whatever it takes, however long it takes' irritated her. Christian's motto where it concerned their relationship. His last words at night before sleeping. But not at Heathrow. Then it had been 'good bye'.

She yanked the radio cord out of the wall socket.

"Whoa! That's one for the Visigoths! Trouble working, Mom?"

Elisabet was illuminated by the light of the refrigerator. She took out the milk container and brought it to the table along with the cookie jar, then, noticing the radio cord on the floor, plugged it in. Christian's song was just hitting the bridge in a lush swell of guitar riffs.

Elisabet frowned in mid-bite and leaned forward, listening. "That voice is familiar, Mamma. Fortinbras? Oh God, it's him!" she exclaimed. "The ancient rocker!"

"Ancient rocker?" Violet queried, amused.

They continued to listen, sharing the last of the cookies, and suddenly Elisabet flushed, hearing Christian's lyrics about sensual mornings in bed and forests – oh yes, Violet hadn't forgotten they'd made love in a forest near the priory, under a yew tree and naked under its canopy and wind burnt, but not caring. It was one of *those* times.

"That song is about you! Oh my God, way too much, *waaaay* too much information!"

"It's a pretty good song," Violet answered, returning to work after Elisabet left the kitchen muttering about being too embarrassed to sleep. Her humor improved then. No one could top that song. They'd be hard pressed to try.

And then Violet started to laugh for the first time in weeks. She remembered the rashes they got as a result of that idyll at dawn in the forest. It took three days and plenty of lotion to recover.

At least, she thought happily, some wounds heal with time.

29

Have Yourself a Merry, Miserable Christmas

CHRISTIAN THREW HIS keys onto the mantle and dropped his suitcases beside the door, pausing a moment to look around. He'd not been to the Priory for almost nine months and nothing had changed, though why he would expect a transfiguration, he didn't know. He'd stayed away on purpose, blaming this old, rambling abbey for everything that happened. The Priory belonged to another life – a contented, happier, time. Christian didn't want to bring Elise here. She'd been asking to come to the place she'd heard a legion of stories about, and he was steadfast in his refusals. Kevin grumbled that the Priory was Christian's Thornfield, the gothic mansion from *Jane Eyre* where Mr. Rochester kept his secrets and a tormented soul away from the world's eyes. But here the secrets were Christian's and the tormented soul was not the unfortunate Grace Poole, but Christian himself.

Christian fell into the great overstuffed chair before the Gothic fireplace in the formal living room. No one, not even his two greyhounds and old Tristan, were allowed access to that chair. Only one other person had been allowed the grace.

He looked up indignantly and then put his head back down to finish his nap when Mrs. Burnes scuffed into the room unannounced to light the fire, it being the coldest December she could remember.

"What is it, Missus Burnes?" Christian sighed, his eyes still shut. He took in a scent of freesia as she lumbered past. A jolt of remembrance made him open his eyes and look around as if for someone.

It was Violet's scent, but Violet wasn't there.

Christian recalled that she'd given Mrs. Burnes a bottle of the perfume when the housekeeper mentioned that she liked it.

"I didn't ask a thing, Mister Christian. Tisn't my business to bother you." "But you will make it."

He now swung his long, lean, body around in the chair and draped his legs over the arm so that Missus Burnes chucked with dissatisfaction.

"That was the Dean's chair! Your father would never—" she protested.

"But it's my chair now, Missus Burnes."

Mrs. Burnes grumbled a protest and started cleaning up the jumble of magazines and newspapers that had lain untouched for several months. No one entered this room or his studio when Christian was away. He kept the doors locked and the keys on his person. It was one of his foibles that annoyed a fastidious housekeeper like Mrs. Burnes. Christian did notice and appreciated the Christmas decorations she had brought in since his arrival. The gardener and his son were putting up a small Christmas tree in a corner and decorating it. Christian noticed the ritual for the first time. He was never home until after the decorations were put up and now he watched, remembering his childhood of breaking globes and ornaments, of being told not to be a bother.

"Sorry I'm late – the weather delayed my flight from Lisbon."

"You should have been home yesterday, Mister Christian. Fortunately I knew to call everyone and postpone the party. Did you enjoy your vacation?"

"Not particularly."

"You'll never guess who keeps calling."

"Don't keep me in suspense, Missus Burnes, I'm dying to know."

"Miss Elise. She says you're supposed to be keeping Christmas in London with her."

Christian grunted and dragged a month-old newspaper over his face to block out the sun that was beginning to break through the clouds and shower down on his face from the window. Missus Burnes reminded him that his bed was a better place for a nap. Soon it was quiet, save for the gardener's annoying whistling of *God Rest Ye Merry Gentlemen*.

"No Christmas party, or New Year's party, then, Mister Christian?" Mrs. Burnes queried.

"None at all. I'm not in a mood to celebrate this year."

"Interesting – since you're going to be married in two months!"

"So everyone keeps telling me, Missus Burnes."

"Something you're not telling me, Mister Christian?"

"Why are you bothering with a Christmas tree?" Christian wanted to know, shifting in his chair to observe the final result of the gardener's efforts.

"It *is* Christmas Day, Mister Christian, but shall I have it taken down now that you've noticed it?"

"Not on my account, Missus Burnes. How you do like to rattle my cage!"

"I could say the same of you, Mister Christian!"

"And we both love it."

"Wouldn't have it any other way, Mister Christian."

Christian settled back into the chair to continue his nap, replacing the newspaper over his face. "Did I get any calls while I was away?" came a mumble from under the newsprint.

"None that were important – you ought to buy one of those telephone message machines. It'd make my life easier, I can tell you."

"That's what I pay you for, Missus Burnes," quipped Christian, waiting for the comeback. She never let one slide.

Mrs. Burnes ignored him and sat upright with a magazine in her lap. The pages had opened to a photograph of Christian with Elise. "Wait a moment! You'll never guess who called only an hour ago to wish you a Happy Christmas!"

"Oh Lord, Missus Burnes, not another guessing game?"

"I shouldn't tell you, should I? You little worm!"

"Missus Burnes, you're only delaying the inevitable."

"Miss Violet called. You'd be a right fair ass if you didn't return the call – at least for auld lang syne."

Christian removed the paper and frowned. "Violet?"

"Your hearing's going with the hair, isn't it?"

"Did she say anything particular?"

"Wanted to know how you were getting on. She sounded sad."

"Is she okay? There's nothing wrong?"

"Why don't you swallow that enormous pride of yours, Mister Christian, and call her? Tell her you're sorry for making such an enormous ass of yourself – yes! You're an ass for not listening to her side of the story! I think she wants to be forgiven and she needs to be. You might as well get things settled before you begin your new life."

"Why didn't you tell me this sooner? You might have called the hotel!"

"And what would Miss Elise have thought of that? For someone who's getting married, well I don't know."

"Give me the damn phone, would you?"

"Now here's a lovely picture! What a lovely girl!"

Christian leaned down and took the snapshot Mrs. Burnes had found among the papers, assuming she spoke of Violet, frowned when he saw it was Elise. Getting out of the chair, Christian took the telephone off its stand and with ten feet of cord behind him, went into the hall and sat on the stairs, ringing up a number.

VIOLET WAS SURROUNDED by Christmas gifts wrapped and those in various stages of presentation. She picked up the remote control to the VCR and pointed it, waited a moment before Zeffirelli's *Romeo & Juliet* started up. She couldn't help it – it was one of her favorite movies. She'd already been through Capra's *It's a Wonderful Life* and

Ingrid Bergman's *Joan of Arc*.

Outside she heard a noise at the garden gate and supposed it was the neighbor's dog scavenging the garbage cans.

Ned was having a time of it dragging the cans to the curb. "Hey! There's no pick up tomorrow," she laughed.

"Well, you'll be ready for – whatever," he replied sheepishly.

"Do you want help with that?"

"Just thought I'd help you."

"You scared the Hell out of me. First I thought you were a prowler, then I thought you were George,"

"George! Now why isn't he here? The fool's crazy about you."

"Dream on. He's a friend and nothing more. He's out of town anyway – in England, but back after the New Year."

"More information than I needed where it concerned just a friend and nothing more," Ned teased.

Violet threw him The Look and then softened, shoving his cap over his eyes playfully. "Come on in. I could use some Christmas cheer. By the way, why are you here so late? Aren't you coming by tomorrow?"

"I came by to drop off the kids' presents. I'm going to Minneapolis to see my folks, Vi. It's been too long and it's about time I patched things up with Mom," Ned explained and took the cup of coffee Violet offered, settled into the sofa cluttered with wrapping paper and laundry. He drank and remembered after one sip that the only thing Violet couldn't do perfectly was make coffee.

"Everyone seems to be doing that of late – mending bridges," Violet murmured. She tipped his cup with her can of Diet Coke. "Merry Christmas."

"Is it?"

"Had better."

"Like last year?"

Violet nodded, saying sadly, "Yes; I tried calling," and

knelt on the floor to resume gift-wrapping, trying to fit one enormous package under the tree.

"What's that thing you're struggling with?" Ned wanted to know, amused.

"A Tonka truck – an earth mover. Complete with all the bells and whistles. It's for Max."

"Say goodbye to your hyacinths and freesia next spring. Is there anything for you under that tree?" Ned asked gently.

Violet searched and came away smiling, shaking her head in the negative. "What I'd like for Christmas couldn't possibly fit under the tree."

Ned slid on to his knees and rummaged through a bag of shining, glittering, bows, selecting a few to place on the earth mover, choosing a foil decorated with tiny angels to wrap Elisabet's CD carrier case. "You never once explained what it was about Christian Walsh. Even all those years ago, I always knew, but I didn't quite understand."

"It was *Dark Forest*. It's one of those songs that you remember the exact day and time when you first heard it. You remember what you were wearing, and what you were doing, and how it changed your entire life."

"Sort of like *A Day in the Life*? *Purple Haze*?"

"I was fifteen. It was late at night, the winter of sixty-eight. Isobel was home for Christmas. We were sharing my old full-sized bed. Anyway, Isobel left her transistor on and laid it between our pillows. I woke around two in the morning and there was Christian Walsh's voice like nothing I'd ever heard before. I felt – well, it was like nothing ever heard. The funny thing is, Ned, that song has always stayed with me. I used to wonder what it would be like to meet Christian Walsh and tell him how much that song meant – how it helped me in the worst of times. I still can't believe that he's the one that fell in love with me, and that I was the one to walk out on him."

"Why did you?"

"Chalk it up to priorities and be done with it, Ned. If I go on I'll start opening up all the old wounds and we'll eventually wind up where it all started so many years ago!"

"The two-bedroom apartment on Spruce Street? Was it really such a bad thing?"

"Yes… and no. Y'know, I should've listened to Isobel about you. She warned me so many times, and she was right! But she didn't think we'd be better friends than lovers."

"If you had, you wouldn't have ended up here to this day, to this Christmas Eve. There'd have been no Sam. No Christian Walsh. From that winter night to this, you have to admit it's been worth the pain."

"Only problem with that, Edmund, is that I get to bear everyone's pain," she mused and then smiled sideways at him. "At least I can say that my relationship with you is the only one that hasn't truly blown up in my face – it's taken a couple of detours into Hell, though."

"And I can always count on you. Merry Christmas, Violet," he whispered and bestowed a gentle kiss on her lips. "Before this waxes into a maudlin, mutual-admiration society, let's get the kids' presents. I have a red-eye to Minnesota."

They were piling clumsily-wrapped gifts in Violet's arms when the telephone started ringing in the living room. After a hasty embrace for the Holy Night, Violet ran breathlessly into the house and managed to avoid injuring herself on Elisabet's bike and various of Max's big, metal trucks. When she finally retrieved the phone from under the reams of wrapping paper and foil, it had stopped ringing.

AT THE PRIORY, Christian was stretched out on the staircase. Mrs. Burnes poked her head around the corner from the living room and gave him The Look.

"So what's it to be, Mister Christian?" she demanded. "What, Missus Burnes?"

"Are you going to Christmas supper at your mother's? Mister William just drove up and he's complaining about the roads to York. Might take all afternoon to get there, thanks to the storm."

"We're not going by horse, Missus Burnes."

"Well, then?"

"I'll be there," he said, watching the lovable old crone shuffle back into the living room. He now considered the telephone receiver droning in his hand and slowly replaced it.

Will grumbled something akin to 'hello' when Christian finally came out and climbed into the passenger seat. "Elise not with you?" Will asked as they circled the driveway and headed towards the A6108 to York.

"She's in London with her parents. I was supposed to meet her after Lisbon," Christian mentioned as he watched the Yorkshire countryside drift past between splotches of rain on the window.

"And she doesn't care?" Will asked, amazed. "I'd be frightened to death of crossing that woman!"

"I'm not married yet."

"That you're getting married at all frightens me to death – especially to that woman," Will chuckled.

"Yes, well, I've got a few weeks left."

"Don't think of it as a death sentence, Chris!"

"There was a time when I didn't."

Will cruised to a stop, waiting for cross-traffic to clear and glanced at his brother. The hair was thinning, graying, and Christian, though tan, looked far from rested, as if the month in Portugal had done nothing to restore him.

Christian switched the station on the radio and switched it off when he heard his voice, then rummaged through his pockets until he found his Gameboy. He played the game quietly for most of the ride to York and just as the towers of Mickelgate Bar were visible on the horizon, was ready to switch it off, noting the words 'GAME OVER' on the gray screen.

It certainly was, wasn't it?

"Will," Christian said suddenly, "there's something you should know, and I'd be glad if you kept your gob shut about it."

"You can confess all you want, but I think you'd be better off not wasting your time telling me what I've always suspected!" Will laughed.

Christian settled into the seat and nodded, glad that he didn't have to say what was on everyone else's mind.

It was one thing to confess sins to a lover, a parent, a beloved brother, but it was another thing altogether to admit to mistakes that hurt everyone one touched.

30

I'll Ride Off Into the Sunset With You –
As Long As I Don't Get Burned

THE CHRISTMAS TREE had been barely taken down and pine needles swept out of the carpet when Violet's marching orders came from the publisher. Advance reviews for *Longing* were good. A book promotion tour was arranged. Twelve cities in ten days, including a shot on the "Tonight Show" at the end of the tour. On her last day before the tour, Ned called Violet into his office.

"Do you have a free moment?" he hinted.

"Sure," she responded, bringing a pad and pencil. Violet never knew when Ned was actually going to do something lawyer-like.

"You're leaving us in a lurch, Violet," Ned said as he closed the door behind her. "If I didn't know how great this was for you, I'd be angry. Here, this is something I've been wanting to give you for a while."

Violet stared at the wooden case now in her hands and then at Ned's ashen face. It wasn't spending the holidays with his parents that had given him the look of a dying man. He needed rest, a decent meal once in a while, not to mention a decent woman. The company and hours he kept would put him in an early grave.

"Open it," he prodded.

She pushed back the lid. Inside was a metal, enamel-painted knight; not a child's toy but a curio. It was heavy and ancient, perhaps made of iron, perhaps nineteenth century in origin. Ned knew she collected knights like she collected handbags and shoes and she had enough to stage a battle.

"It's not like the one, well, I've finally given you a knight on horseback," he muttered.

"Thank you, Ned."

"Welcome."

Ned found the perfect excuse for avoiding her gaze by picking up his pen and signing documents that should have been out of the office days before.

"I do feel guilty leaving you like this," she said. "But I really didn't have a choice, since the publisher expects me to make the appearances."

"You don't. You don't want to have to return that juicy advance, either. I hope the freedom and notoriety doesn't make you reconsider coming back." He finally looked up and smiled, noticed how pale she looked. *It was the pining after that damned singer*, he thought. *She'll never be happy with him.*

"I said I was coming back and I meant it. When did I ever break a promise to you?" she teased.

"Never! Maybe that was the problem with us, Violet," he said quietly, pushing away from the desk. "Maybe now you should break a few more hearts. Success is the best revenge despite what I've always said."

Violet sat on the sofa and Ned joined her, sitting well at the other end. "It sure doesn't feel as good as I thought it might."

Leaning over, he kissed her cheek. "Go on your book tour with my blessing – and my love. If you want to come back, I'll be ecstatic. If not, I won't get over it."

"Ned."

"Don't! Please; not another word. Go on the tour," he insisted quietly. He wanted to kiss her, to make promises that he'd try his damnedest to keep. But why bother? He knew he wouldn't be able to keep them. If she stayed another minute, however...

"You've got my number," he spoke up as she left.

She wasn't coming back, Ned thought as he walked alone to Caffe Malvina for dinner that night.

RICHARD OF GLOUCESTER! The townspeople going about their business on that cold December afternoon moved out of the way for the duke and his armed contingent as it pushed its way through the Southwark street. What could the king's youngest brother want in this neighborhood at two of the clock in the afternoon? Richard dismounted and barked orders at his men to seal off the street and went into Lettie Candlewick's brothel.

The house was in a panic. Lettie herself came down to see what the duke wanted and as if knowing his business aforehand, she had summoned her two strapping sons — just in case there was trouble. Duke or no, she'd give young Dickon a taste of her.

"You have a lady in this house," Richard opened when he was announced, or rather, came into her shabby hall sans invitation.

Lettie's laugh was like soap bubbles on the air. "My lord of Gloucester! I have many ladies here, as well you know. You've tasted only a few of the young ones."

"I think you know my meaning, Mistress. The duke of Clarence paid you to take a lady into your care. Bring her to me."

"Clarence's seamstress? I think not, milord. The girl has vanished."

Richard, never taking his eyes from the woman's, ordered his men to search the house. When one of Lettie's sons looked ready to challenge him, Richard drew his sword quicker than the bat of an eye. Lettie saw she'd be in for more than a substantial fine if she disobeyed the young duke.

"My lord of Gloucester!"

Obeying the call, Richard ran up stairs and found one of his captains standing in a passageway, his sword pointing toward a bolted door. Standing close, Richard heard from inside a muffled conversation and then recognized one voice in particular — soft, low, frightened.

"Anne? Anne are you there?" he called. He knocked and Violet came out of her reverie and found George sitting beside her in the nave of St. Edmund's Church. The damned light from the stained glass windows was throwing a halo into his bright hair and giving him that angelic, holier—than—whatever look she'd first been attracted to. Now Violet looked at him and felt all the emotion she'd ever felt for Christian. And when she felt his arm gently brush hers it made her timorous.

"What's up? I got your message."

"When did you get back?"

"Two days ago; but I have to be on a plane for Boston this evening – seminar at Harvard this weekend, a job interview, and then I have a gallery show in New York, more of the usual. My mum's not well, either, so I suppose I'll be going home for a while. How are you?"

Violet shrugged. "Fine. I'm glad you came, George. I start the book tour today and I wanted to give you something before I went to the airport."

Violet took her sister's religious medal from her coat pocket and held it out, the bright metal flashing in the lamplight. She sighed, continuing: "You once said I didn't need a knight on horseback – Christian said it too. He thought I was enough of a challenge for any dragonslayer. And I've always thought I needed a knight to save me from myself despite what I said. You were right about everything, George. Here, take it." she offered.

He glanced at her throat and saw that Christian's medallion was conspicuous in its absence. "I wish I could've given you a happy ending."

"That was never in your job description."

"I felt I owed it to you."

"It's time to get over it – whatever it was."

"And you?"

"Everything's pretty much fallen into place. And as for those pieces still lying on the ground...you pick them up and make something of them."

"Happy then?"

"I'm contented. For the first time in my life I'm really at peace."

He wanted to tell her he was reminded of another farewell a year ago. Of walking down Marleybone Road on an autumn morning and turning back to see her. A bright stream of gold hair blowing in the morning wind, a silk robe clutched modestly around her shoulders. The hair was dusted with streaks of gray, but the face was still so very youthful, so wondrous. She had been the girl he'd fallen in love with so many years before...

Now, this woman, this incredible woman named Violet who was so much like Bella, but so unlike any woman he'd ever been with. And he had known it from the first moment he'd set eyes on her, up in that tree house with the dusk falling and the last rays of sunlight burnishing her hair.

"George, take the medal. You never know who'll need it next." Violet whispered tearfully when it still swung lazily from her fingers.

"No; you should hold on to it. It might just come in handy."

"Please. For Bella."

He shook his head, smiled sadly, then said: "Okay, but not for Bella. For Violet!"

He kissed her then, not one of his perfunctory, benedictions on the forehead, but a kiss full of passion and on the mouth. "Sometimes when you pray hard enough, you do get what you want," he said, holding her face close to his. "Sometimes it works when others do the praying for you. I love you, Violet."

And then he was gone.

As lonely as Violet suddenly felt at that moment, a profound contentment overcame her as she rose to leave. The medal lying on the baptismal font caught her attention. George had left it there. For a moment she thought of taking it, but no, she thought, let someone find it and think it was a blessing from God. Let that someone believe in miracles, because she, Violet Ellison, had been fortunate enough to have discovered that miracles truly did exist; that for all her faults and sins, she had been wrapped in a love that few people rarely experienced.

As an afterthought, Violet returned to the sanctuary and from her pocket took out the chess piece. For the last time she felt its smooth, ivory, carving and kissing it, laid the knight on the altar.

"IT'S YOUR MOVE, Chris. Chris?"

Christian studied the chessboard and considered moving his white knight, then purposefully moved his white king into checkmate.

"That's the fourth game this week you've let me win," Albert Maesbury guffawed and reached for the decanter to replenish Christian's glass. Christian shook his head and smiled, saying he had a long session at the studio in the morning. After good nights were exchanged all around, he drove back to London alone.

Albert turned to his daughter, who was discussing wedding dresses with his wife. "I don't know what you see in him, Elise. I've only got six years on him, but he's a damn sight older than I am, all things considered!"

"It's the business he's in, Daddy," Elise sighed. "At least he's finally given up the touring. Doesn't that make you happy?"

"I think his face would crack if he ever smiled," Albert sniffed and took solace with his whiskey and soda. Elise ignored his growing litany of complaints about Christian Walsh and concentrated on the pages torn from a bridal magazine her mother now placed at her disposal. She'd talk to him, she promised; it was probably just the holidays. People always seemed to brood and feel melancholic between Christmas and New Year's. Now that the holidays were a bad memory and Valentine's Day around the corner, he might snap out of it.

She was unprepared for what she discovered when she arrived at Christian's London house the next afternoon.

"Missus Burnes didn't answer the bell so I let myself in – what's this?"

Elise's magnificent eyes went from the suitcase Christian was packing hastily to his face. She waited, and Christian forced a smile.

She was plastic and superficial, this exquisitely beautiful Elise Maesbury. Why was it that beautiful women always took up with less attractive men? Christian knew that wasn't saying much for him, but he knew better than to think otherwise. He'd even gone as far as asking Elise what she'd thought of his looks and she merely giggled. Violet's response would have been different – and more considerate. She was staring coldly, those blue-black eyes burning right through him. Everything about her was flawless and it bothered him. Should anything in life be so perfect?

"I didn't think you'd be here until tomorrow," Christian opened as he returned to packing the suitcase. "Listen, I have to go to California."

"California? What's there?"

"Unfinished business – look, I want to call off the wedding."

"Christian!"

"I want to call off the wedding, everything... I didn't think, look, I didn't expect," Christian now sighed and threw a pair of socks on to the bed. *Why not just say it?* He looked at her and said without hesitation, "There's another woman, Elise."

The pupils expanded into the rich color of her irises as her eyes widened and her flawless complexion turned an ashen shade.

"While you've been seeing me? Do I know her?" Elise slumped onto the bed. "Oh God! This has never happened."

"Not while we've been dating."

"Before?"

"There was a misunderstanding, you see. I've never

really given up hope."

"Who is she?"

"A writer from California." Christian was squirming, not particularly in the mood for an interrogation while in the middle of breaking up.

"Screenwriter?" she demanded, the word spat out.

"She writes histories and novels."

"Is she younger, older?"

Christian avoided her intense scrutiny by turning violently to get the toiletries off the dresser. His action over-turned a glass of wine he'd brought up from lunch and now he studied a spreading stain on the lace scarf, watching with fascination as the burgundy was absorbed into the cotton threads in a capillary action.

"Younger than you or older than me?" he queried, mystified that this was of any import. "Younger than me."

"Pretty? Prettier?"

Elise's voice had reached a piercing, irritating pitch, made worse by the fact she had taken up the shirt Violet had made for him and was twisting it angrily. When he gently released it from her destructive grasp, Elise saw that it was his favorite shirt and wanted to rip it to shreds. She knew its history – she heard him tell the story of this famous shirt on a talk show. This shirt graced every photograph of him. He really did wear her colors and his heart on his sleeve.

"You didn't answer the question, damn you!" Elise was shouting now.

He was ready to lose his temper but Christian quelled it with a drink of what was left of the wine. "Nothing like you. Nothing can touch you. But she is so special, so different than anyone – Elise, I never meant for this to happen. Sometimes you make choices and have to live with them. I choose not to. I'm sorry."

"Who is she?"

"Violet Ellison."

He was gone before she could scream at him, call him

an aging, two–timing, lying bastard, or throw something at him. Elise remained on the bed, amazed by what had happened. She was ready to write a filthy, childish message in lipstick on his mirror when she saw the framed picture of Violet Ellison inside a half-opened drawer. Picking it up, she noted a feathery coat of dust protected the carved walnut frame.

All this time! She thought bitterly.

ELISABET'S EYES REMINDED Christian of Violet. She smiled nervously at him and pushed back her curious brothers as they crowded the doorway to see who it was.

"Hi, I'm Chris – Christian Walsh. You must be Elisabet," he greeted, outstretching a hand and offering a bouquet of somewhat wilted flowers. Flustered, Elisabet accepted them and for a moment they stood silently staring at each other. Max pushed his way around Elisabet and held out his enormous stuffed dog to Christian, who sat on his knees and smiled at the little boy. "You must be Max. You do look like your mother. Ah! I remember this dog – Gawain, isn't it?"

"Gawain?" Elisabet asked.

"Uh, yeah – I was with your mother when she – oh! Excuse me, sorry! Hello, I'm Christian Walsh!" Amalie had joined the quartet. "So, is Violet at home?" Christian finally asked.

"Not until tomorrow. She's still on the book tour," Elisabet offered. "Oh God! Did you come all the way —"

"Where's she now?"

"Los Angeles."

He was on the next flight to Los Angeles. Ned offered a ride to the airport as soon as Elisabet called and told him who had unexpectedly shown up on the doorstep. The ride was shared by Elisabet, Alex and Max and lent Christian an opportunity to get to know the children. Alex demanded that he sing the song about Violets – the one he kept hearing on the radio, and Max played a game where he constantly tapped Christian on the shoulder and grinned whenever Christian turned to wink or smile. They were all the best of friends and sworn to secrecy by the time they reached San Francisco International and Christian promised them a summer holiday in England.

"That's if it all doesn't blow up in his face," Ned remarked as they watched him board the plane.

"Like you wish," Elisabet teased, jabbing his side with her elbow.

CHRISTIAN WAS EXHAUSTED but optimistic of his chances by the time a porter brought his luggage into the hotel suite and immediately closed the drapes on Los Angeles.

"Just set everything on the bed," Christian instructed, tipping the porter. "Your usual wake up call, Mr. Walsh?"

"Yeah, sure. Thanks."

Christian held the remote control and channel surfed while searching for his cigarettes and finally landed on the 'Tonight Show' where he left it.

". . . our next guest is a writer from Berkeley, California, whose book *Longing* has jumped from number six to number one on the bestseller lists in three days," said the host; "not since *The Bridges of Madison County* has a book made such a stir. This is her first book and surely not her last, ladies and gentlemen, from all indications and reviews. Please welcome Violet Ellison."

As the cheesy music swelled a curtain parted and Violet emerged, dressed in his brown sweater, a pair of boots, a jacket and jeans. She looked spectacular if casual. Christian's heart raced at the sight of her. The electricity and adrenaline started coursing through him again. He sat mesmerized, watching the interview, a little jealous that the host was flirting with her. Christian took the unlit cigarette out of his mouth and reached for the phone.

"Hello, yes, I'd like the NBC studios, please."

While he waited for the connection, Christian

scribbled the words to a new song on hotel issue note paper and drew little pictures of castles and knights.

"Hello! Hi, this is Christian Walsh. Yeah, *the* Christian Walsh. Well, I don't think any mother but mine would be that cruel to her son and name him Christian...Violet Ellison was just on the show tonight, and – Violet Ellison. She's a writer. She was on the show tonight and I was wondering, um, d'you know if she's still in town... three hours ago? That's right, it's not a live show. Bloody Hell!...no, there's no need... well, thanks."

Christian hung up the phone and then switched off the television. He sat rubbing his face wearily and called for the porter again.

RICHARD OF GLOUCESTER was standing beside Anne in St. Edward's Chapel at Westminster Abbey and was about to kiss his bride when the computer screen froze up. Violet glanced over the monitor to the kitchen clock and puffed out a sigh.

Six-thirty in the morning.

She tried a few DOS commands and whispered a prayer to the God of Microprocessors. The hard drive made a grinding whine comparable to her '67 Mustang on cold mornings. She tried a few more.

Nothing. Nothing at all.

Four hours of work had crashed on the information highway, made an irreparable detour into Cyberspace.

Nothing like modern technology to shock one out of the sanctuary of imagination – that and remembering the garbage cans needed to be dragged out to the curb.

"Damn!" Violet swore as she tripped over something large en route to the front door. She was about to make a mental note of scolding the boys for leaving their Tonka trucks in the hallway when she realized it was her suit-case, deposited there only an hour ago.

"Mamma? Mom?" Elisabet stood at the top the stairs. "When you'd get in?"

"Hi, sweetie. About an hour ago."

"You okay?"

"It's nothing, just go back to sleep. We can talk when the sun's up, okay?"

"Mamma, you had a friend come by last night – he was really anxious to see you."

"Was he?" Violet yawned, fumbling with the door latches. "Whatever it was, and whoever it was, it can wait until tomorrow."

"But, Mamma –!"

"Good night, Beth."

The morning was crisp and clear, the air sweetly pungent. The sun sat on the horizon like a gold coin. Somewhere in the neighborhood the whine of garbage trucks competed with a dog barking. Everything in her world was the same. Her comfortable, safe, predictable world.

What surprised her then was a man at the corner of Oxford and Cedar.

He climbed out of a taxi, and for a moment he paused, as if to get his bearings, then he turned, as if knowing she'd been there and walked toward the house. Violet waited on the porch, just to be sure and when he paused at the gate, she flew down the stairs, almost killing herself on Max's dump truck, and into his arms.

"Hi. Sorry about the hour." Christian apologized in a sleepy yet happy voice. "D'you know you're a difficult woman to keep track of? Oh, here; these are for you." The bouquet of roses were crushed in Violet's embrace. "I've missed you, darling," he whispered between kisses.

Coming back inside, she draped her shawl and Christian's London Fog around Parsifal's highly-polished gorget, removed the 'Earthworm Jim' cartoon from the Ashmolean Knight's face and took the can of warm Diet Coke from the Coronation Chair. A fresh pile of laundry waited on the sofa. She dug under the socks and towels and found the remote control, and clicked off the television set. Christian sat next to her on the sofa, glancing around the living room in wonder. "Violet, this living room is —"

"Don't say it!" she laughed.

"This living room is so very Violet. I love it."

Her eyes widened and then she slid into his arms for a passionate kiss.

VIOLET WOKE JUST as dawn was filtering it's comforting slate-colored light through the bed curtains. It took her a moment to get her bearings, to remember last night, and when she did remember, turned over to wake Christian with a kiss. She found the bed empty, the pillows with barely an impression on them. There was no evidence of Christian having slept in the bed. The familiar sensation of dread and unhappiness began to creep in where elation had been only moments before. Violet sighed and found her slippers under the bed, her bathrobe on the hook behind the door.

The murmur of an early morning news show drifted from the living room as she went down stairs. Violet thought nothing of it; she'd more than likely left the television on.

"Coffee's fresh," Elisabet said between bites of waffle when Violet scuffed into the kitchen.

"Mamma!" Max crowed. "Mamma home! Here, Mamma!" He offered a waffle square soaked in butter and syrup, which she took and plopped in her mouth.

"Oh now that's gross," Elisabet laughed.

"I'm getting a castle!" Alex pronounced with his mouth full.

"Are you? Who's going to give you a castle?" Violet asked as she reached for a clean cup out of the dishwasher. Then she glanced around. "Wait, fresh coffee, waffles, what's going on?"

"Your friend Christian was up before me," Elisabet said with a wink.

Violet poured a cup of coffee and glancing at her amused daughter, went into the living room where Christian was seated on the sofa folding towels and sheets.

"Thought you'd like a hand with this," he said with a wink.

THE LETTER FROM Violet was placed in between the leaves of George's day planner, along with a pressed flower she'd given him, and a photograph of Isobel, Violet and Colin in Berkeley, 1969. He laid aside the planner book and picked up Violet's second novel, turning to the last chapter. His mind started to wander as soon as the familiar words sprung to life.

Violet didn't go riding off with her knight on horseback. Christian and Violet commuted back and forth between the Atlantic, actually. All in all, it did turn out quite well, didn't it? He looked at his watch. There was nine hours' difference in time between London and California. Violet would most likely be taking the kids to school, later a morning stroll with the big Labrador puppy Christian had given her for a birthday present. She named it George. In a week they'd all be in England for the summer – kids and dog, too. He promised to join them in York at Christian's medieval abbey when the term was over. Violet couldn't wait to see him again. The feeling was mutual. She wanted to consult him about her third book – a fictional account of Eleanor Cobham, the unfortunate duchess of Humphrey, duke of Gloucester. The other Gloucester, whose life was just as tumultuous and tragic as Richard's. It was almost finished. The story about Italy was successful and now Richard and Anne's story was doing well in the book stores, for what sold better than love stories with happy endings?

George settled into his chair by the window overlooking the Thames and turning the page, was suddenly back in fifteenth century England, in the north, where, on the road to Heyburn, a royal progress was underway.

Richard of Gloucester and his duchess Anne Nevill were almost to the gates of Middleham Castle. The gray granite roofs and towers were visible for miles. Richard picked up speed, gently urging his stallion to a faster pace, while Anne happily raced to keep up with him. Their trials were over and soon they would have a life together.

Before riding through the gate house and into the ward, Anne leaned across her horse and turned Richard's face to hers, kissing him none too gently before the entire household that had gathered to welcome their lord and lady. One of the grooms held the reins as Richard bounded out of the saddle and, reaching up, lifted his lady wife Anne and kissed her as she slid effortlessly into his arms.

The End

Acknowledgments

Quotation from "The Cat in the Hat" by Dr. Seuss, copyright © 1957, educational edition published by Houghton Mifflin Company, Boston; trade edition published simultaneously in New York by Random House, Inc. and in Toronto, Canada by Random House of Canada, Ltd.

About the Author

A NATIVE of the San Francisco Bay Area, Ellen L. Ekstrom makes her home in Berkeley, California with her family. She serves as the parish deacon for The Episcopal Church of the Good Shepherd, and along with ministry, she enjoys knitting, cycling, a good book and good company. Ms. Ekstrom's growing library of work includes *The Legacy, Armor of Light,* The *Midwinter Sonata* Series, which includes the companion novels *Tallis' Third Tune* and *Scarborough,* and, writing as Caitlin Luke Quinn, *St. Edmund Wood.* This novel, *What She Wished For,* was originally published as *A Knight on Horseback* by Central Avenue Publishing in 2009, and in 2013 the work received Fifth Place honors in the Oklahoma Romance Writer's International Digital Book Competition.

Coming soon: *Ascalon* – the sequel to *Armor of Light*; the third and final book in the *Midwinter Sonata* series, *The Shambles*; and *Swannaeld.*